Dale Mayer

SEALS OF HONOR

BOOKS 20-22

SEALS OF HONOR, BOOKS 20–22
Beverly Dale Mayer
Valley Publishing Ltd.

This is a work of fiction. Names, characters, places, brands, media, and incidents are either the product of the author's imagination or are used fictitiously. Any resemblance to actual events, locales, or persons, living or dead, is entirely coincidental.

ISBN-13: 978-1-773361-69-7
Print Edition

Books in This Series:

About This Boxed Set

Kanen

His best friend's wife is in trouble...

A panicked phone call sends Kanen flying across the ocean to find that she's been held captive in her apartment, tortured for something her dead husband supposedly hid.

Only she knows nothing about it and her husband is, well, dead...

Dead men don't talk – or do they? As they unravel the mystery Kanen has to delve into his friend's life to see what he'd done that put his wife in jeopardy. And find her captor, before he decides to kill her.

Laysa doesn't know what this man wants, but after seeing Kanen again after so long she knows what she wants. But is it a betrayal of her husband? Then why was her husband hiding things?

And why did her captor want them? Even worse, if he got them in his possession, what was he planning to do with them?

Nelson

Nothing is what it seems ... ever ...

Nelson's early morning meeting at the docks with Elizabeth Etchings offers only bad news. Her brother—and Nelson's old friend—has gone missing on his days off while his ship was docked in Ensenada. A trip to where he'd last been seen shows the local color … and reveals Nelson's friend has gotten into bigger trouble than anyone could imagine.

Elizabeth might have had a hand in now sending two men to Baja to look for her brother, but she will not stay behind. Her brother is in danger … and he's the only family she has left.

It doesn't take long for Nelson to realize that Elizabeth has caught the eye of someone who rules that corner of the world. She's now in jeopardy too—possibly more than her brother. Keeping her safe moves up Nelson's priority list.

Until both issues merge, and everything goes south …

Taylor

Murder is a deadly way to start a relationship …

Finally back in Coronado and his own apartment but still tired from traveling, Taylor helps a neighbor by closing her apartment door as she dashes back to work. But, as he does so, a smell he's all too familiar with permeates the air. And he's plunged into a multiple homicide with no meaning or end …

Midge doesn't understand what's happened to her life, … but now her home, her workplace, her neighbors are all in danger and are all suspect. … Taylor is the only piece of normalcy in her world-gone-crazy right now.

But even he can't keep an eye on her all the time …

Sign up to be notified of all Dale's releases here!
https://geni.us/DaleNews

COMPLIMENTARY DOWNLOAD

DOWNLOAD a _complimentary_ copy of TUESDAY'S CHILD? Just tell me where to send it!

http://dalemayer.com/starterlibrarytc/

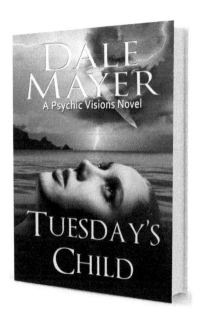

USA TODAY BESTSELLING AUTHOR

Dale Mayer

SEALS OF
HONOR
Kanen

BOOK-20

PROLOGUE

A WEEK LATER, Kanen Larson studied Deli and Jackson, cuddling on the couch, wondering how Mason's magic could have spread for so long and so far. Kanen was happy for his friend. Hell, Kanen was surrounded by men who were so damn blissfully happy it was almost enough to make a guy sick.

But Kanen wasn't jealous—that wasn't part of who he was. Maybe envious. He wouldn't mind finding his soul mate. … But it wasn't why he was here. It wasn't why he was friends with all these men. They were good men—the kind of men to call on when in trouble. The best kind of men to spend time with, whether at work or when it was time to play. He was blessed; and he knew it. These were great guys. And the women they'd met, wow, they were something else. Talk about raising the bar.

Mason had started everyone down this path. They were all helpless to do anything but follow him. And the thing was, not one of them seemed to mind.

Jackson looked at Kanen and raised an eyebrow.

Kanen just shrugged. "You two look good together."

Jackson smiled, wrapped his arm around Deli's shoulder and hugged her up close. "Feels good together too," he admitted.

Just then Kanen's phone rang. He pulled it out and saw

it was his friend Laysa, calling from England. He lifted the phone to his ear and, in a happy cheerful voice, called out, "How is Laysa doing? Trying to whip all those little kids into shape, make them sit up and pay attention?" he teased.

A broken sob was his only answer. He straightened. "Laysa, what's wrong?"

Another sob came and then an attempt to speak. But nothing came out.

"Take it easy. It's all right. I'm here. What's the matter?"

Her voice broke as she whispered, "Kanen."

"Yes, I'm here," he said. "What's the matter?" He could see Jackson staring at him, a frown forming between his eyebrows. Kanen shrugged, not sure what was going on yet. What he did know was Laysa didn't get upset over the little things in life. He hopped to his feet and walked around on the living room carpet. "Laysa, talk to me," he urged. "What's happening?"

She cried again, her tone raspy as if she'd been crying a lot. And it was a tone he recognized. Her husband had been one of his best mates when they'd both served in the navy together for years. But Blake had been killed almost a year ago, and Kanen had talked to her all the time in the beginning to deal with that loss. She'd had a tear-soaked voice all that time then too. But he'd never heard her like this. "You need to tell me what's going on," he urged quietly. "I can't help you if you don't tell me."

Suddenly she shrieked, then sobbed loudly.

"Laysa," he cried out in horror. "What's happening?"

A stranger spoke in a deadly voice. "Laysa can't talk right now. If you want to see her alive again, I suggest you listen very carefully."

Kanen's heart froze. His chest seized. What the hell was

going on?

He spun to look at Jackson, who even now stood in the middle of the living room, his hands planted on his hips over a wide stance, ready to jump in and help. And he didn't have a clue yet what was going on.

"Who is this?" Kanen barked. "What did you do to Laysa?"

"Did you hear me?" the man mocked. "You need to listen to me. And you need to do exactly what you're told to do."

"What do you want?" he asked. "If you hurt Laysa, I swear to God, I'll hunt you down like the dog you are," Kanen growled.

"But that won't really work for me."

"You have no reason to hurt her. Laysa would never hurt a fly."

"No, she probably wouldn't," the man said with casual negligence. "But you, on the other hand, Kanen, would do a lot to save her."

Kanen stared at the phone. He held it out between him and Jackson. It was on Speaker as it was, but the two of them hovered over it. "How do you know who I am?"

"Oh, I know a lot about you. You're one of those who thinks you're better than everybody else. Asshole SEALs. But Laysa's husband never made the grade, did he? He was just a lowly seaman."

"He was a naval officer," Kanen barked. "He was happy to be who he was."

"But he'd have loved being a SEAL with you," the man said mockingly. "But, of course, you didn't stay behind with him, and he couldn't stand up with you, so you moved on ahead of him."

"What's this all about?" Kanen asked, trying to calm down. The shriek that Laysa had let loose earlier had chilled Kanen to the bone. It was obvious she was in bigger trouble than he had originally thought. "What's this got to do with any of us?"

"Blake has something of mine. And I want it back," the man said. "I'm starting to wonder if he planned to keep it—without my permission."

"Impossible. Blake was one of the best men I ever knew," Kanen said. "Besides, he died nine months ago. Whatever he knew died with him."

Jackson stared at Kanen, a question in his eyes, but Kanen had no clue who he was talking to. It was Laysa that he cared about. This asshole was already dead. He just didn't know it yet.

"Blake had something of mine that I want," the man repeated. "It's my insurance." He gave a harsh laugh. "So it's only fair that, if you want to see Laysa alive again, you'll find that item Blake was holding for me. Maybe he gave it to you?"

"What is it I'm looking for?" Kanen asked cautiously.

"Oh, no, no. It's not that easy," he said. "Laysa doesn't appear to know anything. I have been trying to convince her that she should tell me the truth, but it seems like she doesn't really want to talk. So I thought maybe her husband had given it to his best friend, … but, of course, you won't give me what I want without a little persuasion. I'm sure holding Laysa will make you more cooperative."

Jackson sat down hard on the couch. Kanen sat down a little slower beside him. "I don't know what you're talking about," Kanen said in confusion. "Blake didn't give me anything to hold for him. I hadn't spoken to him for weeks before his death."

"Well, that's just too bad then, isn't it?" the man continued in a gentle conversational tone. "Because, if you don't bring me what I want within seventy-two hours, Laysa will pay the ultimate price." The phone went dead.

CHAPTER 1

"**W**HAT THE HELL is going on over there?" Kanen asked. "I need to bug out. If I can't talk Mason into the transport dropping me off near London, then I'm on the next commercial flight."

"I didn't know Blake. What was he like?"

Kanen turned on Taylor. "He was a good guy," he said defensively. "He'd never have done anything illegal—not knowingly."

"I didn't say he would have," Taylor said calmly, holding out a hand, palm up. "But remember that we don't know everyone the way we think we do, and we can't be sure what was going on in Blake's life at the time of his death."

"I'd swear on my honor that Blake would never have done anything criminal."

"It doesn't have to be criminal," Nelson said quietly, facing the two of them. "A friend may have asked him to hold something. Or gave him something innocently, without Blake realizing it was important. Like a code or a key to a safe-deposit box or something like that."

"We need to wrap our heads around the fact that," Kanen said, "Laysa apparently is being held against her will, beaten for information she doesn't have, and her captor is damn short on patience."

"You care about this woman?" Nelson asked.

Kanen ran his hand through his hair. "I've known her for decades. We were all friends growing up together. She ended up marrying Blake. They were happy," he admitted. "I've become closer to her since Blake's death but as a friend. She just needed to know somebody was there for her after Blake was gone."

"That's huge," Nelson said. "Losing anyone is terrible—but a spouse? ... That's got to be a special kind of terrible. She must appreciate that you helped her through that."

Kanen hoped he had been of some solace to her, but, right now, his mind was caught on something else. "Did that asshole go through her Contacts list and find me, or did he already know who I was?"

"Or she told him," Nelson said. "I'll play devil's advocate here for a moment. Can you trust her? Do you believe she would be a part of this? That maybe she herself is looking for something Blake left behind?"

Kanen stared at Nelson blankly as Laysa's cries still rang in his ears. No way was that terror faked. "No. You'd have to meet her to understand. She's a lot of things, but a liar, thief or just plain petty? No, she's not any of those."

Nelson and Taylor looked at Kanen for a long moment, as if trying to read the truth in his face. Then they both gave nods.

Now that they believed him, Kanen let a *whoosh* from his chest. He sat down on the bare cold ground as he dialed Mason's number. When he heard Mason on the line, Kanen explained the situation.

"Location?"

"Ipswich, England."

"How long has she been there?"

He racked his brain, trying to think. "Four years maybe."

"Who does she work for?"

"A preschool. Can't remember the name," he said.

"When did Blake die?"

"September ninth of last year." His tone turned dark. "He was in a car accident."

"Was it caused by another person?"

Kanen froze. He slowly turned away when he answered, as if Taylor and Nelson couldn't still hear his side of the conversation. "No, the police said it was an accident. He ran off a cliff. Possibly avoiding some debris in the road or maybe an animal."

Silence followed.

Then Mason asked in a soft voice, "Do you still believe that?"

"Shit." Kanen tried to think, but his mind wouldn't obey his orders. "At the time it seemed strange because he was one of the better drivers I've ever known. He loved speed, and he used to race cars. That was one of his hobbies. He was hoping to have his own race car someday. He was a pro at the wheel."

"He still could have been going too fast, taking a corner too quickly," Mason said calmly. "That doesn't mean anybody else was involved."

"I know. Yet," Kanen said, his free hand fisted, "I don't know what to believe now."

"You can deal with that later. Right now, I can contact some people in England. I'll get back to you in five." Mason hung up.

Kanen stared at the blank screen on his phone and then checked on flights to Ipswich or London or wherever would get him to Laysa the fastest. By the time he had the data he needed, Mason called.

"MI6 will be waiting for you, no matter where you land."

"*Great.*" Kanen gave a harsh laugh.

"Yeah, they aren't happy to hear one of ours is coming to town either," Mason said. "You know we can't do much from this end without their knowledge."

"You could ask them to assist us instead of hindering us at every turn," Kanen said. "Blake was a former US naval officer with an honorable discharge. I don't care if somebody from NCIS joins me or one of our own unit, but I have to go."

"How early can you get there?"

"If I go commercial, I won't land until sometime after ten tomorrow morning."

"I've got time off coming," Nelson said.

Taylor spoke up too. "Me too. I'm coming with you."

Mason's voice came loud and clear through the phone. "Hold on to that thought, guys. I'll call back in a moment." And once again he hung up.

Kanen addressed Taylor and Nelson. "I'd love to have you two join me, if Mason can afford to cut all three of us loose at once. I don't need an entire team. It'd be nice to have at least one guy for backup. Two would be great." Kanen's phone pinged with an incoming text.

Formal request coming from the US government to MI6, asking for their assistance.

A second text read **Don't book any flights yet**.

Kanen grinned. "Mason doesn't want any flights booked at this time. What do you bet Mason snagged the navy transport for us?" Kanen heard another *ping* on his phone, a text update. **Transport on stand-by for you. Working out**

12

logistics. Will call with names of your team in five. With confirmed pickup time in next text or two.

Kanen nodded and waited to hear who would be going with him.

When Mason called back, he said, "Okay, I've got Nelson joining you for sure. Among his other skills, he'll be especially good for logistics, having spent a lot of time in England. I need to lock down another, someone with some techie leanings too. I'm hoping it will be Taylor, since he's with you as well and has already volunteered." And Mason was gone.

"Nelson, you're approved for this technically off-duty mission. Thanks for lending your expertise. I'm all for it," Kanen said. "Taylor, you're next in line for approval." Then Kanen frowned. "Even if we get the transport, when will they pick us up?"

Taylor shook his head. Nelson gave a one-shoulder shrug.

Kanen snorted. "We're farther than we should be for being only an hour out. Let's head back, double-time, see if we can reach the base of this mountain at top speed without incurring any injuries."

After about a mile of sideways jogging down the mountain, Kanen stopped.

The others did too, staring at him.

"I think I should contact Charles."

Nelson frowned. "Don't know Charles."

"Charles is in the underground line of our work, helps us out when we're overseas," Taylor explained to Nelson, then turned to Kanen. "Maybe wait for Mason to let you know if you're going as a civilian or as a SEAL. If this will be as official visit, then it's hotels all the way. Otherwise, Charles should have the space."

Nelson added, "Ipswich is only like seventy-five miles from London. But, if Charles resides in the capital city, we'd be closer to Laysa if we book into a local Ipswich hotel."

"As long as it happens now, I'm good. Maybe on the navy transport, I can sneak into the country. That way, this asshole can't track me. At least not initially. Might give me some time to sneak up on him."

Taylor grimaced. "If he's a professional hacker, he'll know, transport or commercial. He may have a source in MI6 who'll give you away. I figure Laysa's captor will somehow have immediate notification when you arrive in the country."

"And, if he's such a pro, he'll get into all the databases he needs." Kanen snorted. "Hell, it's probably even easier to do now than it was before."

"Either way," Taylor continued, "we must assume he will know before you enter the country, finding your flight info or whatever. If booking a hotel, make it look like you arrived, then sneak out, in case somebody is waiting for you."

Kanen swore. "Right. Even if I just switch rooms, that could help me lose anybody on my tail."

"Now you're thinking. Plus Charles is a great source of all things that you might need for supplies," Taylor said in a low voice, raising one eyebrow in way of question. "You can always contact him after you speak to Mason."

Kanen understood. He'd never met Charles, but Kanen knew lots of guys who had. Mostly men who worked for Levi. And everybody by now knew who Levi was and the team of ex-military he'd amassed around him. Kanen had spoken to Charles over the years; Kanen just hadn't met him in person. And, as much as he understood Taylor's suggestion to wait for Mason to get back to him, Kanen wanted to give Charles a heads-up. If for no other reason than to clear that To Do item off his mental list and to establish his local contact person. Plus, Kanen couldn't traipse down this mountain and text at the same time.

He tapped his finger on his phone for a long moment, then typed a text to Charles, saying Kanen was in trouble and would arrive no later than tomorrow morning.

The response came back in less than a minute. **I'm always here for you**.

"Maybe double- or triple-book those hotel rooms," Nelson suggested, "to delay that asshole a bit from finding you."

Kanen heard Nelson, but, inside his head, Kanen was numb. He kept glancing at his watch, imagining how scared Laysa must be, how much pain she was in, what the asshole was doing to her and who the hell he was.

WHO THE HELL is this asshole? Laysa asked herself, yet again. He had been hysterical for the last couple hours. He had beat her first, asked questions afterward. But all of it was insensate nonsense. He seemed to be calming down a bit, if only because he got sidetracked by terrorizing Kanen for a bit on the phone.

He wore a black full-face knit ski mask, a muscle shirt and jeans, his jacket on the couch, with a suspicious gun-shaped bulge in one of its pockets. That she couldn't see his face she'd taken great comfort in, thinking, if she couldn't identify him, then maybe he wasn't planning on killing her.

Now she wasn't so sure. His jerky mannerisms made her afraid he had a bullet with her name on it. Not with that rage he couldn't contain. Her body ached; she was already bruised from his initial blows. Although most had been centered on her torso, her jaw would bloom nicely soon.

That he'd pulled Kanen into this made it even worse. She doubted her friend knew any more than she did. She had a simple flat in Ipswich, where she'd lived with Blake. But she'd removed most of his personal items at this point. Kanen had helped clear out much of Blake's things right after the funeral, as it hurt her too much to see them. She had even boxed up more personal items, but they had remained here, until she'd taken time later to go through them—Blake's letters and cards to her and other memorabilia. What if she had already disposed of this thing her captor wanted so badly, not realizing how important it was, like some key that wasn't familiar? What if she'd thrown it away?

Suddenly her captor looked around her apartment. He was not very tall for a man but lean and muscular. His arms showed ripped muscles. His hands were large, yet bony. He turned and looked at her. "Did you always live here with your husband?"

"Yes. Since we moved to England." She remained in the armchair in the far corner of the living room. Every time she tried to get up, he shoved her roughly back down again.

"Do you have a storage unit here?"

"Not here in the building," she said hesitantly, wondering at the look in his eyes, as if he were testing her. "One of those storage units at a yard full of them."

An odd light came into his gaze, confirming her suspicions. "Where is it?"

She frowned. "On Bellamy Street. But I don't remember the exact address. It's one of those big-name storage companies with rows of units."

"What number is your unit?"

"One-thirteen."

"Is it locked?"

She nodded mutely.

"Where's the key?"

"In the kitchen junk drawer," she said.

He walked into her small galley kitchen. She could hear him opening and closing drawers. And then he walked toward her, shaking the container, the keys rattling inside. He held it out. "Which one is it?"

She took the container, stirred around the key mess. Spying the little silver key, she picked it up. The spare was on her key ring. She handed this one to him. "This is it."

He studied her for a long moment, checked his watch, then said, "Stand up. We're going for a ride."

She stared at him, but she couldn't move. He took a menacing step forward.

"What's the matter, bitch? Didn't you hear me?"

"Leave me here," she said in anger. "I've done everything you've asked. Just leave me here when you go look at the stuff."

He shook his head. "No, it could be a trick."

"Like I knew beforehand that you would break into my home before I returned from work? That you would beat me up today, not tomorrow? Like I knew Blake had your stuff? Besides, what could I possibly gain by tricking you? Tie me up if you want. Just leave me alone and go check the storage unit."

He stood for a long moment, as if weighing the pros and cons of leaving her tied up and alone versus taking her where she could possibly escape or attract attention. Then he gave a clipped nod. "I'll do that. And thanks for the idea to tie you up."

He disappeared into the kitchen and returned with the packages of straps she'd forgotten were there. She groaned when she saw them. "Please, not tight."

He zip-tied her legs, one to each of the legs of the chair. And then her arms behind her. He glanced at his watch again, key in hand, and said, "I'll be back in two hours." He narrowed his gaze at her. "Make sure you're here." He turned and left.

CHAPTER 2

THE DOOR SLAMMED shut in front of her. Everything hurt, but she ignored the pain. She had two hours. He'd be back, and she'd be in deeper trouble than she already was. She twisted her fingers, trying to loosen one of her hands from the zip strap behind her. He'd pulled the strap tight, but she had balled up her hands into fists, trying to bulk up her wrists. It worked slightly, in that she had gained a little wiggle room within the tie.

Laysa continued to work her fingers until she got one hand through, then the second to slide out. Immediately she pulled her arms forward and rubbed her sore wrists. She rotated her shoulders, groaning at the pain from just being tied up that short amount of time. Both of her feet were strapped to the legs of the chair. They would be harder to release. The coffee table was beside her. She opened the drawer beneath it, hoping for something sharp. But, no, there was nothing.

She straightened up, and, holding the chair, she hobbled and hopped her way to the kitchen. Soon she had the zips cut. She replaced the chair where it had been. Grabbing her wallet and her phone, she took one last look around her small apartment and slipped into the hall. Afraid her tormenter would be standing outside the building, waiting for her, watching for her, she raced upstairs instead of down.

One floor up, she knocked on Carl's door. He was a friend, but he also was a cop. When he opened it, she bolted in. "Close the door," she whispered softly from the living room. "Hurry, shut it."

When he did, he turned and looked at her.

His wife, Sicily, hopped up and asked, "What's the matter, Laysa? Oh, my God! Are you hurt?" When Laysa choked up with tears and couldn't respond, Sicily added, "I'll get you an ice pack for your face."

Laysa gasped and sobbed, partly in relief at getting free but also because she knew the guy would be back. She explained what had happened, taking the ice pack from Sicily with a small smile.

Carl was on the phone immediately, bringing in a team.

"Send somebody to the storage unit address I gave him," she said. "He'll be there. He should be there now."

"They will send someone," Carl said, then turned slightly to talk into the phone.

She glanced at her watch and nodded. "He's been gone at least fifteen minutes. He could be there already." She looked up at Carl. "Unless he knows I lied. I told him the correct general location. I just didn't tell him the right number for the storage unit. And I don't know why, but asking about this seemed like a trick question, or maybe he already knew about the storage unit. I don't know. ... Nothing there is worth worrying about. But, ... well, they are Blake's things. I don't want a stranger touching them. If he knows I lied, maybe he wanted to follow me to see who I trusted?"

Carl said, "It doesn't matter if he did. We'll get him. Keep that ice on your jaw."

Sicily patted the vacant seat near her and had Laysa sit

on the couch beside her. "I'm so sorry. That must have been terrifying."

Laysa nodded. She fumbled with her phone. "I have to tell Kanen that I'm safe."

"Why would that stranger think Kanen would have something or would know more?" Carl asked. "Were Kanen and Blake best friends?"

Laysa nodded. "We've all been friends for a long time, but Kanen lives in California." She held the phone to her ear. It rang, but there was no answer. Frustrated, she hit the Off button, wondering why it hadn't at least gone to voice mail. She redialed and waited. After ten rings, the voice mail kicked in. "Kanen, it's me, Laysa. I escaped. He will be looking for you. Don't come here. Keep yourself safe. I'll hide until the police capture him." Then she hung up.

She looked at Sicily. "I'm still shaking so badly." She held up her hand, and, indeed, the tremors made it difficult for her to hold the phone steady.

"Of course you are, my dear. Of course you are." Sicily stood. "Let me get you a cup of tea. That'll help."

Carl returned after finishing his phone call. "Let me get some photos," he said. When she balked, he added, "We need them for evidence." He brought out his phone and then stopped, looking at her. "I have to ask, did he hurt you further? Did he rape you?"

She pulled the ice away from her face and shook her head violently. "Thankfully, no. He beat me up pretty good though," she said, reaching to her swollen cheek and jaw. Now that she was safe, Laysa was more aware of her throbbing body. "I'm sure I'll be black and blue everywhere tomorrow."

He nodded. "After your tea, I'll take you to the hospital,

and we'll grab any evidence we can from you."

She winced. "You mean, like hairs or fibers?"

"Did you scratch him?"

She frowned, looking at her nails. "I certainly fought. I clawed at his muscle shirt. I don't know if any DNA is under my nails or not. I did get a good slug into his shoulder or back, but I think it was just my fist, no claws involved. He was wily, staying just far enough away, except for when he hit me."

"That may be," Carl said, "but we have to try."

She nodded but didn't hold out much hope.

Sicily returned with the tea. "It's not superhot. I wanted you to get some of it down fast."

Laysa sagged farther into the couch, her mind spinning in fear. "I feel like I need to get out of this building," she whispered. "I'm afraid you guys will be his victims too. I shouldn't have come." The more she sat here, the more worried she got. She slugged back several big sips of tea, put down the cup along with her ice pack and then bolted to her feet. "I can't stay," she cried out frantically. "He'll be back. He'll try to find me, and he said he'd kill me if I wasn't there when he returned."

Carl reached out and grabbed her. "Easy. I'll take you to the hospital myself."

She stared at him, loving the friendship and the stability he represented in her world gone crazy. "I don't know," she whispered. "This guy is really good. Like, seriously good. For all I know, he's a pro, and I might be putting you in extreme danger." She looked at the front door, then looked at them. Red flags popped up all over in her mind. "I have to go. *Now.*"

She bolted for the front door. She couldn't understand

her panic, but it rode her hard. Just as she reached the top of the stairs, she saw somebody coming up the stairwell from below. It was *him*. Now she knew why she was so terrified. He'd found her Contacts info for Carl and Sicily on her phone. Her attacker was coming up here after them.

She raced back to the apartment and motioned to Carl, then whispered, "He's coming. He's coming. He's coming."

Carl slammed the door, locked the chain on top and called the security office in the apartment building.

She curled up in the far corner of the living room behind the couch, shaking violently, her arms wrapped around her knees, her mind spinning, uselessly trying to figure out what she was supposed to do.

Sicily bent in front of Laysa, holding her hands. "Whatever it is, we can do this," she whispered.

"What if he kills you?" Laysa asked painfully. "I'll never forgive myself. Coming to you for help has brought him to you."

Carl asked from the other side of the couch, "Did he see you?"

"I don't think so," she said, "but he would have heard the door, I'm sure."

"That doesn't mean he knows it was you though," Sicily said quietly.

Just then a hard sound came; wood shattered, and a bullet careened through the front door to land in the opposite wall.

Laysa gave a broken laugh and whispered, "Well, that answers that question."

Carl patted her hand, and she realized he was armed too. She stared at the gun in relief. "I didn't know you were allowed to have guns at home."

He shrugged. "Marksmanship is also a hobby. I do have licenses for them."

"As long as they shoot real bullets," she said, "I don't care if you have licenses or not. I just don't want to be taken by him again."

Carl waited. She watched, worried he was too old for this young, fit madman. But Carl stayed well out of the way and waited. No second bullet came. Nothing. Not a sound. Carl leaned over the corner of the couch, as if to assess the doorway.

Laysa whispered, "Don't go out there."

He looked at her and then shrugged.

She shook her head. "He'll be waiting."

"The cops should be here soon," Sicily whispered.

Laysa wasn't so sure. It seemed like the cops were slow everywhere. But then again, Carl was one of their own. Maybe he commanded a faster response than other people.

Just then her phone rang. She tried to shut it down but realized it was Kanen. Keeping her voice low, she whispered, "Hello?"

"What the hell happened?"

Quietly she explained what happened and where she was.

"And the police are on their way? Tell me they will handle this right now," he asked, his voice rising.

"Yes, that's what Carl said." She realized she'd forgotten to tell Kanen about him. "Carl is a cop."

"Good. I'm on my way to Ipswich. I should be at your apartment building in a few hours."

"No, no, no, no. You can't come."

He snickered. "Too bad. Two more guys are with me."

She shook her head. "You have to look after yourself.

He's after me and *you* now. When you come, he'll capture you too."

"Let him try," Kanen said, his voice hard, rough. "He'll pay for hurting you." There was silence, and then he asked, "Are you okay?"

She sighed. "I'm fine. He didn't rape me. He didn't really hurt me too badly, considering he could have killed me. Carl wants me to go to the hospital and get examined and have the hospital do a forensic something or other." She was still so shocked that her words completely escaped her. "To make sure they collect any evidence there might be."

"I agree. Make sure you're never alone. If you need security until I get there, then you let me know. I'll have somebody by your side."

"No. No, it'll be fine. I can get Carl's help too," she said. Now that she was free, she was sorry Kanen was involved. It had put him in terrible danger.

"Don't ever try to stop me from coming to help or ever be afraid of calling me," he said sharply. "Our friendship goes too far back for that."

She smiled tremulously. "I was just thinking that. But thank you. I need this guy caught. I want this over with."

"I'm sure he's gone," Kanen said reassuringly. "But he won't have gone far. Be extra careful."

"Will do." Outside she could hear sirens approaching. "That's the police now," she said, starting to relax. "If he wasn't gone before, he will be now."

"Good. I'll call you as soon as I land." He hung up.

She cradled the phone against her chest, buried her face in her knees and waited. Sure enough she could hear shouts as the police entered the building and raced toward them.

Carl never moved. When a hard knock came on the

door, he called out, "Identify yourself." The constable replied with his name and number, then asking, "Are you Investigating Officer Carl McMaster?"

Instead of answering, Carl rose and opened the door. "I am. Come on in."

Six men entered, their weapons drawn. They thoroughly searched the apartment, and then two stayed while the other four continued to search the building.

Laysa's captivity was really over.

Taylor's a go. Transport's on another exercise. Available at 1:00 a.m. as planned. To take you wherever you want to go.

"Damn," Kanen said, showing the text to Nelson and Taylor.

"Not to mention," Nelson said, "we could have beat everybody's time on this molehill tonight."

Kanen slapped his newest SEAL buddy on the back. "Thanks, man. Glad you're coming with us."

LANDING THE NAVAL transport took special clearance. Kanen winced at that. *Our hacker asshole will note this special clearance.* At 4:00 a.m. on the dot, UK time, Kanen strode through customs and headed straight outside, ever alert. The minute he was free and clear from the crowds, he called Laysa. Her sleepy voice answered the phone, and he winced. "Sorry to wake you," he said gently. "It's your nighttime here. I just needed to make sure you were okay."

"I'm okay," she whispered. "I spent hours at the hospital, but I'm home now. Well, I'm in Carl's spare bedroom, not my own apartment."

"Good," Kanen said. "I'm walking out of the airport now. I'll be at my hotel soon."

"Why?" she wailed softly. "He'll come after you. You know that, right?"

"Like I said, he's welcome to try. I'll be waiting and watching for him." Kanen's voice was harsh. "If he wants a piece of me, that's good because I want a piece of him. Go back to sleep. I'll call you in a couple hours." Not giving her a chance to argue, he shut off the call and pocketed his phone.

Even at this ungodly hour, he caught sight of three guys in suits—MI6—spread about along the well-lit front of the airport, near the departing vehicles. One gave a gentle tap of his watch, without ever locking gazes with Kanen. He responded by tilting his chin upward ever-so-slightly, as if to say, *Message received.* The watch tap either meant MI6 was watching Kanen or how MI6 would catch up with him later. Or possibly both.

As expected, a shuttle waited for Kanen, and the two men he had traveled with converged here, each giving a subtle headshake. Granted, they had no facial description on this asshole—and he could have sent in any number of lookouts—but the guys didn't see any suspicious-looking characters in their brief tour of the airport. No one seemed particularly interested in them. No one followed them. Nelson had made a side trip to an out-of-the way men's room, while Taylor had gone to baggage claim, despite all three men only having carry-on luggage.

The trio got into the back of the shuttle vehicle. The twenty-minute ride to the hotel was just enough time for the men to get acquainted with their new surroundings. Upon arrival at the hotel, Kanen registered and asked for a rental car to be available as soon as possible—a particularly nice perk with this hotel. The front desk manager explained the car keys would be here within the hour, Kanen grabbed his bags, nodded his thanks and headed for the stairs. The three walked to the second floor. Checking that no one watched, they entered through their door and headed straight for the adjoining suite via a hidden connecting door. Charles had recommended this hotel specifically for that reason and the rental car availability.

Kanen's phone pinged. He checked his alert, shaking his head. "That asshole never sleeps. He's already made us as checked in here."

"So he's a hacker," Taylor suggested.

"Or," Nelson added, "he paid a cabbie to loop around the block until the three of us arrived via the airport shuttle."

Kanen shrugged. "*Or* he could have paid the front desk employee to send him a physical signal or a text." Kanen stared at his phone, then addressed the guys. "I don't think he'll make an appearance this soon. Or ever. He's a bully, hitting women. Doubt he'd attack one SEAL, much less three. But … my money's on him being a hacker, tracking our every move."

In the adjoining suite, with the disappearing door closed and locked, they set up a command center and connected a video chat to their US contact and to Charles in England. Charles's face came on the video. It was really early here, still dark outside, but, according to Ice, Charles always looked dapper and friendly.

"Hello, young man," Charles said with a smile. "Nice to see you again too, Mason."

Mason acknowledged he was available to help any fellow

SEAL abroad.

"I don't think I've seen you face-to-face before, Kanen," Charles noted.

Kanen grinned at him. "No, you haven't. But we've talked."

"There's a first time for everything. I hear you have trouble knocking on your door."

Kanen nodded. "Laysa is now in trouble. Apparently her captor gave Blake something to hold for him. Now the asshole wants it back, but Laysa doesn't know anything about it. Neither do I."

"And neither of you have anything that you're aware of, correct?"

Kanen nodded. "It's not like Blake sent me a parcel before he died, asking me to hold on to it in case anything happened to him."

"We're assuming that's what happened to Blake himself, correct? That somebody did hand him this package and told him to hang on to it for a few minutes, a few months, a lifetime?"

"As close as we can figure from Laysa's assailant's words, yes," Kanen said. "But Blake may have thought it was completely innocent. For all we know, Blake thought he was holding on to a package of mementos of the guy's former girlfriends or something."

"Right. And nothing has been said as to why her captor wants it now?"

"*The situation has changed,*" Kanen paraphrased Laysa's earlier words. "Apparently he needs this for *insurance.* I did help put some of Blake's belongings into a storage unit after his funeral, and her captor headed for that unit, leaving her tied up. But it wouldn't take him long to figure out that, while the address was correct, the unit number was not."

"So she sent him to a storage facility but not to the right unit. Interesting," Charles said. "That almost makes it seem like she does know what he's talking about."

"No. You have to understand it from her point of view. She cleared out much of Blake's stuff immediately, finding it hard to keep so many memories around. We put some in the storage unit for her to deal with later, and some of the more personal items were boxed up but left at home, and lots we gave away. I doubt she even remembers what went where. Although she did say that she had been through most of Blake's personal items, putting his cards and letters to her in their picture album. I don't believe she has much still boxed up at home."

At that, Charles nodded slowly. "She's a very resourceful lady, even under duress." His face was drawn with another understanding. "That does make sense. I'm so sorry for her."

"I am too," Kanen said. "I've stayed in touch with her. We usually talk weekly. And lately she's been much better. We haven't needed to connect quite as often. She's a really good woman, and she was very much in love with Blake."

"So you helped her pack everything away?"

"I helped her move most of it to the storage unit. I didn't pack up anything. I did the heavy lifting. She packed the boxes."

"So you have no clue what was boxed and moved in the storage unit, much less what the assailant is looking for?"

"No. I didn't see anything unusual as she packed up Blake's things," Kanen said, "but obviously we have to go through the storage unit more carefully now to see what this guy is after."

"It could be as small as a CD or a USB," Charles said.

"That makes the unidentified item even more difficult to find."

"I know," Kanen said quietly. "If he's tech-savvy, a real hacker, the best way to handle that might be to set up a team at the storage facility itself. The cops did when Laysa escaped but found no sign of her assailant. We should check it again. And we'll slowly search through the storage items, careful to check out all electronics. I assume this *insurance* entails some sensitive data. So it would make sense that it's computer-oriented. But it could just as easily be paperwork."

"True," Charles said, looking away, then glanced back. "Do you have enough manpower? I could help with that."

"No, we're good," Kanen said. "I have two men with me. MI6 is not impressed we're here."

At that, Charles's face split into a wide knowing grin. "With good reason. They've dealt with a few other US Navy personnel, current and former, coming over and raising a bit of Cain."

"You're talking about Badger, aren't you? I heard through the grapevine how he and his team were here a couple times."

"I never had a chance to meet him myself," Charles said, laughing. "But anything that happens in Levi's world, I'm usually apprised of it, especially when it overflows into my own backyard."

"Too bad Badger didn't contact you," Kanen said. "You probably could have helped him out."

"I think we'll connect sometime in the near future," Charles said with a smile. "People like Badger have to go off as a lone ranger to deal with the emotions that drive them. And then they slowly realize how they aren't alone and that teams are required, and it helps a lot to have skillful and gifted men in your corner. Badger accomplished what he needed to, and, for that, I'm grateful. But I also know England is grateful too—that they left, that is."

Kanen laughed. "I take it a few dead bodies littered his visit."

Charles nodded. "MI6 contacted me back then to see if I knew anything about him. But Levi helped to explain that scenario."

Kanen sat back and smiled. "You know? The more I work in this field, the more I realize how interconnected we all are. Levi is no longer in the military, but he's doing just as much of a service for the world as anybody could possibly do. And Badger is the same. Plus, both remain close to Mason and his various navy teams."

"Not exactly sure what Badger is doing these days," Charles said. "I believe he has some contract work with Levi, and that would be good because, once you're a protector and a defender, it's very hard to turn off those traits. He'd probably drive his partner nuts if he wasn't involved in a similar line of work. Although I guess Kat is his wife now. I did get an invitation but couldn't make their wedding date."

"Yes, so I heard. He's a good man, and, from the bit of gossip I heard, that was one hell of a wedding." Kanen still chuckled as he disconnected his video call with Charles and Mason, then turned to see the guys had set up both audio and video in this room. At his nod, they slipped into the decoy room—where they were booked into for registration purposes—and set it up to look like they had been there, laying out a few pieces of clothing and some personal items, pulling back the covers and making it look like somebody had been sitting on the bed. They also set up more audio and video devices. With the bugs in place, the Do Not Disturb sign hanging outside on the doorknob and a single strand of hair on the door inside to show whether anyone entered this room, they slipped back over to the other side, closed the wall panel so it hid the connection to the next room, and relaxed.

Kanen glanced around and nodded. "This is perfect."

"Need a plan of action," Nelson said.

"We'll go to her apartment and to the storage unit," Kanen said, "and set up electronics with laptops at each place. That way we can open any USB keys and other devices we might find."

"Is there power at the storage unit?" Taylor asked.

Kanen nodded. "There is. I don't know exactly how much though. We'll need to bring a power bar and must be prepared to slip out and get more equipment, if need be. We'll be working in the dark, so as not to give away our position, and thus we have to plan in task lighting. We can't have the door open because this guy is looking for this particular unit. I don't know if he believed the information she gave him. It was the right address but the wrong storage unit."

"That was smart of Laysa to do that," Nelson noted.

Kanen nodded. "If our asshole has access online, or if he's any kind of a hacker, he might find out the names of the renters of the storage units as well. So he could locate Blake's locker without Laysa's help. Even a good sob story is likely to loosen the lips of whoever is in the office. We've seen it happen time and time again. Just because there are rules, that doesn't mean they aren't broken."

Taylor nodded. "We'll double-check that we have every-thing we need before we get there, so we can camp out and go through the place."

"What about letting Laysa know what we're doing?" Nelson asked.

Kanen hesitated. "She'd be pissed if we were doing this without her knowledge. She's kind of a control freak. Probably from her schoolteacher mentality. But we have to get this done regardless. I'm not sure what the appropriate answer is here."

"You should probably involve her," Nelson said.

Kanen shook his head. "Not sure I want to do that. She can be fairly obstinate when she puts her foot down."

"But still, it's her personal belongings," Nelson said. "Her *dead husband's* personal belongings."

Kanen nodded slowly. "Good point. Okay, so I'll tell her what we're doing and that I don't want her going to either place alone. Not until we've caught this asshole."

"He didn't find whatever it was while he was there in her apartment yesterday," Nelson said, "so …"

"What are the chances he missed it?" Taylor asked.

"No way to know," Kanen said simply. "We don't know how big this *insurance policy* is or even *what* it is. But she has lived there for a while."

"It would be faster to search the apartment first, rather than a storage unit," Nelson said.

Kanen looked at him. "Probably, yes. While we were transported here, her place was full of police, taking fingerprints and checking for any DNA. I don't know that she'll sleep there ever again. Seems she was beaten up pretty good. At the moment, she's still in the apartment building, staying with the cop and his wife who she'd run to in the first place. That'll give her a certain amount of protection."

"Well, the cops should be done, so why don't we move on to her place and do a quick search ourselves?" Taylor asked.

Kanen thought about that and nodded. "That works. Her captor will be watching. We can count on that. It might lure him to us."

"That's a good thing," Nelson said. "We need to capture this guy before he tries to snag you next."

Kanen shook his head. "I would welcome that," he said. "What I don't want is him getting his hands on Laysa again. She's valiant, but she can only handle so much. She's had a tough year as it is. I don't want this to ruin her life, to sour her outlook on everything." Kanen checked his watch. "We could get in now, do a full search and get out. It's not yet sunrise."

The men jumped to their feet.

Kanen stood too. "Agreed. Let's do that first. And let's go now."

CHAPTER 3

LAYSA WOKE EARLY that morning. She reached for her cell phone, checking the time. It wasn't even five-thirty yet. She lay here for a long moment, wondering if she could go back to sleep. But, now that her body and mind were awake, all she could think about was getting up. She was normally an early riser, but she was in Carl's apartment and didn't feel she could get up and walk around freely.

She'd also left her laptop in Carl's living room and didn't have a change of clothes with her. She'd love nothing more than a hot bath and to get into clean clothes. Once her mind went from that topic to her apartment only one floor below, it wasn't a far stretch to wonder if she could safely go downstairs and grab a few personal belongings. Surely the police were done looking through her apartment? There wasn't any reason for them to take their time or to work through the night. Surely there were forensics to collect and photographs to take but not anything else to do, was there? She waited as long as she could, but the idea wouldn't leave her alone. Finally she got up, slipped on her bloodstained clothes and crept out to the main part of the apartment. As far as she could tell, Carl and his wife didn't wake up.

Laysa stared at the front door and frowned. Was she being a foolish? She didn't have any fear about going back down to her apartment, so her internal alarm was okay with this idea. It would be risky for her captor to return, even if he didn't have his insurance policy yet. After all, the police had been there probably late into the night. Feeling emboldened at the idea, she scribbled a quick note for Carl and put it on the couch, then walked out the front door, leaving it unlocked so she could return. She made her way quietly to the stairs. The night lights were still on up and down the hallway and in the stairwells.

But outside it was pitch-black. Normal people would be asleep at this time. But not her.

Standing before her apartment door, she used her key and entered. She found no sign of any security—a guard or a camera—or even crime-scene tape. Nothing here let her know if the police were done or if they would return. The place still looked as she'd last seen it, with the drawers dumped all over the place.

With her heart pounding, she took the first step back into her apartment, worried that maybe her captor could have come back around for her. It was a terrifying thought, but there was no reason for it.

Just her fear talking in her mind. At least that's what she told herself.

She headed toward her bedroom and turned on the light. She quickly grabbed an overnight bag and a couple changes of clothes. She didn't know how long she would be upstairs. Part of her wanted to stay among her own familiar surroundings and another part never wanted to return. All she needed was enough to get through the next day or two. She added a light sweater, and, as she zipped up her carry bag, she thought she heard something in the living room. She froze, rushed to the wall and turned off the light.

There she waited, her breath caught in her throat, just to

hear the sound again. She tried to calm down and to convince herself that it was probably something outside. But, in her heart, she knew somebody was in her apartment. And then she couldn't stop cursing herself for being such a fool.

Maybe her captor had been watching. Hell, maybe he had never left the building, and the police had somehow missed him.

Maybe he'd been waiting for somebody to return to the apartment, and, once he'd seen the light, he'd come in. Just the thought sent chills down her spine. She didn't know what to do. Her arms shook, and her stomach churned. She didn't dare get caught by that madman again. She didn't know if she should go in the bathroom, locking the door behind her, and wait, or could she exit the apartment without being seen?

The trouble was, she'd already given herself away by turning on the light.

Her only option was to make a run for it. Counting down in her mind—*three, two, one*—she bolted for the front door, swinging the bag behind her. She made no attempt to be quiet. Then she heard a mumbled shout behind her.

But that brought added speed to her heels. She hit the front door, her fingers scrabbling to grab the knob and to turn it in time to get out. As she was about to cross the threshold, arms grabbed her. She could hear someone calling to her, but she was too panicked to register anything, to understand who it was. Once she was grabbed, her mouth opened, and a hand clasped over her lips. She was dragged back inside.

Strong arms held her firmly. But he didn't move her toward the living room. He just held her tight. Somewhere through the dim panic in her mind, she thought she recognized his smell. She froze and then twisted her head and mumbled, "Kanen?"

He nodded, grinned and eased his grip.

She fully turned within his hold, threw her arms around his neck and clung to him. "Oh, my God! I thought it was *him* back again," She reared back and slugged him in the chest. "Why would you terrify me like that?" Tears welled up. "Do you have any idea how scared I was?"

There was only silence afterward.

Then she flung herself into his arms, her arms tightly around his neck a second time, and whispered, "I'm so sorry. I'm so sorry. I'm so sorry."

He just held her close. Then she heard his deep voice, whispering against her ear, "It's all right. I shocked you. I'm sorry."

She sagged against him and knew it would be okay. She pulled back, the tears burning in the corners of her eyes. "I overreacted," she whispered.

He smiled. "It's my fault for scaring you."

She grinned up at him. "And I'm delighted to see you and not that asshole."

He stepped back slightly, studying her a little more intently. "I can see the asshole's handiwork turning purple already on your chin. ... What the hell are you doing here?"

Two men stepped out from the living room. She froze. They weren't alone.

"They're with me," Kanen said quietly.

She sagged against him in relief. "Thank God for that."

He introduced her to Taylor and Nelson.

She smiled, reached out a hand and shook both men's hands, saying, "Thank you for coming to help."

"Speaking of which," Kanen said, closing the front door

and leading her into the living room. "Tell us why you're down here."

"I woke up really early and couldn't sleep," she confessed. "All I wanted was a hot bath and a fresh change of clothes. I figured the police went home for the night, so they wouldn't be pissed at me for being in here. They searched the building, and the assailant was gone, so I feel a little safer. They also checked the storage unit, but he was gone from there as well." She sighed. "I needed to change clothes."

Everyone seemed to relax at that.

She frowned at Kanen, noticing the change in his body language. "You don't really think I came here for any other reason, do you?"

"I couldn't figure out why you'd come here," he said. "When we entered the apartment, I thought I saw a light flicker out. And I thought maybe the intruder had come back for another look through, but I couldn't tell for sure. Until you bolted for the front door." He gave an admiring look. "I forgot you'd been the best sprinter around."

She sighed. "But I still wasn't fast enough. You caught me." At that, she grinned. "As I recall, you were always the best catcher in our group too."

He chuckled. "That's baseball. Whereas you were the track-and-field star." He nudged her toward the couch.

She sat down, Kanen standing before her, the others nearby. "Now maybe I should ask why you guys are here and how you got in?"

"Like you, we were hoping the police were done and gone," Nelson said. "We figured, if this guy was looking for something, we should start here and make sure it wasn't close by before we headed to the storage unit."

She raised both hands in frustration. "I've done nothing

but think about that damn *insurance policy*. I have no clue what he's talking about. But help yourself. He was dumping left, right and center, trying to find whatever it was. But he never would tell me. I don't know if it was paperwork or a USB stick," she snapped, her ire getting the better of her again. "Another thing is, I haven't even paid for the storage unit. There were no reminder bills. For all I know, the contents have been confiscated."

"Blake could have prepaid for a year though," Nelson said. "That's normal. Maybe he took care of it. But, just to be clear, you're giving us permission to search it, as well as this apartment?" Nelson's tone was neutral, but his gaze was watchful.

She turned toward him and nodded. "Please do."

He gave a clipped nod and disappeared into her bedroom. She winced. "I guess now things get really invasive, don't they?"

Kanen bent closer to give her a tiny shake. "It already has. The minute that guy violated your space, it became invasive. We're just trying to help."

She sagged in place. "I'm sorry." She rubbed her temples with her hands, loose strands of hair flying around her face. "Maybe I should go upstairs and back to bed."

"If you want to, yes, please do." Kanen straightened and pointed a thumb to the door.

She gave a half laugh. "Hell no, I don't want to. What I want to do is visit with you. It seems so long since I've seen you." She stood, opened her arms and wrapped them around his waist and held him close to her a long moment; then she stepped back. "Go do what you have to do. It'd probably be easier if I'm not here. Plus I should let Carl and Sicily know that I'm okay. And I really need that bath." She headed to the front door, grabbed her bag, then turned. "Text me when you're done, and I'll meet you."

He nodded. She opened the front door and walked back up to Carl's place.

KANEN WATCHED HER walk out the door. He followed her to the hallway and waited until she walked up the stairs. She texted him a moment later. **I'm safe inside. Go back to work.**

He gave a half laugh. She knew he'd waited and watched, worried over her. But they'd been friends a long time. Of course he was worried about her. Of course he wanted to make sure she was safe.

Back inside, Nelson stopped what he was doing to look up at Kanen.

Kanen closed the door behind him and said, "Now that she's gone, let's do as thorough a check as we can." And they went at it.

They checked in between cushions—even unzipped the cushions to check inside—then underneath the couch and the bed, behind photos, in the dressers, under the drawers, in the toilet, every nook and cranny they could possibly find. Unfortunately thirty minutes later they were still stumped. They reconvened in the living room, having checked everything but the kitchen.

"I wish we had an idea what we were looking for," Nelson said.

"I know," Kanen replied. "Anything from paperwork to computer disks or USB keys. It could even be a photograph. We won't know the significance until we find it."

Taking sections of the kitchen, they carefully pulled out

every drawer and checked through them, even under them. When he'd gone through the cutlery drawer, Kanen put the drawer back in and pushed to close it, but something caught. He crouched so he could see better and found an envelope taped to the underside.

He made a light crowing sound. The others gathered around. He untaped it and held it in his hand. "Just a blank envelope on the outside," he murmured, "taped but not sealed." He opened it up. Inside he pulled out money, three bills. In between a couple of them was a photograph of someone standing in front of a building. Kanen stared at it, then held it up for the other two to see.

"Do you recognize that face?" Nelson asked.

"It's Blake," Kanen said quietly. "But I have no clue what this means." He turned the photo over. The date on the back was two days before Blake died. Kanen frowned. "Now that is ominous. Blake died two days after this photo was taken." Kanen checked the money and realized the bills were sequential. He walked over to the kitchen table, laid them down in the order they were numbered. Behind each printed serial number were two neatly printed handwritten numbers. He grabbed a pen and a notepad from his pocket and wrote those down. A total of six digits: 263947. He looked at the numbers and then to the men. "Any ideas?"

They shook their heads, frowning.

After a moment, Nelson offered a few guesses. "Safe-deposit box number? Bank account number?"

Taylor added, "It's got to be something."

Kanen pulled out his phone and dialed Laysa. When she answered, he said, "Listen to this number," and he rattled it off. "Mean anything to you?"

Her voice was hesitant when she answered. "It doesn't

sound like a bank account of ours. I'm not sure. Why?"

"Because we found an envelope under your cutlery drawer with three one-dollar bills in sequence. After each of the serial numbers is a pair of handwritten numbers, and that's what these six numbers are." Then the air caught in his throat. "I wonder if they should be read as 26-39-47." He caught the knowing looks in the other men's gazes.

"I don't understand what difference that makes," she said.

"Do you have a locked safe somewhere? This could be a combination number."

"I don't know," she said. "I don't think we ever had a safe where we lived. So I can't imagine what that combination would be for."

"Did he have a locker somewhere, like maybe for a gym membership?"

"Sure, he has a gym membership—well, *had* a gym membership," she corrected. "And he kept a locker there."

"Any idea if the locker is still in his name?"

"I'm not sure," she said slowly. "I never paid any more gym bills. But I think it was paid for annually. I just don't know when that twelve-month period started."

"What gym was it?"

"Gold's Training Center," she said. "He was good friends with Mark, the manager."

"Okay, we'll call you back." Kanen hung up, turned to the guys and said, "Blake was a member of Gold's Training Center. Kept a locker there."

The men pulled up the address. "It's open now," Taylor said. "Why don't we take a quick look?"

"Done."

Kanen turned to look around the kitchen. "Everybody

checked everything possible? We don't want to assume this is the only thing here."

"That should be everything," Nelson said. "She doesn't have an attic here. The ceiling is at a uniform height throughout her apartment and made of wood—not some drop-down temporary panels to hide ductwork or whatever. And there is no optional storage to rent elsewhere in the apartment building. The only thing we haven't done is pull out the fridge and the stove."

The men looked at each other, and Kanen nodded. "Let's do that first."

It didn't take much effort, but they found nothing more. With all the appliances back in place, they took one last look around.

Kanen nodded to the front door. "Let's check out Gold's."

It took ten minutes before they were parked in front of the gym. "This is the building Blake is standing in front of in the picture found with the money. I remember that door trim." They walked in side by side.

One of the staff looked up, smiled at them and said, "What can we do for you?"

"Did you know Blake Elliott?"

The man's face twisted with sadness. "Yeah, I did. He was a good mate."

"Does he still have a locker here?"

"Who's asking?"

Kanen identified himself and then said, "I can get Laysa Elliot to call you, if you want."

Instead the man—whose shirt identified him as Mark, the manager—picked up the phone and dialed a number. "Laysa, I have three men here, asking permission to see inside Blake's locker. You okay with that?"

The two discussed the problem as Kanen watched.

When Mark hung up, he said, "Okay, she's good with it. Honestly, his year's membership would be up in another week or so. I would have called Laysa about it anyway. Should have done it earlier. I guess I just figured I'd give her some time. Come on. It's this way." He led them through the equipment room into the back.

In the changing rooms were banks of lockers, some half size, some quarter size, some full size. He tapped Blake's full-size locker at one end of a bank of lockers and said, "This is it. But I'm not sure I like breaking into it."

Kanen stepped forward and said, "I might have the combination."

He tried the first sequence of numbers. When that didn't work, he did them in reverse. As soon as the third number was dialed, the tumblers fell into place, and the lock clicked apart.

Mark stepped back and said, "Well, that's a relief. It feels like a violation as it is. But I'd hate to cut off that lock."

Realizing Mark spoke as a friend and somebody who had also lost someone close to him, Kanen nodded in understanding. "I hear you. Blake was too good a man to die so young."

Kanen studied the contents of the locker: a jacket, a pair of running pants, a pair of shoes, a pair of socks. He saw a bag with something in it sitting on the floor of the locker. On the shelf above, he couldn't quite see what was there, but it looked like a book bag. He picked up the jacket, handed it to Taylor to check, the pants went to Nelson, and Kanen grabbed the sneakers and the socks.

Finally Mark asked, "What are you looking for?"

"Anything. Nothing in particular," Kanen said absentmindedly. He turned and looked at Mark. "Do you have a plastic bag, so we can return Blake's belongings to Laysa?"

Mark nodded and took off.

The three looked at each other, and Taylor said, "The jacket is clean. So are the pants. So are the shoes and the socks apparently."

With everything folded and stacked to the side, Kanen pulled out the bag on the bottom, and they opened it up to see a water bottle, a fitness watch—one of the latest and best of course—plus a journal where Blake kept track of his progress and his weights. That was it in there.

Kanen reached for the bag on the top shelf. What had looked like a book bag was a leather travel bag. He crouched down with it in front of them and opened the zipper. Inside unsealed envelopes with photos spilling out. He pulled out one envelope and flipped through the photos, then stopped to study a picture of one man who was vaguely familiar. He held it up to the others to take a look. "Anyone know who this is?"

"No, but these look like blackmail photos," Nelson said immediately.

The men exchanged grim looks. Kanen put the photos back into the bag, zipped it up, handed it to Nelson for safekeeping and went through the rest of the locker one more time. When it was confirmed as fully emptied, Mark returned with a plastic bag. They packed it up with Blake's belongings.

Kanen shook Mark's hand and said, "Thanks. We appreciate this." He turned, and the group walked back outside.

"Where to now?" Nelson asked.

"We need to go through this blackmail collection very closely," Taylor said. "Maybe take backup photos, so nothing's lost."

Kanen nodded. "I agree. But where?"

"Our hotel would be best," Taylor suggested. "If we go to her apartment, we might find *him* there as well."

Kanen pulled out his phone and called Laysa. When she answered, her voice was sleepy. "Did I wake you up?"

"No, I'm just dozing," she said softly. "All of this is bringing up memories."

"I'm so sorry," he said.

"No, you don't understand. They are good memories. I miss Blake a lot, but we had a good life, and I realized I'm starting to deal with the loss instead of denying it."

"That's progress then," he said, "but it's still difficult to finally accept the loss. It's a process. Give yourself time. So far, we have not yet gone through the storage unit. But we did find something, and we need to figure it out."

"What did you find?" Her voice was sharp.

"We don't know yet. I didn't want to open anything there in the gym, with all those prying eyes."

"So where can I meet you? Because I want to see this too."

"*Hmm*," he said, frowning.

"Don't try to stop me," she snapped. "This is about Blake's life and about finding that asshole who invaded my home, who held me captive."

"I hear you," he said quietly. "But it might not be that easy a chore."

"Neither was getting beaten up by that asshole, all for whatever you found. If not my place, another place or your hotel. Just name it. I'll be there."

"We'll meet in the lobby of my hotel," he said. "Make that fifteen minutes from now?"

"I'm already leaving a note and walking out of Carl's apartment," she snapped. "I should be there in ten. Make sure you guys are there."

He grinned, hung up and told the others what was going on. "Let's go. She doesn't wait well for anybody."

"She's definitely a woman with a mind of her own."

"That she is."

"Did they have a good relationship?" Taylor's voice was bland, but his gaze was intent as he studied Kanen's face.

Kanen nodded. "They'd been in love since forever. They were best friends who fell in love with each other."

"Were you and her ever together?" Nelson asked.

Kanen laughed. "No. The first time she saw Blake, that was all there was room for in her life. I never quite made the cut."

"That's okay too," Nelson said. "If you wanted a chance, now is a good time."

"Oh, no you don't," Kanen said, shaking his head at them. "Nothing like that is going on between the two of us."

"I don't know about that," Taylor said. "I saw how she was in your arms this morning."

"Absolutely," Kanen said. "But that's what friends are for. To comfort each other. So … *no matchmaking*."

"No matches have to be made," Nelson said with a big grin. "Looks like the match has already *been* made."

Kanen hopped into their rental car and turned on the engine. "That's so wrong," he muttered.

"No, it so isn't wrong. She can hold her own. She'd be prime girlfriend material for a SEAL. We're delighted for you," Taylor said, humor in his tone.

"Don't be," Kanen replied. "That would be like stepping on toes or betraying my best friend. That's something I can't ever do."

"But it's not," Nelson argued. "Look at it from the other side. Blake's not here to be with her, to look after her. He'd be happy to know she was safe and sound with you. He doesn't want her to be alone for the rest of her life. If the two of you are together, you know he'll be up there, smiling down on you and saying, 'Dude, go for it, with my blessing.'"

The trouble was, the way Nelson had said that sounded just like Blake. An eerie voice out of Kanen's past looking down on him. It gave Kanen a hell of a shock. It also made him think. Was that what Blake would be happy with? Kanen and Blake had been best buds. That had never been a question before. But what about now? Would Blake be happy, and would he say something like that? As Kanen thought about it, he realized Blake, being who Blake was, would say *exactly* that.

CHAPTER 4

S HE SAT IN the lobby five minutes ahead of their
appointed time; she couldn't wait much longer. She
didn't understand what Kanen and his men had found, but
obviously the trip to the gym had been worthwhile. It was
early in the day. She kept watch on the front entrance, even
as the hotel manager kept watch on her.

With relief she saw the men move through the lobby
with the same surety her husband had had.

Like somebody in command of his life. A man in charge
of his destiny. She'd always admired that sense of confidence
in Blake.

She'd never had it herself and recognized how valuable it
was in others. Blake had always just laughed it off as being
nothing. But it wasn't *nothing*. He was somebody who had
lived life to the fullest and who understood what he could
handle and what he couldn't. She'd always felt like she
handled life well, but then everybody around her protected
her and stopped her from fully experiencing hardships. And
maybe that was a good thing. She tended to be an all-or-
nothing kind of person. Like meeting Blake. When she did,
she'd fallen instantly. Yes, they were best friends first, but she
knew. Probably long before Blake did. There'd never been
anyone else for her.

Thankfully he'd felt the same all along their relationship

trail—as they shifted from best friends to lovers, then got married. When she lost him, her world had fallen apart. He'd been everything to her—in a very real and tangible way. For the longest time she didn't want to live, had nobody—outside of Kanen—who really cared if she lived or died, other than maybe her students. She had curled up in a cold ball of pain and had refused to acknowledge the world around her. But she had a job to keep and kids to teach, and she now needed that job in order to pay her bills, so she was forced to get up and go to school every day. And that was all fine and dandy until coming home at the end of the day … alone. Reminded of her loss each night.

Kanen had been a huge part of her life. A good friend long before she and Blake were married, Kanen had been a much closer friend since she lost Blake. And she knew perfectly well her friendship with Kanen would be there forever. They'd been through a lot together. When she had miscarried, she had cried to Kanen. Blake had understood, but he was more philosophical about it, … maybe even relieved.

He'd said it hadn't seemed real to him yet, not a child he could see and hold. But Kanen had seemed to understand. That had endeared him to her like nothing else. She and Blake had kept trying, but conception never happened again. When she lost Blake, how she wished to have had his child, a piece of him, someone to hug, to love, to care for. Instead she just had memories from a lot of years together. Kanen had made a point of reminding her how she'd lived life to the fullest with Blake during their best-friends period into their dating period and then their marriage. That she should rejoice in having had the opportunity to have shared all those years with Blake.

Cerebrally she knew Kanen was right. In her heart though, it didn't matter—she wanted it all. She wanted another fifty years with Blake, sitting side by side in their rocking chairs on a porch, holding hands—although Blake had often said that he wouldn't live that long.

He was a bit of a risk-taker, a hell-bent-for-leather kind of guy. But that in itself was okay too. She'd been the opposite. She'd always erred on the safe side. Maybe that was what had attracted her to him. He was the opposite of safe. When he went snowboarding, he was forever going out of bounds and taking risks. When he had his Harley— thankfully, she had talked him into selling that motorcycle soon after they married—it was the same thing, always going way too fast, never really caring if he lived or died, because he lived full-out in every moment. Whereas she sat at home, waiting, hoping he would return to her safe and whole. She never understood that adrenaline-junkie side to him. But it hadn't mattered because she'd loved it anyway. She had loved it because she had loved him.

That didn't mean she liked it. She didn't like the fact that, when he said he'd be home, he didn't come home for a couple hours afterward, and she'd worry and fret before he'd walk in with a silly grin on his face, wrap her up tight in a hug and cuddle her close, and all her worries would go away.

As she brooded on her memories, the men stepped in front of her. Kanen reached down a hand, and she let him help her to her feet. "Don't you look pleased with yourself."

His grin slipped. "Let's go up to the room."

She followed the men to the elevator. They didn't say a word but neither did Kanen let go of her hand. It was hard to know what to think, but she trusted him. And, if he thought this was the best thing to do, then that was fine with her.

At their suite, she walked straight in to find they had a huge suite, with a couch in the central living room area and two large bedrooms with two big beds in each off on opposite sides. She sat down at the far corner of the couch. "So will you talk now?"

Kanen dropped a leather bag on the coffee table. "Do you recognize this bag?"

She looked at it and frowned. "No, I don't think I've seen it before."

He sat beside her on the couch and unzipped the bag.

She leaned forward to see envelopes with photos of all different sizes inside. "What's all this?"

"What we found in Blake's locker at the gym."

"Really? I don't remember ever seeing this."

Kanen nodded. "That's why I'm asking if you know the bag."

Her gaze zipped back to the bag itself. She couldn't remember ever seeing something like this. As a rule Blake liked modern contemporary, manly looking stuff. And this was definitely masculine, but it was older looking. Oval with odd straps, it reminded her of a man's manicure kit but on a much larger scale.

"It's not something he would normally go for," she said slowly. "He had a matching set of luggage, and everything he had was pretty perfect, if you remember," she said, sliding a look toward Kanen.

"I was thinking that myself," he said. "I'm not sure if this is what your captor was looking for or if it's something else entirely." He pulled out an envelope and very carefully upended all the photos onto the coffee table.

She studied them, her mind not really comprehending.

"Lots of these are of the same people," she noted, reaching forward to group related photos together. Her face scrunched up when she saw several were of people having sex. "Good Lord, where did Blake get these, and why would anybody want them?" She shuffled through the very flagrant ones, quickly setting them aside. As she continued to sort the photos, she said, "Not only have I never seen these photos but I don't know any of the people in them."

Unlike her, the men sat on the floor on the opposite side of the coffee table and carefully went through every photo, as if studying the facial features of each person. She watched their actions and knew they didn't care about what activities the couples were involved in. The men were just trying to identify who was in the photos.

"Do you know any of them?" she asked them. At their headshakes, she glanced at Kanen. "Do *you* know any of them?"

"No, I don't recognize any of these men."

Sectioning off another portion of the coffee table, he opened up a second envelope and carefully laid out those photos. This time, instead of dumping them, he pulled them out one by one and put them on the table.

Once done, Kanen took the leather bag to the table and proceeded to empty all the other envelopes. He laid the contents on the empty surface, so they were all spread out, and so everybody could take a look. Trying to be as methodical as possible, Laysa systematically went through every one of the photos, wincing at some of the compromising positions. There were photos not only of men with women but also of men with men and some of women with women.

She personally was of the opinion that everybody should have the right to be happy, and, as long as they weren't hurting anyone else, their sexual preferences were their own. But what if these were prominent figures—and ones who hadn't gone public about their lifestyle? Or what if they were married and their spouses had no idea?

As she stared at the one in her hand, she realized what this was all about. "These are blackmail photos, aren't they?"

Kanen walked toward her. He took a look at the photo in her hand and shrugged. "It's quite likely they all are, yes."

"You can't think Blake had something to do with this, do you?" She hated the worried note that entered her voice because no way she would believe Blake was involved in any of this nastiness. Surely his best friend wouldn't believe it of him either. Warmth filled her heart as Kanen shook his head.

"I know Blake as well as you do," he said softly. "This isn't his style. However, it does make sense that maybe this is the material he was asked to keep."

"Do you think Blake knew what was in the bag?" She waved an arm over the photos. "Do you think he knew what he was asked to keep?" She couldn't stop worrying about the fact that maybe Blake had compromised his own sense of honor by allowing this to come into his possession.

"I guess I would have a hard time," Taylor said, "if somebody I respected asked me to keep a bag for them. I'd want to know what was in it. And, once left in my possession, I would probably open it," he admitted. "Because, as a general rule of thumb, someone you respect shouldn't ask this of you."

She winced at that thought because she figured she would want to know too. "Blake might have asked," she said cautiously. "He might have accepted the man's version of what was in here."

"How do the dollar bills and the combination numbers

fit in with this from Blake's point of view?" Nelson wondered out loud.

"Blake was a lover of all things puzzles," Laysa said. "He loved to hide things—my anniversary present, birthday gift, an extra Christmas surprise—then give me clues to find them."

"He certainly did like to make things convoluted," Kanen agreed. "He used to write down clues for where to meet him later in the day, like is done for scavenger hunts, leading us on a merry chase."

"Maybe Blake was following instructions himself. Maybe he felt he needed to be cautious—maybe thinking his friend was in trouble?" Nelson theorized.

Kanen stared off in the distance.

She studied Kanen's face, worried that all of this would change his impression of his best friend. Impulsively she said, "I don't think Blake had anything to do with it."

Surprised, Kanen turned to look at her, saying, "I don't think he had anything to do with the blackmail, no. Was this just some joke, some game? I don't know. I mean, if you consider how Blake and I talked all the time, who else did he talk to? Can you think of anyone who'd know him this well?"

She shook her head. "No one. And I certainly didn't recognize my captor's physique or voice."

"But Blake had to have another best buddy, another best friend," Taylor said. "No way he couldn't have bonded in the navy, with the teams and the closeness of the units. Once he left the navy, especially moving to England, it must have deprived him of many of those friends. He had to make new ones. Because you don't store something like this for somebody who wasn't a friend. If Kanen had called Blake and had asked him to do something like this, Blake would have done it in a heartbeat. And vice versa."

"But, if he'd been in any kind of trouble, he would have told me before it came to this," Kanen said. "And that's the interesting point here. Because we were such good friends, Blake would have come to me if there was a problem."

"So, from that, we can gather this wasn't a problem for Blake," Nelson said. "And the guy who owned these wasn't as good a friend as you were."

"So we're looking for somebody who was a good friend but not a best friend," Taylor said. He twisted to look at Laysa. "What about at Blake's work? Was he close to somebody there?"

She sank into the corner of the couch, a little more un-nerved at the thought of somebody in Blake's life who she didn't know about. Of course he had had friends, but she thought she knew everyone in his immediate circle. "He didn't talk about work much. At the time I never really worried about it. After he left the navy, he wanted to leave the States and for some reason chose to go into sales in the medical equipment field. Strictly in-house, no traveling. Surprised me that he wanted office work. I know he was constantly busy with stacks of files and always trying to drum up more sales. Like some telemarketer salesman.

"I didn't understand that choice, but I wanted Blake to be happy and to spend my life with him. So, of course, we came here. But I don't remember him ever talking about anybody more than once. A couple people in the office he didn't like. A couple people in the office he thought were useless. A couple people had come and gone over the years who he had no appreciation for. One guy he really did like, but he moved away about two years ago."

"Do you remember what his name was?"

She looked up at Kanen and shook her head. "No, I don't. I'm not sure I ever knew it. Blake just came home one day pretty upset because the only decent person in the office had just quit. He did go out and meet him for a beer a couple weeks later. As far as I know, the guy left the country." She tried to recall the memories from way back when. "It was actually three years ago now, but maybe he returned to the US." Laysa sagged in place as she contemplated what that could mean. "But it's not as if we can say he's the guy who invaded my home and beat me up."

"If he went back to the US, then what would bring him back here again?" Taylor asked.

"No idea," Laysa said. "My captor said *the situation had changed*, and he needed his insurance policy back." She stared at the blackmail photos. "Is that what these are—his insurance?"

"It would make sense," Kanen said. "But why now? Either he stopped blackmailing people and will start again or he knows someone is using these photos as blackmail and plans to do something about it."

"And that will get even more confusing," Taylor said, rubbing a hand to his forehead. "That last suggestion does make a kind of sense. But then you're looking at this asshole as an almost good guy."

"That is what's wrong with this," she said. "These are actual photos. He should still have the digital files."

KANEN LOOKED AT her in surprise. "You're right. If he gave these to Blake even a couple years ago, we had digital cameras back then—our phones took better photos than these—which means, chances are, these are quite old photos." He looked at them to study the backs of several photos and said, "No dates are on them. That's another odd thing. What kind of camera takes pictures without dating them?"

"A lot of the older ones did," Taylor said. "We could assume these are old enough that they came from film that had been developed. There are still a few cameras like that around but not many. But what are the chances that this guy hasn't digitized these photos? It would be easy enough to scan them in, so why wouldn't he have already done that?"

"He *would* have done that," she said in surprise. "No way this is the only copy you have and that you'd leave them with somebody and take off for other parts of the world without having a backup, would you?"

Kanen chuckled softly and sat beside her, patting her knee. "That's the way to think. You and I certainly wouldn't have done that, so I highly doubt your captor did either."

"So then why does he care about these photos?"

The others looked at each other for a long moment.

Then Nelson offered slowly, "Maybe he's lost the digital copy."

"That can happen," Taylor said. "We've all lost digital files. Supposed to be nothing safer but computer files get corrupt, files get lost, the hard drive fails, electronics get junked that shouldn't have been, and you can never find the files again. Obviously, he should have taken very good care of whatever he had in a digital file, but maybe he wasn't doing cloud storage back then. Maybe it was on a hard drive, and he thought it was safe, and then he dropped the hard drive, or it was corrupted in another way. Maybe he lost the thumb drive backup. It could be any of these reasons."

The others nodded, deep in thought.

"That would imply," Laysa said, "that he needs the insurance so he can get a digital copy again, and this is the only copy he has in order to either keep the blackmail rolling or to stop something or someone else."

Kanen sat back. "So what's our responsibility here? This guy wants his photos back. At least, let's consider these are his for the moment. Is there any reason we can't give them to him?"

"Yes," she said, her voice strong, hard. "If these people in the photos don't know he has these, no way I'm giving them back to him."

Nelson grinned at her. "It's nice to know you're honorable. But do you realize that you're pitting your life against these photos?"

Her stomach twisted with nausea. "Surely there's another way than that."

"Nelson is certainly stating the situation in a blunt way," Kanen said. "He is just trying to make you understand how serious this could get."

"There's another option," Taylor said. "We could scan these ourselves. It wouldn't take long. At least then we could potentially contact these people to let them know what the photos are about and where they were taken." At her frowning stare, Taylor answered what was probably her next question. "We'd use facial-recognition software to ID the people if possible. Then we'd use geodata to confirm the location."

"Okay, and then what?" she asked. "If we can't stop the blackmailer, having duplicates just doubles our problem. We could have the asshole after us and also the people in all these photos."

Kanen interrupted. "Our theories are taking us down a very narrow path of possibilities. There could be other options, even if I can't think of what they are at the moment."

She frowned at him.

He laced her fingers with his. "All I'm saying is, keep an open mind."

She pointed at the mostly nude couple in bed. "If that was me, I would want to know every copy of every photo was in my hands."

"That's the problem with the internet," Taylor said. "You can't guarantee that anymore. The internet sends out digital copies forever. It would be almost impossible to destroy these permanently."

She nodded. "Which is the problem with us scanning them in to share with ... one of your guys, I guess. Because then we're duplicating the process, right?"

Kanen sat back and studied her face. "Do you have another suggestion?"

She shook her head. "No, not at the moment, but I wish I knew who these people were, so I could return the photos to them."

"Or we could burn them," Nelson suggested. "Then they don't belong to anybody."

"But what if these people *are* being blackmailed?" she asked. "What if they are being blackmailed and are paying for these photos and never get a copy? Maybe they've been shown digital copies, but these are the originals." She tapped several of the photos on the coffee table. "Which kind of makes sense. These people being blackmailed might want the originals, even knowing the blackmailer could have digital copies still, and then it's up to them to decide if it's worth continuing to pay the blackmail."

"Well, obviously the blackmailer didn't send the damning photos via email," Taylor mentioned. "Otherwise the blackmailer could get a copy of those photos from his Sent folder."

She nodded. "Yes, the attachments are always there. Unless he's locked out of his account."

"It's more likely that he dropped off an envelope with a copy of the picture and his demands. Keeping it anonymous," Kanen said. "The thing is, we have to find out if these *are* blackmail photos. Is your captor a blackmailer? Or does he need these pictures for another purpose, like to save his own hide?"

At that, he felt Laysa start. She turned, staring into his face, and asked, "Is that even a possibility?"

"He invaded your home. He held you against your will there," Kanen said. "He beat you up in order to get information from you. But, if he was really dangerous, he could have killed you or shot you in the leg or wherever."

"He threatened to kill me. But would he have done that before getting his insurance policy?" she asked, looking at the men, who largely remained silent. That made her worry even more. "Plus … he wanted *you* here, Kanen, so he could get this information. Maybe it's more about Kanen and less about the photos. The fact is, I'm half expecting my attacker to walk through that damn door any moment. Something was really, really creepy about him."

"He did break into your apartment, beat you and hold you captive. So he'll seem creepy and scary and pretty damn evil in your mind for a while. To me, he's just another piece of shit, trying to bend another person to his will. Whether he's trying to save his own skin or trying to blackmail these people, it doesn't matter to me. I'm going after him for what he did to you."

He watched tears come to her eyes, and she smiled mistily up at him. He shook his head and wrapped his arms around her. "How can you think I wouldn't be here to help you? Of course I'm pissed off at what he's done. That's not acceptable. But to batter and bruise somebody I know and care about, well, that'll never go down well."

"If you two are done reminiscing about how much you care about each other," Nelson teased, "potentially you could turn all that energy into figuring out how we'll deal with this from here on in."

"I still think we should scan these to use facial recognition software, so we can identify them," Taylor stated. "Then we can contact these people and find out if they *are* being blackmailed. It's possible these photos are being held for a future time. If any of them are political figures, then there might be better times in their careers to be blackmailed, to get something from them or to ruin their careers. Think about elections coming up or bills being passed. If you wanted to sway the political leanings of somebody, nothing like having some nice little photos in your possession to make them do what you want."

She shuddered. "That's terrible."

The men just laughed.

"We deal with this on a global level," Taylor said. "But it all comes down to one man who's usually leading the pack, pushing from behind to get his wants met."

Kanen had seen way too many democracies fall under the power of one man in third-world countries. It was usually about power. It was rarely about the people. He tapped the photos. "Okay, we'll scan these. We'll keep them in a zip file. Who can do the facial recognition?"

"MI6 or maybe Tesla," Taylor said. "She is about the only one with that kind of software which we can access and keep it private. That's if she's available. These people might be too old now for that application anyway. I don't know."

Kanen nodded. He pulled out his phone and sent Mason a text, then glanced at Laysa. "Do you have a scanner at your house?"

She nodded. But she didn't look happy about it.

"May we use it, if we promise this material will never fall into the wrong hands?" It still didn't make her look much happier.

"You can't promise that though, can you? Already you're talking about sending it to someone, which means it'll always be available on the internet."

She was right, and nothing he could do would make her feel any better about that truth. But still, it was what needed to happen.

CHAPTER 5

S HE DIDN'T LIKE Kanen's plan, but it was the only one they had. They crossed the lobby of the hotel only to be suddenly surrounded by several official-looking men in suits.

"It's barely eight in the morning. It's too early for this," Kanen grumbled to the guys.

Laysa came to a confused stop, looked up and said, "Gentlemen, may I help you?"

The three men she was with stepped up beside her, forcing the others to step back.

One of the strangers stepped forward, the other two behind him now, as he held up a hand and said, "We need to talk."

Kanen stepped in front of Laysa. "Identification please," he said, his tone hard.

The two suited men exchanged assessing gazes before the stranger in charge carefully pulled an ID card out of his upper chest pocket. He held it out for Kanen to look at. Of course nobody offered it to her. Kanen studied it, and she caught just the barest grimace cross his face.

She turned to look at the man and said, "I presume you're some special government officer?"

The man chuckled. "We're MI6," he said in a lazy voice. "Julian Normandy, at your service. I understand you might be involved in something a little nasty."

She nodded. "Maybe you can help."

"We're hoping we can." He turned and motioned toward a big black vehicle, like a cross between a sedan and an SUV, sitting outside the hotel's front door. "We'll ask you to join us for a talk."

She headed forward without hesitation. But obviously the three men with her weren't too happy. She glanced at Kanen. "Is this a bad idea?"

He sighed. "No, but it's a curtailing of freedom." He motioned at the man whose ID he'd been given. "Julian has been sent to keep an eye on us while we're here."

"Both informally and formally, depending if you're here officially or unofficially," Julian said with a grin.

She was ushered into the middle seat in the sedan with Kanen on one side and Nelson on the other. It was almost a limo with three rows of front-facing seats. Taylor was in the last bench seat behind her with the two men who had been with Julian. MI6 had a driver waiting in the car, and Julian climbed in to take the front passenger seat. By the time they were all packed inside, and the vehicle was on the move, she turned to Julian and asked, "How did you know we were in trouble?"

"Charles, in a roundabout way."

She frowned. "I don't know Charles," she said hesitantly.

"I do," Kanen said. "But I didn't expect him to call in the reinforcements."

"No, but I think he found something he thought made the two of us meeting up a good idea."

That was unnerving. She stared out the window. "Are we going to Charles's place then?" she asked hopefully. "We really have a situation we don't know how to handle."

Kanen stiffened at her side, but she ignored him. She didn't live in his world of ugliness, and she knew her husband hadn't either. Whatever was going on now was foreign to her, and that made it a very uncomfortable and uneasy place to be. Any help would be appreciated.

"Would you care to explain?" Julian asked.

"My husband died just under a year ago," she said slowly. "Apparently sometime before he died, he was asked to hold something by a man he knew. And he did so without letting me know. Now this person has come back looking for it. He broke into my apartment and held me captive while he searched. He couldn't find it, so he slapped me around to try to get information as to where it was."

At that, Julian crossed his arms and glared at her. "And you didn't call the police?"

She didn't like his tone. She stiffened her back and gave him a hard look. "I was a captive at the time, so I could hardly do it then, could I?"

"But you did get free. Why didn't you call for assistance then?"

She widened her eyes in a look she had perfected a long time ago and said gently, "I did. I contacted Carl, who is in law enforcement. Not to mention at the hospital, the local forensic techs collected DNA and took photos. My assailant had forced me to contact Kanen. So, of course, I had to contact him again when I got free. He's a good friend, so I turned to him for help."

Julian looked at her in surprise, turned to look at Kanen and then back at her. "You're living in England. You have law enforcement all around you. You have *government* law enforcement all around you. And yet, you call an American to come over here and help you? You didn't want to wait for this Carl person to get in touch with the right people?"

"Kanen was already on the way after the first call from my captor. Of course, when Kanen arrived, I followed his lead. It's what he does. He's also a friend, so that was the best thing for me to do."

Julian stared at her in disbelief. "That's not a normal thing to do."

She crossed her arms over her chest, almost imitating him, and leaned back. "I trust Kanen. He was my husband's best friend too. He's also a navy SEAL, although that's not for public knowledge. He and his buddies handle this kind of stuff all the time. If there was anybody I could count on to help me, it was him. My captor insisted I call Kanen because the asshole figured, if I wasn't holding the material, then Kanen would be."

"That makes more sense. Did you ever meet this guy?" Julian turned to ask Kanen.

Kanen shook his head and picked up the story. "Her attacker wore a mask, so we have no facial features to go by. Laysa didn't recognize his voice but noted he was short for a man, and yet, very muscular with extremely wide feet. So, no, I don't believe I've ever met this guy. But we haven't found him, so I can't confirm that yet. And you can bet that, when I do, he won't be talking much."

JULIAN'S FROWN DEEPENED.

Kanen shook his head. "Don't give me that look. This guy holds a single woman hostage in her apartment and beats her up for information she doesn't have. Surely you expect me to at least break the bully's jaw."

Julian appeared to think it wasn't worth arguing about.

"Did you find out what it was he was looking for?"

"Possibly," Laysa said cautiously.

"And that's where I'm supposed to help?" Julian asked, raising one eyebrow.

"No, the only help we need is a ride back to her apartment," Kanen snapped.

Julian glared at him.

Just then Kanen's phone rang. He put it to his ear. "Mason, I'm in an MI6 vehicle, taken to an undetermined location. If you don't hear from us in the next twenty-four hours, you know we've been sunk deep in the ocean."

Mason's lazy voice rolled through the phone and into the vehicle. "I presume that will not happen. Julian, is that you?"

Kanen hit the Speaker button so everybody in the vehicle could hear.

"Hello, Mason. You could have told me yourself what was going on."

"I would have if they had brought me up to date on any of it," Mason said. "But it seems to have all just happened, so I couldn't update you, could I? But I presume Charles has been kept in the loop somehow."

"Yes," Kanen said. "I gave him updates as we were moving about Ipswich, just in case something went south."

Laysa stared at him in surprise. "I think I'd like to meet this Charles."

Kanen laced his fingers with hers. "He's a very honorable ex-military benefactor. He's helped a lot of men."

Julian laughed.

"That's not a bad way to describe him. And he is, indeed, the one who called me," Mason said. "Did you send him a photo?"

"Yes," Kanen said. "I took a picture of one of the photos we found and sent it to Charles, hoping he could ID the man."

Julian nodded. "That's the one he sent to me. So now we're all together on the same page." His smile was big and bright with a tinge of hardness to it.

She didn't need this jockeying around for position. "I get all of this who's-in-charge stuff is important to you guys, but what's important to me is that we catch this asshole. I don't know why he wants this stuff. I don't know what he'll do with it. I don't know who he is or where he came from. I don't want these photos floating around for anyone to see. And I *really* don't want him coming back after me." She leaned forward and glared at Julian. "Got it?"

Surprised at her tonal aberration, Julian smiled at her. "Got it."

Mason chuckled. "Nice to meet you, Laysa. I'm one of Kanen's team members."

Beside her, Kanen leaned over and said, "Essentially he's the boss but with lots of bigger bosses above him."

She nodded. She had asked Kanen years ago for an explanation of how all that military stuff had worked, and he'd given her a brief outline, but it hadn't made a whole lot of sense. An awful lot of titles were involved. She wasn't sure who did all the work. "So then why are you taking us anywhere?" Laysa asked Julian.

"We need a place to talk obviously," Julian said, "and inside this vehicle is private."

She glanced at Kanen.

He shook his head. "No, it's not. It'll be bugged."

Julian looked at him in surprise. "No, it won't be."

Taylor snorted. "Shall I run a test then?"

KANEN

Julian looked at him. "If you have something on you, go ahead."

Taylor was in the seat behind her. She couldn't see what he was doing. She heard a weird hum behind her as he turned in the vehicle and slowly shifted around, as if searching for something.

When he was finally done, he sat back and said, "It's clean."

Julian looked at him. "How could you suspect anything less?"

"Are *you* recording this conversation?" Kanen asked.

"Should we be?"

"You didn't answer my question."

"*We* should then," Taylor stated.

"Stop," Laysa snapped. "Keep all your posturing to yourselves. This is not about who has rights, who has ownership of this problem. We're Americans. And we're on British soil. And these navy men are here to help protect me as much as anything."

"That's the theory," Taylor said.

"Yes, that is the theory," Julian said helpfully. "But the photo that Charles sent us is of one of our current ambassadors. A man of some prominence. And those photos are not ones we've ever seen before. They aren't for public consumption, and that means somebody's violated his privacy, and there has to be a reason why."

"The only reason we can think of," she said, "well, based on my assailant's comment to me about wanting his *insurance policy* back, as things have changed, ... is likely blackmail. Maybe he lost his digital copies and now needs the physical images."

Julian blinked at her a couple times, processing her con-

75

voluted explanation. Then he smiled. "That's all too possible. But these photos are quite old. So who is this attacker of yours, where did he get these photos, and what is he planning on doing with them if he gets them back now?"

"We were hoping you would answer that," she said. "My apartment building might have cameras. I don't know. If you could check who came and went, then maybe we'd find out who he is."

"The gym also has cameras," Kanen said. "I can check with the manager about security footage. That's where we found the bag with the photos. It's possible Laysa's assailant tried to get into Blake's gym locker too."

"But now you have the bag, these photos—correct?"

"We have something," Kanen said. "But I can't guarantee it's what the woman-beating asshole is looking for."

"Did you know about his gym locker?" Julian asked Laysa.

"I knew Blake went to the gym, and it was possible he had a locker there. I guess I just assumed he wouldn't keep anything valuable there."

"Did you need a key to get into it?"

"That's where things get a little odd," Kanen said. He explained about the money and the secret stash of currency that held the locker combination.

"That's very cloak-and-dagger stuff," Julian said. "Why would Blake do something so convoluted?"

Her laugh was strained to the point of almost hysteria. "Let's back up to a year ago and ask him," she snapped. "I have no clue. He was a huge movie buff with dinners afterwards to dissect what we watched. Maybe he saw somebody do something like that in a movie and thought it would work. Maybe he was afraid he'd forget the combination. Maybe this was how he managed to remind himself. I don't know why he did it. I didn't even know he had accepted this bag to begin with."

Kanen squeezed her fingers. "It'll be okay," he said quietly. "We're getting to the bottom of this. We will find this guy."

She closed her eyes and leaned back. "I hear what you're saying," she said. "I just wish we didn't have to dance around each other, so we could get on with it already."

Just then the vehicle pulled up outside her apartment building. She turned to Julian and asked, "Do you want to come up and take a look?"

He nodded. "Thank you. I would like that."

The vehicle parked, and all seven of them got out, the driver again remaining in the vehicle. She led the way to her apartment in silence. Everybody else followed her. At her door she stopped, her shoulders sagged. She looked over at Kanen. "I really don't want to do this."

He took the key from her and opened it.

Julian entered ahead of them.

Kanen said, "Remember that she was held here and beaten by that asshole. Show some sensitivity."

Julian nodded but didn't say a word.

Inside the apartment, nothing seemed to have changed. The MI6 men spread out and did a search. Julian came to the three of them standing in a half circle around Laysa and said, "Where did you find the money?"

Kanen led him to the kitchen drawer, pulled it back out and flipped it, so Julian could see where the tape had been. Then Kanen walked over to the coffee table, lifted a large Atlas and underneath it was the money as he had left it.

Still taped together, still in sequence.

"Interesting," Julian said. "Okay, so now let's get to the basics. Where are the photos?"

The men looked at each other, then turned and looked at Laysa.

She sighed. "You might as well show him. We would probably ask for their help anyway. We need to find out who all these people are."

Kanen took one of the envelopes of photos from an inside pocket to his jacket and lay them out on the kitchen table. The other two men with him did the same thing. By the time the entire kitchen table was full, they turned all the chairs sideways and filled them too.

Julian and his men stared.

"Wow," Julian said. "An awful lot of photos are here."

"Exactly. But we know none of the people in them," Kanen said. "This blackmailer appears to have a more European focus than American."

Julian tapped one of the photos and said, "This is a very prominent British family." He tapped another one. "This was a prominent British family who was accused of several major white-collar crimes and evaded being charged. They are now living in France."

They went through all the photos. Julian failed to recognize only six men.

"So we agree most of these men are in high positions of some kind, and whoever took these compromising photos thought they might be of monetary interest in some way to the people in these photos, correct?" Laysa asked.

The men all nodded.

"That would be a good guess," Julian said. "But these are old photos. Have these men been paying all this time? Did they pay, and this is just insurance that nobody says anything or insurance that the men are forever on the hook for?"

"That could also mean," one of Julian's men said, "what if one of these blackmailed men went after the blackmailer, found his stash and now this new blackmailer is looking to get even?"

"That's possible too," Julian said thoughtfully. "There're three or four likely scenarios. And I think we've touched on them all. None of the photos have dates on the backs."

"I wonder …" Taylor said as he picked up a photo. "A smudge is on the back of each of them, as if some sort of acetate or vinegar solution might have erased the date stamp. Maybe a photo was taken, and it was recorded, but this way they're undated forever."

"And the advantage of that is what?" Laysa asked.

"Because they can be used over and over again."

Laysa's attention was caught by one photo. She stepped closer and squatted down beside the kitchen chair it was on. "She's very beautiful."

The men gathered around behind her.

One of Julian's men said, "I don't know the woman's name, but she married one of our members of parliament, Carlos … somebody," he started. "Although I don't think he serves any longer. Didn't he retire to Spain?"

"He did," Julian confirmed.

Laysa said thoughtfully, "If he paid, this still could have had a great impact on his career. After all, the blackmailer could take the money and could then order Carlos to rule a certain way in parliament. The threat of the photo becoming public is a continuing one. … What if Carlos wants to make sure this photo is gone forever?"

"It's possible. Any and all conjecture is possible," Kanen said. "But short of traveling to Spain and asking him and returning the photo, we won't know."

She shrugged. "I'd be happy to leave the country for a few days. Spain is only a quick hop away. Let's go."

Kanen turned to look at her.

"It's calling for rain in England anyway."

Kanen gave a boisterous laugh. "It's always calling for rain in England."

She beamed up at him. "So what better reason to go for a mini holiday then?"

Kanen chose to look at the MI6 men. "I presume none of you will speak to him?"

Julian grimaced. "No. And why would Carlos talk to you?"

"To tell him that his personal life is his own," Laysa replied, "and I thought maybe he would like this original photo."

"And then what? Just ask him if he was really having sex with her?" one of the MI6 men asked in a derisive tone.

Kanen stiffened and glared at him. "We're not confirming the veracity of the pictures. We're in search of an assailant who knows of the existence of these pictures and may have been the original blackmailer."

"Maybe Carlos can tell us something about him," she said thoughtfully. "Obviously you'll identify the six other men here who haven't already been ID'd, but then what? If you take away all these photos, I'll have a very angry captor returning, looking for goods he can't get back and that I can't give him."

Kanen pulled her toward him, wrapped his arms around her and tucked her close. "You don't have a lot of choice because MI6 is taking over this case."

Julian gave a bark of laughter. "We took it over the minute we heard about it. You guys were just slow to get the memo."

She turned to glare at him.

He held his hands up in mock surrender in front of him. "All in the best interests of keeping you safe, of course.

She rolled her eyes, making Kanen grin. "Then we'll be speaking to Carlos. Your agents can flutter around and look at these old photos. But I think the heart of the matter might be found in Spain."

"I'm willing and game if you are," Kanen said.

She smiled, took one look at Julian and asked, "Do you have any objection to us taking the five photos related to Carlos with us to Spain? I'd like to return those to him."

He shook his head. "Not at all. As long as we have a photo of the original pictures, I'm satisfied." He pointed at one of his men, who pulled out his phone and took a couple snapshots of each photo before handing over the five in question to Kanen. "But do keep in touch. There's no reason to think you'll be followed. But it's pretty easy for somebody to track you from one place to the next."

"We'll keep your advice in mind. But I have three knights of honor here, helping to keep me safe," she said with a big smile. "And we'll all enjoy a holiday in Spain."

Taylor chuckled as he stood at her side. "I've never been, so I'm in."

Nelson laughed. "I have been. But I'm all for going again."

"Decision made. We'll be in Spain." She took the pictures of the parliament member from Kanen. "Giving the originals back to Carlos."

"He may not want to talk to you," Julian warned. "This is a very sensitive issue."

"For that reason alone, he *will* talk to me," she said confidently. "If just to find out that it's over with."

CHAPTER 6

LAYSA WANTED TO dance. How long had she planned to come to Spain? And here they were—10:50 a.m., two and half hours after MI6 had dropped them at the airport instead of their rental car at Kanen's hotel—the four of them driving along the coast. Even though their reason for being here was grim, it still felt in some ways like a holiday. A holiday that she and Blake had wanted to take but just never seemed to make happen. If ever a lesson was to be learned about losing a loved one, it was to make the most of every day.

It had taken her a long time to see the joy in any day after losing him, but finally she had turned a corner. It was good. Even in these circumstances, it was good.

Beside her Kanen asked, "What are you grinning about?"

"It feels good to be alive. And I owe you thanks for that."

He raised an eyebrow. "I'm glad to hear you're feeling better, but it's got nothing to do with me."

She reached for his hand. "Not true," she said. "Regardless of the reason, just having you back in my life, even seeing you, has made me realize what a slump I had gotten into and how I'd forgotten to see the joy in everything Blake and I had. Do you realize we had always planned to come to Spain for a holiday? And yet, somehow, even though we were so close, we never did. That's just wrong."

"Quite true. It would have been a quick holiday for you. But we're here now, even though it's not a holiday and even though Blake isn't with us today," Kanen added. "I'm glad to hear you're happy about it regardless."

She smiled. "Very happy. Even more to realize I'm not caught in the depths of despair anymore," she said slowly. "I loved Blake with all my heart. Losing him was the most devastating event in my life. The suddenness of it. I guess there's no good way for somebody to die. I can't say I wanted him to suffer for five years just so I'd get five more years with him, but, when you wake up one day, and you don't know it'll be the last time you'll see somebody … That was hard, and it reminded me just now how much we had planned to do that we never did. How much we wanted to do that we never made time for. I guess it's one of those lessons you never really understand until you go through something like this and realize how every day is precious."

There was silence in the vehicle as the men absorbed her revelation.

"I think, sadly, you're quite right about that," Nelson said. "Most of us don't learn these lessons the easy way. I think we get so caught up in everything we're doing that we forget to plan for things we might want to be doing."

"What does this trip to Spain mean to you?" Taylor asked Laysa. "I get that you're looking for answers about your own home invasion and assault, but is there anything else? A trip down memory lane for you and your husband perhaps?"

She was silent for a long moment while she thought about it. "I think it's just wanting to make the most of every day," she said quietly. "When we were married, we always thought there was time. We would do it next week, next month, next year, whatever. But it's amazing how much Blake's death and this home invasion event have cemented into my brain that I should take advantage of everything right now because there might not be another moment after this. I want answers to what this is all about, yes. Did we need to come to Spain? No, but it certainly wasn't a hardship. And, if I can make this man's life a little easier by handing back something he might be worried about, then I will do it."

"You realize he's likely to have the opposite reaction," Nelson said, waiting for her nod. "He might hold you responsible. He might think you're involved in some way. He could get ugly about this. He might be old enough that he's completely confused and has no clue what that photo is."

"I know," she said, pinching the bridge of her nose. "I realize my desire to do this is kind of an odd thought, and all those hypothetical responses from him are possible. Still, it got us out of England for a couple days while they track down my captor. I'm more than happy to wander Spain with you guys."

"Likewise," Taylor said. "I've wanted to come for a long time."

"I've never been here," she said with a laugh. "We should stay for a week or two."

"I wish," Kanen agreed with a smile. "But we have jobs to go back to. These guys came to help me out, and we can't take advantage of that."

"I'm so sorry," she said. "You're right. We'll make it as fast as possible." She pointed at the road sign up ahead. "And we're here."

They turned, following the GPS instructions per their rental car. Very quickly they pulled up by a small townhome with a Spanish-looking roof meshed between two other very similar-looking buildings. She hopped out and, with Kanen at her side, marched up to the front door and knocked.

It took a moment before an old man came to the door. and rapid-fire Spanish was shot at them.

When he stopped, she asked, "Do you speak English?"

He said, "Yes, I do. But why is it you think everybody should speak your language?"

She winced. Not exactly a good start. She studied his features and realized he, indeed, was the man in the photo. Although he might be a good fifteen to twenty years older. She pulled out a photo and introduced herself. "This came into my possession. I didn't know if it was important for you to have back."

He looked at the photo. His eyes widened, and a red wash of anger ripped up his features as he spat out Spanish in a deeply ugly tone.

Kanen stepped forward and held up his hand. "Stop."

The old man stared at him, almost vibrating with rage.

In a calm voice, Kanen said, "She had nothing to do with it. She's not part of the blackmail. Her husband, who is now dead, had a bag of these photos he was asked to keep for somebody. She wanted to return it to you. There are four more. She's happy to destroy them. But she didn't know if you wanted to know where the originals were."

As Kanen spoke, she watched the old man's features. Slowly they calmed as he realized they weren't here to extort money from him.

He took the photo from her hand. And then raised his eyes to Kanen's face. "There are more?"

She pulled out the envelope and handed it to him. "Five in all."

He took them from her fingers and shuffled through them, his shoulders sagging. "You had nothing to do with these?"

She shook her head. "No. The first I saw of them was earlier today."

He frowned and tapped the photos. "I paid a lot of money to get these."

"And you didn't get them?"

He shook his head. "I'd hoped to but no. And then I thought maybe they didn't exist and how I had paid for nothing," he admitted. "Now you show up with them decades later, and you're not looking for money?" Doubt filled his gaze as it went from one to the other, including the two men standing behind Kanen and Laysa.

She smiled up at him. "No. But, if these were photos of me, and I was being blackmailed, I would want the original photos back, even though digital copies or the photographic film from an older camera may still be available."

He nodded. "If there are digital copies, or the roll of film itself exists, then I still have to worry, don't I?"

"We don't know that there are digital copies or any film," Kanen interrupted. "We think the blackmailer, or somebody involved in the affair, held the originals as leverage against somebody. Maybe multiple somebodies, people like you. But, for some reason, he has now come back after the originals."

The old man thought about it, but he certainly wasn't slow. "The only reason he would need them is if he had no other copies and needed these originals." He nodded and pushed open the door. "I am Carlos. You may come in," he announced. He led them past a small parlor-type room and back farther to a large family kitchen that opened up to a small garden in the back.

He sat down on a bench in the backyard. "She's my wife, you know. At least she was after those photos were taken."

He looked at the photo, his fingers gently caressing the woman's features. "At this time she was married to someone else, but her husband passed away after being ill for a very long time. I was a politician, so, once he passed, we waited a decent amount of time, then married. But, since I was an upcoming politician, just before I was being voted in as a member of the parliament, these photos were sent to me, with a note saying they would be on the front page of every newspaper if I didn't pay. At the time it would have been terribly damaging to my career," he confessed. "She was fairly well-known, as was her husband, and very well-respected. Our images would have been forever tarnished."

"I'm sorry," Laysa said. "People are opportunists. And they will try to ruin our life sometimes, but we don't always have to let that happen."

He studied her face. "How did you get involved?"

She sat on the bench beside him and explained again how her husband had accepted something from a man who asked him to keep it, and her husband had died almost a year ago. When she came home to her apartment yesterday, she had been held captive for many hours. The stranger tried to find out where the bag was, and he beat her.

Carlos looked terrified at the concept of her being beaten, stared longer at the bruise on her jawline. He kept patting her knee, trying to console her.

She realized she had tears in the corner of her eyes. She

sniffed them back and smiled brightly. "It's okay. Kanen came to help. And he brought his friends. It didn't take long for them to find the photos. But we didn't know what they meant. Or what we were supposed to do with them. If these photos could be returned to their rightful owners, maybe they could have some peace of mind after all this time, and that's what I want to happen the most."

"You have a big heart," Carlos said with a smile. "Anja would have liked that." His gaze dropped to the photos in his gnarled fingers, still working over the surface. "She died five years ago, and a light went out of my world. The older I get, the more I realize the important things in life—whether you live five, ten or one hundred years—are really the relationships you make and keep throughout that life."

She studied his well-worn features, struck by the wisdom of his words. "I agree," she said softly, "because that's exactly what I feel now. Although I lost my husband, I'm so grateful I had the time I did with him."

He held up the photo for her. "You can't stop looking for another relationship," he announced. "Because, my Anja, she loved her first husband. Loved him very, very much. And though she was with me at the end of her time with him, it wasn't because she wanted to be disloyal. It was because she wanted somebody to care, somebody who would hold her, who would let her know it would be okay, even as she had to return to the dying man she loved. But it was a burden for her that she had nobody to share with. I was her friend. I became her confidant, her supporter and then finally her lover. We knew it was wrong, but we couldn't help ourselves from taking these stolen moments. Moments to help us return to the separate worlds we lived in.

"After her Andre died, I couldn't convince her to marry

me. She was so sure we had done something terribly wrong. It wasn't wrong," he said with strength, "but it took a long time to convince her. Finally I did, and together we honored Andre's life by being happy, by reliving the memories of him, by holding him in honor, by speaking about him, by keeping his legacy alive. We did many good things for the community in his name—set up scholarships, set up grants and programs. We did everything for him because it made us happy. He couldn't be here with her, but I'd like to think he was smiling from above, giving me permission to make her happy because he wasn't here to do so himself."

She was touched by that. "And I'm sure he did smile, that he would be happy to look down and to realize it was important for her to carry on and to have a good life too," she said with a smile.

The old man turned to look at her. "That goes for you as well. You cannot stay alone. You are young. You have your whole life ahead of you."

She chuckled. "I don't intend to stay alone. I was very upset, depressed, and I grieved for a long time." She smiled again. "But it's recently been brought to my attention that the time of mourning has come to an end. And it's time for me to face forward and not backward. I can carry the memory of Blake inside, but I can't carry his ghost anymore."

The old man nodded in understanding. "Good. You need to let it go." He held up the photos in his hand and said, "Even though these photos cost me a lot of pain and anger—and a lot of sleepless nights where I wondered what happened to them—I'm very grateful to have them now because they are of an Anja who I knew at the very beginning of our life together. And that Anja was a very, very special woman."

"I'm sorry they are so voyeuristic," Laysa said quietly. "Everybody should be entitled to privacy."

He smiled. "Anja would say that's very true. But she was never ashamed of her body or the joy that being together could bring. So, although she would be ashamed to have unknown people viewing these photos, and I can't imagine how many may have seen them over the years," he said sadly, "she would probably look at the photos, wince and then say, 'Carlos, I look good, don't I?'"

His words made Laysa laugh. "That is a great attitude," she said and stood. "We didn't want to disturb you. Thank you very much for giving us a few moments. We just wanted to let you know the photos are now yours. We don't believe any other physical copies are left, but we can never be sure."

Carlos waved a hand, as if dismissing the idea. "It is not an issue. I am old enough now that any pictures like these are just memories of a time when I was a younger, more virile man, with a woman I loved very much. They don't make me ashamed. They bring smiles to my face with the memories and maybe a little resentment that I have grown old and lost the one I love." Then he chuckled. "I will not pay blackmail again. It is a loser's game. And there's never any peace of mind, even once the payment is met."

Kanen nodded. "That's a very good lesson for everybody to learn. But we all have different reasons for paying off a blackmailer. It might very well have been because you didn't want anything to disturb your rise in politics." His voice was low but deep with understanding. "But I suspect it had nothing to do with that."

The old man turned to look at Kanen, his eyebrows lifting. "What is it you think I did it for?" he asked in challenge.

Kanen studied him and then smiled. "You did it to avoid embarrassing and humiliating and shaming the woman you loved. You would never have paid the blackmail against you alone, except for the pain it would have caused somebody else."

The old man smiled. "That is very true. I would have done anything to preserve Anja's peace of mind. I would never have wanted to humiliate or to shame her. I would never have wanted to shame her husband. They were good people, both of them. That they are now together in heaven is something that brings me peace."

Laysa held out her hand to shake his. "Thank you for seeing us. It makes me feel so much better. We came all the way from England just to hand these to you. But, more than that, I wanted to meet you. I wanted to give you that little peace of mind. Yet you didn't have to see us, and the anger you showed us in the beginning is what we had expected. But I'm really glad to know a much kinder man is on the inside." With that she turned and walked toward the front door, the men still gathered around Carlos.

He called out to her, "Wait. Don't you want to know anything about the blackmail payments?"

She stopped and gave a little gasp, noting the men had not moved. "I completely forgot." She rushed back to Carlos's side. "Do you know who blackmailed you? Was there any way to identify him?"

"Yes," he said. "It was an old colleague of mine. I used to meet him in the coffee shop and make the payments."

"So you know who he is?" Laysa asked.

He nodded. "I tried to kill him at the time. But, of course, that was much too much melodrama."

"Can you give us any information on him?"

The old man got up and walked into the kitchen, then over to a small desk. There he opened the top drawer and pulled out several photos. He handed them one picture, with him and another man. "This is him. I paid him cash for a year, and then I told him no more. He seemed to accept it, shrugged and said it was good for a while." And then Carlos stopped speaking.

"This man is too old to be the one who held me captive," Laysa said. "I don't understand …" She turned to look at Kanen. "How does any of this go together?"

He took the photo from her and studied it intently before handing it to Taylor and Nelson. "I don't know," he said, "but I can tell you one thing. It will connect. That's how this evil works. Somewhere it will make sense."

She looked at the other photos the old man had in his hands. "Who is in those photos?"

He sighed. "I had images of him, wanting to do something to destroy him, as he had threatened to destroy me. I could never go through with it. Joseph Carmel was his name. He had a wife who knew nothing of what he was doing, and he had a son who I knew would be forever harmed by the knowledge of his father being a criminal. So I did nothing. We had an uneasy truce for a long time. I think he knew, if he asked me for more money, I would do something serious to end his extortion. There is an art to understanding your prey, and I think he realized he'd reached my limits."

"Why do we have five photos of you? Did you get any from Carmel at the beginning?"

The old man nodded. "He gave me two. Both were worse than this." His voice went a little faint. "I think that's why it made me so mad, to think he was staring at my beautiful Anja without her permission, without any of us knowing. It was so wrong. And so very invasive."

"Did the blackmail last long?"

"No, no, no," he said, shaking his head. "After I said, *No more*, I just shut him down. We had an uneasy working relationship for another few months, and then he disappeared for years. Ironically he lives close by now, but I don't have anything to do with him." He slowly shook his head from side to side. "I haven't forgiven him for what he did, but I have moved on, just wanting to forget it all happened."

"I think that's what we all want," Laysa said starkly. "I want that man who beat me to disappear, so I never see him again."

"Is it possible Laysa's assailant is the blackmailer's son?" Taylor asked. "It would most logically be somebody who had access to the photos."

She looked to the old man. "Joseph Carmel, how old is he now?"

"Same age as me. Ninety-one."

"And Joseph's son. Do you know what his name was?"

He held up one of the photos. "This is his family. That's his wife and his son, Murray."

She took the photo and studied it. She looked up at Carlos. "May we take this with us?"

He nodded. "Take it. More bad memories I no longer want to have with me. Take them all. I hope you find whoever it was who did this to you. I don't want to ever hear any more about it. So, when you leave, please don't contact me again."

At the door she leaned over and impulsively kissed Carlos on the cheek. "Have a good life," she said.

He grabbed her hand as she walked away. "No," he said gently. "It's you who needs to make a new life for yourself.

My life is old, and it's done. But you—you have so much to live for. So remember. It's all worth living."

Then he stepped inside his house and closed the door while they watched.

"I think those were words to live by," Kanen said. He nudged her toward the vehicle. "Come on. Let's go."

"Where?" she asked, bewildered. "Time to return to England already?"

"No. Time to walk around and to create a few memories of our own," he said gently.

IT OCCURRED TO Kanen that he was walking a fine line. Blake had been his best friend. They'd been so damn close, almost brothers when they were younger. That had changed somewhat when Blake and Laysa connected but not enough to shift the core of their friendship. He'd been so happy for them when they had married. Kanen had never had his eyes on her, never been jealous of either of them. Since Blake's death, he'd done his best to be there for Laysa.

But now he also realized he might be interested in being there for her a little more—make that a lot more. And he struggled to come to terms with whether he was encroaching on Blake's property, crossing the friendship line or reading something into his relationship with Laysa that wasn't there anyway.

Obviously Kanen had been Blake's friend, but now Blake was gone, and Kanen was here. He thought about Taylor's and Nelson's words earlier. It was quite possible Blake would be happy for Kanen and Laysa to get together. That Blake would encourage Kanen to take the extra step to be with her. But he had to get over that feeling of Laysa being his best friend's wife and instead view her as a single woman on her own.

If he'd met any other widow or divorcée, Kanen never would have questioned it. But, because he knew the missing partner, had had a vast and deep relationship with Blake of his own, it made Kanen feel odd.

She squeezed his hand and said, "Penny?"

He chuckled. "It would take several pounds to drag it out of me."

She dipped into her pocket and pulled out a few crumpled bills. "How about this much?"

He shook his head. "No. Honestly I was thinking about Blake."

Startled, she looked at him. "Why? Do you think he was involved too?"

He hated to hear the suspicion in her voice, as if somehow Kanen would betray everything they had shared by believing something wrong about Blake. "No. He would never have been involved in blackmail. I have no misconceptions about who Blake was. He was a man's man, quick to judge and very quick to laugh. He would offer you the shirt off his back, if you needed it, but he also liked to be the best at everything," Kanen said seriously. "He had the best taste in friends and partners."

She chuckled at that.

Kanen smiled because he, of course, had intended her to.

She nodded. "He did, indeed. And you're right. He was quick to judge. But he was also quick to forgive. Although sometimes he didn't like to see anybody else's point of view, once you got him to consider it, he would admit he might not always be right."

Kanen agreed with that too. Blake had been a lot of

things. Kanen couldn't imagine Blake was terribly easy to live with because he had been fairly opinionated. Kanen could also see that, if a buddy had needed Blake to take care of this parcel, he wouldn't have thought anything of it. He would have stuck it in his gym locker and forgotten about it. "I guess I'm worried that his death had something to do with this," he said seriously.

"No, no, no," she cried out.

Taylor and Nelson looked over at him.

"We wondered when you would return to that," Nelson commented.

Kanen nodded slowly. "I didn't want to even contemplate it. Who does?"

"We're not going there," Laysa whispered. "It was hard enough to lose him. No way I want to consider that he was murdered."

"We don't know for sure that he was," Taylor was quick to point out. "Think about it though. It was almost a year ago. Was anything else happening in his life then?"

"Me," she snapped. "I was happening. We were arguing just before his death because I wanted to start a family, and he didn't." There was a note of bitterness in her tone.

After her miscarriage, Blake had said to Kanen, in private, how Blake had been relieved and wasn't sure he would ever be ready to have a family, not with his affinity for risk-taking hobbies.

And yet, Kanen could see that, for Laysa, this would be a big deal. Kanen had planned to visit them anyway and had come soon afterward. He'd held her for hours as she had grieved for her lost child, taking a week off from teaching, yet Blake continued working his job. She'd always wanted a family, a big family preferably, but would be content with just two children if that was all they could manage.

For the first time, Kanen wondered what would have happened down the road if neither would have been willing to budge on that major point.

Kanen frowned as they walked. They'd found the answers they came looking for in Spain. Of course that spawned many more questions, but, in the meantime, they had a free afternoon ahead of them. He wanted to walk through the village, to enjoy the sights, maybe to stop and have a coffee and a treat somewhere along the line. But now that they'd brought up this topic, and he knew it would be hard to come back from.

"Was there anything else happening to Blake at that time?" Nelson persisted. "We have to consider everything."

She shook her head. "I don't like this line of thinking. I get that you have to ask, but Blake wasn't the kind to get into trouble."

Kanen came to a stop at that. He turned to look at her. "That's not quite true."

She frowned up at him. "Since I met him—or rather, since we married—he'd stayed out of trouble," she corrected. "Although he still loved to live on the edge."

Kanen considered her face for a long moment. "That might be closer to the truth," he said. "But, in all the years I knew him, he was always in trouble. In the pub for a friendly drink, he'd always challenged the biggest guy. We ended up in more dustups for a lot of stupid reasons." A huge grin took over his face. "The Blake I knew, he was always happy to jump in and cause a ruckus, just for the joy of fighting."

"Right," she said, "but you know as well as I do that, in the year before we were married, he calmed down quite a bit."

"Quite a bit, yes. But I wonder what he was like at the gym."

Silence followed as she pondered that for a moment. And then shook her head. "I can't imagine it would be any different than what he always was. He was very steady, very stable with me."

"Of course. That's what you needed," Kanen said thoughtfully. "The thing that you really wanted was somebody you could count on. And he was determined to be that."

"There was a lot more to our relationship than that," she protested. "That's a very simplistic way of looking at our marriage."

"Not necessarily," he said. "We all have things we give and take in relationships, and, in this case, that was important to you. Your father had run off on you. Your mother used to take off all the time on you, even your brother did. And I remember you telling Blake very clearly that you wanted someone who would stay at your side, someone you didn't have to worry about deserting you." Kanen cupped her chin, lifting it ever-so-slightly. "Whether you like remembering that or not, it was definitely one of the rules of your relationship."

She tucked her chin down and walked several steps forward. He followed at a slightly slower pace. She hunched her shoulders. "Do you think I stifled the real him?"

"No," Kanen said gently. "I think he was happy to do it because it was important for him to be with you. You were everything to him. And he made a lot of changes for you because he wanted you to be as happy as he was," Kanen admitted.

He hadn't spent too much time thinking about it, but,

now that he was on the topic, Kanen could see how the relationship with Laysa had changed Blake, how he'd pulled back from so many of his rougher activities. He used to box in the ring just for fun. It was fitness for him. But then he loved nothing better than a good rowdy brawl. At one point, they'd contemplated joining a football team in the States, just for the physicality of it.

Of all the things Kanen had done with Blake, Kanen had never gone to the gym with Blake. Definitely not here in England. Never in the States either. *And that was interesting.* Because Kanen didn't know what Blake would be like in that environment. Kanen sighed. Blake was probably much more aggressive in a gym than in a bar fight because he was supposed to fight others there.

Kanen pulled out the gym manager's card and dialed Mark, while the others walked slowly forward, watching him. When the call was answered, he asked what Blake's behavior was like at the gym.

That drew Laysa closer to Kanen again, leaning in to hear Mark's side of the conversation.

"I knew him when we were younger," Kanen explained. "And Blake was quite a punch-up, dustup kind of guy. Always happy to jump into the fray and pound a few faces to the ground. Did he use the gym as an outlet for all that energy?"

The voice on the other end of the phone chuckled. "Absolutely. I had to get in his face a couple times to stop him from getting into everybody else's. We try hard to have a no-contest type of a gym, but gym junkies can be like that. *Who can pull the most weight? Who can bench press the most?* Everybody prides themselves on their upper body, whereas Blake was really, really strong in his lower body. He used to challenge people on lower-body competitions, so he could win. But he wasn't quite so gracious about upper-body competing because he knew he'd lose."

Kanen understood completely. "I wondered if that was the case. Did he ever get into any real fights with anyone?"

Mark's voice was thoughtful as he slowly replied, "A couple complaints were made against him. I had to, you know, like I said, get in his face a bit and have him calm down and back off. People come here to work out. They don't want to get stressed out by having someone else on their case. Every time I would talk to Blake, he'd calm down for a while, and then somebody would piss him off, and he'd go jump into it again."

"At any time was it to the point of him losing his membership? Was he ever that much of a disruptive force that you felt he couldn't come back?"

"Once I warned him that it was his last chance."

"When was that?"

"Not very long before he passed away, actually," Mark admitted. "He got into a ruckus with a bunch of the steadies here. Though Blake had been coming for a couple years, these guys had been coming for a decade plus. And they were pretty fed up with his attitude."

"How bad was it?

"It took all of us to break them up. I reviewed the tapes afterward, and it was obvious Blake had been pushing their buttons. So he got his final warning. If he'd done it again, he would have been out, never to return. He seemed to smarten up then. He apologized, saying he didn't know what got into him. He was just frustrated at home and needed an outlet."

At that Laysa turned her huge wounded eyes to Kanen.

"He was having trouble with his marriage. His wife

wanted to start a family or something, and he didn't want anything to do with that. She'd lost a baby once, and he'd been relieved. She wanted to try again, but that was the last thing he wanted. He was using the gym as a way to get away, a way to drive some of that temperament back inside again so it wouldn't spill over into his marriage. I told him that he couldn't just come here and beat up on other people because he wouldn't come clean with his wife."

"Your guilt kept you from opening his locker all this time, didn't it?"

"Yeah, I guess. It's not like I needed the locker. And every time I looked at it, it just kind of made me feel sad. I wish I'd done more."

"Done more ..."

"I have to admit. Every time I think about him, I wonder if he didn't commit suicide. Maybe things were so bad at home that he took a fast and easy way out."

CHAPTER 7

S*UICIDE?* C*RUSHED,* L*AYSA* took several faltering steps to the side of the road, where a short stone wall stood. She sat on top of it, collapsing, her mind reeling from the suggestion. It had never occurred to her. Why would it? As far as she'd known, they'd been blissfully happy. Blake was a great man. She refused to believe anything differently. So he hadn't been ready to start a family? That was hardly a character flaw.

But how happy could they have been if Blake would go to the gym, picking fights with other guys to work off some of that angry energy? That didn't sound like a happy guy to her at all. As a matter of fact, it didn't sound like a happy marriage either. He'd had a temper, … but that's why he'd gone to the gym.

If she hadn't pushed him about having a baby, would he still be alive? She couldn't let that thought go. It just drilled deeper and deeper into her soul, splintering everything she thought she knew about their life together. She'd never questioned the police. They'd told her it was a car accident, and she'd believed them. She didn't remember the details now. She didn't want to know. They told her that he hadn't suffered, and that had been all she needed. She couldn't bear to hear how bad it might have been.

She presumed Kanen knew. Because he was the kind

DALE MAYER

who wanted details. She was pretty sure he'd said something about getting the rest of the information, and she'd said not to tell her. She'd wanted to remain in her happy little bubble that said Blake had died instantly and hadn't suffered.

She lifted her gaze to Kanen's hard face. He stared at her, a worried look in his eyes. "Is that what you found out from the police? That Blake committed suicide?"

He moved forward and dropped to his knees in front of her. He picked up her hands and held them close to his chest. "No. Suicide was never mentioned, was never contemplated. The evidence at the scene confirmed it was an accident." He paused, then added, "Just like the police said at the first and what I relayed to you."

She closed her eyes as a wave of relief washed through her. "I don't think I could stand it if he had committed suicide to avoid me," she whispered. "Even without him attempting suicide, here I thought we were happy, and instead he went to the gym to beat the crap out of people so he didn't come home and beat me up." She raised her gaze in bewilderment. "I never saw it in him."

"Good," Kanen said with a little more force than necessary. "Think about that. He did everything he could to let all that aggression out a long way away from you, so you didn't see it."

"But then what else didn't I see?" she asked quietly. She knew the other men were listening in. There was really no way to keep this private. But then they already knew so much about her that it didn't matter now. "Maybe he did know this guy? Maybe Blake *was* involved in the blackmail?" She stared at Kanen, her heart sad, her mind confused. "How do I know anymore, when everything I thought I knew wasn't real?"

"Everything you thought you knew about him hasn't changed," Kanen said. "Just because he goes to the gym to let off a little steam, that doesn't change who he was."

She had trouble believing that. They were in this absolutely beautiful little town in Spain. It was so unique and so quaint, and she'd never been happier than when she had stepped out into this area. Just to see the countryside, to see how different it was, wishing with all her heart Blake was with her.

And now she was out here with everything about Blake crumbling at her feet. Was she making too much of it? It just seemed like such an inherently big issue, a huge part of his personality, to have not understood that about him. Sure, people would say she was female, and he was male. They'd say all kinds of things, if they got a chance. But the real issue was the fact that she felt like he'd been hiding who he really was. And she didn't know what to do with that information.

Kanen stood, reached out a hand and said, "Come on. Let's go for a walk."

She shook her head. "I don't feel like it."

"Too bad." He snatched her hand and gently pulled her to her feet. "We'll head over there to that little family restaurant. I'm hungry."

"About time somebody mentioned food," Nelson said. The men seemed eager to have a change of topic. "That looks like a great place to sit down and have a bite."

She knew what they were trying to do. It was just hard to let them do it. She wanted to curl up in a hot bath and dive deeper into this issue, and they didn't want anything to do with it. Was that just another elementary difference between males and females? She couldn't believe how hard this one issue hit her. It was difficult to imagine how different she and Blake really were. It never occurred to her to go to a gym so she could get into a physical fight to expend energy before going home to her spouse.

What did she do when she got stressed?

She'd cry. She'd hit that point where she couldn't do anything about something, and she'd burst into tears. It was so unacceptable to Blake, probably as bad as his fighting was to her.

She always felt so much better afterward, and Blake always felt so much worse. He didn't understand how the crying was a release, how it was beneficial for her. Was that the same thing as the fighting for him? Was it a release? Was that how he felt when he was done? Did he not hurt afterward? She never hurt from crying. Her face might get puffy and hot, but she always felt so much better that it was an easy thing to deal with. She didn't ever remember him coming home with black eyes or a broken nose.

Then she frowned. That wasn't quite true. Several times he'd had some bruising. He just brushed it off. And she let him because she didn't want to know. If he said it was all good, then she was fine that it was all good. So why was it not all good now?

Because now it felt like a betrayal. And she knew she had to get her mind wrapped around that. If nothing else, she would pay better attention to her next relationship, would listen to the actual words—not ignoring the truths staring her in the face, not reading between the lines or thinking she could change the guy—and would open up more herself. She sighed, emotionally reeling that she hadn't learned to do that with Blake, the love of her life. Her soul mate. Her husband. Her friend. And possibly a man she barely knew inside.

She shook her head at those thoughts to keep her tears at

bay, bringing her back to this idyllic Spanish town.

She was tugged forward down the street to the small restaurant with tables and chairs outside, surrounded by a little iron gate. She took the seat in the corner with both Nelson and Taylor beside her. Kanen walked into the restaurant, returning to the table shortly.

Within minutes an older woman bustled out, an apron wrapped around her waist, delivering something that looked like coffee, only in a shrunken cup. It smelled like coffee, coffee on steroids, and Laysa wondered if it was a special kind of espresso. Menus were delivered too, before the woman left them.

Laysa picked one up, looked at the list of offerings and chuckled. "I don't understand Spanish. Does anybody else speak and read the language?"

Nelson nodded. The waitress returned soon afterward, and a rapid-fire exchange followed between Nelson and the waitress. When they were done, she collected the menus and disappeared inside.

Laysa stared at Nelson in surprise. "Wow. You did that easily."

He shrugged. "I was born and raised in Texas. Half of the population there speaks Spanish. The other half speaks English. Most of my friends spoke Spanish growing up. It was a pretty easy language to pick up when you were a kid."

She nodded and asked, "Are we having lunch or dinner?"

"It's after eleven o'clock," Taylor said. "And all we had was a little food on the plane. So I don't care what we call it as long as we get to eat."

She laughed. "So, in other words, you guys are seriously starving, and I—who never eats breakfast in the first place—

didn't even notice. Is that the idea?"

Nelson nodded and gave her a big grin. "You have no idea how happy I am that you finally decided we would eat."

She shook her head. "I didn't. Kanen did, and you could have said something at any time."

"And what? Slow the momentum of whatever it was we were doing case-wise? Oh, no," Nelson said. "I'm good. It comes from our navy training. Work comes first. We eat when we can. We sleep when we can. But now that we're at the restaurant, my stomach is screaming for joy."

She motioned at the menu and said, "Order me something small then."

At that, the men discussed whether they wanted pasta or pizza or something completely different. She wanted vegetables, something that she wasn't sure the guys were all that fond of. It seemed like a heavy meat-and-pasta dish would be the main order of the day.

When Kanen stood and returned the second time, he carried a basket of fresh breads. He set it down with a pot of what looked like whipped fresh butter. She realized she was hungrier than she'd thought. She reached for the first bun, and, after that, the basket emptied almost instantly.

She stared at the men as they almost breathed down the food, as if they hadn't eaten in days. "I guess I really should have said something about food earlier, shouldn't I?"

They all shrugged. "We could have waited a while longer," Taylor said in a boastful voice. "We're all good at starving when we need to. But, when there's food, you can be sure we'll make up for it."

She chuckled. It was such a joy to watch them as they ate. Blake had eaten well, but he hadn't eaten like this. And he'd gone to the gym and worked out. "So do you guys work out like Blake did?"

"To a certain extent, yes," Kanen said. "But never without control. We're there for fitness, not for muscles. We're there to make sure we're always in peak form before we get a call, so we're ready no matter what it is we must deal with."

Taylor lifted his phone just then and said, "There is a bit of good news, there's been no pings on our Ipswich hotel room."

"Good, that's what we like to hear," Kanen said with a nod.

Lunch was delivered within a few minutes. She looked down at her fresh-looking pasta covered in a white sauce and fresh herbs. Somewhere in there was chicken. She ate slowly, savoring the unique flavors. But the men didn't. They seemed to enjoy it just as much as she did, but they ate at twice the speed. And when the empty plates disappeared and came back refilled, she gasped. "You got seconds? Or did you have to reorder?"

They grinned. "She saw how hungry we were and took pity on us," Kanen said, batting his eyelashes at Laysa.

And that set the tone for the rest of the meal. Lighthearted joking and teasing ensued, and her melancholy and confusion were swept aside in the tide of good-naturedness. It was good to have friends like this. Good to have friends who took the time to change whatever was going on into something so much better. She sat back and nibbled on her first bun as the men worked their way through their second platefuls. "What are we doing now?"

"We're set to return to England tomorrow morning," Kanen said. "I highly suggest we act like tourists this afternoon, take in some of the sights, stop and have some wine somewhere. It'll be siesta time soon. A siesta is always good."

Taylor nodded. "Exactly, but a lot of food is consumed during that time too."

She shook her head. "No more food for me. Not until dinnertime."

At that, they pulled out their phones and checked out the local tourist sites.

Ending the silence as they all studied the screens on their phones, she asked no one in particular, "Should we be looking for the son?"

Taylor faced her with a sad smile. "I already did. He passed away two years ago."

She stared at him in surprise. "Really?"

He nodded. "Apparently he had cancer and didn't make it very long."

"So the son is not our home invader then," she said slowly. "What about the father?"

"He's alive and in a retirement home not very far from here," Taylor said. "We were wondering about stopping in to see him this afternoon."

"Is it open during siesta?"

They shrugged.

"It's not very far away. We can always pop in and say hi, if we're allowed," Kanen suggested. "If not, then we can do something else."

She nodded, took another bite of her bun and thought about the little they'd learned that morning. "Still makes you wonder who would care enough at this point to do something like this."

"And some of those photos are of no value—not from a blackmailing viewpoint," Nelson said. "Like Carlos said, he's no longer in parliament. So why hang on to them? Why not just burn them?"

"Because you don't know what could change. You just never know who might pay for something down the road, like a family member who doesn't want Grandpa's legacy soiled," Kanen said quietly, a frown growing on his forehead. "What if we're on a completely wrong track here?" He looked around the table. "What if this Joseph Carmel guy— the original blackmailer—just wants to publish a tell-all book? They seem damn popular. Everything from mommy issues to the size of some guy's privates or details about sexual proclivities appears to be the norm. Maybe this guy is dying and wants to write a book about his life and how he blackmailed all these people."

Silence took over their table as they shook their heads, contemplating a world where reality TV superseded movies for entertainment.

"But then who was the younger guy who broke into my apartment and beat me up?" Laysa asked.

"Could have been just an Ipswich street thug that Carmel hired online," Nelson offered. "Wouldn't be the first time we saw that happen."

"Or maybe," Laysa suggested, "Carmel's ashamed of what he did earlier, now that he's older, wiser. Now that the photos have been found, have resurfaced. Maybe discovered by a grandson or whoever. Maybe Joseph's trying to keep it out of the public eye?" she said.

"Again good guesses, but that's what they are, just guesses," Kanen said. "We might never know for sure. We'll talk to this Joseph and see what he has to say."

She stared out as the hot afternoon sun rose. In her mind there were too many options, but she could remember the desperation in her captor's voice, the anger as he beat her. As she thought about him hitting her, she thought about Blake and that temper he had obviously tried to work out in the gym. She remembered seeing the rippling of her captor's muscles. Her words blurted out. "I think my assailant went to the gym with Blake."

The men froze, turning to look at her.

"Why do you say that?" Nelson asked.

"He had the same hard muscled look as Blake, a similar look to the biceps and forearms. There was a real desperation in his blows. He wanted these photos in the worst way. He said it was his insurance. But who's to say exactly what his reasoning was."

"In which case we need to call Mark, check out who goes to Gold's gym."

"Especially at the same time that Blake worked out. Maybe my assailant was an old friend of Blake's. Maybe the asshole was somebody Blake met there. Although, if that's the case, why didn't the guy suspect Blake kept those photos in his gym locker?"

"Because, to the other guy, these photos were incredibly valuable. And nobody but a fool would keep them in a gym locker with no real security."

She nodded at that. "That makes a twisted kind of sense."

They got up, paid their bill and walked back to the rental car. As they drove past Carlos's home, she turned to look up at the old man's house. He stood in the window, watching them. She lifted a hand in greeting as they sped past. "I wonder what he's thinking about."

"Maybe nothing," Kanen said. "Wondering what kind of fools we are that we're chasing this now."

"Well, for me, it's not such a long time ago," she said

quietly. "That asshole was in my place just yesterday."

As a conversation stopper, it worked. Nobody said anything else as they drove to their hotel for their evening in Spain. Not long afterward, they all walked into their hotel suite. Two bedrooms and a central living room. Just like the guys' London suite. She had one bedroom to herself, and the men were all jammed in the other one.

Good, she thought. The last thing she wanted was any more contact with Kanen right now. She was just tired of the unpleasantness of the whole damn investigation. She had learned disturbing things about her marriage, about her husband. Still, they found no real answers as to who her assailant was and what was his motivation, just more questions. She threw herself down on the bed and closed her eyes. Siesta was a hell of a thing. And very quickly she fell asleep.

KANEN PACED THE living room of their suite. He'd called Mark, the gym manager, twice already, getting more information about men Blake seemed to hit it off with, not to argue with. Mark had come up with two names. Both Ipswich locals.

Kanen waited for Laysa to wake up, so he could ask her about them. But instinctively he figured she wouldn't know them or anything about them, not even their names. Blake had kept a lot of things separate from her, and this seemed like one of them. Possibly not on purpose but it appeared to be his way of having a life outside of their home and their marriage. An interesting mind-set for someone who was so invested in the marriage otherwise.

In a way it made sense because Blake wouldn't want to

be anything less than perfect in Laysa's eyes. He had such a complex about being the biggest and the best. He was one of those guys who would never dare back down—at least not easily.

It didn't mean he wasn't a nice guy because he was. It didn't mean he wasn't generous of heart and a great worker, because again, he was. But he had definitely kept a part of his life separate from his marriage, something Laysa didn't know about—until now. That ability to stay true to himself—even if just partially—must have made Blake feel good. Too bad he couldn't share that with his own wife.

Kanen would ask Laysa what she thought. He wished he could ask Blake what it truly did for him to keep that part of his life hidden. Keeping secrets was never good within any relationship. It usually was for selfish purposes, not for the good of both parties—whether in a business relationship or in a personal relationship. If secrets were kept, it was to do something the other person would not otherwise agree to.

Kanen threw himself into the living room chair, picked up his laptop once again and researched the two men Mark had given him names for. Just then his phone rang. It was Mark again. "Did you forget somebody?"

"Yeah, I did. Somebody from a couple years back," he said slowly. "I didn't think about him because I haven't seen him around in a long time. Blake was working out one day, when the guy stepped into the gym. Blake raced over and almost tackled the guy. He was so happy to see him. The other guy didn't appear to be anywhere near as happy to see Blake, though."

Kanen nodded. "Do you remember what this guy's name was?"

"No, I can't. I have hundreds of guys through here in

any given year."

"Does he have a membership?"

"No. He was a drop-in for a few months. He disappeared as suddenly as he appeared. I remember asking Blake about it once. He shrugged and said that was the kind of friend he was. He would just up and move to another part of the world. Something to do with his job, but Blake was sure the guy would drop in again. And sure enough he did. It wasn't all that long before Blake's death, I think," Mark said thoughtfully. "The trouble is, my memory is pretty wonky, since I've seen probably a total of a thousand or so guys in this gym. It's hard to keep track of them all."

"Any idea how close to Blake's death?"

"Nah, I don't remember. But they seemed to be buds still, and then, when he took off again, I didn't see him anymore."

"You haven't seen him since Blake's death, right?"

"Nope."

"Description?"

"Couldn't tell ya. I see so many guys coming through here. How am I to know this one would be important years later?"

Kanen nodded. "True. Any idea if they were friends in school, friends at work?"

"They talked about one of the local boxing clubs here," Mark said.

Kanen straightened. "Blake talked about one in particular a lot. Barney's, wasn't it?"

"Barney's, yeah, that's it. I heard Blake was really good too. Apparently they'd been in the ring together a time or two."

"And let me guess. If Blake was super friendly with him,

Blake won, right?"

Mark laughed. "I don't know, but it might explain the guy's expression when he saw Blake again. It was kind of a surly damn-it-what-are-you-doing-here type of look."

Kanen chuckled. "Yeah. Blake loved to win, and, when he did, he could be a bit of an egotist and in your face about it."

"Well, they got over it, so that's good." Mark cleared his throat. "You knew Blake well, didn't you?"

"We were friends for decades," Kanen said. "I knew the man as well as my own brother."

"I do remember something else. The guy who came in had a big nose, got it punched a couple times. Looked like it had been broken, set, then rebroken, and all of it badly."

"Dark skin tone?"

"Yeah, that's him. Do you know him?"

"I remember hearing about a guy with a big nose and something weird about his muscles. Blake used to laugh about him," Kanen said.

At that, Mark laughed. "That's the guy then. Because Blake was mocking him when he was here too."

After he finished on the phone, Kanen sat quietly for a long moment. Taylor and Nelson both looked at him.

"Your friend sounds like a complex character," Nelson said quietly.

Kanen's lips quirked. "That's one way to describe him."

"How does that help us now?" Taylor asked.

"I'll contact Mason to have him check with MI6 on the facial recognition issue." Kanen checked the time, realized it was early in the morning for Mason, but he was likely up. He dialed and waited until someone answered. Mason's voice was gruff, growly, but awake. "Too early to call?"

Kanen asked.

"Nah, I've been up for an hour," Mason said. "Just haven't had enough coffee yet."

Kanen laughed at that. "Neither have I. It's almost midafternoon. Doesn't look like a whole lot more coffee is coming my way either."

"What'd you find?"

Kanen filled him in on the old man living here in Spain and his history.

"Interesting but not really relevant."

"No. The blackmailer's son, Murray Carmel, is dead, so he can't be Laysa's assailant. Carlos's blackmailing colleague is Joseph Carmel, and we could stop in later today to see if he remembers anything or has anything to add. He's in an old folks' home up here and in his nineties now. Both the blackmailer and the blackmailee retired here in Spain but have nothing to do with each other. Laysa is having a siesta. It's been a rough day." Kanen hesitated, then said, "Did you hear anything from MI6 about the other photos?"

"They identified two of the remaining six unknown men in the photos. One was a big businessman, and one was a politician. Both have been contacted. Both admitted they did pay blackmail way back when. But it stopped relatively quickly, and they didn't do anything else about it. I'm sure they're worried those photos would come back up again."

Kanen didn't get it. "Why go to the trouble to catch people in embarrassing moments to blackmail them and then stop abruptly? That makes no sense."

"Exactly," Mason said. "These two guys didn't want to look a gift horse in the mouth, but, when it stopped, they kind of held their breaths. When nothing happened, they breathed again. They'd love to have the originals back, as they were shown copies in the first place."

"Hopefully MI6 will give them the originals," Kanen said. "What about the people in all the other photos?"

"Nothing MI6 was prepared to share at this time." Mason's tone was dry. "But you know what that's like."

And Kanen did know. It was all on a need-to-know basis. Generally he never needed to know. He was one of the workers, one of the guys who fought for the world and didn't understand the orders given from the brass above.

"Will talk to MI6 when we get back from the old folks' home." Kanen disconnected the call and looked up to see Laysa standing in the doorway. Her arms were crossed over her chest, and she looked tired. He hopped to his feet and wrapped his arms around her. "How are you doing?"

She gave him a tremulous smile. "I'm better. Still tired but how much of that is emotional, I don't know. I forgot about the old guy Carmel. Let's go see him now, then have dinner. An early night and an early flight would be good."

"We can change the fights and leave tonight if you want," Taylor said. "I doubt it would cost very much."

Startled, she looked at him. "Really?"

He nodded. "If that's what you want to do, we can make it happen."

She appeared to think about it and then shrugged. "We're in Spain, and we might as well at least enjoy one night." She smiled at the others. "Although I might change my mind after I talk to the old guy."

Everybody laughed.

"Before I forget ..." Kanen asked her about the three men from the gym who Mark had singled out, but she shook her head.

"I don't know any of them."

He held out a hand. "If you're ready to go then …"

She smiled, placed her hand in his and said, "You know me. I'll follow you anywhere."

As they walked out of the building and headed across town, still within walking distance, she wondered at her words because she had followed Blake everywhere. Was that what she was thinking here? Was she subconsciously exchanging the two men in her mind? Because that would never do. Yet so much history was shared between her and Kanen that what she'd said made sense. It was still strange. And she kind of worried he thought something of it that she hadn't intended. But it was hard to tell. At least her voice had been low enough that the other men hadn't heard because that would just add to the awkwardness. Something she didn't want.

Outside, she stopped and took a deep breath. It was a sultry, hot afternoon, but the sun was a little bit behind the clouds, giving her a breather from the dead heat.

At a good pace they headed toward the old folks' home. "Good thing Nelson speaks Spanish. It's benefited us before. And it may help us a lot when we get there."

Nelson smiled. "Why, thank you, Laysa. It's nice to be appreciated. Maybe you'll rub off on these guys."

That brought laughter from everyone, even Nelson.

"Leave it to Nelson to add some humor to our days," Kanen noted.

As they approached the front entrance, she looked at the tall two-story almost-cathedral-looking building. "It's a pretty nice place to spend your final years," she murmured.

"Maybe," Kanen said. "Not sure that any of these people would agree with that. It seems a far cry from the life they used to live."

"But their lives have changed now," she said softly. "I think most have come to accept this is where they are. Although it probably took some time to make that adjustment, ultimately I'd like to think they're happy."

He patted her hand. "That's because you believe in the fairy tale," he said. "The happily ever after."

She frowned. "That makes me sound like I'm unrealistic or some Pollyanna," she said. "Like I have no spunk, no spirit."

"Not at all," Kanen said, shaking his head. "You're a spitfire by day—a scrappy fighter when needed—and a romantic by night. ... Kind of like Blake maybe?"

She frowned. "*Hmm.*" She studied Kanen for a couple minutes. But she was thinking about Blake and Kanen's words. "Maybe."

"Now you're not alone. You've got friends here to help you."

"Ha. Until you leave."

The sad note in her voice was unmistakable. "You don't need to *remain* alone. That choice is up to you."

They opened the double doors and walked into a front reception area that rivaled any grand hotel.

She stopped and smiled, gasping at the big chandelier and the large circular desk. "This is beautiful," she murmured.

The woman looked up from the reception desk and smiled. "Thank you. It was an old estate handed over to the city for the seniors to use."

"I approve. And I love your accent. You speak English very well," Laysa said with a smile. "It's a beautiful place to spend your retirement years."

"Thank you. Most of us speak English here," the receptionist said with a gracious smile. "What can we do for you?"

Kanen stepped forward and gave Joseph Carmel's name.

The receptionist nodded. "He doesn't get many visitors," she said, "and none from England or the States."

Laysa just smiled at her. "Is it a problem to see him? We'd like to very much."

The woman nodded, looked at a computer screen, clicked on his name and said, "He should be in the gardens this afternoon. Either there or he'll be playing cards." She gave them general instructions on how to reach the gardens.

They thanked her and walked away. And, sure enough, several older men were outside.

Laysa frowned. "How are we supposed to know which one is him?"

Kanen smiled, motioned to a nurse in a white uniform and said, "I suggest we ask."

Before he had the words out of his mouth, Nelson had walked over to the closest staff member and had done just that. The nurse turned slowly, surveyed the people out in the garden, then pointed to one man standing by the roses. Nelson thanked her with a big smile and motioned in the direction of the older man.

They walked slowly, not wanting to engulf him. When they got closer, the older guy turned and frowned. Kanen stepped forward and introduced himself in English.

The old man shook his hand and then looked at Laysa. "And who is this lovely young lady?

Laysa smiled and introduced herself. "We have a few questions we'd like to ask."

Nelson stepped forward, adding, "About blackmail years ago."

Joseph slowly sank into his wheelchair parked beside

him. He turned to Nelson and said, "If you would push me back to my room, I'd appreciate it."

Kanen stepped forward. "Will you talk with us?"

Joseph looked up at him. It was easy to see he was visibly upset. "There isn't anything to say. I lost a colleague—a man who I would have liked to have called a friend—but for my actions."

"So why did you do it?"

"Because I didn't want him to get the position I wanted," the old man said. "I can't believe this has come back up again. It was over and done with a long time ago."

"But you were never charged, were you?"

The color swept out of Joseph's skin, leaving him pasty-faced. "No. And, at this point, I wouldn't survive a trial. I have to meet my maker over my actions. Isn't that punishment enough?"

Laysa didn't think so, but then it was kind of hard to know what his maker would really say to him. "Somebody had a lot of photos. He said it was his insurance policy. That's how we came to find them. Do you have any idea who would be in possession of these photos now?"

His gaze widened. "No. I have no idea. I'd hoped they had all been destroyed by now."

"Did you take some of the photographs originally?"

He shook his head. "No. I only took two of the prints. And I used them to get money from my colleague," he said painfully. "I've paid for that decision for the remainder of my life. Everything went wrong from that moment on. I lost my wife, and I lost my son. I sit here all alone."

"Where did you get the photos?"

His lower lip trembling, he said, "Honestly, a bag was at a bus stop one day. I sat beside it and noticed the photos inside. Nobody seemed to be around, so I picked out a couple to look at. They were of my friend. We were friends at the time," he explained. "I wanted to get a closer look at the rest of the photos, but a man came rushing toward me and snatched the bag. I didn't see his face. What he didn't know was I still had two photographs in my hand."

"And you used those photos to blackmail your colleague, correct?"

The old man nodded. "That's correct, although that was a long time ago. I'd hoped the world would have forgotten it all by now. I've regretted it ever since."

"How old was that man who took the bag and ran?"

He frowned. "He was young, very young."

"And he didn't explain where he got the photos?"

The old man shook his head. "But he had camera equipment with him, so they were probably his photos. I can't be sure, of course, but I think he was the one taking these terrible photos."

"And you just used his work and blackmailed your friend." Kanen looked at the old man in disgust. "And how many other photos do you think were in that bag?"

Joseph stared, belligerence in his eyes. "I don't know. Hundreds likely."

The four looked at each other.

Laysa turned and, over her shoulder, said, "Thank you for the information you gave us."

"Wait. I know the name of the company."

She spun on her heels. "What company?"

"The photographer's company. It was all over the bag." Joseph smiled in triumph. "It was Finest Photos," he said with a big grin. "Finest Photos, Ltd. See if you can find that after all these years."

CHAPTER 8

A S SOON AS they walked away from the strange older man, Laysa half whispered under her breath, "Find that company."

"Right," Nelson said in an odd tone. "How does that help us?"

"We should have asked him if that was on the back of the photos," Taylor suggested. "What's the chance that was the mark we saw rubbed off?"

"If that's the case, then it is important," Kanen said.

"That may be," Taylor said, "but that doesn't give us the answers we need."

"But we won't know until we take a look," Nelson replied.

"We also didn't ask him if he knew where the company was located," Laysa noted. "Or anything else about it."

"He wasn't too cooperative at that point anyway," Kanen said in a comforting voice. "We can find that kind of information on our own."

"Can we?" she asked.

"Sure," Kanen said. "We just need access to the internet."

Taylor pulled out his phone, checked it and said, "I've got bars. Give me a few minutes, and I can track down something on that company."

They walked in silence back toward the hotel. It was hard not to appreciate the beauty of their unique surroundings. The cobblestone streets absolutely amazed her with how well they fit together. She understood craftsmen did this day in and day out, but this road had to be hundreds of years old, and yet, it was still in remarkable condition. There was a ruddy, rusty red color to it that just added to the amazing color around them. The hotels and buildings alongside the road were in various bright, cheerful colors. It made her smile inside and made her forget those other thoughts in her mind for a bit.

The sun was still high, and some of the clouds whispered past, adding to the postcard-perfect picture all around her. She gave a happy sigh, plunging her hands into her pockets as she walked beside the men. "This isn't exactly how I thought to come to Spain, but I'm so happy I finally got here," she murmured.

Kanen silently wrapped an arm around her shoulders and tucked her up close.

It was pretty hard to not enjoy the moment. Being close like this, her heart against his, the warmth of his body washing over hers, ... it was ... perfect. Did he feel the same way? Then he said something that surprised her, and it let her know maybe, ... just maybe, ... he did.

"Sometimes we just take the moments when they happen," Kanen said.

Suddenly Taylor stopped. "Well, look at that. It's a British company. It had offices all across Europe way back when. They were big-time."

"*Were?*"

Taylor nodded. "Closed down in 1995, from the looks of it."

"And their stock?" Kanen asked.

Taylor gave a shrug. "Who can tell? Have to do a little more research to figure out how and why they closed. Was it the death of the owner? Was it a business going under? Was it rendered obsolete in this digital age?"

"That probably wasn't widespread until the year 2000 or so," Nelson stated.

Taylor nodded and continued, "Of course the real evolution in photography came with the advance of cell phones with camera features—which again began around the year 2000 as well. Sure people still had Nikons and SLRs, but every Joe Blow could take decent photos with their cell phone."

Kanen agreed. "Then the photography business went under. Along with the video rental businesses and many others."

Taylor and Nelson nodded in agreement.

Taylor waggled his phone. "I'll let Mason know. See if he can find anything on Finest Photos."

"Sounds good. A restaurant is up ahead. Are you ready to eat?" Kanen asked everyone. He pointed to an outdoor café, just starting to fill with people.

She smiled in delight. "Oh, yes," she said warmly. "I could really go for some nice vegetables."

The men snickered.

"You can have your vegetables. We'll go for the meat," Nelson said.

"You need to have vegetables too," she scolded with a groan.

"Oh, don't worry," Taylor said. "We will have plenty of vegetables. But we'll get plenty of meat too."

An hour later—after a bread course, a soup course, a

salad course—they were seated in front of gleaming plates heaped high, hers full of sautéed vegetables with some cheesy sauce over the top and a small piece of salmon beside it. She looked at the salmon and smiled. "Seems strange to eat salmon here. Like, don't they have any local fish from this region?"

"Sure, but they also take pride in having the best of everything," Kanen said.

As she looked at his big platter of steak, steamed vegetables and one of the largest baked potatoes she'd ever seen in her life, she shook her head. "How can you possibly eat that much?"

He patted his tummy and smiled. "Easy. Just watch me."

Dinner was an enjoyable affair as they all tucked into that good food and a great bottle of red wine she'd never tasted before and couldn't begin to pronounce. She took a picture of the label in case she could find it back home.

Just as they were sipping the last of their wine over empty dinner plates, Taylor's phone rang. He checked it and held up a finger. "It's Mason."

With the phone to his ear, he spoke in a quiet voice, so she could barely hear. She waited until he was done.

He hung up and looked around at the group. "There was quite a scandal before Finest Photos closed—the owner, one of the Alagarth family members, went to jail for blackmail."

"Seriously?" Laysa asked. "Isn't that a little too easy?"

They laughed.

"We never get easy cases," Kanen said. "Don't knock it when it actually happens. It's probably the only time in the next ten years we'll get something that's easily solved."

"I don't think it'll be quite so easily solved," Taylor said, typing away on his phone. "Alagarth got out of jail after four years. He'd been protesting his innocence the entire time, and, within weeks of his release from jail, he was murdered."

Laysa stared at him. "So he was innocent, goes to jail for a crime he didn't commit, and, when he comes out, the guy who did the crime shoots him?"

"Don't know about any shooting," he said. "I just have news he was murdered. We'll have to dig up the old reports to see how he was killed."

Kanen pointed a finger at her and said, "And that is because you were thinking it was way too easy."

The others all gave sage nods.

And she glared at them. Then, in a mocking voice, she said, "I think you guys just enjoy that this challenge continues. You all want to have this kind of drama in your lives."

Kanen's eyebrows shot up. "Not likely." He waggled his eyebrows. "I can think of much better things to spend my time on."

She snorted.

Taylor hopped up and said, "I don't know about you guys, but I'd like to get back to the hotel and do more research on my computer instead of reading my tiny phone screen. Anything we can find before we return to England could make a big difference."

"Is Mason still looking into Finest Photos too?" Laysa asked.

Taylor nodded. "To a certain extent, yes. But he is heading out on an op and won't be back for four days." He glanced over at the other two. "A trip we're missing, by the way. He's heading up to the Yukon."

"Dammit, we're missing all the fun," Nelson said.

Taylor just chuckled. "Yeah, we're missing the Yukon

horseflies, heat and mosquitoes. While we're sitting here in Spain in the sunshine, drinking great wines and enjoying wonderful meals."

The other two considered that, then nodded.

"Good point."

On that note they returned to their hotel room, where Laysa headed to the jetted bathtub, while the men sat down with their laptops open. The last thing she heard was their discussion about the method of the murder and the blackmailer's guilt or innocence.

After her bath, she dressed, feeling one hundred times better, and stepped into the living room. "Did you guys find anything?" she asked, towel-drying her hair.

The men smiled up at her.

Kanen chuckled and patted the seat beside him. "Come and take a seat. I'll show you what I found."

She collapsed beside him, and he placed a laptop on her lap.

"We have copies of his court case, what was released for public viewing anyway. And we have a copy of the coroner's report on his death. No autopsy was done. He was shot, one bullet between the eyes."

She looked at him. "And does that mean anything?"

"It could mean many things. That's the problem. It could mean somebody close to him shot him. It could mean it was a sharpshooter, like a sniper. It could mean somebody with a pistol had a good aim. It could also mean somebody held the gun against his head and just fired."

"It still seems very sad," she said. "If he spent years in jail for a crime he didn't commit, it would have made him a very bitter person inside. He was probably motivated enough upon his release to come after the person he thought might have done this to him."

"But why would the real blackmailer kill this guy? The case was solved in the eyes of the court and the police. It was a done deal. The guy in jail had probably been hollering about his innocence for years now. Who would listen to him now?" Kanen paused, then raised his pointer finger. "Unless the guy released from jail had some proof. If he had that, likely the confrontation ended with the real blackmailer now being a murderer."

"Was anybody ever charged with his murder?" she asked.

"No. The case went cold and is, to this day, unsolved."

KANEN AGREED WITH her totally. But how did one find a murderer from an old crime like that? He sat back and contemplated their options. "The best place to start might be to find out all we can about the owner of Finest Photos. About his family, those closest to him back then. If he had any close business associates, female companions, or, if he was gay, a male companion. The murder itself wasn't difficult to enact, so either sex could have shot him."

She stared at Kanen in surprise. "Why is it I never even thought the original blackmailer could be a woman?" she asked. "Because that makes total sense. No way in hell she would go to jail. So it was much better to set him up."

That made the men laugh.

"Watch out for her, Kanen," Nelson said. "She'll make sure you go to jail before her."

Laysa shrugged. "I can't imagine either of us ending up in jail. Now you on the other hand …" she said with an evil grin. "Somebody might just blame you for something, and you'll find yourself behind bars."

He gave her a mock look of fear.

She rolled her eyes and went back to the laptop. "So we need to know all of the above information, plus his personal relationships. Did he have any family? Maybe he has a brother he was in business with. Maybe something else was going on," she said.

"He had a brother and a son," Taylor announced from his laptop. "Heavily involved in the business, both of them. Disappeared from public eye after the sentencing. Then it's tough on the remaining family members when someone is jailed. Although, in this case, he protested his innocence constantly—apparently."

"What about names?" Laysa asked. "Same last names, different names, any grandchildren? The guy who accosted me in my own place would be younger, I presume."

"How young?" Nelson asked.

"Anywhere from twenty-five to forty-five," she admitted. "I know that's not very definitive, but it's hard to tell when the guy wore a mask."

"Close enough. It gives us a range," Taylor said quietly. "The owner's wife died while he was in prison. She had heart issues. Seems the son married, had a son."

"We have Grandpa Alagarth, who was killed, a brother who is potentially alive, a son who is alive, and a grandson who is alive, correct?" Kanen asked. "What are their ages?"

"Give me a minute." Taylor tapped away. "Okay. Give me more than minute. I'll get back to you on that."

"Or," Nelson offered, "I'll take over finding the DOBs. You handle Kanen's next questions." Nelson grinned like he was getting the better end of this deal.

Kanen had a notepad opened up on his laptop as he jotted down the family tree. "What about the brother? Did he have a wife? Several wives? Kids, grandkids?"

"Definitely could have," Taylor murmured, typing while he talked. "Not sure anybody beyond the brother is applicable though. The relevance here is, if the brother was heavily involved in the business, he could have been the blackmailer. Nobody would have known he would have used the business as a front, and his brother could have been completely in the dark about it all. Then again, that goes for all the employees as well."

"How much did the sale of the businesses net?" Kanen asked.

"Several million," Taylor said. "I've just lost the page. Hang on while I go back."

"Even though he was charged and convicted of blackmail?" Laysa asked.

Taylor nodded. "He had multiple stores across Europe, a great franchise. It brought in multiple millions. Ten point four million," he announced when he found the page.

"So," Nelson theorized, "what if the grandfather didn't get any of that blackmail money? What if it went to the grandfather's brother and the grandfather's son? When Grandpa gets out of prison, he wanted his share, and they weren't willing to give it to him."

"Conjecture all the way," Kanen said with a light tone of voice, "but I like it."

"The thing is," Taylor added, "we have to track down these people and go from conjecture to reality."

Laysa nodded. "Does anybody have any photos?" she asked of the men. "It's not like I saw my captor's face because he wore a full ski mask, but I certainly saw his body type. Although I guess that can change from generation to generation too, can't it?"

"Absolutely," the men said.

"I don't think photographs would help much. It would probably just confuse you all that much more," Taylor said.

She nodded. "Kind of depressing to think he was there in my apartment for hours, and yet, I couldn't identify him."

"No tattoos? Nothing distinct?"

"No, just like I said, it looked like he was a bit of a gym junkie. Very rip-cord, bulging-veins type of guy. You know what I mean." She looked at the other men's wrists, but they all looked normal. "None of you have anything even close to his, so it's hard to explain." Then she opened up a new tab on the laptop and compared images of bodybuilders and different lean-muscled men, looking specifically for their wrists and their forearms. She found one that was similar. "Like this," she said, holding up the laptop. The men studied the image that showed ropy veins and tendons and muscles up to the biceps.

They nodded. "Yeah, we've seen something like that on guys—gym rats—before."

"But this guy was definitely extreme. His hands were thick, muscled and had zero fat on them. A darker skin tone on his arms too."

"And he had very little body fat all over?" Nelson asked.

"As far as I could tell, yes," she said. "He had on a muscle shirt and jeans and a knitted ski mask. So I couldn't really see much."

"You gave us his basic body mass and his height. I can extrapolate his weight," Taylor said. "There was nothing identifying in the jeans or the shoes?"

"Blue jeans. I couldn't tell you if they were designer or cowboy," she said with a laugh. "And he wore sneakers. That's all I can remember."

"Any idea what kind of sneakers?"

She shook her head. "No, but his feet weren't very big. Maybe because he wasn't terribly tall. Blake wore a size eleven shoe. But this guy's feet were much smaller than that. Maybe an eight or nine. But they were wide," she said as an afterthought. "Oddly enough, they were really wide."

Kanen jotted down the little bits of detail. "All of it helps. When we finally get our man, we can confirm some of the things you saw against our suspect."

"I just don't want you to dismiss anybody who doesn't have a really wide foot," she said, "because what if my memory is wrong? I was extremely stressed, terrified, in fact. And it's very possible I made a mistake. Plus my definition of 'wide' may not be your definition of 'wide.'"

"Which is why we'll keep it in mind," Nelson said. "But we won't take it as gospel."

She beamed at him. "You really are a very nice man."

He glanced at her in surprise and smiled. "Thank you."

Taylor looked at her and frowned. "Hey, what about me?"

She laughed. "You are too."

Kanen frowned. "So you mentioned my buddies as being nice guys, and you don't say anything about me? ... *Sheesh*." He grinned at her, letting her know he had no hard feelings.

It was nice she got along so well with the guys. He knew from them that they admired her guts. But, more than that, they also liked her. She'd shown herself to be somebody they could not only admire but who would fit in with the other guys in their units. A roomful of alpha males would never scare her off.

She leaned over and kissed Kanen on the cheek. "You're much nicer than a nice person. You're special."

At that, the men, including Kanen, went off on a bout of laughter.

She glared at them. "Now what are you laughing about, Kanen?"

He just chuckled, wrapped his arm around her shoulders, a habit he was doing more and more often. It was almost as if he wasn't comfortable or happy if she wasn't in his arms. "They expect the next thing out of your mouth to be an insult," he said. "Don't worry about it. They're used to being teased and to teasing each other."

She sighed and returned to the laptop in front of her.

He checked the time and found it was after nine o'clock already.

"We have an early morning flight," he said, "so the earlier to bed, the better."

She nodded. "Not an issue. But maybe, if you don't mind, may I check my email?"

"Sure, go ahead," he said. "You've got the laptop. You can do what you want."

She smiled her thanks, brought up her email program and flicked through it.

He searched the living room for what needed to be packed. They were good at leaving in an instant, so he wasn't worried they would need much time.

He heard the small gasp in the back of her throat and saw the color leach from her face. "Laysa, what's the matter?"

She swallowed hard and said in a faint voice, "*There's* an email I wasn't expecting." She closed her eyes, took a deep breath.

He squeezed her shoulder gently. "Hey. It's okay. What's the matter?"

She stared up at him.

The other men looked at her, waiting for her to gather her thoughts and to tell them what was going on.

"So, is it good news or bad news?" Kanen asked.

She took a deep breath. "I haven't opened it yet." She stared down at her fingers drifting across the email.

He didn't want to look because it was her confidential email, but, at the same time, he wanted to know what she was thinking. "Are you going to share?"

She lifted her troubled gaze his way and then switched to look at the other two men. "I just don't understand how this could have happened."

"If you don't explain it to us," Kanen said gently, "we can't explain it to you."

She nodded, took a deep breath and turned the laptop toward him, tapped the edge of one email, not opening it but letting him know it was there.

He stopped and stared. He raised his gaze and looked at it again.

She nodded her head slowly.

He faced the other two men. "This email is from her dead husband."

CHAPTER 9

L AYSA STARED AT the email. "How can this be?"
The others gathered behind her. "There's a good chance somebody hacked your husband's email account," Nelson said. "It's guaranteed to have shock value. And that's what you just had—a shock."

"It's also possible to set up an email like that before you die," Taylor said. "I know you don't want to consider that, but Blake may have sent it to you himself."

"But why now?" Kanen studied the email. He sat closer beside her, the laptop on both their laps. They hadn't opened the email yet but just stared at the bold lettering, showing it was an unopened email. "Is it from his usual account?"

"Yes," she said. "His work email."

"That would be much easier for somebody else to get a hold of then," Taylor said. "The naming convention at a job will be the same for each employee."

She understood what he was saying, but it was still rather unnerving. She clicked the email and opened it. It showed a picture of her standing almost nude in a bedroom. It wasn't her bedroom.

"Do you recognize that picture?" Kanen asked softly. He rubbed her shoulders, trying to reassure her that everything was okay. Or at least it would end up that way.

But she felt like she'd gone down a rabbit hole and didn't know how to get back out. "I don't know when this could have been taken," she said. "I'm not even sure where this is."

"And the next question is, why would somebody send it to you?"

She started to shake. "I swear I've never been in that bedroom. I don't recognize the wallpaper. I don't recognize anything about that room."

"Maybe it was altered via Photoshop," Taylor said. "Some pretty sophisticated Photoshop gurus are out there. They could have taken a picture of your head, attached it to a nude body and stuck it in somebody else's bedroom."

She twisted in surprise. "Could they really do that?"

"Absolutely. They can even add a date stamp." He pointed to the far corner.

"It's dated the day after I escaped," she said slowly. "I don't even remember if I had changed clothes that day. Things were a bit hectic."

Kanen asked, "Is there any chance this isn't your back?"

She frowned, thinking about it. "I guess there's one way to know. Here." She sat forward on the edge of the couch and lifted her shirt so the men could see her back. "You guys tell me. Is it?"

There was silence while they studied her back, noting some bruising—which Kanen felt better about not mentioning to her—and then the image in front of them.

"It doesn't have this mole here," Kanen said, gently placing a finger on the side of her spine.

"What does that mean?"

"Your back is also a little fleshier than the back in the photo," Nelson said. "The person in the photo has very low body mass."

She frowned, thinking about that. "I'm certainly not fat, but you're right. My ribs don't show."

"Thankfully," Kanen said smoothly. He tugged her shirt back into place. "So we now know it's not your back."

"If it's my head, you're saying they could have taken it off another photo and put in on this one?"

"Yes, exactly," Kanen said. "It's pretty easy these days to do something like that."

"But for what purpose?" she asked, staring at the photo. "I do have leggings like that." She tapped the bright blue geometric pattern beneath the skirt the woman held in front of her. "I rarely walk around without a bra. And this woman isn't wearing one."

"Again that could have been done with Photoshop software." Kanen studied the photo, then said, "It's not even that great of a job." He pointed out where the two middle sections of her body supposedly joined. Ever-so-slightly they were off. "It's hard to see here, but, if we opened this up in Photoshop, we'd see that discrepancy very quickly."

She sighed with relief. "I have to admit. I'm much happier to think this is a fake photo than to consider somebody took images of me when I changed."

"It's a warning," Kanen announced. "Basically telling you to stop what you're doing, or images of you will show up somewhere you don't want them to."

She turned and looked at the men. "And just what the devil do they think that'll do?"

Kanen shrugged. "The whole point of the photo will be to maximize your humiliation and to expose you. And again, in this case, it's blackmail of a warning nature. Not because they want money but because they want you to stop doing something."

"What we need to know though is who may have sent this to you," Nelson said. "Outside of the image, is there a message?"

She returned to the email. "No, it was sent directly from Blake's account at work," she said slowly. "There doesn't appear to be any other information on it." There was still a sense of violation as she looked at it though. Even though she knew it wasn't her back, she felt weird to think that not only had somebody manipulated her image to the point that other people would think it was her but that somebody was doing this to hurt her. "There has to be a way to find out who sent this."

"Anybody could have sent it if they worked where your husband did, or, if a good-enough hacker, could remotely get into his email account at work," Taylor explained.

"Sure, but he's been dead for almost a year," she said.

"It's still possible," Taylor continued. "After his death the company had to keep the email address working in case they needed to respond to people with current orders or to have Blake's replacement deal with his unfinished orders or to refer back to any customers he worked with and maybe special orders or special pricing. So his email account will be there, but it's probably been retired, maybe with one of those automatic vacation responders, telling people trying to reach Blake to now contact John Doe at his direct email address. So anybody in the company, or anybody who understood how email programs work, would have no trouble accessing it."

She sagged onto the couch. "It's an ugly world we live in."

Kanen's hand squeezed her shoulder. "That it is. We can

get Tesla to look into it, if she's available. She's a software designer and maybe can trace this or at least tell us she hit a dead end. But this is a relatively innocent email."

"*Sure*," she announced. "My dead husband sends me an email to my personal email account with a seminude photo of me, supposedly, and an unspoken message that appears to be very threatening. How innocent can you get?" There was no humor in her tone.

"Time for bed," Kanen said. "We are getting up early in the morning."

She handed him the laptop and stood up without a question. "I'm definitely tired. Maybe if I read something, I can take my mind off this." She smiled at the others. "Good night." She walked into her bedroom and closed the door.

THE MEN TURNED toward Kanen.

He shrugged. "What can I say? Somebody now knows she's on to them. That's the most concerning part of all this."

The others nodded.

"Agreed," Nelson said. "So we have to figure out who and how, based on our investigation so far."

"We'll be back in London tomorrow," Kanen said. "What I want to do tonight is gather as much info as we can on all the Finest Photos' owners and family members who may be involved, see if anybody is still alive and where they're working and living—especially where they were this last week." He nodded at Taylor. "Maybe the younger generations have social media accounts to help with that."

Kanen's voice hardened. "That asshole physically attacked her, and now someone's mentally working on her.

What if they forward that Photoshop email to her school? Or even worse, to her students? She'd lose her job while we gathered the evidence to disprove this. We've got to put a stop to this before somebody decides to escalate it even past losing her job and chooses to take her out of the picture altogether."

"I don't think gathering any more information on these people will help," Nelson warned. "We'll do it, of course, but the bottom line is someone—a single someone most likely—has a purpose for what he is doing. It won't likely involve anyone else. I mean, her attacker seemed to be working alone. This has all the hallmarks of a vendetta. A very personal one. Think of that asshole's anger as he beat Laysa when he couldn't find what he was looking for, no matter how many times she said she didn't know what he was talking about."

"We need to track him down," Kanen said, "and fast."

"Or set a trap," Taylor suggested, "but not until we know more."

Just then a text message came through. "Update from Mason. *Still running down names*," Kanen read out loud. "*Nothing popping so far. Not from our end or from MI6. Keep your heads down and stay safe. Sounds like you've got a lone wolf out there.*" Kanen raised a grim face to the others.

"There you have it." Taylor nodded.

Nelson said, "Mason's right. It goes along with what I was saying. All this Finest Photos blackmail and related events happened so long ago, but—for someone—it's still current. And he's on a rampage to accomplish something. And it doesn't make sense that he would go the blackmail route after so many years, decades even, have passed. So we have to figure out what his angle is."

"He's passionate about his goal. And willing to go over the edge to achieve it," Taylor added.

"As long as that doesn't mean coming after Laysa again." Kanen wanted Laysa safe at all costs.

CHAPTER 10

L ANDING IN ENGLAND the next morning was a big relief. So much was going on, and yet, she had no closure. Laysa wanted the routine of her own life—although the thought of living in her apartment made her cringe now. She'd taken the week off from work, but that was soon running out. She didn't know if she could take off any more time without them replacing her. And that was disturbing in its own right. She'd miss the kids, ... and she needed the income.

If something happened to her, would anybody care outside of Kanen? Her parents were dead; she had no siblings. After Blake's death, she'd had no contact with his family, which had been sparse at best. And that was sad too. It was like all these strings had been cut from her life, and now she felt suspended, on her own two feet, but as if she were alone on an island and didn't really have any way to connect with the rest of the world. She hadn't isolated herself as much as she had allowed herself to be isolated.

On the taxi ride home, Kanen asked her, "Are you okay? You're awfully quiet."

She smiled up at him. "Just realizing how much my world has shrunk. With Blake's death, it changed the dynamics of my life in so many ways. Losing him was the epicenter of even more aftershocks radiating outward. I lost friends we had together, which shows me my girlfriends at the time were more couple-friends. I have hardly kept in touch with any of them. Blake was never close with his family, and we were never close to them when we were married. Now that I'm on my own, it's like a huge chunk of my life doesn't exist anymore."

There wasn't anything Kanen could say to that. Taylor and Nelson shared a grim look.

They got out at her apartment building, and she stared up at it. "Do you think it's safe?"

"Let's find out," Kanen said. "When are you supposed to return to work?"

"I told them that I was sick," she said, "that I would be taking off a full week. So I'm scheduled to return Thursday next week. I don't know if taking off like that'll get me into trouble or not."

"Are you still working at the same preschool?"

She nodded. "Yes, but they could easily replace me if I wasn't there. And missing a week of work at the beginning of the first semester of the new school year is not a way to endear myself to the school administrators or to the children's parents. I'm suddenly realizing that I'm really not important to anyone. And that feels very lonely."

"That's wrong," Kanen said. "You're very important to me."

She squeezed his fingers. "Yes, but, when you return to the US, you'll go back to your job and forget all about me. Yes, we'll talk on the phone a couple times a week for maybe a month. But it's not like you'll be there for me all the time, like these past few days. Any more than I would expect you to be." She paused, embarrassed, as she looked at each of the guys. "I know I'm whining. Just ignore me." She was calm, though, at the same time, her heart ached at the thought of losing Kanen.

"So come back to the States with me," Kanen said. "Nothing is keeping you here now, is there?"

A smirk appeared on Nelson's face. A *told you so* look.

Taylor lifted one eyebrow and tilted his head in a silent nod, agreeing with Nelson.

She stared at Kanen. "My apartment." Even though she'd said it, she shook her head. "I have some friends here." She spoke slowly, then stopped. "No, … nothing is keeping me here." Her voice was low, almost in a dumbfounded way. "I'm not sure I like that."

"What? That nothing is keeping you here?"

"I don't like the reminder of how empty my life has become. When Blake was alive, my life was full. We used to have dinners with other couples. We did things as a couple. We biked, hiked and grabbed books and coffee to sit out in the middle of nowhere and just enjoy being together. Our lives were busy. But now it's just me. All that connected to his life has been removed, and I realize how much of it was part of *his* life. It wasn't *our* lives as much as it was *his* life."

"No," Kanen corrected softly. "When a twosome, you had other twosomes to connect with. As a single person, those couples don't know how to act around you. They don't know what to say to you any longer, how to fill up that empty space at a dining room table. And it makes them feel awkward to invite you over. So they don't."

She nodded.

The guys and Laysa got out of the cab in front of her Ipswich apartment.

"We should be allowed back in, right?" she asked softly. It didn't look like home anymore. Her assailant had tainted that.

"Of course. It's your apartment. It wasn't cordoned off before we left. Shouldn't be now," Nelson said, looking at his silent phone. "I'm surprised MI6 hasn't tagged us yet. Somebody should have been pinged that we're back in the UK."

As they walked to the elevator, she asked, "Do you think we should ask anybody?"

"You mean, ask MI6 for permission to enter your own apartment?" Taylor asked. "Hell no. I tried to get answers earlier from MI6 on other matters. I didn't get very far."

Now at her apartment door, she unlocked it and pushed it open. There was no sign of anyone having been here.

Regardless, the guys spread out and did a quick search just to be sure.

She walked into her bedroom, dumped her travel bags on her bed and said, "Doesn't look any different." She walked back out to the kitchen, where she put on a pot of coffee.

While she waited for it to brew, she looked around her apartment. It was an empty shell and symbolized so much of her life. Nothing was on the kitchen counters, except the coffeemaker. She had no toaster, no blender, nothing. She had put it all away after Blake's death because she didn't use them anymore. She rarely ate bread herself, and she hadn't ever baked anything here. She didn't care if she had a cookie or a cake ever, whereas Blake had loved his sweets. They had routinely visited a nearby bakery so he could get his sugar fix.

She walked back into the living room and sat down. She booted her laptop up and waited for it to load. "What's next on the list?" she asked.

"What do you want to do?" Nelson asked. "I can't say I

had enough to eat on the plane, and we didn't have breakfast before we left because it was such an early flight. So food right now wouldn't be a bad idea."

She chuckled. "There's the kitchen. Help yourself." She expected him to give her an argument, but he didn't.

He hopped up and walked into the kitchen, checking out her fridge and the cabinets. "You've got eggs. Do you have any bread?"

"Nope, I sure don't," she answered.

He rummaged a bit more, poked his head around the corner and said, "Do you mind if I make pancakes?"

She turned to face him in surprise. "Sure. Absolutely. If there's enough to make some for everybody, that's a great idea." She smiled as he puttered around in the kitchen. She looked at Taylor. "Do you cook too?"

"I can," he said. "Don't have much call for it in my world. I tend to do barbecues more than anything."

She nodded in understanding. "Men gravitate more to outdoor barbecues."

"Men gravitate to protein," Kanen said with a chuckle. "Big fat steaks."

"Well, you won't find any steaks in my fridge," she said, "but, if Nelson can make pancakes for all of us, that's perfect." Even the thought of it made her mouth water. She hadn't had homemade pancakes in a long time.

Before long, they all sat around her small kitchen table, enjoying a wonderful breakfast. She smiled at Nelson. "You can cook for me anytime."

He chuckled. "You're welcome at my table anytime too," he said with gentlemanly politeness.

She smiled and snagged another pancake off the stack. "These are really good. Blake used to make pancakes."

"Man food," Kanen said. "Something to stick to the ribs."

She nodded. "He often said stuff like that too." She waited a few minutes, while the men continued to eat. Then she asked, "How long can you stay in England?"

"Another two days," Kanen said. "I can stay longer if need be, if we haven't found this guy. But I can't stay too much longer."

She nodded. "I'd hate to be here alone if he hasn't been caught."

"Which is why," Kanen said, "you should come back with me."

"You mean, *run away?*" she asked, working up her face in distaste.

"Staying alive to fight another day," he corrected.

"Blake never ran away from anything," she said slowly. "I can hardly run away myself. Particularly if something is odd about his death."

"We're a long way away from having any proof of that," Kanen said. "Honestly I wouldn't go down that pathway at all. It's just going to twist you up inside."

She nodded. "I understand, but …"

"Did you want to pull that thread?" Kanen asked, watching her expression change. "Just tell me if you decide you want more facts, and we'll see what we can do."

She nodded, her mouth a grimace.

As the men finished the pancakes, she rinsed the dishes before loading them in the dishwasher. "What's next then?"

"We'll contact MI6," Kanen said. "Make sure they share whatever information they may have found on those photos. Then we'll continue our research to see if we can track down any Alagarth family member still alive or anybody who knows about Finest Photos and what happened to them."

"A historian? A genealogist? ... Selfies on social media?" she quipped with a roll of her eyes.

"There are all kinds of choices," Kanen said. "In a way, MI6 might even be the best option, if they'll cooperate with us." He got up from the table, filled his cup with coffee. "I'll be in the living room, seeing if I can get a hold of anyone on a weekend."

It *was* Saturday. Maybe nobody would answer. In the living room she heard Kanen speaking to somebody. She continued washing up, and they all half listened to the conversation.

Finally Kanen came back in and said, "Well, I got them on the phone. Surprise, surprise. And they're still tracking down a few other unknown people in the photos. They did come up with a couple more. One is dead, and the other one is in a coma from a car accident he had a long time ago. The family has been fighting the courts not to take him off life support."

"Interesting. Do we think the death of one and the accident of another are related?"

"I doubt it. Seems the death was natural and much more recent," Kanen said. "These photos were likely blackmail material from years ago. I think our best bet is to track down the couple known family members of the jailed alleged blackmailer. They have the best motivation for wanting the pictures back."

"But what motivation?" she asked in bewilderment. She snagged a tea towel and dried her hands. "I get that there has to be some reason why they are important to someone, but it seems like the actual blackmailing itself is no longer viable."

"I think MI6 is coming to that same conclusion," Kanen

said. "That's why we should find the rest of the people in this alleged blackmailer's family. You look to those closest to the victim or to the perpetrator of the crime, usually family members. If somebody knows about these photos, somebody has a reason for wanting to hang on to them. And usually that is to use them as threats. To stop somebody from doing something. We still have to get to the bottom of the who, what, how and why."

After she finished cleaning up the kitchen, they sat around the table with their laptops, searching and making phone calls as they tried to track down the last few living members of the alleged blackmailer's family.

Kanen got another text from Mason.

It's possible the Alagarth family moved to the US after the grandfather was convicted. We have proof the son was in Maine for a few years. But the grandson appears to have returned to England.

We'll look for him. Kanen read his message as he typed it into his phone for the others' benefit. **We need to write him off as part of this or put him on the plus side and keep him as a suspect.**

Pressing Send, Kanen said, "That means the grandson is likely still here in England. Why is it we haven't found him yet?"

"Because we were looking for a Robert Alagarth. I suspect he's using the name Bob instead," Nelson said. "Because we found several Bob Alagarths. One in London working as a photographer."

"Are we thinking the grandson followed in the grandfather's footsteps?" she asked. "Are we also thinking he's a blackmailer?"

"No way to know. I suggest we pay him a visit," Kanen

said.

"I'm up for it," Laysa said. "If he's even there on a Saturday."

Next thing she knew, Nelson was making a call. "Yes, I wanted to stop in this afternoon but didn't know how long you were open." He smiled. "Thank you. We should make it." He hung up the phone. "They're open until five o'clock today."

She marveled at how quickly they got things done. They had been moving nonstop since arriving in England, accomplishing a lot on their list, even though not yet at the finish line. Before she knew it, the men had already set up a plan of places to go. They had two more Bob Alagarths who they considered viable suspects. Once they were packed up and ready to go again, she looked around her apartment wistfully, wondering when she'd get a full day to herself to just sit and do nothing, without a care in the world.

Kanen wrapped an arm around her shoulders. "You ready?"

She nodded and followed them out of the apartment.

They went to see the first Bob Alagarth on their list, the closest one to her apartment. They walked up to his flat and met him; he was probably in his late seventies. Definitely not the person they were looking for.

They carried on to the second one on the list. He appeared to be the right age, but it couldn't be him; … he was black.

With that suspect crossed off the list, they headed to the photography shop. "What's the chance this is our guy?" she asked.

"As good as any," Kanen said cheerfully. "The question is whether you'll recognize him when you see him."

"It will be interesting to see his reaction when he sees her. So, take as much time as you need to recognize him and to take a good long look at him," Taylor said as they got out of the vehicle parked outside the shop, "I want to track this guy's reaction. That'll be as telling as anything."

They walked into the photography shop. It was bigger than she'd expected. "He seems to be doing quite well for himself here."

The shelves were full of lenses, cameras, supplies and other accessories. They wandered the store for a long moment, looking for the one person they were searching for. Two women worked at the counters.

Laysa walked up to one and asked, "Is Bob here?"

"He's in the back room. Did you have an appointment with him?"

She smiled. "We called and said we'd be coming. If it's possible, it'd be nice to talk to him."

The woman headed toward the offices in back. Because of what Taylor had said, Laysa stepped back behind the men. No reason for this guy to recognize Taylor or Nelson. He might recognize Kanen if he was tracking him through England's airports. But the guy would definitely recognize her if he saw her in the store.

The woman quickly returned. "He'll be out in a minute."

The men nodded and wandered the store. She deliberately kept herself hidden behind everybody, wondering if this Bob Alagarth could possibly be her assailant.

Soon a man in a business suit stepped forward, a bright smile on his face, asking the men what he could help them with.

That voice ... She studied the owner and realized she

couldn't tell just from that if it was him or not. She looked at his wrists, and, sure enough, he had the same ropy muscled arms as her captor, but was it really him? There was only one way to find out. She stepped forward into the middle of the men, smiled up at him and said, "There you are. We finally found you."

KANEN JOLTED AT her wording. He immediately turned to the man, looking for the response that would trigger a conviction one way or the other.

Bob swallowed hard and said, "I don't know anything about you."

She gave him a hard smile. "And that just convinced me even more. Your voice caught my attention first. You should have some scratches along your right shoulder." She immediately smacked him hard where she'd scratched him before.

He took a step back, glanced at the men and bolted.

The women in the shop screamed as Kanen jumped over the counter and raced after Bob. Kanen didn't waste time worrying about Laysa because he knew one of his two men would stay with her, the other right behind Kanen.

Bob disappeared into the back offices and out the rear exit. As Kanen blasted out the door of the building, he saw a small blue car already turning from the parking lot onto the road. The vehicle was older, more of a patchwork kind of a blue, as if different parts were taken from multiple vehicles of all different colors. It would be very hard to hide that vehicle. Kanen came to a gasping stop, furious to think this guy had gotten away from them.

Taylor stopped by his side, glaring down the road. Then he turned to him. "Are you sure that's him?"

They both studied the rest of the parking lot, looking to see if they spotted anyone else.

"It's just as likely he could have gone off on foot, using that vehicle's exit as a distraction." Taylor motioned inside. "If you want to check with the staff, I'll keep looking around out here."

Kanen returned inside and asked one of the staff what kind of vehicle the owner drove.

"He's rebuilding a small blue car," she said in confusion. "What's happened? What's he done?"

He pulled the woman gently outside to the parking lot. "Is his vehicle here?"

"Oh, you can't miss it," she said. "It's a wreck. It's got various bits and pieces that he's using until the parts he wants come in. And, no, it's not here."

Sadly that confirmed what Kanen had already assumed—they'd lost him. "We need a way to contact him. Do you have his phone number, his home address?"

But the staff member got irritated. "Hey, I don't know who you are or what you're doing here, but, if he took off, he had a good reason."

Kanen wasn't about to let her get away with that. But he didn't have to because suddenly Laysa was there in front of them.

She snapped at the woman. "Oh, he had a reason all right," she yelled. "He broke into my apartment, held me captive there and beat me up because I didn't know where his precious *stuff* was. Turned out to be blackmail photos."

The staff member took several steps back, her hand going to her chest. "That's not possible. He's a good guy."

But Laysa was pretty damn convincing as she explained what had happened. "See this bruise on my jaw where he planted his fist? More photos like this are on file with the police department, if you care to check."

The woman backed up another step.

"We've been hunting *Bob* ever since he attacked me. I'm still sporting his other bruises and have a few scars from the rough treatment he gave me." She spoke bitterly. "But I recognized him, both his voice and his arms. And I have no doubt that's who he is. He's the one who took off. Remember?" she snapped at the woman, getting the better of her again.

Kanen gently rubbed her shoulder. "We'll catch him, now that we know who he is and where he works. The police will nab him."

The woman stared at them in horror. "But I've known him for ten years. He'd never have done something like that."

"Maybe not before," Laysa said, "but he certainly did now. So we need to know what you know about him."

But the woman wasn't willing to cooperate. She stormed back inside.

Laysa followed her and started taking pictures of the store with her phone, Kanen right behind her.

The other staff member came over and said, "You can't be here. We don't know what the hell's going on, but we trust our boss."

Kanen nodded. "You can trust your boss all you want. But we're staying right here until the cops arrive."

"And MI6," Laysa said in a hard voice. "If you think they're not involved in my finding my assailant, you're wrong."

The women looked at each other nervously and then went back to their jobs.

Kanen didn't blame them. They had jobs to do, problems with their boss or not. "You might want to contact the higher-up boss if you have one," he offered helpfully.

The woman shrugged and said, "Bob owns the company."

"Then you better be looking for another job," Laysa said, "because he's going to jail for B&E, battery and extortion. Maybe even murder."

The women shook their heads and remained quiet.

Kanen had to admire that kind of blind loyalty, if that was what it was. More than likely it was a case of they didn't know what else to do. And he could understand that too. It wasn't like they'd given the women any warning or proof.

At that thought, he noticed the framed photographs on the side wall that Laysa was taking snapshots of. He pointed them out to the guys. One by one they studied these black-and-white pictures. They appeared to be of old photography stores.

"What's the chance these are Bob Alagarth's grandfather's stores? What if this is about revenge? About his grandfather's wrongful incarceration?" Kanen glanced over at one of the women. "Did your boss's father ever come into this store?"

The woman looked up at him nervously and shook her head, then went back to her work.

"Given his likely age," Nelson offered, "chances are he has nothing to do with his father's business, Grandpa Alagarth's chain of European stores. And, if Father Alagarth is still living in the States since about 1994, then he never was involved with his son's subsequent business either."

"So why did the grandson want that package from Blake?" Kanen asked in a low voice. "Unless he's trying to protect someone."

It was just too much for Laysa. She walked over to the closest chair, pulled it far away from the women and sat down. "How long before the police get here?"

"We called MI6," Kanen said. "They'll be here first." And, sure enough, he looked up to see two men in suits striding in the front door.

Their hard gazes searched the store. They came toward him with a strong determination that wouldn't be swayed. Neither of the women who worked at the store spoke.

Kanen explained what had happened. The men in suits took notes and then, when questions were completed, Kanen, Laysa, Nelson and Taylor were escorted from the store. Outside on the sidewalk, it dawned on Kanen. "Surely you'll do a full investigation?"

"Of course," one of the MI6 men said. "But we want to get our hands on him first. The store is just that. ... It's a store. It's nothing more than that."

"No, there you're wrong," Laysa said. "The history of the Alagarth family business is on the walls. The grandfather was wrongfully accused of blackmail, jailed, murdered. His assailant was Bob, the grandson and owner of his own photography store, this one. Those photos on the walls inside are interesting as far as the backstory of the family."

One of the agents turned to look at the double glass entrance doors. With a few quiet words to the other man, he headed back inside, as if to look at the photographs.

Laysa looked up at Kanen. "He needs to pull them off the wall, all of them, and take them in for evidence."

Kanen chuckled and tugged her a little closer. "They know how to do their jobs. Besides, they aren't really evidence. They are mementos of this guy's history."

"No," she argued. "They are evidence of his motivation. And that counts." She shoved her fists into her pockets and glared up at the men.

They stared back at her with calm, bland faces, knowing it was best to not say much at this moment, without getting into an argument with her. "Come on. Let's go back to your place," he said quietly. "We'll get the details soon."

She resisted but finally gave in. As she turned to walk away, she looked back at the two MI6 men and said, "Please catch Bob before he comes after me again. He beat me up and threatened to kill me."

The look on the agents' faces eased, and one of them nodded. "We plan on it."

As they walked toward the car, she turned to Kanen. "It's not fair. Bob was right there. He was so damn close."

"It would have been nice if you had pointed that out to one of us, instead of antagonizing Bob right off the bat," Kanen said gently. "We could have set a trap for him. As it was, he had the advantage of a familiar location and a clean line out of the building and a vehicle to run away in."

"I know," she said. "I didn't think. I'm sorry. Once I was convinced it was him, I confronted him to get confirmation."

Now in their rented vehicle, they headed toward her apartment. Kanen was a little worried. She kept staring out the window listlessly, as if Bob's getaway was all her fault. He slid his fingers through hers. "It's okay. We'll get him."

She nodded but didn't answer. Outside her apartment, she looked up at the windows. "It doesn't even feel like home anymore."

"Once this is all over," Nelson said with forced cheerfulness, "it will feel different, hopefully better."

She followed Taylor through the front doors. Kanen brought up the rear. He stopped to look around the streets. As long as her assailant, this Bob Alagarth, was loose and on the run, Kanen didn't dare leave her side. This Bob guy was just as likely to run to the main continent, but, if he was angry or wanted to put a stop to this, he might easily come back after her again.

Kanen stepped inside. As the rest of them entered the elevator, he said, "I'll take the stairs." He waited until the door shut and headed to the stairwell. He ran up the stairs quickly. On the third floor, he got out and walked toward her apartment. There was no sign of her.

He walked back to the elevator and saw it hadn't made it to the third floor, stopping on the floor below. Swearing profusely, he bolted back down to the second floor and came out of the stairwell ready for a fight, only to see the three of them talking softly outside the elevator. He came to a dead stop in front of them and reminded himself not to yell. "Jesus! I thought something had happened. What's wrong?"

She turned to him and raised both hands in frustration. "I don't want to go home."

He reached for her hands. "Then we don't have to go back there," he said quietly. "If you're nervous, or if you think something is wrong, if your instincts are telling you that you can't go there, then that's fine. We'll go to my hotel for the night."

He heard a heavy sigh and watched the relief cross her face. He enveloped her with a hug and held her close. "Look. You had a traumatic event in your apartment," he said quietly. "Of course you don't want to be there. Just say so. We won't force you to do anything. We're here to help keep you safe and to catch this asshole Bob. But let's not make fear be the reason you do anything."

She nodded and squeezed his back. "I know. I feel like we should avoid my apartment. I know I'm being foolish, but, at the same time, knowing that guy's out there …"

"Which is exactly why the three of us are here with you," he said. "Now do you want to go back and make sure everything's okay? Will you feel better if you see that your place is the same as it always was?"

She tilted her head to the side as if contemplating that idea, then nodded. "Yes, I will."

They went back to the elevator, but she balked at the doors.

"No, I don't want to get in the elevator."

The other men exchanged worried glances, but Kanen grabbed her hand and said, "The stairs are fine."

They walked up the last flight to her apartment. There she unlocked the door, and Kanen pushed it open and entered. While they waited outside, he did a quick search of the entire place, ending his search in the bedroom, even checking under the bed and in the closet.

He walked back out to where they waited. "It's empty. No one's here. Come on in."

She walked in slowly.

He wasn't sure why it bothered her this time versus the last time, but he had to respect her feelings.

She stopped and pointed at the couch. "That is new."

Kanen inspected her couch, pulling out a note stuck between the cushions. He showed it to Nelson and Taylor.

"What does it say?" she asked.

"It'll be okay," Kanen began. "It seems Bob stopped by here while MI6 questioned us. He left a note saying, *I'll be back.*" He grabbed Laysa's shoulders. "We won't let him get to you again."

She nodded, trying not to focus on those three words.

"Hey," Kanen said, sucking her out of her thoughts. "You called it. You followed your instincts."

She nodded.

"No, really. You followed your instincts. It was a good call. Continue doing that. Always let us know when you have these gut checks, okay?"

She remained silent, still nodding her head as if unable to stop.

"Okay?" he asked louder.

"Yes." She smiled a weak grin. "Yes," she said in a stronger voice. "It scared me."

"As he meant for you to be," Kanen said.

"But I'm getting madder as I think about it."

Kanen and the other guys laughed. "You got it, Laysa. Turn that fear into fight mode." She'd gone through a horrible ordeal, and Kanen could well imagine she no longer had a feeling of home here. He'd be more than happy to take her home with him. All she had to do was agree. They'd been friends since forever. And she was definitely pulling at his heartstrings.

Now that Blake was gone, he shouldn't feel guilty about his feelings. It would take a little time to adjust to seeing her as someone in his life, not just as Blake's wife and as a longtime friend. He glanced at her, realizing it wouldn't take any time at all. He was almost there now.

She sat on the far end of the couch—opposite from where Bob's note was found—and stared up at Kanen, a wistful smile crossing her face. "It would have been so nice to have seen you before all this," she said. "Now it feels like we're not equals anymore."

At her odd wording, he sat down beside her. "We've always been equals. What do you mean?"

"I feel like I need you to protect me right now, and that makes me less than what I was before."

He shook his head. "That's so not true. We all need help sometimes. Even SEALs need help. Right now you need us. And that's fine. You might not need us tomorrow. You might not need us next week, but, for the moment, you need our help, and that's what we're here for. It doesn't make you any less in our eyes. In fact, I admire somebody who can accept the help when it's required."

She chuckled. "I forgot what a cheerleader you always were."

"I am what I am," he said with a lopsided grin. "And I have to admit that, right now, I am hungry."

She stared at him. "No way. You can't always be so hungry."

He shrugged. "Why not? It's got to be at least lunchtime, if not dinnertime. I've lost track of the time of day."

She snorted. "Well, if anyone wants to make something, go ahead, but I don't think I have enough food to feed all of us."

Nelson jumped to his feet. "Challenge accepted." He raced into the kitchen, with Taylor right behind him, both of them laughing.

She looked over at Kanen and smiled. "I like your friends."

He leaned over and kissed her gently on the lips, whispering, "They like you too."

CHAPTER 11

LAYSA WAS SURPRISED at the kiss, and yet, why should she be? They'd been heading toward this since he'd arrived to help her. She looped her arms around his neck and kissed him back. "I like you too," she whispered.

He settled her into his lap, and they sat here, cuddling. She thought about how long it had been since she'd been held by somebody who really cared and realized it had been way too long. "I've missed this," she announced quietly.

He looked down at her. "What?"

"Being touched," she said softly. "Cuddling. Just being with somebody who cares. After Blake died, it seemed like my world collapsed. I was so alone, like walking through a constant dark, cold night. And there would never be any sunshine ever again. Of course, eventually you pass through that phase, and you stare outside, and you start to reconnect with the world around you. But you're single now. There isn't anybody to hold you in the middle of the night when you had a bad day or a nightmare. There isn't anybody to pick up the phone and call or to send a happy face text to in the middle of the day just because you were thinking of them. Everything is geared for a two-person world, and, all of a sudden, you are cut in half. It feels so foreign, so strange and, most of all, so very cold."

He hugged her gently. She rested against his big chest.

She'd never thought of him as anything more than a good friend, … until recently. At the same time, she wondered why not. He was incredibly sexy, one of those strong and capable kinds of guys who oozed power and charm at the same time. She knew he'd had lots of girlfriends, but nobody he ever got close to.

She leaned back slightly, looking up at him. "Why did you never marry?"

He jokingly said, "Well, I could say because you were already married."

She wrinkled her face up at him. "No. I mean, why did you never marry?"

"Because I never met anybody I cared enough about to make it permanent," he said calmly.

She had to wonder at that. And his initial joke. Was this the time to ask him about that?

Just then Taylor poked his head around the corner, saw the two of them together and smiled. "Now that's much better," he said, "to see the two of you like that."

She raised an eyebrow. "Ha. You don't know anything about us."

He shrugged. "And? That doesn't change anything, does it? Not really. But the reason I'm here is to ask if you had any plans for some of the stuff in your freezer, or can we help ourselves to whatever we need?"

She waved a hand at him. "I doubt much is in there. Have at anything you want."

Kanen called out, "It's better if we use up everything anyway. She won't be staying here, so the less to move, the better."

Taylor gave a big nod with a happy grin. "Got it." He disappeared again.

She leaned back and turned to look at Kanen. "What are you talking about?"

"You don't want to be here. You don't really have a job you can't live without. You're all alone. And you just said it's like a half life. The dark half. I want you to come stay with me," he said. "California is warm and sunny. Leave the rain here. I have a two-bedroom apartment, so plenty of room, and I think you could make a new life for yourself there."

"I'm not a charity case," she warned.

He snorted. "Nobody in their right mind would call you a charity case." He tilted her chin up. "Is that why you keep ignoring me when I ask you to come home with me?" He studied her a moment, but she kept silent. "Can you look me in the eye and tell me that you really want to stay here all on your own?"

She winced. She tried to pull her chin away, but he wouldn't let her. She glared up at him. "I don't know what I want."

His gaze warmed.

She sighed and smiled up at him. "You're right. I don't want to be here alone. The invasion of my home and the beating was enough of an experience, without factoring in the loss of Blake, so I don't want to stay in this apartment. But moving back to the US is a big step."

"You moved here with Blake, but California has always been your home. Is there any reason you don't want to go back home?"

"It doesn't feel like home," she said. "Even though I lived there for so long, it doesn't feel like going *home*."

"Good point," he said. "But does this place feel like home anymore?"

She had to think about it, for like two seconds. Her

shoulders slowly shrugged, answering him. She shook her head. "It hasn't really felt like home since I lost Blake. It's his furniture. I wanted something different, but he really loved this, so I was okay with it too." She spoke slowly. "The wall colors are his choices. I wanted bright and cheerful, but he wanted the browns and caramels."

"You could buy new furniture and repaint the walls, if that was the only issue."

She shook her head. "No, it was Blake who made this home. Without him, well …" She shifted from Kanen's lap to sit beside him again, subconsciously separating herself from him.

He let her go, but he didn't completely release her.

She stared down at their fingers laced together. "I have some friends here but not good ones."

"And what about your friends in California? Do you still have them?"

"Well, there's you," she said with a bright smile. "And I never did thank you for coming to my rescue."

He shook his head and placed a finger against her lips. "No thanks needed," he whispered.

She kissed his finger and watched as his eyes deepened in color. "Are you sure we should walk down this path?" she asked hesitantly.

The corner of his mouth kicked up. "I don't see any reason why not. Do you?"

She didn't have any reason, except a part of her still held back because it felt wrong. "I just wonder if Blake will always be between us," she said hesitantly. "And moving to California seems like leaving him behind."

Understanding lit his gaze. He gathered her in his arms and cuddled her close. She didn't fight him, just lay against his chest.

"I wouldn't want him to be there, always between us, and I think, if we were to become more than friends, he would be," she finally whispered.

"Blake will be wherever we put Blake," Kanen said firmly. "He was a friend to both of us. He was your husband, but he was my best friend. And he's not here with us now. So I understand that he'll always be there in our memories, our thoughts, but I don't think he has to be *between* us. There's no reason he can't sit off to the side and be a part of our lives. We don't want to forget him. We don't want to avoid using his name. We want to remember the good times. Some of our memories are shared. Sometimes we had the same adventures with him. The last thing we want is to be worried about not bringing up his name in a conversation. If we try to avoid having him with us, that's what will happen. So I suggest we just let things develop naturally between us and don't worry about it if Blake memories arise."

She chuckled. "Is life so simple for you?"

He shrugged. "It makes it a little easier to get through everything in my world with the least amount of stress."

She thought about that and nodded. "Okay, just so you know, there will be times when I get worried about you and your career."

"Okay, just so you know, there'll be times when I may get worried about you too," he commented.

She frowned. "What would you be worried about?"

He smiled. "About the fact that you might always be comparing me to him."

"What?" She shook her head. "I'd never do that. You're so very different." She thought about it and realized, "It would be subconscious if I did."

"It would be natural if you did." His voice was full of acceptance.

She nodded in understanding. "You're both so very different, and I love you both," she said quietly. "It's hard to comprehend he's gone. But, after almost a year, I've finally come to terms with it—I think."

"Good," he said, giving her a big hug. "Because I like what you just said."

Startled, she looked up at him. And then realized she'd said she loved them both. She smiled. "You know I love you. I've told you often enough."

"But there's *love*, and then there is *in love*," he said. "I'm quite happy if you go from one to the other."

She shook her head. "Oh, no, no, no. Not unless you'll go there too."

"How do you know I'm not already there?" he asked with a chuckle. "There's a lot you don't know about me."

"And there's a lot you don't know about me." She smiled back at him.

"Well then, I suggest we keep the communication line open, and we get to know each other a little better, even though we think we've always known each other. This is the perfect time to see just what might be there."

"How are we supposed to get to know each other under these circumstances and with your two friends around?"

He smirked and said, "We'll find a way."

KANEN PICKED HER up in his arms and carried her into the kitchen. The men were there, waiting for them, big grins on their faces. With great ceremony, they pulled out a chair at the head of the table, let Kanen place her there, and Nelson said, "Madam, your meal is served."

She laughed out loud. "Hey, I don't know what to do with you guys spoiling me so much."

They shrugged, and Taylor said, "Sometimes you need that."

What followed was a meal anybody would have been proud of. Kanen's eyebrows rose as he saw pork chops grilled to perfection with an absolutely delicious-looking hollandaise sauce draped over the top, a sautéed vegetable mix he'd never seen before and even biscuits on the side.

Nelson said, "It's a bit of an eclectic mix, but we were working with what we had."

She held her hands together in delight. "I don't care what you call it or how eclectic this looks because it smells delicious. I had no idea this much food was in my apartment."

Just then Taylor returned to the table and placed a rice dish beside her. "This one needed an extra minute."

It was yellow and fragrant and had spices all over the top, plus dried herbs. She sniffed the air and said, "This is fantastic. You guys can cook for me anytime."

They chuckled as everyone sat down.

Kanen was about to take his seat, when his phone rang. The others looked at him. He stepped back out to the living room to answer. "Mason, what's up?"

"I just heard from MI6," he said. "I understand you had a crazy afternoon."

"We did," Kanen said, realizing he'd forgotten to update Mason. "Did they catch him?"

"No. They put out an all-points bulletin for Bob. His vehicle was found ditched on the side of the road, with no sign of the driver."

"Of course not," Kanen said with a groan. "Which means he could be anywhere. The women at his store were very loyal. They would easily have lent him their vehicles, if needed."

"The MI6 guys thought of that, and the employees' vehicles are being watched."

"Good," Kanen said.

"How is Laysa holding up?"

"Bob left her an *I'll be back* note in her apartment. First she was scared. Then she got mad. She recognized him in the store, even though he wore a balaclava while holding her. He has very distinctive wrists and forearms," Kanen said. "And that made a big difference to her. She could easily identify him and recognized his voice. Once he realized the gig was up, he bolted."

"Which always makes a guilty man look guiltier," Mason said with a chuckle.

"Exactly."

"Makes MI6 more cooperative too."

"We're just about to sit down to a hot meal. Then we'll get back to it."

"MI6 is tracking down everybody in the blackmail photos. They've identified and found the last two previously unknown men, both who admitted to being blackmailed but said the blackmail is of no value now because their circumstances have changed."

"So, if the photos are no longer of any value," Kanen said, "why the devil does Bob care?"

"We'll ask him when we find the man and hopefully get answers to end this mystery."

"True enough." Kanen pocketed the phone and went back into the kitchen, where everybody dug into the food. "I hope you left me some," he protested.

Laysa chuckled. "Those who come late to the dinner table will have whatever dregs are left," she misquoted with a grin.

He protested again loudly.

She quite happily handed him whatever was left on the platters. There wasn't much. Still, it was a full plate by the time he had dished up servings of everything. Then he told them what Mason had said.

The conversation dimmed from laughter to the looming specter over their world.

She nodded. "We need to figure out why he's doing this, and everything else will come together."

"Money, sex or power," Kanen said. "Those are generally the reasons we do things."

She stared at him. "Surely not. There has to be a lot of other reasons."

"You mean, like jealousy?" Nelson asked with a smirk. "That could go under sex or power."

Her face wrinkled up. "I don't think you guys have a very good attitude."

They chuckled.

"We do have a fairly balanced one," Kanen said. "The problem is, we've seen an awful lot that you haven't. You're just now being touched by it, realizing how absolutely twisted many people are. But, to the bad guys, their motives are always reasonable. To them anyway."

"So it's reasonable, to Bob, to hold me captive. To beat me up."

"If he needed those pictures and had left them with Blake, absolutely. He thinks it's the means to the end. That it's totally justified."

"At least he didn't kill me," she said. "So, from that perspective, the damage to me is minimal."

"True," Kanen said. *But for how long?*

They finished eating and were doing the dishes when a knock came at the door. Everyone froze. Kanen motioned Nelson to take her to another room, and Kanen stepped up to the door. There was no peephole, and he hated that. He opened the door to see a stranger. "Yes? May I help you?"

The man frowned. "Where is Laysa?"

From the bedroom Laysa called out, "Carl, I'm here."

Kanen recognized his name, the man who she'd stayed with that first night. Kanen motioned to the living room. "I'm a friend of hers. Come on in."

But Carl didn't appear to want to step inside. He looked at Kanen suspiciously. "When did you arrive?"

"A couple days ago," Kanen said. "Right after she contacted me, I came running. But then long-term friends are like that."

Carl looked at him and said, "How long have you been friends?"

"Long before Blake passed away," Kanen said.

Laysa suddenly appeared at Kanen's side. She smiled up at Carl. "Hey, how are you?"

He looked at her with relief on his face. "Are you okay? I came down yesterday, and, when you didn't answer, I got worried."

She reached out a hand and grasped his. "I'm sorry. I should have let you know we flew to Spain and back. I have been out with the guys quite a bit, trying to find my assailant. This is Kanen, the friend I told you about. He's been looking after me."

She turned to Kanen. "Carl is my neighbor and a policeman, who opened his home to me when I escaped and kept me safe until you arrived."

Kanen reached out a hand with a smile. "Thank you for watching over her. She went through a terrible ordeal."

Carl nodded and shook Kanen's hand but still looked suspiciously at Kanen. Carl motioned down the hallway for Laysa to come out there to talk to him. It was all Kanen could do not to yank her back to his side. He waited at the doorway with his head cocked, trying hard to hear their conversation. But he didn't hear much, just whispered voices.

Then she smiled at Carl and said, "It's all right. Everything's good." And she headed back toward Kanen. With her apartment door closed, she said, "Carl was afraid you looked a little too dangerous to be on my side. He wanted to make sure I was safe and not being held captive again."

Nelson snorted. "Yeah, that's our Kanen. Dangerous to look at."

"At least he had your well-being in mind," Kanen said. "He seems like he cares."

She nodded. "He's been a good neighbor. He lives just one floor above me."

As far as Kanen could tell, anybody close to Laysa deserved a second look. Just to make sure Carl really was a good guy and not involved in this mess. And that brought up something else Kanen should have considered. No one had ever questioned if Bob could be working with a partner. Kanen caught Taylor's eye, who appeared to be thinking the same thing.

Taylor walked back into the living room, sat down with his laptop and opened it up.

In a casual conversational tone, Kanen asked her, "How

long has Carl lived here?"

She shrugged. "I don't know. A few years before Blake and I moved here."

"What's his last name?"

That was one question too many. She planted her hands on her hips and glared at him. "There's nothing wrong with him. He's a good guy. A cop. You be nice."

He opened his eyes wide and gave her an innocent look. "Anyone connected to you is someone I will take a second look at," he said. "So I get that you don't want me prying into people's lives who may have nothing to do with this, but I won't know they have nothing to do with this until I pry."

He waited for her answer. He could see the younger version of the woman in front of him. As a child, she would have stomped her foot several times in frustration. Right now all she did was glare at him.

Then she turned to face Taylor, narrowed her gaze. "Are you in on this?"

He turned a bland face in her direction. "I don't know what you're talking about."

She raised both hands, palms up, in mock surrender. "Fine. Whatever. His name is Carl McMaster." She spun around and sat on the couch with more force than necessary. "His wife's name is Sicily. She's lovely too. They are good people."

The men busily tapped away on their keyboards.

Kanen sat beside her and said, "Remember that, whatever we do, we're doing for your sake."

She released a heavy sigh and nodded. "I get that. But it's still very intrusive. Not to mention the fact no one wants to contemplate that Carl could be involved."

"A lot of people could be involved on a peripheral level,"

Kanen said. "That's why we do these checks and balances."
Once again Kanen's phone rang. It was Mark, the gym
manager. Kanen answered it quietly, keeping an eye on her.
He was a little worried about how this all affected her.

"Hey, should have called you earlier. We had a break-in
last night."

"Oh?" Kanen straightened and stood, walking to the
living room window. "What was taken?"

"Nothing was taken, but Blake's locker was broken into."

Half under his breath, he whispered, "Shit."

"Exactly. So I presume whatever you took out of that
locker …"

"I'll make the same assumption," Kanen said. "Do you
have video feed from last night?"

"I do, but the guy wore a black mask and kept his face
away from the camera."

"What about outside in the parking lot? Any idea what
vehicle he was driving?"

"No, I don't. The camera angle stops at the front door."

"Have you called the cops?"

"Should I? Nothing else was damaged, and I don't really
want the added aggravation. Once people see the cops
hanging around, all hell breaks loose."

"How about a quiet pair of MI6 agents coming through,
looking for fingerprints?"

"Good idea. The guy on tape didn't wear gloves. So, if
there are fingerprints, they would be around the locker."

"I'll call you right back." Kanen hung up and called his
MI6 contact. "There was a break-in at Gold's gym last night.
Somebody breaking into Blake's locker, presumably to find
the bag of blackmail photographs."

MI6 arranged for a small team to go in and to take fingerprints after-hours.

"I'll call Mark back and warn him. I'll tell him to make sure nobody else touches the locker."

"You do that," the MI6 contact said. "But chances are it's already too late."

"I know." Kanen hung up and redialed Mark. Once he explained about MI6, he said, "I know it's probably too much to ask, but, if you could make sure nobody touches the locker or the door frame, lock, etc., it would be appreciated."

Mark gave a half laugh. "As you saw, it's the last locker in a bank of lockers. I have no idea how many million fingerprints would be on it, especially since men often grab on to it as they swing around the corner."

"Understood." Kanen hung up, turned to look at the others and said, "Our photographer guy is getting closer. He broke into Blake's locker at the gym last night."

"He obviously had the same idea we did," Nelson said. "And maybe he even saw us go into the gym and had to check for himself."

"He'll either assume we have it or he will keep looking for it," Kanen said.

"We didn't check the storage unit though," Taylor reminded them.

"No," Laysa said, frowning at them. "I completely forgot about it."

The men checked their watches.

Kanen said, "I suggest we go now. We have several hours of daylight. Let's make good use of this time. Even though we think we have what this guy is looking for, maybe we can draw him out, see if we can set him up and take him down at the storage facility."

She brightened. "Particularly if he sees us leave here."

Kanen smiled. "Exactly." He met Nelson's gaze over her head and knew they were both thinking the same thing. There had to be some way to set a trap for this guy. But how?

CHAPTER 12

L AYSA LED THE way to the storage unit. They'd parked
farther down on the street, so nobody would know easily
where they went.

Kanen came up to her side, reached gently for her hand
and whispered in your ear, "Give us the number. Let us take
a look and make sure nobody's here or anywhere around."

She shot him a look, then shrugged. With Nelson once
again standing at her side, Kanen and Taylor took off. She
faced Nelson and asked, "How come you're on babysitting
duty?"

"Because I love looking after babies," he said with a
smirk.

She shot him a sideways look.

He grinned and said in a more gallant one, "It's an hon-
or to look after the lady."

"Don't you miss out on the action?"

"I get plenty of action," he said.

Something in his tone made her think he was talking
about a completely different kind of action. They waited on
the spot in silence. She glanced around and realized Kanen
had left her in a rather unique area, a path leading to the
back of the storage units. They'd already gone through the
gate, but they were surrounded by tall cedar trees and were
out of everybody's view.

"It's really isolated here, isn't it?" she asked.

"It is. It's a great place for an ambush."

Instinctively she took a step closer to him.

He chuckled. "That works every time."

She smacked him lightly on the shoulder. "If that works with all the girls, you should be ashamed of yourself."

"Oh, I am. I am." He tried to sound serious.

She just rolled her eyes at him.

Suddenly Kanen stood in front of her, his gaze going from one to the other.

Was that worry in his eyes? "You okay?" she asked.

He looked at her in surprise. "I'm fine. The coast is clear."

He reached out a hand, and she placed hers in it. As they walked along together, she looked around to see that Nelson had disappeared. "What's going on?" she asked. "You show up, and now Nelson leaves. Like musical chairs. Plus, when you arrived, you looked worried."

"Of course I'm worried," he said. "What if you prefer Nelson to me?"

"As if," she snorted. "A new friend is always nice to have, but it certainly isn't a replacement for an old one."

"No, but a shiny new penny is always more attractive than the dull old one you've been carrying around."

She realized his tone held a note of insecurity. She squeezed his fingers and whispered, "I don't prefer him over you. I don't prefer either of them over you. Honestly, you're the best man I know."

He squeezed her fingers now, then stopped her as she started to go around the corner.

She hesitated, watching as he studied the surroundings, never losing that sharp attentive look as he searched through the buildings, almost as if he had X-ray vision, seeing what went on inside each one.

"Do you really think he'd come here?"

"I think he has no choice," Kanen said. "We're only here to check it out, to make sure nothing else is here that we should know about."

When he felt it was safe, he took a step forward, tugging her gently along behind him, always protecting her, always keeping his body between her and any assailant. She wondered at that. Was there ever a more certain man born with a protective gene? Was Kanen born with that instinctive need to look after others? She certainly hadn't been born with it. At that thought, she wondered what kind of a mother she'd make.

For a long time, that was all she'd thought about, but, since Blake had been so against having children, she had tried to not push it too hard.

Apparently she had, though. Blake had struggled with that. And that was sad. She hadn't wanted to bring him any heartache. Yes, she wanted a family. But she wondered if she could look after her child as well as Kanen looked after her.

Or maybe that was a genetic skill that blossomed when you got pregnant and had a child. She'd never even babysat when she was growing up. She was an only child and had basically been orphaned at a young age. Now she had to wonder about her mothering instincts. Did she have any?

Luckily those thoughts were interrupted as she neared her storage unit. She pulled her key ring from her pocket and found her spare key to open the lock on the door. This was a key lock, not a combination lock. She studied it for a long moment, trying to remember when they'd put it on. And why this kind of a lock versus the other? But she gave up.

She had no way to know what was in her husband's mind at the time.

As she stepped back with the lock in her hand, the men grabbed the handles on either side of the rolling garage door and slowly raised it. She hadn't been here in a long time and assumed nothing had changed. But, as they flicked on the lights, she realized everything had changed. "I don't know what all this stuff is," she said.

"What do you mean?" Nelson stepped forward, blocking her view. She was forced to look at him. "Are you saying this isn't your unit?"

She looked around him, returning her attention to the contents. "I don't know. It's my lock." She held up the key still in the lock in her hand. "But I don't remember the unit being this full." He stepped out of the way as she walked forward, looking at the furniture. "For all I know, Blake, being Blake, might have let somebody else put their stuff in here too."

"*Interesting,*" Kanen said. "More questions we should have asked him before he died, huh?"

She didn't know what to say, but Kanen seemed to have second thoughts about Blake. She spun to look at Kanen. "But you know what Blake was like. If anybody needed anything ..."

Kanen nodded. "I do, indeed, know all about that. And it is definitely something he would do. If you only had a portion of this storage unit filled, he would easily help somebody out by offering them the free space."

"He had the unit before we got married. We stored some stuff in here, but it wasn't even close to full. You and I moved some stuff here after Blake passed away, ... but again it wasn't this full. Someone put more in here after Blake's death." Several narrow walkways seemed to be between items, as if people had been back and forth, among all this stuff. "The thing is, I'm the one with the lock and the key. So, unless somebody has duplicate keys ... Well, Bob did force me to give him my spare key, but I didn't give him the correct unit number." She studied the couch underneath a few boxes. "I don't even know whose couch that is," she said in confusion. "I've never seen it before."

She walked farther down this path and stopped in front of a filing cabinet that was easily accessible, enough room so that the drawers could open. She tried to open one, but it was locked. She glanced back at Kanen. "This isn't my filing cabinet. And it's locked."

He pulled a small tool kit from his back pocket. "It's your storage unit," he said, "so let's find out what's in here. Maybe it'll tell us whose stuff is stored here."

He quickly broke into the filing cabinet. She didn't even see how he'd done it, he was so fast. She studied the tool kit in his hand, then raised her gaze to his.

He gave her a crooked smile and said, "My SEALs training has offered many avenues for future career potential." He pulled open the top drawer, finding it full of files.

As she flipped through them, she gasped. "These are all photographs. *All* of these are photographs." But they weren't photographs of people in compromising positions, they were like portrait photos. As they checked the folders, names were on the top. "Are these proofs? So people can call and ask for more copies or something?"

"That's how it would have been done in the olden days," Kanen said, "but, with the digital photos now, it's obviously very different."

She nodded. "But this points to somebody hanging on

to all the old photos."

"True."

They went through drawer after drawer after drawer. "These literally are all from one business, Finest Photos," she said.

"And they're all old," Kanen confirmed. "If you look at the dates, they're all from before 1995, when the poor man was charged with blackmailing his clients and was sentenced to jail."

She spun around. "None of this makes any sense. Why is this Finest Photos stuff in my storage unit?"

"A question we'd like to ask you ourselves," said two men from the entrance.

She spun to see the same two MI6 officers who had been at the photographer's shop. She frowned at them. "Oh, did Kanen tell you we were coming here?"

"Yes, but we should have known about this unit earlier."

Unbelievably she looked at them. "This is a storage unit my husband and I have. But this isn't my stuff."

"Can you prove that?" the first man said, his voice soft.

Her blood froze. "You can't possibly think I'm involved in this."

Kanen pulled her closer. "Nobody thinks you're involved," he said in a hard voice, his gaze never leaving the two men in front of them. "The agents might try using the element of fear, to see if they can shake some answers out of you, but that obviously won't work now either. And it's certainly not a technique I approve of."

The two men stared back at him, their faces bland.

"Kanen?" she asked, her voice low. "What are they doing here?"

"We'll all find answers together. Unless," he firmly said

to the men, "you're planning on charging her with something right now."

The men measured each other, and then finally the MI6 agents shook their heads. "We came here for answers. We're not ready to charge anyone yet," the first man said, but he left that threat hanging in the air.

Kanen felt Laysa tremble in his arms. He held her tight and said, "It's all good. You've done nothing wrong."

"But what if Blake did?" she whispered in a voice so low and so full of pain that nobody could mistake how the thought hurt her.

"We're not going there until we have a real reason to," Kanen said. "Blake was my best friend too. If he was involved in something, we can't ask him questions because he's gone. We can only pick up the pieces of what he's left behind and hope we can sort it out properly."

The agents came forward. Even though it was cramped in the storage unit, they pulled open a drawer to the filing cabinet and took a look for themselves.

"Don't look at me," Laysa snapped at them. "I'm just as confused as you guys are."

Taylor, from the other side of the unit, said, "Let's all calm down and start analyzing what we've got here. Obviously somebody has used this place for a long time. But why and who? What's the chance Blake found the bag here and moved it to the gym locker?"

The color drained from her face. "In which case you're implying my husband *was* involved in some way."

He shook his head. "No, only that he found what he thought were incriminating photos and decided to pull them out of the equation. We don't know anything yet, but I suggest we take the opportunity to find out."

THE NEXT HOUR was spent sorting through as much of the storage unit as possible. There were boxes full of paperwork, which appeared to be all the leftover files, photos, prints and negatives from the grandfather's chain of stores that closed in 1995. It didn't help in finding the current owner of this collection, but it was fascinating reading.

One box she got excited about. "It's all the court documents," she said. "Look."

Kanen flipped through the files and realized they were transcripts of the court case, copies of legal documents filed on the man's behalf. "I'm sure it's fascinating reading," he said, "but I'm not sure how important it is to us now."

"But we know there's a connection," she said. "I just don't know what it is."

Out of the corner of his eye, Kanen caught a movement. He spun to look at the front entrance. Some of the sunlight was fading, but it was still light enough inside to see clearly.

Leaving her in the middle of all the men, Kanen stepped out to the open side of the storage unit and took a look around. A truck was parked near another unit. The truck bed was open, and people were moving furniture out of the unit into the back of the truck. Taking a chance, Kanen walked around the block of units. There were ten storage units in each of the blocks, five facing one way and another five backed up to the others, facing the other way.

He walked to his right through the back and around to the front, looking for a sign of anybody having been here. But he found no new footprints in the grass, and, from the front, the area appeared to be empty.

As he returned, one of the MI6 guys stepped forward and asked, "Did you see anything?"

Kanen shook his head. "I can't help feeling we're being watched anyway."

"That makes sense. We have two men on watch."

While Kanen felt much better hearing that, he didn't like anything else about this. Bob was desperate to get whatever it was he wanted. As far as Kanen was concerned, it was the photos from the gym locker. What he wanted to know was how did the guy know the images had been here? Was it just a lucky guess? Maybe he'd seen them here?

Or ... did this come full circle back to the gym manager—Mark?

Kanen pulled out his phone, and, as the MI6 guys worked beside him, he called Mark. "So who did you tell?" he asked without preamble.

Silence loomed for a long moment. "What are you talking about?"

"You heard me. Who did you tell that we'd been to see Blake's gym locker?"

CHAPTER 13

S HE HEARD KANEN'S voice somewhere in the vicinity of the storage unit's opening, but she was kind of stuck in the back, busy looking in boxes of paperwork. It was fascinating to think that the entire photography shop business had ended up here. But also made her think Bob had to have been the one to store this here. Who else would have all this material? But none of that explained how this stuff ended up in *her* storage unit.

With all these thoughts rolling through her head, she wasn't sure what to think. She looked up, peered around the boxes but saw no sign of Kanen. She turned to Taylor and Nelson and asked, "Where did he go?"

Neither man looked up. "He's doing a perimeter walk," one said. "Nothing to worry about," the other one added.

"Are you sure about that?" she asked. The back of her neck twinged; she didn't feel anywhere near as confident as they seemed to be.

Nelson looked up and studied her. "What's the matter?"

"I think something is wrong." She snapped closed the file in her hand and stormed toward the front of the storage unit. There she looked around but still found no sign of Kanen.

Both Taylor and Nelson joined her. They stopped her from walking outside near the main roadway. "You're not going after him," Nelson said, his voice hard. "Let me contact him, and we'll see what's up."

She waited anxiously, her nerves getting the better of her as she waited for Nelson to text Kanen. The problem was, if he was in trouble, he needed to stay hidden, and the *ping* of texts would give him away. A phone call could be much worse. If Kanen didn't have his cell on Silent mode, it could put him in a lot of danger.

When there was no answer, Nelson and Taylor exchanged hard glances. They marched her back to the MI6 men. Taylor said, "She stays with you. We'll look for our friend."

Instantly the suited men were on alert. "What's happened?"

"Kanen has disappeared and isn't answering his phone," Taylor said.

The men pulled weapons, tucked her behind them and motioned for Taylor and Nelson to go.

She could hardly breathe now. She kept thinking about all the things that could have gone wrong with Kanen. But the agents weren't interested in listening to her attempts to get them all to go after her friends.

The agents stared at her, their faces bland and hard.

"And what if the other two are walking into a trap?"

"Then they're walking into a trap," one agent said.

She wanted to call them Cheech and Chong, just so she had a way to tell him apart. Both men were about five foot, ten inches tall. Both had dark brown hair. Both were long and lean and had a mean look on their faces when they wanted to. Most of the time, they looked like ordinary men. Maybe that was part of the magic of MI6 agents, that they had the ability to be completely unassuming and to blend into a crowd without any discernible, memorable features.

As it was, she wasn't in any way happy to be left behind. She pretended to go back to looking through the files. And then she smelled something at the rear of the storage unit. She turned and yelled, "Smoke!"

It came from a small hole underneath the storage unit. Suddenly flames shot through the hole.

She watched as the boxes of paperwork caught fire. The men hustled her forward to the front of the unit. She looked at them and said, "You do realize what they're trying to do, right?"

They didn't say a word, just shunted her between them and rushed her in between the two blocks of storage units. All of them were accessible from the outside. She presumed these units backed up into other units.

She turned to look at the agents. "Somebody started the fire in the unit behind this one. Go check it out!"

They just crossed their arms over their chests. She glared at them. "Then I will." She dashed forward. One of the agents tried to grab her and missed. She picked up speed, raced around the corner, counting off the same number of units until she came to the one that backed up to hers.

The door was down. A lock hung on the outside. Swearing to herself, knowing the agents were right on her heels, she went to lift the lock—finding it just resting there, not clicked together—when a bullet pinged into the door above her head. Now she was really in trouble. Someone outside was shooting at her.

She flattened to the ground, noting the fading sunlight. She decided to quickly stand and pop the lock, dropping again to push up the big rolling garage door, enough that she'd get in this adjoining storage unit by crawling underneath the door. She was a sitting duck in the unit, but at least the door was between her and the bullets.

Inside, with the storage unit door about six inches up off the floor, she turned on the light and stared. Wisps of smoke trickled along the back wall, shared by this unit and hers. This unit was almost completely empty, except for a desk that had been set up like an office. As she inspected the bulletin boards around the desk, she realized this was more of a central station, a control room, so to speak. Whoever was doing this had used this particular storage unit as his base for whatever his plans were. How strange. But it also meant he knew she was in here, and, with the light on, she was beyond just a sitting duck. If he didn't get to her, the smoke would soon enough.

She quickly moved to the desk to see if there was anything of interest. There were pictures of gyms. Pictures of weightlifters. Even a picture of her beloved husband.

She reached out with two fingers and stroked his face. It had to have been taken close to a year ago, just before he died. He'd had a mustache then. It had been a relatively new look for him, and this picture showed him with one. She didn't understand why Bob, the photographer, her assailant, had these gym photos. *Unless Bob really had met my husband at the gym?*

Just when she thought she might have a chance to figure it out, the big door behind her shifted. The light went out. She swore and squatted, hiding underneath the desk, the only item in the whole unit.

Bob said, in a mocking voice, "You really expect to hide here? You think I don't know where you are?"

She groaned. "It's you! How the hell did you know my storage unit was on the other side of this one?"

"That's easy," he said. "It used to be my unit. The reason your husband ended up with it was because I told him that I had some space, and I let him use it."

"You let him use it?" She was distracted momentarily by the increased smoke gathered around her on the floor at the back of this unit. *This is not good.*

"Basically I subleased it to him. And then asked him if he minded me adding some material to it. He said he didn't care. But ... *then* he did care. However, after he was dead, it didn't matter because you didn't seem to even know the storage unit was here. And I wanted the space, so I moved all my shit back over there again. I would get rid of your stuff eventually, but there didn't seem to be any point since you never came here. It was just more work, and I didn't need more of that."

In the darkness she could hear the same raspy voice of the man who had beaten her. "Did you find what you were looking for, Bob?" She stifled back a cough, refusing to appear even more helpless to this asshole.

"No," he snapped. "And, for that, I blame you and those asshole men you hooked up with. Blake would have given it back to me. And, if he hadn't died, we wouldn't be having this problem."

"If he hadn't died, *I* wouldn't be having a lot of problems," she cried out with anguish in her voice. "Do you even hear what you just said?" Then she let her voice drop in volume as she stared into the darkness in the direction he'd spoken from, her eyes now stinging from the smoke. "Did you kill him?" She hated to bring it up, but she had to know.

"Hell no. That wouldn't have served me well, would it?"

She closed her eyes, her shoulders sagging in relief. "Oh, thank God."

"I wondered if he didn't commit suicide though," Bob said, his voice thoughtful. "He sure bitched enough."

She didn't want Bob to continue. She didn't want Bob to break the lovely memories she held of her husband and their relationship. But it was like the asshole knew it was her weakness.

"Blake kept complaining about how you wanted a family, and he wanted nothing to do with that. But you wouldn't stop nagging him."

Each word was like a little stab wound to her heart. Had she really been so hard on Blake? It had been important to her, but they could have talked more. He could have told her how much it bothered him. Why hadn't he? She can't read minds.

"You know he was planning on leaving you, right?"

She sucked in her breath.

"I guess not. At least not from your shocked reaction. He really liked a woman at the gym. I figured he might go for it. But, even then, he seemed to pull back. Torn between two options. That's one of the reasons why I wondered if he'd chosen suicide as an easy out. Couldn't stand the idea that he'd break your heart or something foolish like that. But obviously he wasn't happy. He needed to get out from under you."

She swallowed hard several times, hating what he was implying. "I don't believe you," she whispered, unable to control her coughing now.

"I don't give a shit if you believe me or not," he said, coughing too. "I still want those photographs."

She closed her eyes, realizing the pictures were what he wanted. "MI6 has them all," she said wearily. "What difference do the photos make? They're old pictures. All the blackmails have been paid, and the victims don't give a shit anymore. Some of them are even dead."

"I know," he said, coughing more. "I've always known that."

She shook her head. "So why do you care now? What difference does any of it make?"

"Because my great-uncle was the blackmailer. And my grandfather paid the price," he said in a conversational tone. "My great-uncle is a very wealthy man now. He's insisting I don't get any of it. I want those photos to go with the other information I have, which proved he was the blackmailer. Because, if nothing else, I'll see his carcass rot in jail for the last years of his life. But, before then, I'll blackmail him for all the goddamn money he stole from all these people, ruining my grandfather's life as well as mine."

"Did you kill him?"

"Hell no," he said, "But I can thank my great-uncle for that too."

"Your great-uncle has to be quite old by now."

"Not as old as you might think," he said. "My grandfather was the oldest, and my great-uncle was a step sibling from yet another marriage. He was a good twenty-plus years younger than my grandfather. He was almost the same age as my father. And, for that reason alone, I thought my father should have done something to fix the problem, but he was too weak. Either too weak or too easily swayed by my great-uncle. Not that he and Grandfather ever got along very well, but Grandfather was a great man. He built a huge business across Europe. He was well-known for his work. And my great-uncle ruined him, ruined his name, ruined our family name and took away the legacy that was mine by rights."

The sordid tale of betrayal and murder was something

that could be told and retold at any street corner around the world. Was there anything more vindictive and hateful than a family member consumed by jealousy or greed?

"I'm sorry," she whispered, coughing more often now. "I'm sorry for your grandfather. That must have been extremely hard on him."

"You have no idea," the younger man in front of her said.

"So why did you wait all this time? You had the photos."

"Because he has yet another wife, and this time there's a child," he said, his voice turning vindictive. "And my great-uncle made it very clear that I would get nothing. He stole everything from our family, and now he'll give it to that baby who knows nothing of his ill-gotten inheritance."

"And now … you think these photos … will make a difference?" she asked, among coughs, not quite understanding. She could certainly understand the trigger when the great-uncle had a family to hand down the fortune to. "Did he tell you … beforehand … it was all yours?"

"He promised it was all mine, if I kept my mouth shut," he said, his words interrupted by coughs. "Because he was already ill, I didn't think anything of it. … For the last few years, I took whatever he would give me, … just small sums to tide me over, but he wouldn't give me … very much. Or enough to live on." Bob was overtaken by a spate of coughing, then resumed his explanation. "Despite his illness, he got a young woman pregnant. … Supposedly pregnant. … The first thing I wanted to do was test for DNA, but he wouldn't let me. … He's tickled pink at the idea of finally having a son. And … he also made it very clear that, … if I did anything to disrupt his family, I'd get nothing."

"So don't disrupt his family, and you still get everything," she said, finding it harder to breathe, to keep her wits about her. Surely it was worse for Bob, right? Didn't smoke rise? Aren't we told to drop and roll?

"Are you a fool?" More coughing ensued. "No way he'll give me anything." Bob drew a labored breath.

She could hear him moving about, probably moving closer to the opening, hoping for less smoke there.

"He now has a son of his own. … The last thing he wants is to give anything to my family."

"But they're just old photos," she said. "None of it is enough to prove anything."

"Except that I have the bookkeeping ledgers that relate to the men in the photos. And that's the proof I need to confirm the blackmail payments. Because I also have the case files from my grandfather's court case. … And, because he was murdered, this is the motive for his death. I get revenge on my grandfather's murder. I'll blackmail my uncle so he turns the money over to me, and I get to watch him suffer through his last few years, poor and broke, like my grandfather suffered. … If my great-uncle won't cooperate, then I'll turn over everything to the cops, and they can prosecute the real blackmailer and murderer." Bob chuckled. "Regardless, if my great-uncle cooperates or not, I'll turn him over to the cops anyway."

"What about giving the money back to all those families he blackmailed?"

"That's their problem. They're the ones caught being fools," he snapped. "They've already lost the money. They paid it for silence, to wash away their sins." Bob let out a cackling laugh, ending in more coughs. "I won't be the same fool."

"So why did you give those pictures to Blake to hold?"

"Because he bragged about having the safest holding spot ever. That nobody would ever find his new hiding spot."

Laysa frowned. "Blake?"

"Yeah. I already knew about his gym locker. But, if he had a safe somewhere, I figured that would be one of the best places to hide everything."

"That makes no sense," she said. "Absolutely none."

He sighed. "No, you're right. It doesn't. That's because I'm lying. I was hoping to keep the last vestige of your beloved husband alive." His tone held heavy mockery. "Blake saw everything I had when I moved it all into the storage unit. He went through it and found the bag with all the photos. He stole it. … It's how he would finance his exit from your marriage. He wanted money for it all. He knew how much it meant when he saw my reaction. … He showed me the damn bag, then said he had the safest hiding place in the world. At the time I pretended indifference, and I walked. … But I didn't walk far. I was trying to figure out what to do. So I tracked him. No, I didn't kill him. He truly died in an accident."

At this point the blows were coming too hard and too fast. She sat here stunned, completely overwhelmed by what Bob said. "I don't believe you," she cried out, tears washing the smoke out of her eyes and prodded along by the emotional pain Bob had inflicted.

"I don't give a damn if you believe me or not," he said, then seemed to fall to the ground or dropped to his knees.

Was he seeking oxygen? Was he overcome with the smoke?

"I've been working on this project for a long time. If my great-uncle hadn't produced an heir, I probably wouldn't have given a damn, thinking the money was coming my way.

But, after I talked to him and realized how things had changed, I couldn't let it go. ... And I wanted the photos back from your bloody husband. Once he realized they had value, he wanted money. But I didn't have any. So I waited, biding my time. ... Until the fool got himself killed. Then I went after you. I'd checked the storage unit but gave up. Then you made me think to look again. More time wasted as I couldn't find them here."

She bowed her head, wondering about the things he said. *Could they be true?* She really desperately wanted them not to be true. But how was she supposed to determine the truth? "And what now?" But he didn't answer. "I've told you that MI6 has the photos. When you go back to your great-uncle, just tell him you have proof—you still have the ledgers—and that he's to hand over all the money regardless."

"No," he said, scrambling to stand it seemed. "He'd just tell the cops that I forged the ledgers. No, I need those photos. I want to see the look on his face when he realizes I've got them."

"Or maybe just hand over the ledgers and the rest of what you've got to MI6, and they can turn it all over to whatever jurisdiction needs to try your great-uncle."

"Either way, I need those photos."

Frustrated, she raised both palms. "Then talk to MI6. How many times do I have to tell you that?" By now she was choking from the smoke from the other side. "What if the photos were in there? In my side of the storage unit?" she asked. "Everything else, the court case files are in that unit too that you just burned up, not to mention all my own personal belongings."

"If you cared anything about Blake, you would have

come by sometime in the last twelve months," he said.
"Believe me. Everything important to me in that storage unit
is digitized—the ledger, the courtroom documents. I did that
once I realized your lovely husband stole the original
blackmail photos."

"You mean, you didn't digitize them earlier?"

He waved a hand. "No. Do you have any idea how
many hours it took? But it's done now," he said wearily. "All
except for those damn photos."

She started to cough heavier now. People banged on the
outside of the large door to this unit. She screamed out for
help, using up what little oxygen she had. She could hear
people pounding, trying to open the door. She looked at Bob
and said, "You've locked it, haven't you?"

"Yes," he said. "I figured, if you die without telling me
where the photos are, those men will just throw me in jail.
Then I really don't give a shit. Maybe I can sneak out with
the smoke, when they open up the door to this unit. I don't
know at the moment. I'm not sure I give a damn."

"What about all that vengeance?" she asked. "What
about all the revenge in your heart? You wanted to get back
at him, at your great-uncle."

Now Bob coughed too.

"What about just surviving for yourself?" she asked in
desperation. "If you didn't kill anyone, you don't have much
you can be charged with. Yes, you held me captive in my
own home and beat me up. But that's what, a year, two years
maybe? Probably just a slap on the wrist and probation." Her
voice was bitter, knowing the judicial system and how
fruitless it was if he was a first-time offender at least in the
US but she had no clue here.

He started to speak and then bent over double, hacking

and coughing heavily.

She crawled to the big door, trying to lift it. There was just half an inch of space underneath the door. She lay closer to it on the floor, sucking in fresh air. "I'm in here," she cried out. "I'm in here."

She could hear the men doing something on the other side, but she wasn't sure they'd get to her in time. Smoke inhalation was ugly, and even now flames licked at the back of this unit. Not that much was here to burn, but there was a little. And the flames sucked up every bit of oxygen she had available.

She gazed at her captor, now rolling on the ground coughing, holding his chest. In the din she could hear Kanen calling to her, "Hang on. We're getting there."

Suddenly a knife cut the rubber edging right in front of her face, giving her a couple more inches of space for oxygen. She breathed in deep. She couldn't see him but for one eye, and he was right there, smiling at her.

"We're getting there, sweetheart. We're getting there."

And suddenly a heavy groaning and creaking came as the door broke free and rose. He reached for her, pulling her to him. She had one last heavy coughing spell and collapsed in his arms.

KANEN HAD NEVER been so damn scared in his life. When that garage door finally lifted, and all the smoke poured out, he thought for sure she was a goner. She collapsed in his arms, and he started CPR to clean out her lungs. He knew the medics were on the way, and the men collected around Kanen. They already had collared the asshole, Bob. But he'd passed out from the smoke too.

As he was loaded, handcuffed, into an ambulance, Kanen stood to the side and made sure he was secured and transported out of there. He also didn't want Laysa in the same ambulance with her captor, just in case. Thankfully a second ambulance showed up at the same time.

He rode alongside her as the paramedics worked on her. He could do nothing but hold her hand, urging her to keep fighting.

His mind was completely overwhelmed with everything he and the other men had heard. Although the big door had been down, it hadn't been soundproofed, so Bob's and Laysa's voices had easily carried outside. It was just stunning what this was all about. Revenge, greed, hatred.

If Bob was correct, his grandfather had served time for a crime he didn't commit and had been murdered by the same person who'd done the crime, Bob's great-uncle. Kanen knew the cops and MI6 would be all over this one, and he hoped they caught the asshole great-uncle. But he didn't think this Bob guy deserved to get any of the money. Not one dime. Not after what he'd done to Laysa.

Finally she was removed from the ambulance into the emergency area of the hospital, and thereafter, with tubes and an oxygen mask, she was tucked into a bed, stable but still not out of the woods. He sat in a chair beside her, holding her hand, kissing her fingers every once in a while and bowing his head to rest his forehead against the back of her hand as he whispered, "Come on, Laysa. Fight."

Finally she squeezed his hand, and he bolted to his feet. She tried to speak and started coughing. A nurse came in and removed the oxygen tube under her nostrils, pouring water into a cup and leaving it nearby.

"Call me if needed," the ER nurse said, leaving them

alone again.

Once the coughing cleared, Laysa had a sip of water and collapsed against the pillow, the bed at an angle so she could breathe easier. She smiled up at him. "Thanks for saving my life."

He shook his head, leaned down and kissed her hard. "Now that I've saved it, it's mine," he said. "Enough of this. You're coming back to California with me. You're moving into my apartment. Hopefully into my bed. And we'll have as many years as we can together. And, if life is good to us, we'll start a big family and live happily ever after. Blake's death highlights that obviously there is no guarantee we'll grow old on rocking chairs side by side, but, if I could ask for just one thing, it would be for that. I want to keep you safe and at my side forever." He was as serious as he could be. He watched tears come to the corner of her eyes and wiped them away. "Sweetheart, don't cry," he whispered. "Please don't cry."

She smiled and reached up, her hand covering his against her cheek, and she whispered, "That's what I would wish for too. Just keep me close." She closed her eyes and rested. Then her eyes popped open. "Get me the hell out of here so we can share a bed tonight. You can just hold me in your arms. I doubt I'm up for much more." She coughed again. "But it would be nice to not be in a hospital, not having anybody chasing after us, just for it to be the two of us. Just hold me please."

He snagged her into his arms, settled himself on the hospital bed and whispered, "As soon as you're discharged, we're getting out of here."

She rested her head on his chest and fell asleep.

CHAPTER 14

W HEN SHE WOKE the next time, she was being moved
into a wheelchair. She stared up at Kanen. "Do I get
to leave already?"

He nodded. "We're breaking you out," he said in a
whisper. But his big grin belied his words. "Charles arranged
it."

She smiled and said, "Ah, the secret, shadowy Charles.
Will I ever meet him? Not right now though. I'm still so
damn tired."

"And your chest will hurt for a long time," Nelson said.
"There can be no exertion. Wheelchair all the way."

She wrinkled her nose up at him. "I'd rather not."

"Just to the cab," Kanen said. "I promise. And, before
we head stateside, we'll stop in and meet the elusive but very
excellent Charles."

He bundled her up in a blanket, and the cabbie drove
them back to her place, where Kanen carried her to the
elevator and up to her apartment.

She looked at him. "I knew you were strong but ..."

"Sweetie, no way you're walking. No way I'm letting you
out of my sight. Besides, right now, all I want to do is hold
you." He carried her into the apartment and all the way to
the bathroom, dropped her gently on her feet, and said, "Get
ready for bed and then straight under the covers."

She coughed and nodded. "I can handle that."

Her nightgown hung on the back of the door. She changed into it, and, when she opened the door, her face scrubbed, her teeth brushed, he was right there to assist her across the room.

"I can walk, you know," she said and then started coughing. "You don't have to keep looking after me."

"How about we forget the looking after part, and stick with the keep part." He said flashing her a big grin. "I'll just *keep* you period." He kissed her gently then helped her into bed. "I'll get you a cup of tea. I'll be right back."

She nodded. "Fine."

By the time he returned, she was nodding off. She opened her arms. "Can you lie down with me?"

He chuckled. "I'm getting into bed with you." He closed the bedroom door, stripped down as he walked to the bed and crawled into it beside her. He wrapped her into his arms and drew her close. "Now sleep."

She smiled and murmured, "Thank you," and closed her eyes again.

But her dreams were full of bad guys and fire and smoke and chasing after Kanen because he had disappeared. She woke up, remembering. "Where were you?" she cried out, sitting up slightly.

He woke from his sleep and stared at her. "Did you have a bad dream?"

"The only reason I left the storage unit was because you were gone for longer than you should have been. You didn't answer your phone either. Do you know how terrified I was?"

"We were searching for Bob. And I couldn't answer my phone or the backlight would give away my position. When

I got back to the storage unit, it was engulfed in flames. I thought for sure you were still in there," he said.

She smiled at him. "Oh." She collapsed beside him again. "That makes sense." She leaned up on one elbow and kissed him. And then kissed him again and kissed him again. "You taste smoky," she said.

"No, I think it's you who tastes smoky," he said with a chuckle. He rolled her over gently onto her back. "You should be sleeping. You're still keyed up and sore from the CPR. It's too early for you to be awake."

"I'm fine," she announced, rolling over atop him again. "Besides, this is my bed, and you're in it. And I've thought about this a lot over the last few days. I'm really not prepared to let you leave until I'm ready."

His eyes lit with interest. "Oh? What did you have in mind?" His hands already tugged her nightgown, taking it over her hips, up to her ribs.

She could feel his bare skin beneath her, and a very interesting ridge nestled against her hips. She wiggled ever-so-slightly, watching his eyes turn a smoky color, and she chuckled. "I'm up for anything. Maybe a little gentle to begin with, but, after that, I suggest we see what might appeal."

One eyebrow rose. "Sweetheart, I'm up for anything anytime you are." And he bumped his hips up against her, so she could feel exactly what was up.

She chuckled, leaned over and kissed him gently. "Maybe you should prove that to me. I'm not exactly sure how this will work."

"I'm sure you understand how all of it works," he murmured teasingly.

His tongue traced the shape of her ear, sending shivers

down her back, his warm breath against her throat sliding down to warm the space between her breasts. When he cupped her plump round breasts, she moaned gently. She arched, filling his hands fully as she whispered, "But I've never done this with you, so maybe you're full of tricks I don't know anything about."

"No tricks," he murmured, "just love. Maybe now it's our time."

She sighed as he took one nipple into his mouth and suckled deeply. Feeling an answering tug deep in her groin, her belly tightened, and her body softened. She stroked his arms, sliding her fingers through his hair, kissing where she could reach.

As he shifted them both on their sides, facing each other, he gently and carefully treated her like a china doll as he explored her from one end to the other. By the time he slid his fingers along her leg, tickling the back of her knee, then to the inside of her thigh before finding the curls at the apex, she was already moist, ready and more than willing to take the next step.

As a matter of fact, she was past willing. She slid into demanding. She tugged on his arms, "Come to me," she ordered. "Now."

He chuckled. "So impatient," he murmured.

"Absolutely," she said. "I hate being thwarted when it's something I want." She grabbed his hair and tugged him gently toward her.

He rolled her to her back again, separating her legs wider as he hooked his arms under both her knees, and sat up, whispering, "Are you ready?"

Open, vulnerable and never more in love than she was right in that moment, she whispered, "Absolutely."

And he slid home. All the way to the heart of her. She cried out, her body tensing against a long year without any form of intimacy. He gave her a moment to relax, releasing her legs, his hands gently stroking her thighs and hips before cupping her breasts. Then he started to move.

She gave a cry of joy, her hips rising and falling, meeting him, matching him stride for stride, loving the feeling as the two came together, in a way of celebration, in a way of joy.

When he finally neared his release, she moved with him, harder and faster, a cry of urgency inside. She was so damn close.

Then he reached down between them, found that little nub between the folds of her skin, and her body exploded with her own climax, then his.

She lay shuddering in his arms, their bodies slick with sweat. She whispered, "That was a long time coming."

He rolled over, brushing her hair off her face and whispered, "No ghost?"

She knew what he was referring to. At some time she'd tell Kanen what her captor had said about Blake. She wanted to believe it was all lies, but she knew, no matter what was the truth, Blake was a part of her. And Kanen? ... Well, Kanen was a part of her too. Hopefully a permanent part of her future. She kissed him gently on his lips and whispered, "No ghost. Only angels singing. Because you gave me a touch of heaven. And it's a place I want to stay."

"With you in my arms," he whispered, "we're both in heaven, now and forever."

USA TODAY BESTSELLING AUTHOR

Dale Mayer

SEALS OF
HONOR
Nelson

BOOK-21

PROLOGUE

NELSON BROWN SAT on Laysa's living room couch the next morning. He folded up the blanket and set the pillow on top. He and Taylor were leaving the UK and heading back to the States today. Kanen was taking a few days and staying behind with her. Nelson wasn't exactly sure what Kanen and Laysa planned to do long-term, but they were committed to each other, and she was happy to leave behind her apartment in England with the good and bad memories she had there.

Everything in the storage locker she'd owned with her late husband was lost in the fire. However, their apartment was still full of stuff and had to be dealt with. Whether she and Kanen rented it out, which wasn't a bad idea, or sold it, it would still take some time to decide what to leave behind, like for a furnished apartment to rent, what to give away and what she wanted to take with her. Nelson figured in another few days that Kanen and Laysa would arrange for her remaining belongings to be shipped over stateside as they flew back to California together.

Taylor was making coffee. They'd already booked flights for eleven o'clock this morning, heading back to their regular jobs.

Then Nelson and Taylor were scheduled for training— training they were anxious to get to, into an area where torpedoes were made. It was more of an information session, but it fascinated Nelson. He wanted to see how the bombs themselves were made. There was a lot of science and engineering that went into them.

Taylor came toward him, holding up his phone. "Hey, apparently we've got some officer training at the same time."

Nelson wrinkled up his face. "Great. That may not be fun."

"A couple engineers are coming as well. They'll be on staff, working on the deployment of these new torpedoes. They're integrating a new chute system into the battleships."

Nelson nodded. "Well, that part at least makes sense."

"Yeah. Remember that woman who gave the lecture we went to? She was talking about how maintenance was so important on these chutes, and you got mad at her because you felt she was implying the navy wasn't doing its job?"

Nelson frowned. He shook his head. "Sort of. She was being kind of arrogant, right?"

Taylor nodded. "She was, indeed. But she'll also be part of this torpedo operations tour that's happening in Coronado Bay."

"Where's the tour?"

"On the USS *Independence*. It would be good to go to the manufacturing plant, but that's not happening. At least we'll see these new torpedoes on the ship. She'll be there to show us how they are different."

Nelson shrugged. "What difference does it make? They'll still have a certain payload. They'll still have an automatic delivery system. I doubt anything's changed that we'd have to retrofit the battleships."

"Apparently, something is different about these." Taylor smiled. "As one of the engineers working on the project, she's a keynote speaker."

"It doesn't matter to me," Nelson said. "I barely know the woman."

"That's good, but apparently she knows you."

Nelson looked up and frowned. "What are you talking about?"

"I just got a text from Mason. Let me read it to you." He flicked through the texts on his phone, stopped and said, "*Make sure Nelson comes back with you. The engineer wants to speak with him specifically before the tour starts.*" Taylor looked up at him. "Does that mean anything to you?"

Nelson shook his head. "No. I don't know the woman. What the hell does she want with me?" Just then his own phone buzzed with a text from Mason.

Meeting one hour in advance of tour tomorrow morning, 0800 on shore. At the dock.

Nelson texted back. **What's this all about?**

Engineer wants to talk to you.

About what? he asked.

Mason wrote **No clue. But she mentioned you specifically.**

I don't even know the woman.

Maybe but she knows you. Be there, 0800 sharp.

Nelson tossed the phone on the coffee table and snorted. "Who the hell is this woman? And why the hell does she give a damn about me?"

Taylor brought over two cups of coffee. "I guess you'll find out tomorrow morning, won't you?"

Nelson just stared at him, disgruntled. "Maybe. That's if I show up."

But that was only Nelson's bravado speaking. When the navy called, he stepped up each and every time. But it sure didn't stop him from wondering who the hell this woman was and what she wanted with him.

CHAPTER 1

NELSON ARRIVED AT the docks the next morning in good spirits. He hadn't given much thought to the appointment before his training until breakfast, when he realized he really had no clue what was going on. He wasn't sure who else would be at this morning's meeting, but he hoped it was somebody he might know. For all he knew, this was a case of mistaken identity. He barely knew the woman who had requested this meeting.

As he walked down the long pier, a small group of people waited for him. Nelson recognized Mason's aide but not the other seaman. Only one woman was with them. *That must be the engineer.* He checked his watch and frowned. As he approached Mason, he smiled and said, "I'm not late."

Mason's stern face nodded. "No, you're not. You're fine."

As Mason spoke, Nelson checked out the woman who supposedly knew him. He had met her at a lecture, as Taylor had reminded him. But that was a while back. He reached out a hand to shake hers, smiling. "Nelson Brown, at your service, ma'am."

One eyebrow raised at the *ma'am* part.

He might have done it just to piss her off. He didn't know. He'd been in an off mood all morning. Nothing like having something like this coming down with no one giving him any heads-up as to what was going on. From the stiff demeanor of those around him, it was obviously serious.

"I'm Elizabeth Etchings." She eyed him coolly. "I believe you know my brother."

It was his turn to raise an eyebrow. "I'm not sure I do. What's his name?"

"Chris," she said. "Chris Etchings."

He frowned as he thought about it, then shook his head. "I'm not sure. That name doesn't ring a bell."

She sighed. "You probably know him as Skunk."

Nelson's face broke into a wide grin. "Absolutely. I know Skunk." He chuckled. "I'm not sure I ever knew his real name though."

"I know," she said. "How sad is that? Hardly a nickname to go through life with."

"And how is Skunk?"

"He's missing," she said abruptly. "That's why I asked to speak to you this morning."

"What? How long has he been missing? Have you contacted the police?"

"He joined the navy," she said, "which means NCIS is involved. But honestly, they haven't found anything."

He nodded slowly. "But you're still not telling me anything. When did Skunk go missing and where?"

"He was last seen docked in Ensenada, in Baja, California."

"Well, if a seaman's got shore leave, Ensenada makes for a nice tourist spot, a place to play ..." But, under these circumstances, with Skunk missing from his ship, other elements came into play. And, like any seaport, there could be the darker elements involved. Drugs came immediately to mind. But Skunk wasn't into drugs. And the navy had never been Skunk's dream. "Why the navy?"

She frowned at him. "He was never happier than when he made it into the navy."

"I haven't seen him in a few years," Nelson said. "But I doubt he's changed that much. As I remember, the navy was something he fought against."

"He fought against our father," she said wearily. "And essentially, for Chris, that means the same thing. But the bottom line is, he's been in the navy for a couple years now. He had days off and was due back on board four days later. He was reported missing twenty-four hours thereafter."

"What does this have to do with me?"

"NCIS traced his number and have a list of his calls," she said. "They read some of it to me but wouldn't send me a copy of it. But you were on that list. You were the last number he used. Since then it's not been used again."

Nelson understood the gravity of the situation. Mason shot him a look, basically asking if he had an explanation. Straightening, Nelson gave a tiny imperceptible shake of his head. He had no clue what was going on. "He may have tried to contact me," Nelson said, "but I didn't talk to him." He pulled out his cell phone. "Do we know when he tried to contact me?"

"Seven days ago," Elizabeth said. "Friday night at 9:05 p.m."

Nelson handed his phone to Mason. "You check."

Mason checked through the messages. "There are no phone messages."

"No, he sent a text," she said.

Mason flicked through and said, "There's nothing here from anyone under either name."

"What about at the specific time frame?" she asked.

Mason slowed as he got to that particular time, went through the text messages once more, finding a lot of them, and looked over at Nelson with a smirk.

Nelson shrugged. "Hey, we had a party. What can I say? There was a lot of wild chatter back and forth."

"Was that at Dane's place?"

Nelson nodded. "He got engaged. Remember? That party was quite something." He gave half a smile to the woman who stood watching him. "Sorry, but one of our friends was recently engaged, so that weekend we had a pretty wild time of it."

"And that's likely when the text went through," she said.

He nodded. "Honestly, we had a good twenty or thirty texts bouncing back and forth as we collectively gave Dane hell. I might have missed Skunk's message."

Mason checked through the texts and held up Nelson's phone with one pulled up so Elizabeth could see. "There's one here from an unknown party." Then he showed it to Nelson.

He frowned. "I might have seen that but didn't know who it was from. I likely just ignored it."

"What if it was from Skunk?" Elizabeth held out her hand. "May I see the text again?"

Mason held it up for her.

Out loud she read, "*I'm in trouble. Need help.*" She looked over at Nelson. "When somebody sends you a call for help, you just ignore it?"

It was Mason who answered. "If you understand the party he was at that weekend"—he pulled up other texts to show her—"you'll see many are along the same line. They were teasing Dane into not going ahead with the engagement."

Elizabeth stiffened. "You guys don't like her, I presume."

"Not at all. Absolutely, we like her. We love her," Nelson said cheerfully. "It was all in the spirit of what would follow. You know? Having surprise triplets, getting old and gray by the time he got to forty."

She watched him intently for a long moment. Her shoulders sagged. "I was really hoping you might have known something about his disappearance."

"I'm sorry. I don't," Nelson said. "I wish I did. Skunk is a very special friend of mine. But, like I said, I haven't seen him in the last couple years. Obviously not since he joined the navy, or I would have already known about that surprise."

"Then how special of a friend can he be for you?" she snapped.

"I get that you're worried about your brother," Mason said, "but you asked to meet Nelson here to ask him a few questions. He has answered them."

She nodded and took a few steps away. The expression on her face had Nelson speaking up. "Look. I can contact a few of our mutual friends and see if anybody has heard from him."

Eagerly she turned and looked at him. "Would you mind?"

"Hell no," he said, "if I'd known he'd gone missing, I'd have done so on the day of his disappearance. I just can't believe NCIS hasn't found him."

"The last I heard," she said bitterly, "they think he's AWOL."

"No way. That's not Skunk," Nelson said in outrage.

A small smile played at the corner of her lips. "No, it isn't. But that doesn't stop them from building a case that's got nothing to do with the truth. They say he has effectively walked away from the navy."

Nelson groaned. He'd heard of similar stories. NCIS did the best they could, but, if they didn't come up with a solution fairly quickly, it would almost always be assumed that the seaman had deliberately left his post and was hiding out to avoid being found. That rarely ended well. "Did anybody he worked with have anything to say?"

"Not really. But NCIS said they were going on the theory he was unhappy with his new commander."

"Aren't we all?" Nelson snorted.

At that, she gave a half nod of acknowledgment. "It does appear to be a common theme."

"I think most job dissatisfaction has got to do with bosses and coworkers, no matter where you are or what sector you work in," Mason said. "It could possibly have had nothing to do with his commander."

"Did anybody ask the commander?" Nelson asked, already knowing the answer.

She shrugged. "Good luck getting that information from NCIS. I don't know if you've ever worked with them, but they're remarkably tight-lipped. And they have no intention of sharing anything they don't want to share."

That was a sad truth in many ways. "Civilian law enforcement is exactly the same," Nelson said slowly. He looked at Mason. "I do have a couple days leave coming. I am here for training but could attend the next session instead."

Mason studied him for a long moment. "Don't go alone."

"Any chance we can make it official?"

Mason shook his head. "Not likely. NCIS will close the

case as soon as they can, figuring Chris will surface again soon, and they'll get him then."

"I might be able to help," Elizabeth said.

Mason turned toward her. "In what way?"

"NCIS did say, if they could do anything to help …"

"So, you'll do … what?" Nelson asked. "You think NCIS will share more with two navy seamen taking over their investigation? Highly doubtful."

Mason added, "You might get them to hold off on closing their case. That might work."

She pulled her phone from her pocket. "If I can do it, I will," she said. "All I have is my brother. I don't want to lose the only family I have left."

"You do realize," Mason said, "it could already be too late."

She froze in the act of dialing a number, then nodded. "I know. But I can't help but think Chris is in trouble and has gone underground or somebody else is holding him. The fact of the matter is, he did send a message to you, Nelson, asking for help on the night he disappeared. And it's not who he is to go AWOL."

"I'll regret not having done something more about that text for the rest of my life," Nelson said slowly. "But I didn't recognize that number. And that night was pretty crazy. But, I can guarantee you that if Skunk had called me from his regular phone, his name would have come up on my Caller ID. And I would have answered his call or responded to his text."

"Chances are, he lost his phone or dropped it somewhere, for whatever reason, after whatever happened. Sent that SOS text to you from a friend's phone or, hey, asked to borrow a local's phone." Elizabeth held up her phone to her ear, waiting for somebody to answer.

"Or he was using a burner phone he bought immediately afterward," Mason said quietly. "If he was in trouble, it would be the smartest thing to do. But then again, because he just sent a text and didn't call, Nelson had no clue who it was. We all get texts we ignore, particularly ones that come in the middle of a big slag of texts from other guys."

She nodded. "I get that. What I don't get is what happened to Chris. And that's where my priority lies."

Nelson faced Mason. "Do you think you can get brass approval for a few days off for me and a partner so we can check it out closer?"

"Possibly with this text. With Elizabeth's say so as well."

She nodded. "I would hope I have some pull with the navy after working with them all these years."

From behind them were calls to see if they were coming. Nelson checked his watch and held it up to Mason.

Mason nodded. "Yeah, the day needs to start, and you're one of the key speakers, Elizabeth."

She nodded. "Go on in and tell them I'll be there in a minute. How many men do you think you can get together to do this?"

Mason shrugged. "The brass won't pay for more than two."

A frown furrowed her brow.

He shrugged again. "If you ask for too much, you won't get anything. Make it reasonable. If Nelson goes with one other, that's all you will need."

She looked at him in surprise. "Really? Because all of NCIS couldn't get answers."

Nelson gave her a hard smile. "But they aren't me." And he and Mason and the others left to pass on Elizabeth's message about her delayed arrival for the training session, leaving her alone on the pier.

AS SOON AS Elizabeth got off the phone, she sent Mason a text. **Confirmed. He has four days.**

Mason sent back an immediate response. **He's not here. He's gone to pack.**

I want to go with him, she texted in response.

No, Mason said. **You'll only hold him back.**

Okay but he reports to me.

He reports to me, Mason said. **We'll be sure to keep you in the loop.**

She had to be satisfied with that. Except, as the day went on, she realized not only was she *not* satisfied with that but she had no intentions of being satisfied with that. If her brother was in trouble, four days wouldn't be enough, and two men wouldn't be enough either. They needed a whole team, and she had some connections—not a ton, but enough to help.

Four days. She shook her head. She had Chris's last port of call written down in her pocket. As soon as she was done speaking at noon, she'd look at it, then make reservations to Ensenada. She could probably drive down there faster than flying at this rate, even with the delay at the border crossing, known to sometimes be up to two hours each way. It was just a matter of timing.

At noon, she immediately pulled up her laptop and checked the airlines for departure times and costs. It didn't take her long to dismiss that option, wondering why it took twelve hours at the least to get from one international airport in San Diego to another one in Tijuana—the closest she could get to Ensenada from her quick Google search. *The equivalent of driving twenty miles. Wow. And she had seventy more to go to reach Ensenada.* She quickly realized she could drive there maybe by seven p.m., even allowing the time to get a rental car. Much better than flying out and not getting there until the wee hours of the morning. She'd drive and catch up with the men, who should be arriving at Ensenada within the hour.

Surely they drove too, unless they got a military transport or whatever. She shook her head. She had her own travel arrangements to deal with. A hotel was about twenty minutes away from the docks where Chris was last seen. It wasn't likely the best area of town, but, as long as it got her into the neighborhood where her brother had gone missing, then she was good with that. She booked it immediately online. She was still castigating herself for not having gone there immediately. But NCIS had said they would handle it.

Until she'd gotten word last night that NCIS still had no answers, she'd been content to let navy law enforcement investigate. But now that they had given it a cursory check and deemed no more answers were to be had, her brother would be court-martialed when he was found. It set her nerves on edge and terrified her.

Because, if NCIS wasn't looking for him, nobody would be. And that wasn't acceptable. That's why she had had to speak to Nelson this morning. And she was glad she did. She was also glad that Mason had stepped up, had helped her set this up, with Nelson and his partner now allowed to search for her missing brother. She headed home, packed a bag with several casual outfits, drove her car to the San Diego International Airport, so she could rent a car easily, not worrying about the possible unavailability of a car at one stand-alone lot.

Did she say *easily*? Most places flat-out denied her a rental, not allowing their vehicles to cross the border. She found that odd, considering San Diego's proximity to said border. Others tried to dissuade her by jacking up their rental fares. She was getting more and more irritated. She had cash, but that cash was to exchange for Chris, nothing more, nothing less.

She didn't bring her emergency credit card with her, not wanting to worry about losing it in Mexico. She had her debit card. That was it. And she had drained a big chunk from her checking account, leaving little left. She had a money-market fund, but it took twenty-four hours to make a transfer on a weekday. And this was Friday. So no money until Monday effectively. *Damn, should have done this online too.* Thought being in person would make for a quicker selection. *Wrong.*

So she had to waste further time haggling with these people, trying to get across the border without dipping into the wad of cash she carried with her and had earmarked for Chris. *Only* for Chris.

She finally found one company who would allow her to drive into Mexico without hiking up their rental fees.

Then it was another fight about the amount of insurance needed to cover the rental car.

"In Mexico, we expect some damage to our vehicles, from previous experience over the years, even for a day trip," the man behind the counter explained. "But, for your four-day trip, you must purchase full-coverage insurance, to ensure the car is covered for any eventuality."

"Like what?" she asked, when she probably shouldn't bother at this point.

"Tire damage, windshield damage, breaking into the vehicle to steal your luggage, or even theft of the vehicle itself."

She didn't have time for this. "Full-coverage it is."

"It's four times what the basic rental charge is when crossing the border." He frowned at her.

It would leave like ten dollars in her account. But she had other accounts. "Done." Like that would keep her from her brother. She handed over her debit card. "Get me on the road."

She ran all the way to the car, throwing her carry-on bag into the passenger seat, and drove south with a long sigh.

When she arrived at her hotel at seven-fifteen p.m. and parked her vehicle—in the unlit, uncovered, unenclosed grassy area to the windowless side of the hotel, clearly marked Hotel Parking—she shook her head. "Good thing I bought full-coverage insurance." Making sure all of her personal belongings were no longer in the car, she locked her rental, saying a silent prayer. If worse came to worse, she figured she—and Chris—could get a ride home with Nelson. She entered the hotel, checked in with the front desk and hurried to her room. There, she tossed her bag onto the bed, grabbed her black jacket and headed outside.

She had several photos of her brother, some in uniform, some in civilian clothes. She knew it wasn't the smartest thing to do, to advertise she was a basically a tourist and a female on her own in an unfamiliar place, but she started at her hotel, asking if anybody had seen him. Out on the street, she found six more hotels, two normal-looking bars, and a seedy-looking bar that she wasn't sure she wanted to go into in the first place. But it looked like a seaside dive, so it was probably exactly where her brother had been.

After she asked around the hotels, she tried the two bars, then walked into the seedy bar. A wave of loud music and Spanish filled her ears even as the aroma of too much alcohol filled her nostrils. There was nothing like a seedy pub to add flavor to a night in Mexico. She almost backed out. Then she saw Nelson and somebody else sitting at a table with beers in their hands. She walked over and sat down beside Nelson.

He glared at her, leaned forward and asked, "What the hell are you doing here?"

She gave him a bland look. "I'm looking for my brother." She held out the photo. "Have you seen him?"

He groaned. "We can handle this. You know that, right?"

"I put my trust in NCIS," she snapped. "And seven days later, they tell me nothing except that he has left on his own and that he'll be court-martialed when he returns. I'm not putting my trust in the wrong men again."

CHAPTER 2

S HE SAW THE surprise in his eyes. "Why the surprise? Or did you think I was wrong to put my trust in them in the first place? Or did you not realize what they said about Chris?"

"I realized it," he said smoothly. "I'm just surprised they said anything to you about that. Normally that's not good PR to tell anybody, particularly family members."

"What it did was make me angry," she said. "Now I've got you two helping." She looked over at the stranger beside him and frowned. "I got you two for four days to look for my brother. But no way I'm being left out of the loop. If NCIS couldn't find out anything in seven days, the two of you will need a hell of a lot more help to find out anything in four days. So I'm here."

"Now that's insulting." Nelson sighed. He squared his shoulders, then sagged. "Look. I understand why you want to be here, but this is hardly the area for you."

"I'm in a hotel on this block," she said shortly. "So whether it's where I belong or not, my brother doesn't deserve to be ignored. If we find out he's dead in the river, then I'll deal with it. What I don't want to deal with is to find out he's been kidnapped and being tortured or any other horrific concepts."

"Aren't you maybe exaggerating a bit?" the second man

asked.

She glared at him. "What's your name?"

He reached out for her hand and said, "I'm Taylor."

She shook his hand. "No, Taylor, I'm not. My brother has always been a bit of a partier. He's always been a bit of a ladies' man. And he hasn't always been too fussy about exactly where he found his entertainment. A part of me has always half expected him to end up in a back alley, shot by a jealous husband. But, since he went into the navy, he's a completely different person. He's proud of who he is. He loves being who he is. He would not have walked away on his own."

Nelson grabbed her hand and said in a very low tone, "No, you stop right there. Because all kinds of circumstances might very well have caused him to walk away on his own."

She turned that glare on him. She wanted to rage at him for taking that tack. He should back Chris up. He was her brother's friend … But clearly he wouldn't budge on this, interrupting her as she opened her mouth.

"You need to understand that shit happens sometime. Often without our having done anything to make it happen. If Skunk saw something, and he thinks he'll get blamed for it, he might have run. If he saw something, and he knows he can't fight it, he might have run. If he saw something, and he was threatened, he might have run."

"He wasn't spineless," she snapped.

"What if *you* were threatened?" Nelson asked in a hard, low voice. "As you said, he's your only family. Anybody who wanted to make him do something could easily have applied pressure on him by saying *you* would be the first one they took out if he didn't do what they wanted him to do. If he thought getting away and getting out from under them was the only answer, he'd have done it. But he'd have done anything he could to keep you safe."

She sat back. Of course Nelson was right. How could she not have considered this? Because she'd been so sure she was right, ... that she knew her brother. But she hadn't considered the circumstances that might have surrounded him. Like she was doing, he'd do anything to keep her safe. Her heart heavy, she slumped into the chair.

Just then a waitress came by and asked in a mix of Spanish and English, "Buenas noches. Do you want a beer too?"

She looked over at the men's mugs of beer and nodded. "Yes, please." When it arrived, she took a long slug, downing one-third of it.

The men looked at her with respect.

She wiped the foam mustache off her lip. "Okay, so then where do we start?"

"*You* don't start anywhere," Nelson said. "*We* have already started."

She brightened. "What have you learned?"

He just gave her a flat stare.

She frowned and leaned forward. "You can't get rid of me that easily. That's not who I am. You also need to remember that I'd do anything to help my brother. So don't try to chase me off with any kind of excuse. And don't say, *Just go home and wait.*"

Nelson sighed. "But that's what you need to do. We have things set up. We have a relay system back home. We have connections. We'll let you know if we find out anything."

She lifted her beer mug, had a second sip and put it down. Then she pulled out the hotel's business card she'd picked up and wrote her room number on the back with her cell phone number and slid it across to Nelson. "You'll do better than that. You'll tell me before you go to bed tonight exactly what the hell happened here. I get this isn't the time or place, but no way you're walking away without letting me know how much you've learned."

And, with that, she picked up her mug, tossed back the contents, pulled out some money to cover it, threw it on the table and walked out.

"SHE WON'T BE an easy person to deal with," Taylor said.

"No," Nelson agreed. "But, if you think about it, she's right. It's her brother. NCIS can't find anything, and we are down here because she managed to give us this window of opportunity. Of course she wants answers."

"Yeah, but I wasn't thinking we would have to look after her too."

"True," Nelson said. "But you got to admit, she's got class."

"She's classy only because you like women who drink beer," Taylor said with a grin. But then he nodded. "She's a good-looking woman. The fact that she's also an engineer is huge. She's got brains and beauty, although she might be missing a little bit of that feminine-wiles stuff." His grin widened.

"Oh, I don't think so," Nelson said. "I think it has everything to do with being concerned about her brother. You can't really blame her. You know if it was one of us, we'd have gone to hell and back to make sure we found him."

Taylor nodded. "And we have many times before. ... I guess this time it's your turn."

Nelson looked at him in surprise. "What are you talking

about?"

Taylor chuckled. "I'm talking about you're single and part of Mason's team. It looks like you've got somebody already in your corner."

"Corner?"

"*Keepers*," he said. "Don't tell me that you didn't think of that? No way not to, with so many of your buddies finding successful matches by now."

Nelson shook his head. "Don't even go there. What we've got is a woman who doesn't want to believe her brother has done wrong. That's all. Besides, you're here too. Maybe it's your turn."

"She's not for me. You don't believe what she said about her brother either, do you?"

Nelson thought about it. "When I knew him, he was a party skunk, and that's one of the reasons he got his nickname. He used to pass wind so violently after he drank heavily that he'd gas us all out. And he drank like a fish, and I tell you, he left a room smelling like a skunk had been through there. It was unforgettable."

The two men chuckled at the thought.

"But what was he like morally and ethically?"

"Well, it's funny because I didn't think he was interested in the navy. His father was navy, and of course, his sister works for the military as an engineer."

"When did their father die?"

"That's a good question." Nelson looked off in the distance. "If it's recent, I wonder if that's what triggered his behavior."

"You should phone and ask," Taylor said. "We need all the information we can find up front."

Groaning, Nelson grabbed the card Elizabeth had given

him and sent her a text, asking about her dad. When the answer came back, he whistled. "Eight weeks ago."

"That also explains why she's so stuck on finding Chris. She's already lost one male in her life. She doesn't want to lose the other one."

"Exactly," Nelson said. "But we also need to know how he died."

He texted her the question, but, instead of getting the response texted to him, his phone rang.

"He died on base," Elizabeth said. "They still don't know what happened. They say he had a heart attack. I'm pretty sure it was drug-induced. They said too much heart medicine."

"And you didn't think to tell us that?"

"NCIS said it wasn't related," she said. "So I figured that's what you would say too."

"We can't say anything if we don't know."

There was silence for a moment, then she asked, "Do you have his file?"

"No, we don't," Nelson said. "We don't have either file. And I highly doubt NCIS will give us access."

"I have copies of both," she said. "I'll email them to you."

He gave her his email address. "We'll be here for another hour or two, waiting for more people to saunter in. Then we'll head to the hotel."

"Good," she said. "You can fill me in then." And she hung up.

CHAPTER 3

THE WALK BACK to the hotel was relatively short, interrupted only to get some food to-go, but Elizabeth fought with her nerves as way too many people appeared to be watching her. Every step she took brought catcalls and whistles from both sides of the streets. She shoved her hands in her pockets and wondered if it was even safe to be out in the dark in this area. The shadows shifted and moved beside her. She glanced nervously around even as she put steel into her spine.

Had she been foolish to choose this hotel? There was really no way to know yet. But to think that her brother had been here, well, she wouldn't be any less diligent than he was. If she had disappeared, he would have come after her. She could do no less for him.

Finally she made it back to the hotel, dashing up the front steps. Inside, the clerk at reception was welcoming, giving little credence to the seedier nightlife loitering outside.

At the front desk, the nighttime manager looked up and smiled. "Buenas noches senorita, nice night out there?"

"Maybe if you're a male," Elizabeth said bluntly, thankful he spoke English. "It's definitely not the place a female should be walking at night. At least not alone and not if she's not in the escort business."

He nodded sympathetically. "If you're alone, that's true

enough. We haven't had any problems with anybody on the street, but there's definitely lots of interest if you're looking for a quick hookup."

She winced at that. "No, I certainly am not looking for a quick hookup. Any messages waiting for me?"

"Not since the last time you asked." He looked at the take-out bag in her hand. "That's the best Chinese food place around here."

She smiled as she looked at the small bag in her hand. "That's what I was hoping for. I left without realizing how dark it would be on the trip back."

"You made it," he said cheerfully. "That's what counts."

She walked past the desk and headed to the elevator. Her room was on the third floor. Once there, she sat down with her dinner. She hadn't eaten earlier, preferring an empty stomach while she traveled, even by car. She didn't want to waste any time looking for bathrooms along the way. It was much easier for her if she kept her food to a minimum.

Since her father's death and her brother's disappearance, food hadn't stayed down. Her dinner smelled divine.

She sat on the chair at the desk and opened the first box, proceeding to have several bites, then opened the second box. She'd picked up a beef and broccoli dish with fried rice. That was about all she thought she could handle. But they had thrown in a couple egg rolls and something else. She opened the something else to see it looked like a piece of chicken. Surprised and delighted, she ate that too—delicious flavors that filled her stomach and eased her stress levels. The trip back to her hotel had unnerved her more than she'd realized. Still, it was easy to relax now that she was back and had a full tummy. Plus she had enough leftovers for breakfast.

She knew she could be wasting her time by making this

trip to Mexico, but, at the same time, she wouldn't lose anything by being here for four days. She could still work on her laptop.

Her commitments allowed for some time off, and she was really bad at not taking her holidays as it was. She definitely needed more breaks. But it was hard to do that when there were so many problems to fix. Work problems. Life problems. Emotional problems. Burying her father had been a difficult task. The last thing she wanted to do was bury her brother.

Glumly she stared at the TV, and the never-ending list of Spanish speaking programs, flipping aimlessly through the channels, avoiding thinking about what a second funeral would cost her emotionally. If it had to happen, it had to happen—she didn't have much choice. But she really hoped the men would find out something that would lead her to thinking Chris had run away, was truly AWOL. It was much preferable to finding his body, which she would be forced to deal with and to grieve over.

She contemplated all the options Nelson had brought up as to why her brother might have run. She had to admit a couple possibilities were in there.

Damn, should have checked on my rental. I bet it's been stolen already. With a sigh, she decided to do that tomorrow. No way was she stepping outside her hotel, *any hotel, at night* in this area.

It was still early as far as any kind of nightlife around town. The men wouldn't leave the bar for yet another hour at least. They hadn't confided their plans to her but waiting was hard. She wanted the evening to be over now. For them to call and report in.

Moody, upset, out of sorts, she prepped for bed. She lay

on top of the covers waiting, hating that sense of being dependent on somebody else to contact her. She had a terrible time with that at work too. You'd think people would have the decency to contact her to let her know what was going on. But instead, she lay here, completely frustrated and in the dark.

Just then her phone rang beside her. It was Nelson. "What did you find out?"

"Hi. How are you?" he asked in a dry tone. "We're fine. Thanks for asking."

She sneered as she wrote down his Caller ID number. *In case I lose this phone like Chris lost his.* "I have no time or patience for small talk," she said, "when I'm waiting for news about my brother. I highly doubt I'll have any patience anytime soon."

He groaned. "Are you always so serious?"

"Are you drunk?" she asked in response. "Because that question you just asked doesn't make sense. Think about the subject matter regarding why I'm down here."

He sighed. "We found out your brother was here at the bar a week ago."

Shock wrapped around her heart. She sat upright. "Seriously?"

"Yes," he said.

Silence.

"That's why you chose that hotel, isn't it?"

She winced. "Okay, I wondered if this was the hotel he stayed at."

"Why would you wonder that?"

"Because he sent me a text telling me that he was at the Wayward End."

"But that's not the hotel you're staying at," he protested.

"No, but it is the bar right beside it."

"But lots of hotels are up and down that street."

"I know that," she said, "but this was the closest one. I figured it was a place to start."

"True enough," he said. "He was at the bar a week ago. He was also at the bar every night for the previous six nights before that. And, before you ask, they haven't seen him since. And no they didn't see him with anyone either. Male or female."

"Oh," she said in a small voice, her heart sinking. She sank back onto the bed. "So we have no idea where he went from there?"

"No," Nelson said. "We're still here at the bar. I just came out to the back alley to let you know. We've had a couple drinks, just mingling with the locals. They won't take too kindly if we ask too many questions."

"Of course not," she said. "So what's next then?"

"We'll probably try every place on the strip, see if anybody else has seen him. What we need is to have a sighting between now and the last time he was here."

"And yet, if he left because of trouble," she said, "he won't be hanging around, will he?"

"No, he won't. But we need to know what hotel he stayed at and when he checked out or was he staying somewhere other than a hotel? Either way we need to know. Then we'll take a look at how he could have left town. Either rented a car, hopped a bus, hitchhiked, something," Nelson said. "Somebody never disappears completely."

"At least you hope not, and, the last I heard, he was at the Wayward End," she said. "As far as I know, my brother didn't have the skills to disappear completely. So, if he is gone, I would suspect foul play."

"But we aren't going there," he said. "At least not yet."

"Fine," she said. "I could call the local rental companies and see if they have any record of him."

"You could," he said. "Good luck with that. It's late Friday night."

"Right, of course."

"Get some sleep," he said. "We'll see you in the morning."

At that, she brightened. "Bright and early?"

"Not too bright and early," he said. "Depends how late we stay out drinking."

"Yeah. It's a tough job." A sour note entered her voice.

"You could have stayed home," he said, "but, with your wandering around, asking questions with that photo, it was definitely getting some attention."

"Isn't that what we want?" she asked.

"Not if it's the wrong kind of attention," he said. "Think about it. If there *is* foul play involved, what are the chances that same person who might have made your brother disappear permanently is still around, and now he may have to get rid of his sister, who's sticking her nose in where it doesn't belong?"

She sucked in her breath. "I never thought I would be in danger from something like that."

"No." His voice softened. "Of course you didn't. You're focused on finding your brother. But we don't always like the answers we do find. And sometimes, when we stir the pot, it's a hornet's nest instead. And there are consequences to that. Now, please, get some sleep tonight. I'll call you in the morning." And with that he hung up.

She didn't like this one bit. Nothing about that call helped. It just made her feel even more useless. Well, enough of that. She pulled out a pad of paper and jotted down notes of things they could do to find out if her brother had left town. He had to have gone someplace. And he had to get there somehow. Buses, taxis, planes, and honestly, he could have left by boat. She frowned as she thought about that. He could have gone with a friend who rented a boat. He could have hitchhiked, like Nelson said. The options were too vast for her comfort.

And maybe Chris had booked it from Ensenada. It was only ninety miles south of the base in Coronado, which was just a hop, skip and jump away from San Diego, where Elizabeth bought her new home. They'd both spent a lot of time down in Mexico with their father. They had family down here too. Distant relatives but family nonetheless. Why hadn't she considered that in the first place?

She pulled out her phone and checked the family contacts and sent off a couple messages, asking if anybody had seen Chris. Most of them should be asleep by now, but several texted her back and said they hadn't seen him in months. Of course, they wanted the inevitable questions answered.

She worked up a quick, short answer and she copied her message to them all, telling them nobody had seen or heard from Chris in seven days. The responses that came back afterward were anything from **Oh, my God** to **Ha! He's probably off with a girl for some R&R.** And of course, that was very much who her brother was.

Skunk had a female following which Elizabeth had never understood. But he'd been happy, so she hadn't worried too much. She'd like to think he wasn't leaving a whole lot of little Skunks behind, but she couldn't guarantee it. And it wasn't her job to police him or his love life. She'd only wanted to be a loving sister.

Finally with everything done that she could possibly think to do, she curled up in bed and crashed.

WITH TAYLOR BESIDE Nelson, they moved from bar to bar, casually asking the waitresses the same questions they'd been asking everyone. Nelson knew that some of them would have taken particular notice, but, at the same time, that was what he and Taylor were here for. They read body language as well as listened to people when speaking. If Nelson had to stir the pot a little bit, then stir it he would. Somebody had answers; somebody had seen Chris; somebody knew more than they were saying.

At the last stop, the waitress took one look at the photo Nelson still carried, the printed copy Elizabeth had left behind, and the waitress tapped it. "Are you looking for him?"

"Yeah, we are," Taylor said with a smile. It always amazed him when he was in Mexico how many people spoke English here. Sure there was enough Spanish flying around him to remind him of where he was but it was easier to question people if they spoke the same language. "Have you seen him?"

"He was a regular here for a few nights," she said. "Haven't seen him in a while though."

"Can you tell me what *a while* means?"

She thought about it. "Six nights ago, maybe five nights."

Nelson straightened slowly. "That soon, huh? I figured maybe you hadn't seen him for at least a week."

She shook her head. "No. He came in a disguise the last

night I saw him, but I still recognized him. I kind of laughed at him, told him that he should have done a better job dying his hair. He got serious and said he'd fix it. I don't know if anything was really wrong, but he looked pretty serious."

"That's interesting. Not too handy with hair dye, I guess," Taylor said with a grin.

The waitress rolled her eyes. "I don't imagine too many men are, at least straight men," she said with a laugh. "He didn't look happy that I had recognized him. He paid for his drink and walked out."

"You haven't seen him since then?"

She shook her head. "Nah, but that's the way this part of town is. People come and people go." She dropped off their mugs of beer, waited for their money, and then she took off with a hefty tip in her pocket.

Nelson and Taylor looked at each other, but neither spoke. They both knew what the other was thinking. The disguise meant Chris had remained here in Ensenada, testing the waters to see if he could fit in without being noticed. When that had failed, he'd obviously gone to a different tack.

It also gave credence to NCIS's position that he had disappeared willingly. Not good. The last thing they wanted was something like that to happen. If Chris had a good reason, it was all to the good, but it would still require an investigation by the NCIS.

As they drank their beers slowly, just looking around at the patrons, Nelson realized just what a hard lot they were. He thought this was one of the better bars on the strip, but it had seen better days—much better days. The clientele had dropped the later the hour. The Spanish became thicker, more guttural as more beer was drunk.

As they got up to leave, two men stepped in front of them. "Strangers?"

Nelson nodded, his hands casually resting in his pocket. "Yep."

"You should buy the house a drink."

Taylor snorted. "There's got to be forty people in here. Another time perhaps." He brushed past the men; Nelson followed. The two stopped outside and looked around. There was a seediness to the shadows, and muted music from the multiple bars could be heard. A reek of alcohol permeated the air.

"Nothing more here for us to do tonight," Taylor muttered, and they walked back toward their hotel, still about ten blocks down the road. As it happened, they were in the hotel beside Elizabeth's, but then there were four of them here with a couple of bars in between. "You going to update her?"

Nelson nodded. "In the morning. That'll be soon enough." He heard an odd sound just as the streetlight beside him went out. The men looked up at it, looked at each other, both their faces turning grim. They separated slightly and continued to walk. They knew the light hadn't gone out on its own. Those weird splintering sounds happened when somebody throws a rock at a streetlight. Nelson could feel the hair on the back of his neck rising, waiting for the attack. But, when it came, it was from in front of them. That was new and different.

A woman, looking like a motorcycle gang mama in full-leather, stepped in front of them. She held up a hand, stopping their progress. "Why are you asking about him?" she asked, her voice hard.

"He's gone missing," Nelson said quietly. "He has family

who's worried about him."

The woman shook her head. "That's not what he said. He said he had no one."

Nelson frowned. "Maybe he didn't think his sister was worth mentioning. He's still grieving for a father he lost recently."

But the woman wasn't having anything to do with it. "He's gone, and you two need to disappear and to stay gone too."

"And if we don't," Taylor asked, "then what?"

She brought out a switchblade so fast it was easy to see she was comfortable using it and probably had threatened more than a few people with it. "People who piss me off," she said, "end up dead."

"We have no intention of ending up dead." Nelson's tone was cool and hard. "We're after our friend, so, if you know something, I highly suggest you tell us."

"I don't give a fuck what you suggest," she snapped. "We don't like anybody asking questions around here."

Nelson heard her backup coming behind them. He exchanged a hard glance with Taylor. "It's worth money if you do know something," he said with a casual shrug as if he didn't give a crap about her or her people behind them. "And often it's much easier to cooperate than it is to take a beating."

"I won't be the one taking the beating," she said with a sneer. "And we got money. We don't need your bribery money."

"Paying for information is hardly bribery," Taylor said mildly. He shifted his stance to the balls of his feet even as he stepped sideways so he faced the new threat coming up behind them.

She laughed at him. "Do you really think that fancy footwork will help? Only two are here right now, but I can get another half-dozen to come in less than five seconds."

"And why would you do that?" Nelson asked. "What are you so afraid of? Just to talk to us? You can't even handle the streets alone? You have to bring in your little bodyguards?"

Her back stiffened, and she glared at him in outrage.

But he already had her number. "You're just the queen in the streets, but you're nobody without all this backup."

She jumped forward and tried to poke him with her switchblade.

He grabbed her wrist, flipped it around and slammed her arm behind her back, popping the switchblade from her hand into his, holding it up against her throat as he turned to show her bodyguards who had the upper hand. Both men stopped in their places.

"Like I said, you're nothing without your bodyguards," he sneered. "And here we were being nice. We're looking for one of our own, and we won't stop until we find him." He shoved her forward so she was moving toward her two henchmen.

She swung around and glared at him.

He held up the switchblade and said, "You forgot this." He flipped it toward her.

She caught it midair by the handle her glare glacial now.

"Now the offer still stands," he said with a carelessness to show her that he didn't give a crap if she wanted to come at him again or not. "We'll pay for information. He's wanted and loved. And we want to know what happened to him. And, if something bad happened to him, we want to know that too so we can mete out our own punishment." And then, in a daring move, he turned his back on her and walked up the hotel stairs.

But she didn't make a move. He turned at the top of the stairs to see her and her two bodyguards had disappeared.

He looked over at Taylor. "She's got a temper."

"I forgot how good you were with blades." Taylor chuckled. "Although I'm not sure you've got such a smooth attitude with women."

"She was a little too arrogant for me," Nelson said at that.

Taylor burst out laughing.

Up in their rooms Nelson sat down and checked the laptop to see if they had any messages. He'd felt each vibration as they had come to his phone, but bar-hopping and street-fighting weren't the time to get into the details. Mason had sent him the little information he had gleaned from the NCIS, but they were not being very helpful. On the other hand, Elizabeth had come through and had emailed both reports.

He fired off both reports to Taylor and to Mason. "Taylor, if you want to look into her father's file, I'll read her brother's."

They sat down, one at the desk and one on the bed, and went over the two files.

"So their father did have a heart attack, but there's also a suggestion of suicide. He took a large amount of his heart medicine."

"Any reason for him to commit suicide?"

"Not listed here," Taylor said as he flicked through the pages. "There isn't a whole lot actually. They didn't investigate it too closely."

"If they didn't investigate it too closely," Nelson said in exasperation, "how did they know somebody didn't force that medication down him?"

"Apparently, he had no bruising at the mouth or signs of restraints, so they assumed the medication was self-inflicted."

"It might have been at that. Did the autopsy reveal any disease, such as cancer or a brain tumor or anything? Something to explain the suicide. Financial ruin? Depression? Blackmail? Criminal activity?"

"I don't have a copy of the autopsy report here." Taylor hesitated. "We should ask Elizabeth."

"Better you than me."

"I'll pick my time."

"Don't wait too long. It might be connected."

"You think it's related?"

"I don't think anything at the moment," Nelson said. "But it's all too possible, if Chris is in trouble, their father might have been originally in trouble. Just think if somebody coerced the father into doing something, and, rather than that, he committed suicide. Now it's falling to Chris. We need the NCIS file on their father."

"None of those scenarios sounds very good. What's in the other file? Open it up and get to reading," Taylor invited.

"Again almost nothing's here. NCIS did a bunch of interviews, checked with everybody on board ship as they put into port here in Ensenada, checked with the crew members he'd gone on shore leave with, and they came back without him."

"Did they say why?"

"Chris refused to come. Said he would stay and party on. If he was reported not on board, then you know the consequences would not be something he wanted."

"Maybe he woke up the next morning, realized he was in

trouble, and decided to just screw that whole life anyway."

"That's the easy answer. Wouldn't it be nice? He'd pay the penalty for not reporting in on time, but then he'd get his life back," Nelson said.

"Do you think he's alive?" Taylor asked suddenly.

Nelson thought about it for a moment and then nodded. "I do. At least I haven't found anything that would lead me to believe he wasn't. He's a healthy young man, and, if he thought something was going on that he couldn't fix, he might have just walked."

"Did he take the easy way all the time?"

"No, he didn't. But he also knew when to cut his losses. So, for the moment, I'll hold out hope he's alive."

On that note Nelson went back to reading. Just as he finished going through the file, he heard something at the door. The two men hopped to their feet. Nelson slid to the door, only to find a piece of paper. He opened the door and looked outside, but the hallway was empty. Frowning, he snatched up the piece of paper, came back in and locked the door.

When he read the message, he snorted and held it out for Taylor. "*Get out of town. Your friend is gone. Deal with it*," he read aloud. "That's not exactly helpful, is it?" Nelson said. "How do we send a message back?"

"Good question," Taylor said, now looking over both sides of the note. "It's not like they left a return address." He put down the note, took a picture of it, sent it to Mason and texted, **We're getting a great reception here. People are so friendly.** And he sent it off.

Mason sent a text back. **Watch your back.**

Hey, don't I always? Taylor asked in the next text.

Mason's response was **Maybe, maybe not. It's quite**

possible Skunk has already met up with foul play. We won't have you two ending up the same way.

You mean us three, Taylor typed. **Or do you not know Elizabeth came down here too? She's in the hotel right beside us. We were sitting in the bar, looked up, and there she was, asking everybody in the damn place if they'd seen her brother.** His phone rang. Taylor hit Speakerphone.

"She what?" Mason barked. "Are you serious? She's down there with you?"

"Oh, we're very serious," Nelson said. "And she's already being a pain in the ass."

"Now you have to look after not only yourselves but her too," Mason warned.

"I know," Nelson said. "Why do you think I said she's already being a pain in the ass?" And he hung up.

CHAPTER 4

ELIZABETH WOKE UP the next morning, disgruntled and out of sorts that she had not heard from the men. She hopped out of bed, had a quick shower, dressed to step outside to find her car gone. Not exactly surprised, she reported the theft to the day manager. He was not surprised either. With a big sigh, she returned to her room, figuring out what to do next—as far as finding Chris. As for her stolen rental car, she'd report it later to the rental company, when she was stateside once again.

What she needed to do now was contact the men and prove to them how helpful she could be. But where the hell were they staying? It wasn't like they had given her the name of their hotel. She'd handed over her contact information, but they hadn't reciprocated. And she hadn't gotten any clues from them.

"Of course not." She laughed out loud. "That would be way too easy."

She wandered downstairs, through the front lobby area and out onto the street. Six hotels were nearby. What were the chances the men were staying somewhere close? It was an obvious choice to stay in the same area where her brother had last been seen.

On impulse she walked into the next hotel and asked if the two men were registered here and was delighted to find out they were, indeed. "Any chance I can get their room numbers?" she asked. "I want to deliver breakfast to them."

The man looked at her, giving her a tilt of his head.

She winked at him and said, "I know one of them really well."

He sniggered. "So it's *breakfast* you want to give them?"

She gave a nonchalant shrug. "Hey, you never know what might come of it."

He leaned forward. "Not supposed to tell you, but they're on the second floor."

"And a number?"

"It starts with the two, and you add two and then you add two," he said, "but I didn't tell you that."

She beamed a smile at him and walked over to the coffee shop around the corner, picked up two coffees, then added a third for herself. As she studied the breakfast array, not a lot was here, but she added three muffins to the tray she had picked up and headed to the cashier to pay.

Walking past the guys' hotel clerk, she winked and headed toward the elevator.

On the second floor she walked up to Room 246 and knocked. She could hear scrambling noises from inside the room, then dead silence. She stepped to the side and waited. When the door opened, she smiled up at Nelson. "Good morning. Coffee delivery," she said cheerfully.

The look of surprise and then the frown that immediately followed lightened her heart.

She brushed past him. "You see? I do have some uses."

Taylor sat up in bed. He caught sight of her and the coffee and grinned. "Hey, if you'll deliver coffee in bed every morning, you absolutely have your uses." He reached for one of the cups as she held it out to him.

"How did you find us?" Nelson asked in a growling voice.

She turned toward him. "You're not the only one who can figure things out. And stop growling. I'm not going away. Especially since my rental car was stolen almost immediately. So you guys have to give me *and Chris* a lift home." She laughed when Nelson crossed his arms and widened his stance. "Very combative early in the morning, aren't you?"

She picked up a coffee and a muffin and sat down. "I guess I should have brought you cream and sugar, huh? You're kind of sour in the morning." She glanced at Taylor, busy munching away on his muffin. "At least you appear to be a morning person."

He flashed her bright grin. "You brought food and coffee," he said. "That's always an icebreaker."

"For you, yes," she said. "For me, no." She unwrapped her muffin, took a bite and watched Nelson, who had grudgingly picked up his coffee, taken the lid off and sipped. He hadn't touched the muffin so far. "So tell me what else you found out last night."

"Not much," he snapped.

She stared at the note on the coffee table in front of her. Finally the message emblazoned through her brain. "Oh, my God! *He's gone?* Who sent you this?"

"It was shoved under the door last night."

She turned to look at him. "You think Chris is really gone?" She couldn't help the shocked tone in her voice. Or the shortness of her breath, the constriction of her chest. She tried really hard, but the only way to function was to keep all thoughts of her brother being dead at bay. Otherwise it would crush her.

"No," Taylor said firmly yet softly. "We don't work on assumptions. Or threats. When we find proof about Chris, either way, then we'll know something for certain. And we'll share that with you. In the meantime, all possibilities are out there, but none are for sure."

She nodded but didn't say anything. Taking five deep breaths, she could feel her heart rate slowing. She wasn't hungry, but nervously nibbled at her muffin, studying the writing. "Looks like a woman's hand," she announced.

The men turned to look at her.

She shrugged. "It's got lots of loops and tails. Very feminine looking."

Nelson took a look at the note and then nodded. "You're right. We sent it to Mason last night. I don't know if he can match it with anyone."

"Not likely," she said. "Who's he matching it with? NCIS won't give a shit. And who they'll really be looking at, most likely at this point, would be other crew members. There isn't a navy database for handwriting like there is for fingerprints and DNA. It's a good idea though, but there's no money to create one much less update it."

"Too bad," Nelson said. "I heard they would soon be archiving palm prints and potentially cheek impressions."

Elizabeth's gaze widened as she looked up at him. "Are you kidding?"

He shook his head, sat down at the table across from her with his muffin in hand now. "No, and apparently no two ears are the same either."

"Interesting," she muttered. She nudged the note farther away from her so she could finish her muffin without having it in her face. "What's the plan for today?"

"We'll track down the woman who attacked us last

night," Nelson said. "She had information, and we want it."

"You were attacked?" she asked in shock. "Seriously? Was it connected to my brother?"

"Yeah, no big deal. She was just there to give us a warning. Basically the same message as the note there," Taylor said with a nod at the paper beside her. He gave Elizabeth a quick rundown on the incident.

"What makes you sure that this woman would give you information today when she wouldn't last night?"

"Last night she had men around her," Taylor said calmly. "The trick is to get her alone. She's weaker then. The men are bodyguards, a shield, and she won't talk in front of them."

"So you can threaten her?" She tried to not let it bother her, but the idea of these men isolating a woman so they could forcefully question her was unnerving on some level.

"Where she doesn't have to be the big chief and prove herself," Taylor corrected. "She can be herself without all that outward bravado."

"Or she'll be more aggressive as she'll feel cornered." Elizabeth considered that. "That might help though. Especially if I'm with you. She might talk to me, woman-to-woman."

"I don't think she's part of any girls club or had any intention of joining one," Nelson said sarcastically. "She was leading this trio. Don't forget that. She's a dangerous one to turn your back on."

"She doesn't have to be," Elizabeth said calmly. "But she might understand, if she knows it's my brother I'm looking for."

"She's pretty streetwise, hardened," Taylor said. "I think the only thing she'll understand is cold cash."

"Or a gun in her face," Nelson added.

Elizabeth glared at him, then ignored him. Addressing Taylor, she said, "Maybe that money route is okay too." Elizabeth sighed. "I don't have a ton of money, but I do have some."

"Did you bring any cash with you?" Taylor asked.

"Yes." She took a deep breath. "Five thousand dollars."

Silence filled the room, but Nelson gave her a healthy glare too.

She shrugged. "It did occur to me that I might have to pay for information. I just didn't know what the going rate was."

"I hope to God you are not carrying that much cash on your person. And let's hope it doesn't come anywhere close to that amount," Nelson said. "But some might help get information out of the Queen of the Block. I think money did matter to her. At least that's the most popular currency anywhere."

"How will you know where to find her?"

"I think she lives in the first hotel on the block, across from the bar, just outside where we were accosted. She was lounging on the top step when we came out. She probably thought I didn't notice her, but she was pretty hard to miss."

"Okay, as soon as we're done here, we'll go talk to her," Elizabeth said. "Anybody from the base have any more information? And did you guys read the files?"

"We did. I'm sorry about your father," Nelson said. "That's tough."

"Also why I don't want my brother to be dead right now too. It's hard enough to deal with one major loss, but, to deal with a second one, that's more than I care to experience."

"Do you believe your father's death was natural?"

Elizabeth shook her head. "No, I don't. And that's also why NCIS isn't interested in talking to me about my father's death anymore. As far as they are concerned, they investigated my father's death and are happy with their conclusions. It's case closed for them. Neither do they want to talk to me about my brother's disappearance."

"Why is that?"

"Because I really pushed to have them investigate my father's death."

"So now they think you're making a big deal about your brother being missing too. Is that it?"

She nodded sheepishly. "I admit, my father's death was fast and maybe a decent way to go, considering some of the alternatives, but it was still hard to accept."

"Did they do an autopsy?"

She shook her head. "He had a heart condition already, and he was seeing a cardiologist. So, when he dropped dead, they decided he had taken too much of his heart medication. Maybe he thought he had missed a pill, so, due to his confusion and panic, took two in the same day—or something to that effect."

"You could have pushed for a more in-depth investigation."

"I did push, and they cited budget limitations," she explained. "They had to save it for cases where they actually needed it. There was absolutely no reason to believe my father's heart attack was anything other than that, when he already had a known heart condition." She hesitated, then added, "I think they believed he'd killed himself but were avoiding making that official. And a part of me wonders if they weren't correct. My father battled depression off and on for years after my mother's death." She gave them a sheepish smile. "And maybe a part of me doesn't want to know."

Taylor nodded. "Makes sense on their part. If there was nothing obvious to suspect foul play, then it makes sense they wouldn't put out that kind of money."

"Maybe, but now that my brother's missing, they're looking at Chris's reaction being one of grief and loss. That he's just decided to take a walk because he can't handle life after losing our father."

"I gather you don't agree with that," Nelson asked, eyeing her closely.

She shook her head. "No, I don't."

He stayed quiet after that.

Although she was grateful, she was also irritated. Finally she burst out, "I'm not making a big deal out of this. You know that, right? Chris is missing. If he *wanted* to go missing, I'm sure he would have said something to me. We've always been close."

"I can see that," Taylor said. "If it's just the two of you, and you were close, you would think he would contact you."

She nodded. "Exactly."

"Then you know what it means if he didn't," Nelson said shortly.

She glared at him, realizing exactly what he was saying but not saying. "If he's dead, then there's nothing I can do to help him. But I need to know one way or another. If he's in trouble, I'm here for him. And, if he decided to walk away from me too, then I need to find that out. I'll deal with it one way or another. The worst thing is not knowing."

NELSON HAD TO agree with her. Endless questions and always waiting for the phone to ring, for someone to walk in through the door—never getting any answers—that was the worst thing. He'd seen families worry over missing loved ones, not knowing what happened to them for decades. Anytime somebody who'd been listed as MIA was finally identified, there was such a relief to the family. They could finally find closure. The only problem with closure was there was no longer hope. So it was a double-edged sword.

From her perspective, it would solve a lot of her sleepless nights if she knew her brother had voluntarily disappeared or if his body could be found. She'd grieve, but there would be daylight at the end of that long process. As it stood now, she'd worry about her brother's disappearance forever. It would haunt all aspects of her life.

Not that Nelson had come down here looking for a body. Skunk was one of those guys who always seemed to slip through the cracks and do well for himself, regardless of the situation. It didn't seem to matter what was going on; he always turned up smelling like roses. But this time Nelson wondered if his friend had had enough good luck to get somewhere safe. It wasn't in Skunk's nature to just walk away. So, in his heart of hearts, Nelson figured something had gone wrong, and Skunk had been forced away, or he was no longer capable of going anywhere.

He brought up his laptop as he sipped his coffee, and he did appreciate the coffee but would have preferred she hadn't risked coming over here, letting anybody know who might be watching them that they were connected. Keeping her safe was paramount, and she just might have put herself in even more danger. Her intentions were good, but she didn't understand how dangerous her actions were.

Which then impacted his ability to do the job he came to do.

As he flicked through his emails, checking for any updates, he lifted his gaze above the laptop. "You do realize you have put yourself in danger by coming here, right?"

She shrugged. "I'm in danger just because I'm associated with my brother. I don't have any illusions about that."

"But if we had managed to keep our association apart," Nelson said, "you wouldn't have been dragged into the muck if we go down."

She stared at him in surprise. "I blew that last night. Today won't make any difference."

He chuckled. "You got a point there. We were avoiding too public a display of what we are doing here. We were also showing pictures and asking people about him but were discreet about it."

"Why?" She tilted her head as she looked at him. "How will you show people what he looks like discreetly?"

"By finding a few select people who might have known him," he said. "Not flashing a picture up and down the strip so everybody knows he's missing and that you, a woman alone, wants answers. Even if they aren't being truthful, we can get a read on them, know who to follow up with."

"You have your method," she said. "I have mine."

Nelson looked to Taylor. "You got any updates, any interesting emails?"

Taylor shook his head. He brushed the last of the crumbs onto his napkin he'd been using as a plate, cleaned up his garbage and said, "Looks like it's time to move." Casually he got up, just in his boxers and walked into the bathroom. Not that he had much choice as she'd come into their hotel room.

Nelson glanced over to see if it bothered her. But she seemed completely relaxed as she worked on her phone.

She looked up and frowned. "If Chris came on shore, what would he have done here? How much trouble could he have gotten into? Although, we have all those exits to consider too, checking for him at the airport and the bus depots. Which would he most likely take?"

"Bus," Nelson said. "They don't check ID as closely as other modes of transportation."

"Makes sense. Anything that makes it easier for him, makes it harder for us to track him." Elizabeth got up and paced the small room. "So can I come with you while you meet this woman?"

"I'd rather you didn't," he said. "If we judge the meeting isn't going well, then I might bring you into it. But it's probably better if it's just the two of us first. She won't like any surprises—although we don't have a formal meeting set up, so this will be a shock and not a pleasant one, so let's not push it."

"Right." She glared at him. "So I'm supposed to just go back to my room and wait again, huh?"

"You don't like waiting much, do you?"

"Do you?" she challenged.

He shrugged. "I don't think anybody does. Particularly not in this scenario. It doesn't change the fact that this is a waiting game until we can find the right lead to open up some information here."

She studied him with a frown. "I still think I could be helpful with this conversation."

Taylor came out of the bathroom fully dressed and said, "Nelson, I think she's right. It might make us seem less aggressive."

"I don't think this woman will be concerned about how aggressive we are. She's the one who got aggressive last

267

night."

"I get that," Taylor said. "But we can keep an eye on her, see how it goes, and if need be, you can approach her on your own, and I'll stay back with Elizabeth."

"And that's where the problem will start," Nelson said in exasperation. "Already we have to split up."

Elizabeth stood. "Let's go now. If I'm in the way, then I can come back. If it doesn't work this morning, you can always try again later, just the two of you."

"We don't have a lot of time, remember? We have four days. And yesterday probably counted as Day One to NCIS, even though we didn't arrive until early afternoon. So we have three full days left. And that's it." Nelson tossed the rest of his garbage, his coffee cup as well, and closed his laptop, but he gave in. "Let's go." He glanced to see what kind of shoes Elizabeth wore and nodded. "Make sure you are always sensibly dressed while you're down here. You never know when we'll go for a full-on sprint."

She winced. "Sounds lovely."

"No," he said, "it won't be. But it could be very necessary."

As soon as everybody was ready, he led the way. They took the stairs down the back exit. Out in the parking lot, they walked around to the front of the building and down to the end of the block. It was early, and the streets were mostly deserted. The air was as fresh as it was likely to get in this corner of town.

Nelson checked his watch. "Almost seven. You'd think some traffic would be out here."

"I think they all enjoy the nightlife too much to care about early mornings here," Taylor said in a low voice.

"Plus, it's a *Saturday* morning," Elizabeth said.

NELSON

Taylor nodded. "Most of them aren't awake yet."

"Good," Nelson said. "Maybe we'll get lucky, and she'll still be in bed too."

At the corner of the building they were interested in, they took a look around, saw no sentries on duty. They walked up to the front entrance and pulled open the double doors.

With Elizabeth literally pinched between them, the three walked into the building. If somebody was supposed to be at the front desk here, they weren't now. Nelson frowned, walked around the desk and checked to see if they had a list of who lived there. But there was nothing.

Suddenly a voice behind him said, "Hey, what the hell are you doing?"

Nelson straightened, turned to look at the old guy pouring a cup of coffee. "We're looking for the queen bitch around the place."

The old guy cackled. "What the hell do you want with her?"

"Information," Nelson said.

"She doesn't even crack open her eyes until noon. What kind of information? Maybe it's something I can help you with, particularly if there's a reason."

Taylor stepped forward and pulled out a one-hundred-dollar bill.

The guy's face lit up. "A guy can buy a lot of booze for that."

"Yeah, but we're looking for *particular* information," Nelson said. "A man went missing a week ago."

The clerk shrugged. "You know how many people go missing around this place? That's a day-to-day thing."

He'd barely finished speaking when Elizabeth shoved a

269

photo of her brother in front of his face.

The guy looked at it, scratched his scraggly beard and frowned. "You know what? I think I've seen him."

"Here?"

He scratched his beard again. "I can't remember."

"Well, be sure because there won't be any more money if you don't remember," Taylor said in a dry tone.

The guy studied the one-hundred-dollar bill, looked back at Nelson and said, "That kind of information could get me killed."

"We're afraid that kind of information already got our buddy killed." Nelson's voice was hard. "We need to know if he's alive or dead."

"When I saw him last, he was alive," the clerk said. "But that was not quite five nights ago. I could be misremembering." He grabbed his book, flipped through it a couple pages back and said, "Chris. Chris Etchings. Is that his name?"

Elizabeth stepped closer. "Yes, that's my brother."

"He was here Monday night. That's all I know."

"Did he stay here before then?"

He nodded. "He was here for a couple nights. He was here with some other people as well. But the last night he was alone."

"Do you know who the other people were?"

The clerk slid a sideways look toward Taylor. "You'll need a second one of those bills for that information."

Taylor pulled out a second one and waved the two of them in front of the old man. "Who did he spend time with?"

Making sure nobody was listening, he leaned forward and said, "The queen bitch."

"And her guys?" Nelson asked.

"They're never separated," the old man said.

"Are they looking out for her, or are they watching to make sure she doesn't get into any trouble?"

At that, the man cackled. "So you noticed that, huh?"

"I noticed something," Taylor admitted. "It's a little hard to tell though."

"She belongs to somebody, and you don't want to piss that somebody off."

"Did my brother piss him off?"

"Not necessarily. But we get a lot of seaman through here. They spend a lot of money in this place. We certainly won't do anything to slow down that business."

"And did he have something to do with that?"

"He was drunk and making a lot of accusations," the old guy said. "Accusations that were making other people uncomfortable. At this kind of a place, it takes a lot to make somebody uncomfortable."

"Can you tell us what the accusations were?"

He shrugged. "Something about seeing some men murder a man. Deep-sixing the body in the water and that they needed to be stopped."

"If he saw something like that, why didn't he tell anyone before?"

"Something about the rest of his rank closing in on him, and his life would be in danger if he said anything. He wanted somebody on the docks to say something. But down here, we keep our mouths shut. It doesn't matter what you see or when you see it, no reason to tell anyone about it." Just then a door opened. He lowered his voice. "And that's all I'll say about it."

"Wait," Nelson said urgently. "What's queen bitch's name?"

"Chelsea," he said, "but I got no clue what else but that. First name only."

"And the guy she belongs to?"

He just cackled. "We call him King." His phone rang. He snatched the two hundred-dollar bills from Taylor's hand and then answered the ringing phone and refused to talk to them anymore.

They slowly walked back out onto the street. "That's interesting," Nelson said. "That would give Skunk a reason to disappear."

"Or it gave others a reason to make him disappear," Taylor said thoughtfully. "And maybe he couldn't get to the commander. Maybe it just happened, and he was looking for help to do something about it."

"He could have gone to the police though," Elizabeth said. "No reason to not go to the local authorities."

"Maybe," Nelson said. "And maybe the threat scared him enough that he didn't want to go back on board. Sometimes it's not easy. The crew can be pretty rough. And, if you're considered a traitor, it can get ugly."

"So he knew something he shouldn't, knew he was in trouble, missed returning to his station, and now he's in trouble with the navy because he didn't return to the ship? If he even mentioned bringing in the cops here, and some seamen did kill somebody, ... that'll get him killed," Taylor finished.

"So help me understand," Elizabeth said. "No matter what Chris does, he loses. Sounds like he's safer here than on his own ship. Yet he doesn't get back on board because he's too scared and has missed reporting in. That's hard to swallow too."

"Don't judge him for that. I'm not kidding when I said

it can get really ugly. What if he thinks his friends were involved in the murder? Then he wouldn't dare go back on board particularly if they know he *knows*," Nelson said, emphasizing the last word. "I've been in the navy a long time, and there are a hell of a lot of good guys there. But you get some bad ones in the mix too. And it's nothing like being up against your own homegrown soldiers who know how to kill. It happens. If Chris even thought they saw him, his life was in danger."

"Okay, so he's here in town for a couple days on leave. He sees his friends do something shitty, figures out they know he saw them. He doesn't go back on board because he's scared what they'll do to him. So instead, he goes on a bender to try to forget what he saw, realizes he screwed up his life. And that's where I get lost. Why didn't he tell someone?"

"If he told a Mexican cop down here," Taylor said easily, "it's possible he told the wrong one. A lot of cops would just look the other way in this corner of the world."

"So some crooked navy and some crooked cops?" Elizabeth asked in outrage. "How can anybody get that much of a shitty deal?"

"Apparently, Chris can," Nelson said in exasperation. He looped his arm through hers. "Come on. We need more food, and I need more coffee."

CHAPTER 5

A S THE THREE of them walked along the street toward the restaurant, Elizabeth said, "I guess this is all helping me, but it just confused the issue more."

"Not at all," Nelson said. "Now we have a direction and some people we need to talk to."

"Who's that? Chelsea, the queen bitch, by any chance?"

"Yes, but it changes things to know she's owned by somebody. Means she's not free to talk."

"So what do we do?"

"We need to meet with King," Taylor said easily. "She can send a message to him. But whether he grants us the meeting, I don't know."

As they walked toward the restaurant, Taylor pointed to one of the doorways. "Isn't that one of her henchmen?"

Nelson, in a surprise move, jumped up the steps to stand in the guy's face. The guy tried to tower over him, his fists clenching. Nelson slapped him back against the wall. "Take a message to King for us," he snapped. "We want a meeting, and we want information on where Chris Etchings went. We want it today." And then Nelson released him so he could sag against the wall. Nelson turned his back and hopped down the steps to join Taylor again. "Message sent," he said with a laugh.

They walked into the restaurant, and Elizabeth continued to stare at him. "Did you just threaten that big guy?"

"They're usually the best ones to pick on," he said. "They always think they're so damn big and dangerous looking that they don't expect it." Nelson still smiled but gave her a one-arm shrug. "Besides," he said, his voice lowered, "you gotta stand up for yourself in this neighborhood. Never show fear. Never back down. They don't respect you if you don't get in their face. Just like that schoolyard bully we all grew up with, you have to confront them."

All Elizabeth could think was, *Well, that might work for you and Taylor* ... Like she had told Nelson before, there was his method, and then there was hers. "And what if we *don't* get an audience."

"We'll create one ourselves," Taylor said. "I suppose if we pick up his lady, that might do it."

Nelson chuckled again.

They took a seat, ordered fresh coffee, and, when the waitress tried to give them menus, Nelson said, "I'd like huevos rancheros on the hot side. And tortillas, double the normal amount."

The waitress wrote down his order. When it was Elizabeth's turn, she said, "I'll be fine with just coffee, thanks."

Nelson looked over at Taylor and asked, "Times two?"

Taylor nodded. "Sounds good to me."

The waitress disappeared, leaving the three of them with coffee.

"How long until the message is received?" Elizabeth asked.

"He's already got it," Nelson said.

"Seriously?" Elizabeth asked. "That fast?"

"Yeah. The henchman would have turned around and

gone straight there."

"So now we just wait?"

The waitress returned with a plate of toast she put down in front of Elizabeth, who said, "I didn't order any toast."

"I ordered it for you," Nelson said. "A muffin an hour ago was not enough food to run on."

She wasn't sure about his term *run* but remembered what he had said earlier about being able to sprint. With a sigh, she slathered on jam and took a bite.

It wasn't too long before the food arrived.

She looked at the mountain of food placed in front of the men. "How did you know they would have food like that here?"

He shrugged. "Almost everybody in here looks to be a big single male. The only reason for that is if there's good grub."

She laughed out loud but watched in astonishment as the two men devoured their plates. "Hungry much?"

"Not so much now," Nelson said, reaching for his coffee and drank it down.

By the time they were done and on their third cup of coffee, Elizabeth said, "Are you waiting for something?"

Nelson nodded. "Yep. Should be anytime now."

She frowned.

All of a sudden, shadows came up beside her. She glanced up at the new arrivals to see two big men standing here; one of them was the man Nelson had spoken to earlier.

"King wants to talk to you."

"Good," Nelson said. "When?"

"Now," the man said without moving a facial muscle.

"Good," Nelson said. "We weren't waiting much longer." He stood up, tossed money on the table to cover the bill, and then grabbed Elizabeth's arm, helping her to her feet. "Where?"

"Follow us," the man said.

Elizabeth glanced over at Nelson, but he shook his head as if to just say, *Don't ask.* So she didn't. But she wasn't terribly comfortable with that. And then she remembered her words this morning about doing whatever they needed her to do. Well, right now she needed to shut up and watch apparently. She hoped this went well. But she had no clue why it would. They were on somebody else's turf, and apparently that mattered.

As they walked outside, two more men joined them. Taylor stiffened on her other side. She asked, "Is that a problem?"

"Hell no," he said cheerfully. "That's only to make sure they have peace."

She pondered what he meant as they were led down the street into an alleyway and into a back entrance. She studied the area, hoping to find a way back out, providing these guys let her walk out of here.

As they went inside and downstairs, a door was opened ahead of them. They came to a large lounge area where a massive black man, seated at a piano, gently played.

She smiled. "That's a lovely song," she said. "I haven't heard it since I was a child."

He looked up at her. "It's one of Bach's lesser-known pieces. Not too many people know it."

She smiled. "I used to play, but it's been a while."

He moved to one side. She sat down beside him and tested the keys, sliding her fingers up and down the ivories. He watched her play, joining in every once in a while with a couple notes as they sat for a few minutes enjoying the music. As she looked up with a happy smile, she caught Nelson staring at her with a quizzical look. She smiled at the big man at her side. "Thank you. I'd forgotten the joy of playing."

He stood from the piano bench. "It's all yours. Play something your heart wants to hear."

She shifted to the center of the bench, letting her fingers ripple once again up and down the keys. "I don't remember anything fully," she said good-naturedly.

But then she remembered her favorite song—"Amazing Grace." Her fingers fell into an old pattern. She played this every time she was upset when she was growing up. As her fingers whispered across the keys, she could feel the words bubbling up inside her soul.

Keeping her voice low, she sang the words to the song. When she finished, and the music fell into the silence in the room, the huge man standing beside her clapped.

"Now that," he said, "was lovely."

She beamed up at him. "I haven't played that in forever," she confessed. "Thank you."

He grinned. His mouth was full of flashy gold teeth.

Although she had been relaxed as she played the piano, and totally in love with what she was doing, the dynamics and the mood had changed. She stared at the man. "Are you King?" she asked him.

He nodded. "I am. What's this I hear about you missing somebody?"

In a voice gone soft and full of sorrow, she said, "My brother. He's been missing for nine days now." She pulled the picture out of her pocket and unfolded it, handing it to King with reverence. "We are very close. He's my last relative. Our father died several months ago."

King took the photo from her hand and studied the printed page, then nodded. "He was here, maybe a week ago."

"We haven't figured out where he went after that," she said with a heavy sigh. "Nobody saw him leave …"

"Do you think he's still here?" the big man asked.

"I hope not," she said, "because that would most likely mean he's dead." Her tone turned bleak. "And that's something I can't really deal with right now."

"He was alive the last time I saw him," King said. "He was calling for the police, and that's something we don't condone here."

"So what did you do?" she asked. "Beat him up and toss him at the bus stop?" When a ripple of laughter was heard around the room from all the henchmen, she sighed. "Am I being too naive? You said he was alive when you last saw him. That doesn't mean he was alive when your henchmen saw him last. Did you have him killed?"

"No. I probably should've, but I didn't."

"So do you know where he is?"

He shook his head. "If, as you say, he's gone missing, then I don't know." He held the photo of her brother out for her.

She creased it back up into the same folded form and put it in her pocket. "Can you tell me where he was dumped, so I can at least pick up the trail from there?"

"Down at the dock. Do you know what he said he saw?"

"Rumor has it," she said, "he saw a man being murdered. He saw men beat up this guy, then drop the man into the water. Possibly Chris was too scared to go back on board his ship because the others knew he'd seen them. He was looking for help," she cried out plaintively. "And it seems like all he did was run into more foul play."

"Not necessarily," King said. "We did warn him to shut up and to get the hell out of here. Otherwise, he would get into real trouble. No way to know what he did after that warning."

She added, "If I at least knew he'd gone to the bus station or the airport or someplace, so he could have gotten a ride out of town, it would help. I don't know what's happened to him."

"He hasn't contacted you?" King asked.

"No," she whispered, hating the emotions choking her when considering why he might not have called his only sibling. "It scares me that he hasn't. If he was in trouble, you'd think he'd have called for help. The only reason I can think of why he didn't is because he was trying to keep me safe."

"That would be a shame to put you in danger," King said with a brief smile. "Anybody who can play the piano like you did, shouldn't be silenced."

She chuckled. "That's the nicest thing anybody's said to me in quite a while. Thank you."

He nodded. "I'm sorry I can't be of more help, but we sent him back to the dock. So maybe go check down there and see if anybody saw him."

"He could have gotten onto a boat from there, couldn't he?"

"He could have," King said, "particularly if he found anybody he knew. They might have let him come on board and work his passage one way or another. I highly doubt he was broke. So it's possible he just bought a passage home again."

"He wouldn't call me if he was out to sea, would he?"

"Not necessarily," King said, as if giving the point a considered thought. "Maybe he's getting his head wrapped around what's coming. Once he goes to the brass about what he saw, he'll be investigated too."

"True enough." She stood and held out her hand. "Thank you. If you do hear anything else, I know you won't want to tell me, but I *would* appreciate it. He is the only family I have left."

King gripped her fingers lightly and placed his other hand over his heart. "I promise."

She smiled at him, squeezed his fingers and led the way to the door. Nelson and Taylor fell into step at her side.

As they walked through the door, she had to admit she worried they'd be stopped. But they were allowed to leave.

They walked down the steps to the alley and back out onto the main street before anybody said a word.

As soon as they hit a more public spot, Nelson grabbed her arm and tugged her to face him. "Are you okay?"

She stopped in the circle of his arms, needing the support for just a moment. Her heart pounded, and her insides twisted in confusion. It felt nice to know somebody was here, to know somebody would hold her and help her get through this. "I am. I'm glad to hear there were more options to what might have happened to my brother. The fact they took him to the dock worries me because there's a chance he drowned. Did they leave him at the dock or leave him in the water at the dock? I have no illusions about who King is. I just figured as long as there was a connection between us, I'd use it to get what we could."

"It was nicely done," Taylor said. "If we had gone in with the same questions, he wouldn't have been as forthright."

She chuckled. "You never know how a piano and two people with a love of music can connect."

"Apparently, you did very well," Nelson said. "Now what do you want to do?"

"I want to go to the dock," she said, "and walk it and make sure nobody's underneath the wharf. Make sure my brother isn't feeding the fish in a way I don't want to contemplate but can't get out of my head."

"On any given day, I'm sure a bunch of different bodies are down there. But we'll go. We have all day. Let's take a look, see if anybody is down there, ask if anyone saw anything or knows anything. Maybe we'll find somebody who saw the original man killed there."

"You mean, a witness other than my brother?" She looked at him with trust, then thought about it. "That would help. The problem is, Chris figures he's up against the whole system, and nobody'll listen to him."

"That's true to a certain extent," Taylor said. "But we know a lot of good guys in the navy. They're not all rotten. It won't take long for Chris to renew his faith in his fellow servicemen. Or in humankind, once we get a chance to connect with him."

"That's what we need to do," she said, certainty in her voice. "So now, how the hell do we get to the docks?" She turned back to Nelson and asked, "Do you know?"

He hooked her arm through his. "Act as if the two of us are together," he said in a low voice. "We don't want anybody here to think you're on your own."

With a chuckle she said, "That's a far cry from what you said last night about not wanting me to be connected with you."

At her side Taylor chuckled. "That's us. We're always

looking out for which way something'll work better."

GETTING TO THE docks wasn't simple. Nelson looked down at Elizabeth's shoes. "Are you up for a several-mile walk, or shall we take our car?"

She looked startled. "So you two drove? And your car hasn't been stolen yet? How did that happen?"

"Mason hooked us up."

"It's practically an armored vehicle," Taylor said, all smiles. "It's loaded. It did cause us some delay at the border crossing, but we had papers to help us through."

"Papers?"

"Yeah, papers stating we're military attachés, which makes us almost deemed diplomats."

Elizabeth just stared.

"Anyway … it has airless tires, bulletproof everything, two GPS systems, two securities systems and two kill switches."

Elizabeth frowned. "What's to stop them from towing away your car?"

Nelson smiled, shaking his head, looking Taylor's way. "Not happening."

"That's the best part. It's loaded with tear gas canisters all over that eject at the slightest sensation on the undercarriage or at the door panels and elsewhere." Taylor's animated face said it all. "It's a beaut."

"Well," she said, "I guess the motor pool guys on base know how to work around all that. And you guys should have no problem driving me and Chris back home, right?"

"No problem," Nelson with a knowing look and a smirk.

"So," she continued, "how far away are the docks?"

"Depends," he said. "The Saturday tourist traffic and crowds could make it more complex."

"I thought it was just a few blocks away."

Nelson nodded. "But I don't know how far along the docks we'll have to walk."

She shrugged. "Let's go for it."

Dodging the heaviest of the crowds, they moved from the seedy area to the touristy area, then to the industrial section.

"I'm amazed that, in just these few blocks, foot traffic has picked up immensely," Elizabeth noted.

By the time they got there, Nelson could see the fatigue on her face. He should have gone with his instincts and called for a cab midway. At least he knew they could take one back to their hotels.

As soon as she saw the large wharfs, she nodded. "This looks like the photos Chris used to send me."

They walked along the water's edge, and she could see how many miles they'd have to search. And how vast the ocean was.

She groaned. "Even if they had drowned him, the tide could take him all over the place."

"Often if somebody drowns around the wharfs, they get stuck underneath, caught up on the pylons," Taylor said. "When the tide goes out, it's easier to find them. But, by then, the fish have had a good feeding."

"And nobody knows who went into the water, correct?"

"All we've heard in the last twenty-four hours is that Chris might have seen a murder. We don't know who was murdered. And we don't know how they disposed of the body. Just because they threw him in doesn't mean he drowned. Now if they tied cement blocks to his legs, that's a different story. If they held his head under, that's a different story. If they ran him through a propeller, that's a different story," Nelson said. He tried to keep his tone even, but it still caused Elizabeth to blink at him. He shrugged. "Look. I'm just telling you that, when you get a gang of men in a murderous rage, and they have a purpose, usually a self-driven one, it can get pretty ugly."

"Wow," she said, staring down at the water as it lapped against the piers. "And here I was thinking how beautiful it is. No way in heck I would swim down here."

"Not too many people swim along here. The beaches are farther down." He pointed along the edge.

She smiled. "The rockier and harder-to-access points are not what I call a beach—or at least the kinds I'm used to. But then, maybe you and I come from different parts of town. I happen to think a beach should be long miles of white sand."

"You might," he said, "but that doesn't mean it's the same everywhere."

As they wandered, Nelson kept an eye out for where he knew bodies could be underneath. Chances were good these men had sunk the evidence pretty deep. And, even if the body did get free, like she said, the body could have floated anywhere down the beach. As he looked at the docks, he wondered, why *these* docks? Well, no traffic, public or industrial, appeared along this area. Not for another block or so. Under the cover of darkness, men could have thrown a body in here. Could have easily weighed it down without being seen. Would Chris have been in this area though? Or had he seen something off and came to investigate. Was he then seen? Or had he disappeared into the shadows and then returned to his hotel, not sure what to do next? That would make more sense.

They continued to walk until she asked, "Can we sit down?" She pointed at the rocks. "I want to just sit here for a bit and look at the water."

As they made their way onto the rocks, Elizabeth sighed happily and settled down. "In the dark, nobody would have known anything, would they?"

"No, but the men could have been carrying lights. If they heard something, they would have turned on the lights and quite possibly caught sight of Chris. Or Chris might have followed them, wondering what they were up to, hoping they weren't doing what he thought they were. When the deed was done, and they saw him, they would have chased him. He could have disappeared into the slips, an empty boat even, and, from there, made his way back to the hotel. As soon as the navy ship left with his buddies, he would have tried to do something about it. But it would have been too late."

"It's hard to believe how being in the wrong place at the wrong time can go so bad," Elizabeth said soberly.

"And remember. We're just listening to hearsay. As soon as we find your brother, we'll find out more. But, in the meantime, we don't know anything for sure."

"I know," she said in a groan. "So now what?"

Nelson stood on the water's edge and took several photographs of the area. "This is just for the file," he said.

As they studied the area, they couldn't see anything.

"I'm glad, you know?" she said. "I'm standing here, expecting to find bodies, but I'm really hoping we don't. The longer we don't find anything, the more I realize the chances are almost nil that we will."

He understood what she was saying. He helped her onto the dock, and they walked back up and down the wharfs. She was fairly methodical, even though he knew nothing would likely show up. He turned to find Taylor had gone to talk to a couple dock workers. With gesturing hands, they appeared to have an animated conversation. Nelson wanted to join them and hear what was going on but didn't want to disturb them.

As he approached Elizabeth, he stopped and looked between two moored boats. One looked to be a Zodiac; the other one was a small speedboat. They were on the public side of the docks now. As he looked down, he caught sight of something floating.

As she walked toward him, he held up a hand. "Stop."

She froze.

He leaned over the wharf and took a closer look, inching one of the boats to the side. Sure enough, there was a hand. He couldn't tell yet what it was attached to, but it wasn't moving.

Just then Taylor came toward him. "Hey, did you find something?"

"Yeah. Did you?" Nelson asked, still peering at the water.

"One of the guys said there'd been a fight, but, when they got here, the crowd had dispersed."

"Look at this."

Taylor joined him at the side of the wharf. Elizabeth too. Taylor crouched beside him. "Shit."

"Yeah, but we don't know who it is."

"Are you sure anything is attached to that arm?" Elizabeth asked at his side. Her voice was raspy, but she was holding her own, and he had to admire that. Not too many people could look at a corpse hanging off a boat like this and not be shocked.

"Do you think he reached up to get help? His fingers look like they're wrapped around that line."

"I'd feel better if I could see the rest of him," Taylor said.

He shifted to the other side of Elizabeth and pulled one boat back so the two boats weren't rubbing up against each other. Almost immediately they could see the head floating upward from the arm.

Elizabeth cried out in horror.

Nelson looked at her. "Do you recognize him?"

She nodded, tears in her eyes. "Yes, I do. It's not my brother, but it's one of his navy friends."

CHAPTER 6

ELIZABETH PEERED DOWN the long dock to the wharf, her arms wrapped around her chest. Several times Nelson had tried to stop her pacing, but a jitteriness inside her needed movement to keep it in check. She kept trying to breathe, yet her breath would get stuck in her chest until she could ease up enough to draw in more air.

Finally she stopped at the far end, where the water lapped up against the boats, pushing them against the wharf. The ambulance and police had arrived at the wharf end of the dock. Elizabeth turned to look back toward the shore. A small crowd had gathered, but she wondered if anyone truly cared about this poor man or if they were just curiosity seekers. Then, like her, they wouldn't know much. How could they, unless they'd been involved? Nelson walked toward her. She gave him a wan smile. "I really am okay, you know."

"I know you are," he said quietly. "Finding a body like this is a shock for anyone. But to find somebody you know makes it that much harder to deal with."

"Yet I can't even remember his name," she said, hating the guilt inside. She stared up at him in pain. "Somebody is dead. Somebody should remember who he was. *I* should remember who he was."

Nelson grabbed her shoulders and gave her a light shake.

"Why? Why are you supposed to remember? Why do you have to do everything? His name will come to you eventually. And we'll find out from the coroner's office when they ID him. This is *not* your fault."

She reached up and rubbed her head. "I can't get away from the idea it's the man my brother saw killed, and Chris could be next."

"That's very possible," Nelson said. "In a way it would be good news if it was that man killed by his fellow seamen because it would lend credence to what we've been told so far. As soon as we find a body, we have a hope of discovery forensic evidence. We can work with that. We'll find out who's responsible, and maybe we can track it back to your brother. And, if it nails anybody on his ship, that's good too."

All of a sudden she crumpled against his chest, his arms holding her close. "But what if it is Chris the next time?"

He rested his chin on her head. "I know that's the first thought that came into your mind when you saw the arm. Obviously I thought it too. But it's not your brother, and, because of that, we hope that he's still out there, doing his best to survive. We can help him if he is."

She gave a strangled laugh. "Nobody was there to help that poor man," she said, gesturing at the body.

"I know," Nelson said. "And we can't do anything more for him either. I'm sorry, so sorry for his family. But right now, we focus on finding Skunk before the men who killed this guy find him."

"I guess in a population like this, finding floaters isn't all that unusual, is it?"

"No, unfortunately it's not," Nelson said in a hard tone. "There're a lot of suicides. There're a lot of accidents. And unfortunately water makes a great murderous medium." He turned her slightly so they could look at the paramedics as they raised the body out of the water. The coroner bent over as they all discussed the body.

"I feel so damn bad," she said. "He's somebody's son, likely a brother, possibly a father. How horrible to lose your life like that."

"Loss of life when it's not your time is always difficult," Nelson said. "We're doing what we can."

"But this now brings the local police into it, doesn't it?"

"Yes, it does. Since he's navy as well, it'll bring NCIS back into the issue."

Her shoulders sagged. "They won't like that we found him."

Nelson gave a bark of laughter. "They won't like that anybody found him because it means more work for them. It also means they'll take another look at your brother's investigation. Still, they will do their best by this man."

Elizabeth looked up at him hopefully. "Do you really think so?"

He nodded. "I really do because it's not easy to dismiss the connection."

"Only then, what's the chance they'll think my brother drowned him himself?"

Nelson made a startled movement as if he hadn't considered that.

She nodded. "You know that's the easy answer and that would be NCIS's reason for why Chris has gone AWOL. How the two seamen probably had a falling out of some kind, somehow my brother killed this guy, and, being aware of what he'd done, knowing the repercussions, he bolted."

"Yes," Nelson said slowly. "I can see them trying for

that."

"Also, if Chris knew his friend was here and dead, why didn't he come find the body?"

"Just because his body's here right now doesn't mean he was killed here," Nelson said. He pointed up the coastline. "His friend could have been dumped in all kinds of places. A cliff's up there. It's quite easy to throw him off, have him hit the rocks below. Then the tide picks him up and carries him down where he got caught up in the boats."

Elizabeth shuddered. "What a horrible thought."

"We need as much proof as we can get," Nelson said. "And, in the next twenty-four hours, before the autopsy and the ID is completed, NCIS will get involved. If he's not navy for some reason—maybe he got out of the service and you didn't know about it—and he happens to be somebody completely unrelated to the navy, then it has nothing to do with Skunk or us."

"And yet, we found him," she said.

"So his family would probably thank us for that," Nelson said. "Not knowing anything, as you are aware, is the worst."

Another shiver ran down her core. Feeling it, he pulled her into his arms. "This is not a setback. Though it's hard to see a dead body, it's a relief because it isn't Skunk."

She nodded her head. "I get that," she muttered. "But it's tough to think about. I don't want to be found hanging on to a boat by strangers and give them nightmares for the rest of their lives."

"It'll give you a nightmare for the rest of your life if we don't solve it. Time will help ease the details."

"But *should* time be allowed to ease the details?" She looked up at him, her gaze direct, searching. "A man lost his life. Whether by accident or intent, it's still important to remember his life. I don't think his details should be blurred."

"No, they shouldn't. But our psyche keeps us moving forward and helps us to deal with trauma, and, over time, those details will blur. It's easy to do a memorial card with his name and the time and date and any other details," he said steadily, "and pull it out every once in a while as a reminder how he shouldn't be forgotten, but our mind does, over time, help us to ease back on the sharpness of the memory. There's no other way to function."

She took several deep breaths, calming herself. "Maybe that's what I'll do instead of looking at this, hating that this happened. I should do something to help celebrate his life." She could feel Nelson's welcoming squeeze of approval on her shoulders. She looked up at him. "Have you seen many dead bodies?"

He stilled and then gave a crisp nod. "Unfortunately, yes. And you never get used to it."

"You never should."

They watched until the body was moved off the wharf. Several policemen wandered through the crowd, taking photos, talking to people. As soon as the body was taken away, Elizabeth and Nelson walked down the wharf toward the uniformed officers.

"Question time," she said.

"Yes," Nelson said, still holding her. "Taylor has been talking to them."

"Now we just line up our stories," she said on a broken laugh.

"No," Nelson said. "We answer the questions as honestly as we can."

She looked up at him in surprise. "That's not what I expected you to say."

"No point in confusing the issue or lying. I always find the truth comes out in the end. But don't offer any information. Answer their questions and only answer their questions."

"Got it," she said. "Now if only I can remember it."

Two policemen approached. One had a kindly face. He said, "Sorry, folks. That's a bit of a rude awakening, huh?"

And that brought the tears to her eyes. She tried to brush them away. "Do we know who he is?" she asked. "I feel so sad knowing he's been lying there for who-knows-how-long."

"We haven't ID'd him yet," the second police officer said. "But we're hoping to quickly."

She nodded. "The worst part of all this is that his hand was up, as if looking to grab that line."

"He was hanging on to the tie rope, but it looks like his hand might have seized and given out at the end. It was enough to stop his body from floating away."

She nodded, but the tears wouldn't stop spouting.

Nelson tugged her close. "I understand you need to ask us some questions. Any chance we can get to them quickly so I can take her away from here?"

The men nodded. "We just have a few here to go over with you." The first question was asked. "What are you doing in town?"

Nelson answered each and every question.

The officers turned toward Elizabeth and said, "And what about you? Do you have anything to add?"

She thought about it and then shrugged. "No, I'm here for the same reason he is."

"It's your brother who's missing?"

She nodded. "Yes, it's my brother. When I saw the body in the water, I thought for sure it was him. And now, I mean, I'm grateful it's not, but, at the same time, it's like I can't get that poor man's face out of my mind."

"Understood," he said. "We'll let you know when we confirm ID."

As they turned to walk away, an officer held out a card. "If you think of anything else, you can use this to get a hold of us. We have your contact information. We'll call you if we have any more questions. When are you leaving?"

"In three days, counting today," she said. "Three days." She let her sad voice drift away because she realized now three days wouldn't be long enough to get any of this sorted out.

They stayed where they were as the cops walked away. As soon as they were off the dock, Taylor strolled toward them and said, "The police found an ID on him. They probably didn't tell you, but his name was Peter Patnik."

Elizabeth stiffened. "That's it. That's his name."

"Now they'll be hunting your brother. You do know that, right?"

"I know," she said softly. "I told Nelson they would think he was the murderer."

"We'll find him first," Taylor said. "It's the only way he'll be able to defend his innocence."

Elizabeth looked up at him. "Thank you for believing he's innocent."

"I've seen enough scenarios like this," he said. "It could go either way. But I'm happy to believe your version for the moment. If we get any evidence to the contrary, then we'll deal with that. But, for the moment, we're going on the assumption your brother got caught up in something he shouldn't have, and he's on the run for his life."

Her shoulders sagged. "I could use a drink."

"Coffee or something stronger?"

That burbled a laugh out of her. "Well, both actually. How about coffee with a shot of whiskey in it?"

"Happy to oblige," Nelson said cheerfully.

As it was, they ended up with just coffee. They went to the closest coffee bar, which was beside the pub. Only a dozen people were inside when it probably could hold three or four times that amount.

She took the table in the farthest corner while the men picked up the coffees. When they returned, she looked up at them and asked, "So how do we find out where my brother went?"

"It depends on what Mason has found out," Taylor said.

She looked at him. "What's he looking for now?"

"He's looking into travel methods out of town, airlines, buses, rental cars … At least the ones we can track. If there's any sign Chris took a bus somewhere, we'll start with that."

"And if he went down to the docks and caught a ride with a stranger …"

"Then we hope that stranger is an honest-enough person and won't deep-six your brother out in the ocean," Taylor said bluntly.

Elizabeth gasped.

"When you consider the neighborhood," he said, "people will do something like that for the price of a good meal."

She closed her eyes. "God, I hope not."

"I suggest we head back to our rooms to grab our laptops, go over our notes, figure out what our next step is," Taylor said. "We need to update Mason on this news, and we need to find the connection between Peter and Skunk."

"They were both navy." Elizabeth had her phone in her hand, scrolling through her brother's texts. She held up one. "Here he's talking about the two of them having leave together."

"How long ago?"

"This was months ago," she said, "but I think they were stationed together."

"Good to know," Nelson said. "That definitely means NCIS will be involved."

"How quickly will they be breathing down our necks?"

"Within a few hours probably. At least as soon as we let Mason know, they'll let NCIS know. The cops down here probably won't be in a rush to send Peter's ID onward."

"Then let's go back to the hotel." Elizabeth stood, looking at the two men. "Maybe I should be in the same hotel with you?"

The two men shrugged. "We'll discuss that when we get there," Nelson said.

As they headed out of the coffee shop, they found several of King's men close by.

"Looks like King is involved again."

She looked around for him. "I don't see him anywhere."

"You won't," Taylor said. "It's his men, keeping track of us. They probably already found out about the body."

One of the henchmen stepped forward and addressed Elizabeth. "Is it him?"

She looked up at him and gave a half smile. "No, it isn't. It's a friend of his. Likely the one he saw killed."

The man nodded and stepped back.

As they watched, King's men melted into the shadows and disappeared.

"Wow, that's quite the system they've got here," Elizabeth muttered. Feeling a chill in the air, she wrapped her arms around her chest and followed Nelson and Taylor to their hotel. Hers was right next door with her laptop and notes. "I need to go to my room and grab my stuff. At least my laptop. We might as well compare notes."

"We'll go to your room," Nelson said. He turned to look at Taylor. "Why don't you go up to our room? See if you can get some grub brought up for an early lunch. I'm already hungry again. I'll go with Elizabeth and bring her back."

With Taylor rooting out some food from one of the local vendors, Nelson and Elizabeth headed to her hotel.

She waved at the clerk and headed up to her room, pulling out her key. It didn't work. Frowning, she tried it again.

Nelson took the key from her and checked the door. Realizing something was wrong with the lock, he pulled out the tools from his back pocket and unlocked the door, pushing it open.

Elizabeth gasped as she stared into the room.

"Well?" Nelson said. "Apparently somebody knows you're staying here."

She shook her head. "What difference does it make? I don't have anything here. Why would they care?"

Her bag had been upended, and her laptop was missing. Her paper notepad was still here, but she had torn off her handwritten notes and stuffed them into her cross-body tote bag. She'd wanted to go over them with Nelson and Taylor when she had picked up coffee first thing this morning. She carried her small tablet in her big tote bag too, but she had brought her laptop in case she could get some work done at night.

"They stole my laptop," she wailed. "I need that."

Nelson said, "I think it's still here." He dug in the debris and pulled it loose. "Looks like they checked it out, couldn't get into it and threw it."

"Well, they weren't after items to pawn for money then, as that's a valuable laptop, at least here," she snapped, taking her laptop from his hands. She opened it, turned it on and watched as her login page came up. She typed in her password and got on to her normal pages. "Okay, it appears to be working. But that means this wasn't a burglary. I know it's not the highest-priced laptop, but it's certainly a decent one and would have been worth a couple hundred bucks, if nothing else."

Nelson nodded. "That's what I figured too. They were after information."

"When they couldn't get it, they were either disturbed, or they chose to leave because they were out of time. Or they couldn't find anything of any value."

He motioned at her belongings. "What do you want to do?" He picked up her clothes, laying them all on the bed.

"I want my money back on this room," Elizabeth cried indignantly. "I want a different one. Obviously somebody broke into this one."

Nelson reached for the phone on the night table, called down to the manager and told him her room had been broken into. When he hung up, he turned to look at her. "The manager is coming up."

She nodded. "What do I tell him?"

"The truth," Nelson said cheerfully. He sent off a text as she watched.

"Now who are you contacting?"

"Taylor. Just brought him up-to-date."

Elizabeth sagged onto the bed. "I guess it's a good thing

I didn't bring much with me."

"What about your passport and wallet?"

She tapped her tote bag. "I always keep them close. And the spare money hidden in the false bottom of my bag. If the hotel doesn't have a safe, and I didn't feel the hotel here would have a safe I could depend on, I keep it all with me."

He nodded. "Tickets?"

"Online booking," she said.

"So nothing's been ruined or stolen." Nelson stood, took a look around with his hands on his hips. "Can you tell if anything is missing? That'll be the one of the first things the manager will ask you."

She went through her clothing and carry-on bag, which had some of her work. Her paperwork copies were still there, which had been opened and flipped through, but nobody understood what they meant unless they were a mechanical engineer working for the US government on submarines. She'd brought a few manuals she'd wanted to check out if she got a chance. They were still here too. She walked into the bathroom. Her toiletries were still there, though the lipstick was open; so was the eye shadow. She looked at them with revulsion. "Talk about feeling violated."

Nelson stepped into the bathroom behind her. "I gather you didn't leave them like this?"

Elizabeth shook her head. "What possible reason could they have for opening my makeup?"

"Checking to see if you had anything hidden in there."

She shot him a sideways look. "Do I look like James Bond?"

He laughed. "Not necessarily, but I guess they didn't know what kind of connections you had, or if you had people behind you. Like if you're CIA or FBI or something like that."

Her jaw dropped. "Seriously? Is that what they're looking for? Proof I'm a government agent?"

"I would be looking to see if you had any interesting connections if I was searching your room," Nelson said. "Obviously you don't, and they didn't find anything because you aren't connected in that way, and that'll be the saving grace here."

"Who do you think did this?"

"My first choice would be King," Nelson said with a smile. "Double-checking he didn't get taken in by you. Making sure you are who you say you are."

She sank down at the end of the bed. "There's no trust anymore."

He shook his head. "Hell no. More than that, it makes good sense on his part to have checked you out. But it would have been nice if they hadn't destroyed the place in the meantime."

"Do you think we'll see more of him?"

"Obviously they're taking note of everything we do, so the answer will be *yes*."

"Good," she said. "Then I'll have something to say to him about the way he left my room."

Just then a knock came at the door. Nelson looked at her and said, "That's likely the manager."

She groaned, walked to the door, checked through the peep hole and pulled it open.

The manager came in, took a look around and shook his head. "Was anything taken?"

"No, it doesn't appear to be," she said, "but everything has been tossed. The door is broken. The lock on it is jimmied, and I certainly don't feel safe that somebody got into one of your rooms."

He gave her a half smile. "Normally it doesn't happen. I'll get the lock fixed right away."

"Doesn't matter," Nelson said. "She's checking out."

The manager turned to face him. "Oh, there's no need for that. We'll be happy to upgrade her room and give her a much nicer one."

"She's not safe here." Nelson crossed his arms over his chest. "She won't be able to sleep, knowing the locks are jimmied so easily."

"They aren't," the manager said, examining the lock. "I don't understand how that happened."

"Well, it did happen," Elizabeth said. "So no way am I staying another night here."

The manager appeared to want to argue, but then he nodded. "I'll arrange for your checkout then. It's past the normal time, but, considering the issue, I'll waive any fees."

As he walked out, Nelson snorted. "Good thing."

"I feel like I should get some compensation as it is," Elizabeth said. "But it's not worth the fight. I just want to get out of here."

With his help, they made short work putting the rest of her belongings together and repacking. With one final look around the room, they left. She said, "Presumably the manager will straighten out the rest of the room."

"He can't offer that room again until the lock is fixed."

When they got to the main lobby, she finished checking out. The manager had profuse apologies this time. She just ignored him, accepted the paperwork and left. She was certainly not in a high-end hotel, but she hadn't expected it to be broken into either. She turned to look at Nelson. "So where am I going then?"

"Taylor has already booked the room beside ours. It connects to the one we have," Nelson said. "We can talk easier, and we'll hear if anybody tries to break in again."

That was great news. She wasn't looking forward to sleeping in a new room on her own. "Good," she said. "And then, being closer, we can work together better."

NELSON HAD TO really hold back when he saw her room. He didn't want her to realize just how dangerous this mission had become. Her room was a targeted attack. A warning. He wasn't sure exactly what they were after because there hadn't been anything for them to take. He figured it was King. Now Nelson and Taylor needed to send a message back to leave her alone … or else. He walked into his hotel and checked her in, then moved up to their rooms. He walked into his room with her and opened up the connecting door. He motioned at the adjoining room. "This one is yours."

Elizabeth dropped her bag on an overstuffed chair, and they left the connecting door open between them. Back in his room she sat down at the table with her laptop and said, "Any hope Taylor is coming back with food soon?"

Nelson chuckled. "He'll be back when he gets back."

She looked up at him. "Are you not worried about him? Maybe King wanted to talk to him again."

"I think we need to be more worried that Taylor didn't go and talk to *him*."

She gasped. "He wouldn't do that without you as back-up, would he?"

Nelson gave her a hard smile. "We're not pushovers, and we don't like it when somebody close to us, particularly a defenseless female, has her room searched."

She nodded. "I get that. But I don't want Taylor injured either. Finding one dead body today was more than enough."

"It won't be Taylor next. I think even King realizes he'll bring more down on his head than he wants if anything happens to Taylor or me."

"Why? Do you guys have a badass rule between you?"

"No," he said, "but we understand each other, King and I."

She smiled at that. "I think we're dealing with the opposite meaning here."

He chuckled. "Just relax. Taylor will be here soon." He opened his laptop and sat down across from her.

"I suppose you're telling Mason now."

"I am," he said. "And Mason's talking to NCIS."

"Which means, they'll want to talk to me again."

"Which is good. Any open dialogue is good. And they'll look at this from a whole different perspective now. You might have been a pain in the ass for them before, but they might now see you as a valuable resource."

She shuddered. "That's hardly what I'm looking for."

"We're all just looking for answers," he said. "Keep that in mind."

She smiled. "I don't have anything to do, so, if you don't mind, I'll bury myself in some other work. It'll help calm me down and get my mind off this morning."

"Go for it," he said absentmindedly.

He was flicking through emails from Mason, making sure he hadn't missed anything. With the new Gmail system, so often the emails got stacked up, and it was easy to miss one. Just then his phone rang. He pulled it out. "Mason, what's up?"

"NCIS will be calling you in about an hour. Peter was, indeed, an active seaman. He went missing the same time Skunk did."

"So it is related then?"

"We'll proceed on the assumption it is," Mason said.

"Are they sending somebody here?"

"There'll be one investigator coming later this afternoon. That's what the call is about. They want to meet with you."

"Okay. I'll be prepared." He had no sooner hung up when his phone rang again. He frowned. "So much for an hour from now." He answered it formally and waited for the identification at the other end.

"This is Special Agent Stan Johnson. I'll be there in approximately four and a half hours. I'd like to meet up."

"Pick the place," Nelson said, "and we'll meet then."

"I believe you have Elizabeth Etchings there as well. Is that correct?"

"Yes, that's correct. And Taylor."

"Yes, he's on my list. If the four of us can meet all at once, I can conclude everything in my investigation and get back home."

"It might not conclude that quickly," Nelson said. "We have one death and one missing person."

"Likely connected," the officer said. "We'll sort it out when we speak this afternoon." And he hung up.

Nelson laid the phone on the table. "That didn't go well."

"He thinks they're connected, correct? And my brother's responsible," she said.

There was such a fatalistic tone to her voice. "Correct," he said, "so we don't have much time to find new evidence before he gets here."

"We aren't likely to," she said sadly. "But that doesn't mean we can't continue to find evidence after he leaves. NCIS will come in to cross their *T*s, to dot their *I*s, to make sure they weren't negligent, and then they'll leave."

"Yes, but only on a basic level. They already have somebody to pin it on. And I'm afraid your brother is it." He nodded grimly. "They can do whatever they want to do. We'll find out the truth. I promise you that."

"But how?" She sounded defeated. "As long as my brother runs, he'll never be there to face the accusations."

"I know that," Nelson said. "And the problem is, if we don't have something to help clear Chris of these accusations, as soon as Stan arrives, Chris will be considered guilty. All kinds of shitty events will happen to him then. Sure, he has to be found before he can be punished, but the longer he's missing, the guiltier he'll look."

Elizabeth nodded. "No wonder he ran."

"Right? No one wants to be blamed for something like this. Not to mention that, unless there is forensic evidence on the body that leads to who might have done this, Skunk could still take the fall. He was seen with these men, and it's his word against several men. He's connected to the case no matter what."

"That forensic evidence would be very nice," she said. "But so far we haven't had an easy run of it."

"It's not all bad," he said. "We've found out a fair amount."

She snorted at that.

Just then they heard sounds at the door. They could hear Taylor's voice asking for help. Nelson opened the door to let Taylor in with his bags of takeout. The room filled with warm smells.

Elizabeth hopped to her feet, closed her laptop and made room on the table as Taylor set his burden down. "Now that smells wonderful," she cried out.

He nodded. "We've got to eat to keep our energy and our spirits up."

She chuckled. "I'll take it for energy. I don't know that there's anything to keep my spirits up."

As Nelson moved his laptop, Taylor looked at him. "What's changed?"

"NCIS. The inspector is supposed to meet us in four hours," he said, checking his watch.

"Great," Taylor said. "And I presume they'll take the easy answer and walk away."

"We would hope not," Nelson said, "but you know they're on a budgeted time frame too."

"Not to mention absolutely nothing proves my brother didn't kill his friend."

Taylor opened the bags. "It's what we expected. They'll do an investigation, but we can't blame them if there isn't much to find. The case will stay open, and your brother will be a wanted man. If we have something to prove his innocence, then we can hopefully track him down, bring him in and get his name cleared."

"Sounds like a tall order." She picked up a piece of fried chicken and chomped away at it.

Nelson chuckled. "That's good. Take your temper out on that poor chicken leg," he teased.

She flushed. "I figured it was easier than taking it out on your hand."

He pulled his hand back in mock shock because he'd been reaching for a piece of chicken too.

She laughed. "Go ahead. I share."

The next hour was enjoyable. They ate comfortably and made a plan for the afternoon. It wasn't much of a plan, but, short of hounding the local detectives for information, there wasn't much they could do.

"I wonder if King knows who killed Peter. If he has any evidence, photos, anything like that?" Elizabeth said.

"It's possible, but he won't let it go easily."

"Or cheap, I presume," she snapped. She finished her second piece of chicken and put down the bone, grabbed a napkin and wiped her fingers. "Nothing quite like the comfort of a hot meal."

When Nelson's phone rang yet again, he groaned. "Can't even have a decent meal in peace." He wiped his fingers, answered his phone, and then turned to look at Taylor in surprise. "Absolutely. We can meet in half an hour," he said. He put his phone down. "That was one of King's henchmen. Chelsea's henchmen rather."

"What did he want?" Taylor frowned. "That's not cool that he got your phone number."

"They want to meet, and, no, it isn't." He turned to look at Elizabeth. "Did you have my cell phone number in your room?"

She flushed. "Yes, I did. I wrote it down without thinking," she said. "I do that. I doodle all the time on napkins."

"That explains how they got your number," Taylor said. "But I wonder what King and Queen want?"

"They'll want to deal," Elizabeth said.

"But what'll the price be?" Nelson asked. "He didn't look to be suffering."

"No, not money. But I don't think the henchmen ever have enough," she said.

"No way to know until we show up," he said. "And is it the henchman we're meeting or Chelsea or King?"

"I don't know which one to hope for," she murmured.

"I suggest we talk to King," Nelson stated. "He's the boss, not the second in command, if she's in command of anything."

They continued to eat; then the men cleaned up. When the phone rang again, Nelson looked at it and said, "It's the same number. Yes," he spoke into the phone. "What's up?"

"King wants you to bring the girl to the meeting. Ten minutes. Don't be late."

And before he had a chance to say anything, the call was cut off.

He glanced at Taylor and then Elizabeth. "We're meeting in ten with King, and he wants to make sure you come too."

She shoved her hands in her pockets and nodded. "That's fine. He doesn't scare me."

"He should." Taylor's voice was hard. "Don't be fooled by his affable manner. He is and always will be a kingpin. That means he runs a lot of people's lives, and they do his bidding, from murder to prostitution, whether they like it or not."

That unsettled her. She nodded. "Got it. He's not a nice man."

"No, he's not, but it's possible he might have some leads," Nelson said. "So we'll play the game his way. Until that no longer works for us."

"Do I bring cash?"

"Yes," he said, "but give it to me to carry."

She walked through the connecting door and turned to look back at him. "How much?"

"I hate to ask but maybe a grand?"

She sucked in her cheeks, nodded and continued to the other room.

Nelson looked back at Taylor, asking, "What do you think about that price?"

"I don't think you'll get anything important out of him for less."

"But does he have anything of value?"

"Let's find out," Taylor said. He grabbed the garbage. "No point in leaving it here. We'll dump it on our way out."

The three together, Nelson holding the cash, walked down the stairs and out the front door. At a streetside garbage can, Taylor dumped all their trash into it, and they kept walking.

They ended up at the same hotel they had been to before. It opened for them as soon as they reached the top step. Nobody said a word as they walked in. King once again was at the piano. He looked up and smiled. "You want to come and play the piano with me?"

As if understanding her role, Elizabeth smiled. "I'd love to."

At the piano she sat down beside him. He played a set of scales. She matched her finger movements to his, and together they ran the scales, laughing.

Taylor watched, but Nelson stared. She seemed so natural and comfortable in King's presence that it blew Nelson away. Nothing seemed to faze her. Whether that was good or bad, he didn't know. They waited until the recital was over.

King looked up and said, "We hear you found someone."

"His name was Peter," Elizabeth said quietly, her fingers still lightly stroking the ivory keys. "He was a friend of my brother's."

"Do you think your brother killed him?"

"No," she said. "I think he watched his friend get murdered."

"That's what the word is on the streets," King said.

"We're waiting to see if the body holds any forensic evidence that will help us identify his murderers," Nelson said.

King looked at him directly. "My men didn't have anything to do with it."

"Good," Nelson said, "and we didn't either."

King didn't say anything for a long moment. He appeared to be thinking. "One of my men saw something."

"What did he see?" Nelson asked.

"A face," King said. "One he didn't recognize. He thought he'd seen it around in the bars, but he didn't know him by name," he added.

Elizabeth looked up at him. "Any chance you have somebody who can draw a picture of him?"

King shook his head. "No, he would probably recognize him, but no way he'll look through photo books down at the cop station." His tone was dry.

Elizabeth laughed, her voice light and cheerful. "Of course not. I wouldn't want to do that either."

That surprised King; he ended up in a roar of chuckles. As he finally calmed down, he said, "I do like you."

"I like you too. And I'll like you more if you can help us figure out what happened."

"My guy only saw a face, but that's because he wasn't heading out to the end of the wharfs. He was heading back toward one of the bars."

"Which bar would that be?" Nelson asked. "Any chance it would have a security feed which your person could look at?"

"I own the bar," King said. "And I do have the security feed. He hasn't looked at it though, to see if the face is on it."

"Will you let Nelson look?" Elizabeth asked, her voice guileless and innocent.

King's gaze went from her to Nelson. "For a price."

Elizabeth stiffened, then nodded. "I guess that's the world we live in, isn't it?"

King nodded. "It is, indeed, little one. It is, indeed."

"And for this price what is it we get?" Taylor asked, speaking up for the first time.

"My man will go through the feed and see if he can identify the person."

"And can we get a copy of the feed?"

King seemed to consider that, then shrugged. "Sure. Why not? It won't help much."

"No, but identification will give us one piece of the puzzle and finding other associates will allow us to find more puzzle pieces."

King nodded. "As long as my men don't get involved."

"But you know as well as I do, if they had nothing to do with it, it doesn't matter."

"You can have part of the feed," King compromised.

Nelson chuckled. "Okay, as long as we agree on the same piece. We want all the feed that has any images of this guy and any of the men he appears to be eating, drinking, talking or hanging around with."

"As long as I okay any other activities being shown on the same feeds."

"Agreed. When can this happen?"

"When can you pay?"

"Depends on the price," Nelson said.

"It depends on what it's worth," King said with a calculating tone of voice.

"It's worth a lot," Elizabeth said. "It's my brother. But that doesn't change the fact I don't have a ton of money."

"But you do have enough to pay something?"

"Business is business, so, yes," she said. "I can scrounge up some. I just can't scrounge up much."

He nodded, his fingers going to the ivories.

She picked up the tune he played, playing the exact same refrain on the lower octave.

He laughed. "I do miss having somebody to play the piano with."

"I don't have a piano at home," she said. "But this reminds me how much I would enjoy it."

"You should get one," he said.

"Maybe I will when I get back, after this mess is over," Elizabeth said with a slight incline of her head. "It might help me deal with the trauma of being here and seeing what life is like outside of the comfort of my own space."

"True enough. You probably live in a lily-white tower and don't deal with the outside world."

"I deal with it enough," she said. "But, when you start losing family members, and you're down to the last one, it gets a bit dicey."

"One thousand bucks," he said.

She gasped.

King sent her a sideways look. "That's cheap. Normally I charge ten times that."

She looked at him wide-eyed. "Wow. I'm in the wrong business."

And that set him off to huge guffaws of laughter. When

he finally stopped, Nelson stepped forward with the money in his hand, a clip around it. "That's all she brought."

"Good," he said, "then it was the right figure." He put the money in his pocket and motioned at two men standing nearby. "He'll take you into the security room where the monitor is. You'll run through it, and he'll see if he can find the man he thought he saw. If so, we'll pick out the pieces of the film you want copies of."

Nelson headed toward the room, then stopped and looked back at Elizabeth.

King waved at him. "Go. Your girlfriend will be here when you get back. We'll just play the piano together for a while." And, with that, he played Beethoven's Fifth Symphony.

With a delighted laugh, Elizabeth dove in and played with him.

Nelson shook his head, looked at Taylor, who just shrugged at him, and the two men walked into the security room. They were taking a chance leaving her, but they were also taking a chance going into this room themselves. At the moment Nelson figured Elizabeth was safer than they were.

They stepped forward, and the door closed behind them.

CHAPTER 7

"T HEY WON'T HURT them, will they?" she asked King.

"Nah," King said. "We only break bones when people are uncooperative."

"Good," she said. "Because I wouldn't want to stay up all night and look after them. I make a lousy nurse."

And again he burst out laughing. "My goodness," he said, "you are a breath of fresh air."

"Maybe," she said, "it's from living in the ivory tower."

As soon as they finished Beethoven, she ran her fingers in a rendition of Mozart. Then, in a completely different move, she played John Denver and rolled into a Stevie Nicks number.

He sat back and listened, watching her fingers. "How is it you don't have a piano at home?"

"I work too much. I don't have much space, and these are very expensive instruments," she said.

He was silent for a moment and then said, "You're right. A good one is. But you're very talented."

She shook her head. "No, not like so many are. My piano teacher was always complaining that I didn't practice enough. The problem was, I wanted to play the songs in my heart, not the songs in *her* heart. It is such a joy to play again," she admitted. Her fingers flew across the keyboard, as if they had a mind of their own. They swung from an Adele number into reggae and then into jazz. As she played the jazz piece, she slowed and closed her eyes, letting her body sway to the music as she played.

Finally her song ran down, and she dropped her fingers to her lap, still in a trance. She stared at the keyboard and then over at King and smiled. She wiped the tears from her eyes. "Thank you," she said. "That was lovely."

He stared at her in surprise. And something else too.

Just then the door opened, and Taylor and Nelson returned, their faces grim.

"We found him," Nelson said. "We need you to look at the feed to see which pieces we can have."

King walked toward him. Elizabeth slipped off the bench and ran toward Nelson. He reached out and caught her up close to him. "Do you recognize him?" she asked.

He shook his head. "No, but we should run through it through our databases with some good facial recognition programs."

"The question is, whether he's a local?" she said. "Or if he's a seaman?"

"He's a seaman," King said, looking at the monitor. "He's not from around here." He went through several of the film stills and then pointed out which ones they could have. Then the henchmen printed off the images. And they cut part of the video and emailed it to Nelson.

With prints in hand, Nelson, Taylor and Elizabeth walked toward the front door. On impulse, Elizabeth turned, smiled up at King, sitting at the piano, and she said, "Thanks for a wonderful piano session."

His face gentled, and he nodded. "You're more than welcome."

As they stepped out the door, and it closed behind them,

Nelson wrapped her up tight and said, "Stay on guard."

She almost stumbled. She'd been in a happy daze from the music. The reality of what they were doing now wasn't something she had expected. In a whisper she asked, "What is it you expect?"

"While you were having fun playing with him," Nelson said, "the woman who accosted us the first evening looked to be incredibly jealous. And what you don't know is, she stood in the far corner behind you, glaring daggers at you. She wasn't there when we came back out. I wouldn't be at all surprised if she isn't ahead of us somewhere, looking to teach you a lesson."

Elizabeth stiffened. "I forgot about her."

"I know," Nelson said. "But I'm not kidding when I say these people are serious about every detail. And, if Chelsea thought King was sweet on you, or that you were trying to steal him from her, you would not survive the night."

"We're not far from the hotel." She glanced around. "So hopefully we're safe."

Just then Taylor said, "On your left."

Nelson's arm tightened around Elizabeth, then he shoved her behind him as he pivoted toward the threat.

Elizabeth peered over both men's shoulders to see two of the henchmen and indeed a hard-looking female in front of them.

"You keep her away from here," Chelsea spat. "I don't give a fuck how high up in the white tower she is. She's history if I ever see her again. Do you hear me?"

Elizabeth wanted to defend herself, but the men were shoulder to shoulder, keeping her behind them. "I didn't mean to upset you," she called over their shoulders.

Chelsea snorted. "You didn't. But I protect what's mine.

And King is mine."

"I just bought him an hour of peace through playing the piano," Elizabeth said. "Music is something he doesn't get enough of."

"What are you talking about?" Chelsea snarled. "He's on that damn piano all the time."

"That's because it brings him peace," she said. "He tries to lose himself in the music but often can't get deep enough to be transported out of his normal world."

The men separated ever-so-slightly. Elizabeth could see the confusion on Chelsea's face.

But almost as quickly it shut down, and she growled, "Get her out of here now. And I don't want her coming back to see him anymore. Better if she disappeared." On those words she blended into the shadows.

Elizabeth reached up and gripped Nelson's arm. "But I didn't do anything to make her feel like she was being replaced."

"You're missing a piece of the puzzle," Taylor said.

Nelson wrapped her up close, and this time Taylor walked behind them.

"What piece of the puzzle am I missing?" Elizabeth asked Taylor.

"What you're missing is the fact that King takes what King wants. And if he decides he wants you to play the piano with him, as far as he's concerned, you're there for the grabbing."

"What if I don't want to be grabbed?"

Nelson looked down at her. "Remember? That's the point about not understanding this world. He controls a lot of people. He controls prostitutes and murderers. People do things on his behalf because they're too terrified not to. So, if he asks them to kidnap you, then they would do so. Not only that, they would do it with a smile on their face because it would be making him happy. And, after that, if he kept you, it would be in whatever capacity he wanted you in."

Elizabeth could feel the joy of the evening drain away, and her stomach clenched in panic. "I was too nice, wasn't I?"

Nelson sighed. "I hate to say it, because there shouldn't be such a thing as too nice, but yes, you were too nice."

She groaned and flung up her hands. "What am I supposed to do? I can't stay on guard all the time. It's not who I am."

"Of course not," Nelson said. "But I would be happy if you never saw King again. Sometimes I wonder if the reason we weren't called there was just so he could visit with you again."

"He did give us a good price for that video, or was that all part of the sales pitch?" Elizabeth turned to look at Taylor. "Right. Maybe that was just all part of the same slimy deal."

"Doesn't matter," Nelson said, "because we did get something useful. And now we have a lead on the man who was followed from the dock after Peter was murdered. If we can identify him, we'll identify those he hung out with."

"That's perfect then," she said. "Let's get back to the hotel and track down who this person is."

"We can't do that," Nelson said. "That'll go through NCIS, the local cops and Mason."

"Why Mason? It seems like you're always in touch with him anyway."

"He's the one who got me assigned to this," he said. "And his wife has an incredible computer system at home that can access all kinds of government software."

"Legally?"

"She has very high clearance," Taylor said with a laugh. "And she'll use it every once in a while to help us out."

"That makes her a very good person to know," Elizabeth said in admiration. "Wouldn't it be nice to think that was something we could all have access to?"

When they reached their room, it still smelled of fish tacos and fried chicken. "Is there more?" Elizabeth asked.

"We only ate the chicken," Taylor said. "There are lots of tacos. Help yourself."

"Is there anything else we have planned for this evening?"

"After our meeting with NCIS Special Agent Johnson, no. Depends on what we come up with. At the moment, nothing. Sit down and eat."

"Maybe I will then." Elizabeth grabbed a box. "Do we serve it or am I just eating out of the box?"

"Eat out of the box," Nelson said. "We are big enough to share. And we're a little short on dishes."

"Got it," she said with a laugh. She sat down on the bed, picked up the TV remote and clicked on a news station with a story on the body found at the wharf. There were just enough pictures to realize it was the body they'd found. She could speak some Spanish but not fluently, still, this report was hard not to understand. Hating to, but knowing she didn't dare miss any tidbits of news that would help find her brother, she turned up the volume. Both men came around so they could watch too. There was film of the body being removed from the water. She noted herself and Nelson down by the dock. They weren't identifiable that far away, but it was the same location and scene. "I wonder who gave the news station that footage," she asked.

"That's not a bad question to ask," Nelson said. "We also need to figure out if they have found out anything we don't already know."

But there wasn't anything new, until the cameras panned away. Elizabeth jumped forward. "Did you see that?"

"See what?" both men asked.

She tried to hit the Stop button, but of course it was live TV, not a recorded movie or anything she could pause. "Damn it," she said. "I thought it was that man down at the bar, the one we went to King for and got the stills of."

They held up the picture, and she shrank. "I hardly had time to look, but, yes, it looked like him."

"Interesting," Nelson said. "Because that would mean he went back to the scene of the crime. Not back to the ship—if he was a seaman too."

"Quite likely he's telling his other seamen buddies what's happening," Taylor said. "Somebody had to stay behind to see if anybody finds the body. The longer that body stays gone, the less forensic evidence they will find. Imagine if it was six months later."

"Right," Elizabeth said. "But we found the poor man late ourselves. It's been a week in the water, which I guess is pretty nasty in terms of what happens to the body, but there might still be something usable to find."

"Which means this guy is telling the rest of his buddies what happened."

"Definitely. And we know who his buddies are," Elizabeth snapped. "Seamen aboard Chris's ship." With the news done, she flipped through the other channels, looking for something to take her mind off things. She went past a murder mystery and settled on a chick-flick. When she brought it up, she grinned. "This could be good."

The two men looked at the TV and groaned. "Seriously?"

"Hey, what's wrong with it?"

"It's a chick-flick, for women," Nelson said. "Hardly guy content."

"What do you guys want to watch?" She glared at them. "The sports channel, I suppose?"

"Yes," Nelson said, "that would be a good answer. Or a good fantasy movie or something action-based would be nice."

"Agreed," Taylor said. "However, we're working over here, so, if that'll help you get through the rest of the afternoon until our meeting, then fine."

Elizabeth nodded. "Good, because I want to watch it." She hit the remote's Start button. With half an ear, she listened to the two discuss what they were doing, what they'd found, but she quickly lost interest because it seemed like they were doing nothing but sending emails and looking at maps. Finally, when the show ended, she rolled over on the bed. "So what's next?"

"We're waiting to hear from everyone," Nelson said. "So the investigation's at a standstill."

"Did any of you think to follow my brother's money?"

"I believe the cops are on that. They said something about his credit cards hadn't been used, and his bank account hadn't been accessed."

"Oh," she said in a small voice. "Here I was thinking it was a great avenue to consider."

"It's one of the first things law enforcement does," Taylor said. "Everybody needs money."

"He has multiple bank accounts," she said. "So I don't

know if law enforcement is checking every one of them."

"You know what banks?"

Elizabeth nodded. "Sure. We shared a couple. It's a good way to move money back and forth between us as needed." She logged on to her bank account, showing them the two accounts. "This one we've had for a long time. You can see there's almost nothing in it. But this one, when I needed money at school, he used to drop funds into it for me, and I did the same when he ran into some trouble. He was traveling in Europe at one point and ran into difficulty when he crashed his bike. I put money into that account so he could access it over there."

"Bring up the details on that account, will you?"

She clicked on it and then gasped in surprise. "Money was taken out two days ago."

"How much money?" Nelson asked.

"Two thousand dollars," she said in amazement. She turned to the men. "That means he's alive, doesn't it?" she asked hopefully.

"It's definitely some of the best news we've had since this began," Nelson said. He checked the account over her shoulder. "He hasn't accessed any of that money for months beforehand."

"No, he usually just keeps it as another source of income if he needs it."

"There's still five grand left, so he'll be fine for a while," Nelson said. He looked over at Taylor. "We should tell Mason about that. We might find the ATM machine it was taken from and get a shot of the person who removed the money. That would let us know if it was Skunk or some asshole who stole his bank card and password."

Elizabeth wrinkled up her face. "I was ignoring that possibility."

"We can't," Taylor said. "No blind spots here. It's the only way we'll survive this. Full awareness and consider all options."

Nelson added quietly, his fingers busy on the phone, "Unfortunately the chances of getting any feeds from anywhere around here is likely nil. The country is not known for their IT skills or security concerns, and aren't as advanced as what we're used to. But I'm texting Mason to see if anything is available."

She sagged and nodded.

★

ELIZABETH STEPPED OUT of the way so Nelson could sit down. He checked the other bank account. "Nothing here, but I have the transaction number written down." He texted the information to Mason. **Not sure who else you want me to contact.**

The answer came back immediately. **Give us ten.**

Nelson dropped his phone on the table and walked over to the kitchenette where he grabbed a glass of water. "They'll get back to us in a few minutes." He glanced over at Elizabeth. "Does your brother have another house? Any place you know he would go to ground?"

"Just my place," she said softly. "He had an apartment but sold it when he joined the navy. I told him to keep it so he'd have a place to come home to, but he just shrugged and said he didn't want the responsibility or the headache when he would be traveling the world. He figured he'd have to call on me to deal with renters. Headaches all the time. And I admit, I appreciated that because I didn't have a whole lot of free time in my life then either."

"Have you two always been close?"

"Pretty close," she said. "Growing up, there was just the two of us. I helped him through many drunken years where he used to go out and party all the time. He'd wake up, spewing his guts out the next morning because he was still drunk."

"I remember a few of those days too," Nelson said. "I'm still surprised he went into the navy."

"Yes, and no," Elizabeth said. "You know how he idolized our father. But he could never quite make the grade as far as our father was concerned. And that's where the problem was. When Chris thought about it, he really did want to go into the navy. He had hoped that maybe, just maybe, our father would finally admire his choices."

"How sad is that?" Nelson asked. "Go into the navy because that's what *you* want." He shook his head. "Not because that's what you think your father wants."

"It doesn't matter because he did want to and loved his time there. It was more a bid for respect. That's the sad part. I told him to enjoy the years he had, and, if he came to a point when he was ready to leave, he could leave."

At her terminology both looked at her.

"I didn't mean he could just walk away. I meant he could do whatever he had to do to legally leave."

The men turned their gazes back to their laptops.

Nelson said, "It's almost time for the meeting."

Mason texted back. **No camera on ATM. Transaction has been identified to location but no other information available.**

Nelson sighed and told the others.

"You two go on now if you want," Taylor said. "I want to be here to run communications. I'm going to send out some questions to NCIS on their father and to check for forensic information on the body."

"Good. That's what I should be doing too," Nelson said. "I shouldn't even be thinking about leaving. I'm just feeling a little closed in."

"Understood," Taylor said. "Waiting is always the hard part. But I'll be right behind you. Give me about ten minutes."

CHAPTER 8

I T FELT WEIRD heading out in the hottest part of the day this time. It was late afternoon, and they were out in a seedy part of town. And besides, it wasn't like Elizabeth could forget Chelsea's sudden appearance last time. Even the reminder had her walking closer to Nelson.

In a smooth and natural movement, he wrapped an arm around her shoulders. "Are you okay?"

She nodded, murmuring, "I am. Just I particularly don't want to meet someone right now.'

"Or anytime," Nelson said. "Particularly given your interactions up until now."

She winced at that. The afternoon held a deep mugginess, the smell off the ocean stronger than normal. She usually loved the salty tang, but today it had a sourness to it.

They walked in silence. But the air was filled with loud music, reeking of alcohol, drugs and cheap sex. They made their way to the coffeeshop and the far back corner where they were supposed to meet Special Agent Stan Johnson.

"Why here?" she murmured, as they sat down.

"Our request," Nelson said. "Otherwise, it would be in an office and likely not until Monday. This way we share information—" She snorted at that, but he continued, "And it's over faster."

"Okay, that makes sense." She was cheered to know she

329

was in a very different situation than the last time she spoke to NCIS. Nelson and Taylor had supported her every decision, even when they hadn't been the best choices. She appreciated that. "Thank you."

Nelson slid her a sideways look. "For what?"

"For working with me and not treating me as a useless featherbrained female," she admitted. "I know I haven't been the easiest to live with, work with. But it's because I care about Chris so much."

He squeezed his arm tighter around her, tucking her up closer. "You've been fine," he said. "Sure, we weren't too happy when you showed up, but we adjusted. We all want the same thing—Chris home safe and sound."

"Exactly." She beamed at him. "Anyway, thank you."

A tall lean man arrived before Nelson could answer. It wasn't hard to identify the austere look on the man's face. Nelson stood and quietly introduced themselves. "Taylor should be here in ten minutes."

"Call me Stan," said the stranger with a brief smile as he sat down beside Nelson. A waitress came, took their order and disappeared. And returned almost immediately with their coffees. Elizabeth really didn't want caffeine at this hour but ...she might need it to get through this.

Stan pulled out his tablet, set up the keyboard and said, "What do you have for me?"

She stayed quiet as Nelson filled Stan in on what they'd learned about Chris's disappearance. Nelson kept the discussion minimal regarding King and Chelsea. Elizabeth found that interesting. Yet it made sense as NCIS needed to know some stuff, but did they need to know it all? How much was enough? She was glad Nelson talked to Stan, although she knew her turn would come.

There were several questions back and forth.

"And what say you, Elizabeth? Why do you think Chris is missing?"

She stiffened. His words were fine but the tone? "Because he got into trouble he couldn't get out of easily."

"What kind of trouble?"

"Seeing something he shouldn't have seen kind." She kept her tone cool, level. The last thing she wanted to do was lose it on him. It wouldn't help Chris's case. Yet, she knew she wouldn't hold back if Stan threw accusations around.

"What information do you have for us?" Nelson asked.

The NCIS officer shrugged and said, "Not much more than you. He's missing in unusual circumstances in which a murder has occurred. Obviously it doesn't look good for him. However, we're still looking into his case." He lifted his head and looked directly at Elizabeth. "We won't jump to conclusions, but the longer he's missing, the worse it looks for him, so if you have any way to contact him and to convince him to return, it will help all of us."

She opened her mouth to snap at him but felt Nelson gently grip her hand and squeeze it in warning. "I'm more concerned that my brother is a second victim here," she said flatly. "I'd just as soon he did kill his friend than be found floating like we found Peter. But"—she leaned forward—"I know he'd never do that without a hell of a good reason, so I'll keep looking for him and for the truth."

She stood. "If you have nothing else to offer us, and obviously we have shared what we know with you, I'll say good night." And she turned and headed out to the street. She didn't know if Nelson would follow, neither did she care. She was done.

NELSON STOOD IMMEDIATELY. "I guess we're done here."

Stan stared at the door, where Elizabeth had disappeared. "She's pretty touchy."

"With good reason," Nelson said. "No one wants a family member, particularly one who isn't here to defend himself, accused of murder."

"I didn't accuse anyone." Stan was quick to defend himself.

"No, but you certainly implied it." Nelson dropped his card on the table and said, "That's how you can get a hold of us, if you have more questions. And we'd like to know what's going on with her father's death."

Stan's face thinned. "Nothing. We suspect he either took his own life or got so depressed he mistook his medication. She's seeing shadows where none exist. He's completed a distinguished career and we're not going to mar it with anything other than death from a preexisting condition."

"And you don't believe he was helped to his death?" Nelson asked searching Stan's face. But the look of surety convinced him that at least in this Stan believed in the facts as they stood. "Not in any way."

"Good, then we don't have to worry about his death being connected to Chris's disappearance."

"No you don't."

On that note and feeling better, Nelson exited in time to see Elizabeth cross the street at the end of the block. Taylor joined him from the shadows and laughed. "When's she mad, she can move."

"She can." Nelson laughed too. "She held it together nicely in there though. I was afraid she'd get emotional and blow up."

The two men jogged to catch up, just in time to see

Queen and her two henchmen making a move on Elizabeth. Nelson and Taylor both took off at a stealthy run. Queen was closest to Elizabeth, and Elizabeth was completely unaware of what was going on behind her. She was so angry still, which made her clueless to her surroundings.

Nelson and Taylor each took down one of Queen's henchmen with a single powerful chop to the neck that laid them out and didn't even stop Nelson or Taylor or hinder their strides. Covering a few more feet, they overpowered Queen, who immediately started yelling for help.

Elizabeth gasped and turned. "What is going on?"

Taylor grabbed Chelsea's arms and not very gently yanked them behind her, causing her pain if she remained still and even more pain if she moved. She finally settled down.

Nelson bent over her, nose to nose. "You don't listen so well, do you?" She tried to spit in his face, but he pulled her arms tighter making her gasp in pain. "I don't believe in hitting women. Not even if they are hitting me. I will talk them down or subdue them, like Taylor here is doing with you. But you keep crossing the line. So next time I won't hold back. You've threatened Elizabeth one too many times."

When she opened her mouth, Taylor twisted her arms. All that came out was a cry for help.

"So listen up. We won't hurt you if you leave us the hell alone. Agreed?" He stared at her.

She seemed to be considering her options.

"Too long," Nelson said and pinched the nerve at the back of her neck, lowering her to the ground as she dealt with the paralysis. She'd be fine but it would stop her from coming behind them. She lay beside her henchmen on the sidewalk.

"Now what?" Taylor asked.

"Leave them here. It's our message to the locals. And it's a humiliation to her. I just hope it takes her a while to regain full motion." Nelson turned to Elizabeth. "And I know you were mad, but you can't walk around here all caught up in your mind. You need your wits about you. Understand?"

She seemed flustered, looking at both of the guys.

"It's okay. You've had enough thrown at you for one day. Let's get to our rooms." And he again put one arm around her shoulders and pulled her near. They were quiet the rest of the way there.

The three were together as they walked into their hotel rooms.

"After that less-than-stellar meeting," Elizabeth said, "I'm thinking about getting ready for bed and putting the TV on in my room and watching a show until I fall asleep."

Nelson nodded. "Go then. We'll leave the connecting door open. Just make sure all the other doors are locked." But he hadn't once checked her room since they'd come back. With one hand up, he stepped in front of her before she went in the connecting room and searched the other bedroom. He checked that the doors were locked and that the glass balcony doors and windows were also locked. He smiled with a nod. "You're clear."

She grabbed her nightclothes and headed into the bathroom. Nelson went back into his side but stuck close to where the connecting door was.

"You going to worry about her all night?" Taylor asked.

"Probably," Nelson said. "I'm really not sure what to think about King."

"I was thinking the same thing. I'm not sure he's ready to replace his ladylove, if that's the woman we keep getting accosted by, but I think King finds Elizabeth something special, unique in his world. A lot softer than he's used to. And she certainly made him laugh."

Nelson remembered the amount of amusement King had seemed to find in their conversation. "I think she surprised him several times. I think it's been a long time since he remembered the softness in life."

"If he ever had any," Taylor said, not looking up from his laptop keyboard. "Sometimes guys like that are born in the gutter, raised in the gutter, and never climb out of it. Who knows where he learned to play the piano. Maybe self-taught?"

"Good point," Nelson said.

The bathroom door opened on Elizabeth's side. She came out wearing short boxers and a camisole that clung to every inch. Nelson swallowed and forced his gaze away. He glanced at Taylor and noted that knowing look in his eyes. "Don't say it," he said.

"I don't have to say anything," Taylor said. "You're already saying it all yourself."

"I hear you. It just took me by surprise," Nelson said.

"You shouldn't have been surprised," Taylor said. "You've been heading in this direction for a while."

"Hardly. I only truly met her yesterday."

"Maybe," Taylor said. "But I think you recognized something happening on a different level."

"Nothing happens this fast," Nelson said. "I don't believe in love at first sight. Lust, yes, but not the other."

"I think Mason's group has made most of us take another look at our beliefs in that department," Taylor said.

"Hah. I've been ignoring all those rumors," Nelson said. "Besides, we're on a job."

At that, Taylor really laughed. "As were every other one of the men when they fell. Whether it was a job, a mission sanctioned by the military, or it was a personal mission, like what we're currently doing, it was always some type of job when the men met their match."

"I hate those terms, *met their match* and especially *fell*," Nelson said without rancor. "*Fell* makes it sound like the men are less than what they were. Whereas a relationship should make them more than they are."

"Oh, they are definitely more now," Taylor said. "But I think the initial meet is a complete and total wipeout of expectations because you see something that hadn't ever occurred to you that you wanted or needed."

Nelson frowned at him. "That doesn't make a lot of sense, and I'm pretty sure we all know what our type is by now."

"I don't think so," Taylor said. "I'm keeping an open eye. When you think about it, what you think you want versus what you know you want, or what is actually better for you, can often be at very different ends of the scale. We don't always know ourselves as well as we'd like to think we do."

"Maybe," Nelson said. "But I'm not heading in that direction."

Just then Elizabeth walked around the bed and bent over to put away her clothes. He swallowed hard as the boxers rode up perfectly rounded cheeks and very long legs. With a muffled oath he got up off his chair and stormed across to the bed where he threw himself down and grabbed the remote. "I need something to do," he said.

"Definitely—if you want to get any sleep tonight," Taylor said with a chuckle. "But nice to know you're as affected as the rest of us."

"Are you interested?" Nelson stared at Taylor with a frown. "I didn't think she was your type."

"She isn't," Taylor said. "But that doesn't mean I'm not interested. The thing is though, she's interested in you, not me."

"Hah," Nelson said. "Not likely. I'm just here helping her find out what happened to her brother."

"More than that. Every chance she gets, it's you she goes to. And you might want to acknowledge that it's always you wrapping your arms around her."

"Sure, but it's better if we appear as a couple. Gives me an excuse to be here and gives her my protection as being my girlfriend." Nelson knew it was a feeble excuse. There was really no better answer he could give. And it seemed foolish, but he wasn't quite ready to acknowledge it, although she had felt wonderful in his arms, and no way could he look at her barely clad body without having a physical reaction. It would make life very difficult for him tonight. Just the thought of her sweetness lying close to him was enough to make his body react. He took several deep calming breaths.

"Would it be so bad?"

Confused for a moment as he was caught up in his own thoughts, he turned to look at Taylor. "Would what be so bad?"

"If something did happen between the two of you?"

Instantly, all the work he'd done to calm down his body was like it had never happened. He took a deep breath. "I'm not into one-night stands anymore."

"Nothing one-night stand about this," Taylor said. "You both live in the same town, you both have a lot of similar interests. You know there's no reason you couldn't have a relationship."

"That's true," Nelson said, "if, back at home, she still wants anything to do with me. But, while we're on a job, no."

"Ah, we're back to being honorable again then, are we?"

"I'm always honorable," Nelson said quietly. "Taking advantage of a woman while she's desperate for answers, looking for help, that's not my idea of a relationship."

At that, Taylor nodded. "I agree totally. But she'll be home in a few days. You might want to follow up on the advantage you have now."

"Well, if it's an advantage," Nelson said, "it's still not something fair then, is it?"

Taylor looked at him in exasperation. "Stop being so nitpicky. There's obviously an attraction between the two of you. You'd be fools to not see where it went when we go home."

"Possibly," Nelson said. "And I'll keep your comments under advisement." He turned back to the TV and tried to bury himself in a horror movie. It suited his mood right now.

CHAPTER 9

ELIZABETH LAY IN bed, wondering if the men had any idea how easily their words carried. Or were they speaking deliberately loud so she did hear? No, they weren't the type to play games. At least she didn't think so. She remembered her brother talking about Nelson years ago, being a bit of a wild card and a definite ladies' man.

She could see both in him, but maybe it was the navy that had made a man out of him, not just a playboy. There was something extra about the package that definitely appealed. Dark hair, square jaw, and those piercing blue eyes. How was it he had longer eyelashes than she did?

So not fair.

In the background she could hear them talking, but their voices were softer as if they were either getting into bed themselves or suddenly aware she might hear them.

Her night was not ending the way her day had begun— it was better. There was something comforting about not being alone right now. Especially after seeing her other hotel room trashed.

The men's voices picked up. She sat up to listen. Then realized they were talking about tomorrow's schedule. She lay back down quietly, feeling like she was eavesdropping, but she didn't care.

It was their fault. She'd had the television on and was

puttering around the room getting ready for bed when she heard their conversation start. It was all she could do to not rush in and hear the half of what she was missing. But some of it stuck with her. Most of it she agreed with. Certainly the fact that there was an attraction between the two of them.

And, yes, she did turn to Nelson every time she could. And he did wrap her up in his arms often. And maybe it was because of the job, but she also felt something much more, something much deeper was between them. And, if he wanted to pick it up when they got home, she was on board with that. In fact, she looked forward to it.

She also agreed it was a good thing not to start something like this while they were both dealing with difficult emotions, particularly her. That didn't stop her heart or mind from heading in the direction.

And her body? Well, it had a mind of its own.

There was a warm glow around her as she lay here. It had been a while since her last relationship, and that one was more of an office romance. Two people thrown together, who liked each other, and things had progressed from there. But it hadn't had that same glow to it that she currently felt.

She turned out the light, eager to go to sleep with hopefully happy dreams. Tomorrow was a whole new day. And maybe, just maybe, they'd get some answers. Time was running out. She didn't know how long she could stay, but she knew the men only had two more nights. Then she'd decide if she was going to stay longer.

She closed her eyes and sent out a whisper to her brother. *Stay safe. Stay alive. We're coming.*

NELSON HAD ALWAYS been a light sleeper, but whoever

walked down their hallway right now needed to work on his technique. He attempted to be stealthy but was anything but.

Nelson slipped out from under the bedcovers, turning to look at Taylor. Taylor's eyes gleamed in the darkness. He also slid out of bed.

The footsteps went past their door and slowed. Nelson pulled on his jeans as he tiptoed across the opening to Elizabeth's bedroom. He went to her bedside, clapped a hand over her mouth and whispered in her ear, "Wake up."

Her eyes opened wide, but she didn't struggle. She just lay here and stared at him.

With her ear still close to his mouth, he whispered, "Looks like you've got company." He could feel the shudder work through her. "Know that I'm here," he said. "I'll stay down on this side of the bed. Taylor is closing the door between us. But it's not shutting him out. It'll be slightly ajar so he can push it open and get in here."

Again she didn't say anything. She stared, her eyes huge, the pupils almost indiscernible in the darkness.

He heard somebody at her door. Elizabeth shifted so she could watch it. He held her close, gave her a hug and said, "I need you to pretend to be asleep."

She nodded.

He released his hand over her mouth, pulled the covers up, gave her a squeeze on the shoulder and whispered, "I'm here. Remember that."

She settled as if his words were finally drifting into her psyche. With her head back on the pillow, she closed her eyes, facing the door.

He knew that was instinct. Nobody wanted to be turned away from the door, waiting for that attack to come. As long as she didn't open her eyes and give it away.

He also couldn't take the chance that somebody would just stand at the door and shoot her. The intruder was still working on the door. He crept past her bed, up against the wall where the bathroom was. They had to come in at least enough to see her. That should allow him time to grab any weapon.

He held a finger up to his lips as the door finally went *click*. Elizabeth slammed her eyes closed. Her body, although tense, appeared relaxed. He held his breath, not daring to breathe as the door swung open.

A little bit of light from the hallway filtered inside. But it wasn't a fancy hotel where subdued running lights were out there. It was more of a dim shadow from the one remaining bulb still on.

The door was closed behind the intruder. Soft footsteps crept forward and then halted. He wasn't sure if the person's eyes had adjusted and could see Elizabeth or not, but, sure enough, an arm came up. An arm holding a gun.

Nelson didn't waste any time. He grabbed the arm, shoving it upward, and, with his right hand, connected with the jaw of the person who had come into the room. He had expected a fight. He had expected something much more solid. Instead the person completely collapsed on the ground. *Unconscious.*

Taylor burst into the room and turned on the lights. And there on the floor was King's ladylove. They looked down at the gun, then back at Chelsea.

Elizabeth got up from the bed, walked over and stared down at her. "Why would she do this?" she whispered.

"I warned you," Nelson said. "She didn't like the attention King was paying you."

Elizabeth wrapped her arms around her chest and, realizing how little she wore, grabbed her bathrobe.

Nelson was sorry to see her pull it on, covering such a soft silky material that clung to all her curves, making her even more seductive. She went to him and snuggled up close. He wrapped an arm around her, remembering Taylor's earlier words. Still, he held her closer as she snuggled in deeper.

"Now what do we do?"

"We need to get word to King," Taylor said. "He needs to know what his ladylove is up to."

"Will he kill her?" Elizabeth asked.

Both men turned to look at her.

Elizabeth shrugged. "Okay. I get it. She tried to kill me, but it was out of jealousy, or maybe it was out of self-preservation."

"What do you mean by that last bit?" Nelson asked.

She tilted her head to look up at him. "If King's such an ugly character, what are the chances he would order her to either be a hooker on the street or have someone take her out in the back and shoot her?"

Silence.

"Because, if so, that would explain why she's gone to such lengths to get rid of me."

"But she still can't go unpunished," Taylor said. "She won't forgive you for trespassing on her man. She sure as hell won't thank you for getting her killed by her man or for showing some compassion here for her."

"So then what the hell does she want me to do?"

The scratchy voice from the floor said, "Die would be nice."

Nelson looked down at the woman, seeing the hate in

her gaze. "We get that you're jealous. We get that you would like Elizabeth to disappear because King showed her attention. But she's mine," Nelson stated firmly. "And I don't give up anything of mine I don't want to."

"You won't have a choice," Chelsea said, waving her hand as if he was nothing. "If King wants her, King gets her."

"And the only way you saw to stop that was to kill me?" Elizabeth asked in disbelief. "What did I ever do to you?"

Chelsea snorted. "You think I give a shit about what you think? I have to maintain my position in that hierarchy."

"And just exactly what is your position?" Elizabeth asked. She shoved her hands into her bathrobe pocket and glared down at the woman. "What are you? His whore? You're hardly a girlfriend or a wife or a mistress, not if he thinks you're disposable."

"I'm no man's whore," she snapped viciously. She tried to kick Elizabeth, but she was too far away.

Nelson stomped on her thigh, crushing her flat onto the thin carpet.

"Oh, big man," the woman snapped. "Do you really think I haven't felt a man's fist or his boots before?"

"I'm pretty sure you have," Nelson said. "The question is, if this isn't a life you want, why don't you change it?"

Chelsea gave an almost hysterical laugh. "What do you think I could do to change it?"

"What do we do with her now?" Elizabeth asked.

Taylor walked into the other room and came back a few minutes later with a shirt and jacket on. He made some sort of motion to Nelson before slipping out the door.

Nelson called out to Taylor, "Watch your back. Her two favorite henchmen will be out there."

"I know," he said. And with that he was gone.

Nelson looked down at the woman on the floor. "How much do you want to keep those two henchmen?" He watched the consternation across her face. He shrugged. "What did you expect? You came here to kill Elizabeth. No way I can allow that, so you have to find another way to solve this problem."

"There is no other way," Chelsea said bleakly. "I've seen it before. And it doesn't matter what you think. King has spies and killers everywhere. If he wants her, he'll mow you down to get to her."

Elizabeth sank down on the bed. "I don't want anything to do with him. We enjoyed some fun on the piano, and that was it."

"That fun is a connection he's never had with anybody else. It's a connection he desperately wants. And it's a connection only you can give him. So what the hell did you think you were doing?"

Nelson winced at the accusatory tone in Chelsea's voice. "I don't think she was *thinking*," he said gently. "I think she was just *feeling*. *Enjoying* the moment."

"Yeah, well, that moment is about to ruin my life and possibly a bunch of other people's lives."

"Who else could possibly be affected?" Elizabeth asked in astonishment.

The woman sneered. "You. And him. And the guy who just left. King just wipes you all out. Buries you deep. Nobody ever knows where to even go looking."

"Did he kill my brother?" Elizabeth asked in horror. "Did he bury him deeper so there's no way I'll ever find him?"

"No, surprisingly enough," the woman said. "I don't

think he had anything to do with that. I know he laughed about how screwed up the seamen were. He's often made comments about how they talk about being the best in the world and how disciplined they are, yet they go and kill one of their own, and another one is off and running. You see? People are the same no matter what field they are in. And, at the bottom of it all, men are just animals."

"You can get away from it all," Nelson said. "Right now. You could leave. Go a long way away."

"I know too much," Chelsea said quietly. "I'll just get buried too. It won't be today. It might not be tomorrow. But very, very quickly I'll just turn around, and the bullet with my name on it will find me."

"Why did you get into this life?" Elizabeth asked.

Chelsea shot Elizabeth a look of disbelief and amusement. She turned to look back at Nelson. "Is she for real?"

"Yes, she is," Nelson said. "She doesn't belong in this world. She doesn't know anything about it."

"She would learn fast enough," Chelsea snapped. "Or else she'd die."

"No," Elizabeth said. "I don't think I could."

"He won't give you the choice. That's what you don't understand. I was born on the streets." Chelsea's voice was glacial and hard. "And don't feel any sympathy for me. I know these streets inside and out."

"What made you hook up with King?" Elizabeth asked as if she really didn't understand.

Nelson had a pretty good idea. Women tended to gravitate to the biggest protector they could find. Chelsea had had a very difficult life on the streets. No way she avoided all the abuses that went on regularly.

"He wanted me," Chelsea said with a toss of her hair.

She scrunched back so she was sitting up, leaning against the wall. "He desired me. I was the most beautiful woman around."

"And now you're afraid your looks are fading?" Nelson asked. "You're afraid he's looking for somebody new?"

"I wasn't worried about her in the beginning." Chelsea darted a hard, angry glance toward Elizabeth again. "But now, obviously she's an issue."

"No, I'm not," Elizabeth said. "I have no intention of taking your place."

The woman just shook her head. "You really don't get it, do you? I keep telling you, you won't have a choice."

Elizabeth shrugged. "I trust Nelson that I won't end up in that situation."

The woman looked at her, puzzled. "This is King we're talking about."

"And this is Nelson," Elizabeth said quietly. "They're fairly equal. Nelson doesn't have an entire team of killers at his beck and call. And he doesn't need them. Because we don't live that lifestyle. But I think King understands us. And I think that King realizes I'm not somebody he can just pluck off the street and keep as his own little pet, that there will be people who would stop him and even more people to bring justice to this part of the world."

Chelsea sneered. "God, you're unbelievable."

"Yes," Elizabeth said. "I am very different from you. I get that. We're not here to cause trouble. We're here to find my brother. That's it."

Chelsea, in a sudden move, jumped to her feet. But she was weak and could only lean against the wall, her arms across her chest. She looked at Nelson. "Since you are some sort of big hero to her, what exactly is it you'll do to me?"

Nelson smiled. "Depends what Taylor tells us when he comes back."

Chelsea glanced nervously at the door. "Where's he gone?"

"To find King," Nelson said. "No way we'll watch our backs with you all the time. Obviously you've got to be stopped. But we don't want to have you killed or taken out."

As Nelson watched, the color drained from Chelsea's face. She clenched her hands tight together, her nails biting into her palms.

He nodded. "I get that you're terrified. But maybe if King realizes why you did what you did …"

"Are you kidding?" she cried out. "You've just signed my death warrant."

"And I should cry why?" Elizabeth asked. "You came prepared to shoot me. Prepared to kill me while I slept. And now I'm supposed to be worried you might get the same punishment you planned to send my way?"

Chelsea looked hopeful for a second, and then, as if her history had piled in on her, she knew what would be. Nobody would save her. She sagged against the wall again. "Oh, there's no help for it. It's been a decent run, but I always knew it would come to an end."

The door opened behind her, but she didn't appear to notice as Taylor came in.

"In what way did you figure it would come to an end?" Nelson asked.

"King is always after younger, prettier women," Chelsea said sadly. "There is no such thing as love or longevity. The minute my looks fade, which I presume is happening now …" She rubbed her face tiredly. "I'm gone. I'm replaced. That's why he's looking at *her* anyway."

A harsh voice rattled through the room. "Cut the bull-shit," King said. He stood there in the hallway, glaring at Chelsea.

Chelsea backed up, then dropped to her knees.

He looked at her in disgust. "You came here to shoot Elizabeth because we played piano together?"

"Of course not just because of that. You want her." Chelsea looked up at him. "What else was I to think?"

"You were to think with your brain, not from your fear."

Nelson raised his eyes at the phrasing.

King crossed his arms over his chest and said, "What the hell am I supposed to do with you now?"

Elizabeth piped up, "Forgive her. Make her feel like she's appreciated and cared for. Not that you'll replace her at the drop of a hat."

King looked at Elizabeth and laughed. "Damn, I wish you were somebody I could pick up and keep in my parlor," he said, "if for nothing else, you always make me laugh." He reached down for Chelsea's arm. "Chelsea, get out." He marched her to the door, then turned to look at Taylor, who now stood beside them. "Thanks." And he walked out, shutting the door firmly behind them.

Silence settled.

CHAPTER 10

"**D**O YOU THINK he'll really hurt her?" Elizabeth hated the guilt sitting inside her gut. She felt terrible about Chelsea's future.

"If he's a regular kingpin, yes, he will," Nelson said. "But we really have no choice. She had to be stopped, and King can stop her. The last thing I want is to constantly make sure she's not coming after you. We've got enough trouble on our plates without that."

"Do you think this will stop her?"

"I can only hope so," Nelson said quietly. "We don't really have a lot of choice."

Elizabeth sagged on the bed, shuffling farther back so she could lean against the headboard. "I don't even know what time it is. But that was a hell of a midnight awakening."

"Sorry about that," Nelson said. "We heard the footsteps come down the hallway."

"And you both woke up?"

Both men nodded.

She couldn't believe it. "That's just a little too bizarre. I'd have slept through getting shot." She stared out at the half light creeping in through her widow. "Is it morning already?"

"It's five-thirty," they both said.

She wrinkled up her nose. "I doubt I'll sleep again, but

I'd like to try."

Nelson and Taylor turned and walked toward the connecting door.

"Get some sleep," Nelson tossed back. "Who knows what today will bring."

He closed the door between them.

Elizabeth hopped up and opened the door. "If you don't mind, I'll leave this open," she called out.

"Don't mind at all," Nelson said. "See if you can grab another hour or two."

Elizabeth crawled back into bed and lay there. But her mind kept spinning. She wanted to plead with King to not hurt Chelsea. But neither did she want to feel the back of his hand. He could likely go from the really nice piano player to a killer in a heartbeat. She didn't know how to help Chelsea or if she even wanted to help. Elizabeth couldn't imagine being raised in the streets, having that be her normal world. It was so foreign to her that it didn't bear thinking about.

"Sleep," Nelson called through the doorway. "You're keeping us awake."

She frowned and sat up. "What are you talking about?"

"You're thinking too loud," Taylor said. "That's pretty obvious, isn't it?"

She snorted and lay back down again. Still, just because they told her to shut it off didn't mean the fountain of thoughts would comply.

As she lay here, she wondered if they could do anything about King. And then she realized just how much he had been a help already. And, when she started down that path, she knew she wouldn't sleep after all.

She tossed and turned for a few more minutes, then gave it up. She got up, figuring the other two would be sound asleep, and sneaked over to the window, where she looked out into the alley below. It was definitely not a nice part of town, but, with the sunrise, it was surprisingly beautiful. When she heard a sound, she turned to see Nelson standing in the doorway, wearing just his boxers. She looked him over appreciatively. "I didn't realize you were into wandering around without your clothes on."

"I have as much on as swimming trunks," he said easily. He walked to the window and looked outside.

"Isn't it beautiful?" she asked him.

He dropped a glance her way.

She shrugged. "So there's lots not to like, but there is lots to like. I can focus on that happily enough." She checked her watch. "Honestly, I did try to sleep. But I couldn't."

"I know," he said. "I've been working on my laptop for the last hour."

She turned to him in outrage. "Really? You mean, I could have been there on my laptop too?"

"Sure, why not?" he asked. "Taylor and I are working."

She glared at him. "If you tell me that you have coffee, I'll really be pissed."

He chuckled. "We were letting you sleep."

She growled. "Don't bother. I never did go back to sleep. I've been tossing and turning the whole time."

"You look like you need more sleep," he said bluntly.

"Whether I look it or not"—she glared at him—"doesn't matter because I can't get back to sleep. Maybe later this afternoon I'll lie down for a nap, but I doubt it. I'll wait until tonight to sleep. But what I am is hungry." She darted into their room. "Is there leftover food?"

Taylor nodded. "But it's cold."

She snatched up the taco and shrugged. "I've eaten

worse." She had several bites and then put it back down again. "I really would rather have coffee."

"We can head out for breakfast if you want." Taylor closed down his laptop and stood.

She noticed he wore just jeans. Both men had the lovely muscled bodies of men in their prime. "I don't want to disturb you though," she protested.

"Already disturbed," Nelson said cheerfully. "Besides, I'd like something other than cold tacos for breakfast."

"They should have microwaves in these rooms," she said. "We could heat this up."

"Maybe," Nelson said. "A coffee shop is a couple blocks away. I suggest we go there."

"Any word from anybody yet?"

"No, nobody has gotten back to us. NCIS is running the photos from King's place through the navy database. If this guy we're hunting is a seamen, it should pop."

"Doesn't mean NCIS will tell me much. I don't think they consider they owe us anything," Nelson said. "They're a bigger bureaucracy than any governmental body."

She sighed. She thought about breakfast and perked up. "Okay. I'll get changed. Be ready in five." She dashed back to her room, sorted through her meager selection of clothes, grabbed a few pieces and went into the bathroom where she washed her face, braided her hair, brushed her teeth and got dressed.

When she came back out, she packed up all her stuff so it was easy to grab, just in case. She returned to their room with her tote bag on her arm and her carry-on bag in her other hand. The two men looked at the bag and looked at her, and she shrugged. "Figured we should probably keep everything together. I don't know if my stuff is safer in your room or mine, but it obviously wasn't very safe where it used to be."

Nelson grabbed the bag, putting it with his. "Is anything valuable in here?"

Elizabeth shook her head. "I'll take my laptop with me this time. If we're at a coffee shop, who knows what we might need it for."

"Okay, give us a chance to grab our stuff."

Within a few minutes they stood in the hallway, locking both doors. They walked down the stairs instead of taking the elevator. Outside, Elizabeth took several deep breaths. "I'll never forget this trip," she said heavily. "There hasn't been a whole lot good about it yet."

"It's the *yet* that we have to worry about," he said. "There's an awful lot of leeway between now and when we leave."

"Isn't there though? I was really hoping my brother would contact me."

"At least you know he has money, and he can get food and a ride, if need be."

"I guess," she said moodily.

They walked up the block to the restaurant. It was early enough in the morning for the place to be empty.

She glanced around and smiled. "This is probably the nicest time of day for this area."

The men both nodded in agreement. They walked into the coffee shop, spotted a table in the back and headed right for it.

"Any reason not to tank up?" Taylor asked. "Don't want to do that if I'll have to do a ten- to twenty-mile run." He had a big grin. "But I admit to being really hungry."

"What about the tacos and chicken last night?"

He looked at Elizabeth with an injured look. "But that was last night. That has got nothing to do with now."

She sighed and sagged in the closest seat.

Just after they ordered, Nelson's phone rang. He checked the number, looked around, and saw the place getting busy. He answered it, whispering to Taylor, "I'll walk outside and take this." He stepped out in the front where they could see him, but at least he could hear and have some privacy.

Just then the waitress brought over their dishes.

When Nelson returned and took his place, Elizabeth asked, "Good news or bad news?"

"Any news is good news," he said. "In this case, we're getting some confirmation of what's going on."

"It's the seaman?"

"Recent ex-seaman Private Hogarth," Nelson said. "He already had several black marks on his record and is currently under investigation from his time on active duty. Suspected of doing some smuggling, some thefts of navy property from the supply rooms, that kind of stuff. Now we track him down."

"That would be good," Taylor said, "because NCIS definitely wants to talk to him.

"So navy seamen were involved in smuggling whatever, and maybe Peter witnessed this, so they killed him to save themselves?" Elizabeth's look of horror said it all.

Nelson nodded. "It's hard to swallow that some of our own have gone bad. But that is our working theory at this point."

"Maybe Hogarth knows where my brother is," Elizabeth said.

"NCIS also wants to question him about Peter's murder," Nelson added.

"So they did find evidence he was murdered?" she asked.

They both nodded. "Yes, blunt force trauma. But they haven't found any forensic evidence on the body."

Elizabeth sagged in her chair. "I figured he was murdered, but something about hearing there's evidence made it more vivid in my mind."

"Exactly," Nelson said. "But now we need to find Hogarth. That's our first priority. As soon as we do, NCIS wants to know."

"What about local law enforcement?"

"It's possible they might get a second phone call," Nelson said, "because we'll need a place to keep Hogarth hidden until NCIS gets down here."

"How do we find him?"

"Apparently he hangs around this area a lot, if that video we saw on TV is anything to go by, so we'll see if we can throw stones at anybody who knows him."

"Does he have an address?"

"No fixed address," Nelson said. "A point of contact was family out of Hawaii."

"Really?" Elizabeth shook her head. "There's gotta be more to the story than that."

"There probably is," Nelson said, "but we need to find him before we can get him to talk."

"Even more than that," Taylor said, "we need to find him alive because dead men don't talk at all."

APPARENTLY THE NAVY had been looking for Hogarth for a long time, calling him a slippery lying weasel, able to wiggle out of too many bad circumstances he found himself in. The chances of shaking him out of thin air weren't very good. Nelson needed a moment to tell Taylor that.

NCIS was more than a little anxious to put their hands on Hogarth. And he was considered armed and dangerous, with special weapons training. In other words, he would be a bad case and ugly to take down. But it was what it was. If he was involved with her brother though …

NCIS didn't appear to be too surprised that Hogarth might have been involved in Peter's murder. At the same time, they weren't willing to commit that he'd had anything to do with the murder until they got more evidence. Nelson couldn't blame them for that. A court-martial within the military was different than civilian law enforcement. But they still had rules they must follow. And apparently this asshole Hogarth didn't like anyone's rules, was a slippery lying weasel.

Nelson dug into his breakfast, his mind spinning on what they could do.

"What do you think? How will we find him?" Elizabeth asked. "We never did ask King about that, did we?"

"No, and we're not likely to ask him now either," Taylor said. "The less contact, the better at this point."

"I agree," Nelson said. "There're other bars around. There're other people around. We need to just keep asking."

"Or," she said, "we could just trip across Hogarth."

The two men looked at her in surprise.

Nelson put down his fork and shoved his empty plate back. "What are you talking about?"

She gave a slight head nod toward the window.

Nelson turned to look behind him and damn if it didn't look like the man they were hunting. He shoved his chair back and, in a hard voice, told Taylor to stay with Elizabeth.

And he walked out the front door.

Hogarth walked quickly down the block. He had his head tucked low, wasn't looking where he was going. Obviously he knew the path well. Or he was trying not to be recognized.

Knowing Taylor would look after Elizabeth, Nelson fell into step behind the guy. This was Nelson's one chance to figure out where the hell Hogarth was going. If Nelson surprised Hogarth now, he would run, and they'd lose him forever in this mess.

Keeping a decent distance, Nelson followed Hogarth for the next ten to fifteen minutes. Hogarth took a left and then a right and went up an alley. That made it a little harder to follow him unnoticed. But Nelson managed it.

When he saw Hogarth coming out of a building, heading out of the alleyway, he picked up the trail again. He ended up going into the back door of a bar. Nelson stopped, quickly texted Taylor as to where he was and looked up to see rented rooms were above.

He opened the rear door to find a stairwell. He crept up the stairs, seeing five different doors. He frowned, not knowing which one he was looking for. And likely nobody here would help. Five doors would be too many to search without being caught or giving Hogarth notice.

Just as Nelson crept up to one door, another of the doors opened, and a woman came out. She looked like she rented her apartment by the hour. She gave him an appraising look. He smiled and said, "I don't need your services, but I will pay for information."

Instead of being delighted, her gaze narrowed. "About who?"

He pulled out a photo of Hogarth.

She snorted. "That asshole? He owes me money for the last couple jobs I did for him."

"I followed him in here, but I'm not sure which one of the rooms is his."

She motioned up to the next flight of stairs. "Top door on your right." And she marched past him.

"Thank you. Don't you want payment?"

"Nah. He never paid me, so you got this one for free. Go kill the bastard." She sauntered out the door.

Almost laughing, Nelson went up the second flight of stairs. There he found another set of five doors, but the one on the right was the one he cared about. He put his ear to the door and could hear somebody walking on the other side. With a quick text updating his location, he knocked on the door and waited. Instead of somebody coming to the door, it sounded like somebody scrambling, then there was dead silence. Nelson's mind flashed through what Hogarth could be doing, anything from loading a rifle to packing up and leaving out the fire escape. And that made Nelson mad because he'd forgotten to check if there was one.

On a sudden hunch, he grabbed the knob and opened the door. It opened easily under his hand. He stepped off to the side in case shots were fired, but there was nothing. He pushed the door farther open and walked in. "Hey, Hogarth, you in here?"

No answer.

Nelson went through the small space and saw a living room window had been opened. He pushed it up and stared out. Hogarth jumped from his railing to the railing below it. Nelson stepped onto the railing, grabbed the man's hand and said, "No, you don't."

Hogarth pulled back hard to get free, but Nelson hung

on tight. The position he was in was awkward because the guy's hand was under the railing, and he was hanging off the deck itself. Somehow he had to lift Hogarth up and over.

"Let me go," Hogarth squeaked.

"No, and killing yourself ain't the answer either," Nelson snapped.

"Fuck you," the guy said. "I have no intention of killing myself. But I don't like guys following me."

"Yeah, well, you don't like guys apparently," Nelson said, "because you had a hand in killing Peter, didn't you?"

"Who the hell are you?" Hogarth roared, struggling to free himself. But he was a small wiry guy, and Nelson managed to grab him by the wrist and pull him up higher. Once there, Nelson dragged him over the railing, dropped him on the fire escape and followed him down to pin him in place.

"You're not getting away so easily."

As soon as Nelson shifted his weight, Hogarth freed himself and ran into the apartment, but Nelson caught him and slammed him back down again. With Hogarth's arms pulled behind his back, Nelson looked for something to tie him up with. An old stretched-out sock lay on the floor. He grabbed it and twisted it around Hogarth's wrists, tying them together.

With Hogarth's arms secured, Nelson found a discarded belt and did the same with his legs. Hogarth swore a blue streak all the while.

"Who are you, man? You got nothing on me. You come busting in here, you got to be after something."

Nelson just let him run off at the mouth while he found two T-shirts to tie his bound hands and his bound legs to one chair. *That should keep him in one place for a while.* He knew Taylor would be coming at any moment. For that matter, if Nelson put out the word, a dozen NCIS and local law enforcement would arrive to cart Hogarth's ass out of here.

When Nelson finally had his prisoner secured, he flipped him over and propped him up on a chair. "Now that you aren't going anywhere," Nelson said with a lazy smile, "you can tell me all about Peter."

The guy just shrugged. "Don't know who you're talking about."

"That's fine," Nelson said. "As much as I care that Peter, the poor guy, was murdered, and he was young, and he had his whole life ahead of him, I'm more concerned about Skunk." And that's when he caught it—that shiver, that blink of Hogarth's eyes.

"I don't know anything about a skunk," Hogarth said in disgust. "If you can't keep track of your own pets, dude, you shouldn't have any."

"Hogarth, you funny man," Nelson said. He wandered the apartment, checking out a few things.

"Hey, leave that alone," Hogarth cried. "Get the hell out of here."

The closer Nelson got to the laptop, the more frantic Hogarth's speech became. Nelson sat down and tapped the keyboard. It was already open and logged in, so Hogarth had been doing something before he heard Nelson arrive. He brought up Hogarth's email from the task bar and sorted through the stack. "Oh, now look at that. Just a little bit of blackmail here, huh?"

At that, Hogarth seemed to lose it. He was bouncing his chair to the point he got dumped sideways, but his mouth just never shut off. He swore and cussed some more. It was almost funny the way he was raging because there was absolutely nothing else he could do. And that was okay with Nelson too.

Nelson ignored him. At a pounding on the door, Nelson checked out the peephole. Instead of it being Taylor, it was another stranger. A great big beefy guy.

"What the fuck, Hogarth? Open up."

Nelson walked back to Hogarth. "Should I open it for him? Because maybe that guy is interested in making a few hundred bucks telling me all I need to know."

Fear whispered through Hogarth's face. "No, no, no, no," he said. "You don't want to talk to him."

At that, the door slammed open, and the stranger walked in. He took one look at Nelson; then he saw Hogarth tied up and chuckled. "Serves your skinny ass right," he said. "You owe me fucking money, and I want to see it now."

"I don't have it," Hogarth whined. "Look. You can see I'm in a bit of a bind here."

"That's great," the big guy said. "Don't mind if I take a layer or two off your hide, now that I got you in my hands."

Hogarth screamed.

Nelson stepped between the two. "You know what? I don't have a problem with you doing that, but I need information from this little weasel first."

The big man laughed. "You can't trust anything that comes out of his mouth. He's a liar. He's a snitch. He's a cheat."

"I also want to know if he's a killer," Nelson said. "A bunch of seamen killed a guy not long ago, and Hogarth was at the scene, noted coming back from the same area."

The big guy looked at him. "I don't think the little weasel has the balls."

They both turned to Hogarth. He shook his head like crazy, muttering words, but they were coming out over the top of each other. They didn't make any sense.

Nelson held up a hand. "Slow down."

"I didn't kill anyone," he said. "And I don't have your fucking money."

"Why don't you have my money?" the big man asked, his rage barely banked in his voice.

"Because I don't have it, that's why. I just don't have any."

The big guy took a step forward.

Nelson put up his hand. "I get that you're angry."

"Angry? This little weasel cheated me out of three hundred bucks."

"Maybe I'll replace that three hundred bucks," Nelson said, "if you can give me some information on this guy. I think he may have something to do with the murder, but I need proof."

"I didn't see him down there, so I don't know what I can give you."

Inspiration struck. "Have you seen this guy?" Nelson reached into his pocket and pulled out the picture of Skunk.

He looked at it and nodded. "Yeah, that guy was here for a couple days. He was hanging around Hogarth. Someone should have warned the kid that Hogarth was a shit deal." He sneered at Hogarth. "I'm really glad to see your skinny ass tied up like that. You're such a fucking loser."

Nelson turned to Hogarth. "When did you last see him?"

"A couple of days ago. I took him to the bus, okay? He wanted to get out of town. He wanted to get out of town fast."

"And how much did you charge him for that?"

Hogarth glared at him. "The kid had money. What the hell do you care?"

"He didn't have that much money," Nelson said, "and he was getting away from the guys who had killed his buddy. But, of course, you didn't mind. You took advantage, right, Hogarth? Because that's what you do."

The big guy laughed. "That's exactly what he does. He's such an ass."

"Hey, you're no bloody angel. You're the one who pimps out stolen goods for everyone," Hogarth whined. "It's not my fault the stuff I brought you wasn't worth what you thought it was."

"Maybe it would have been if you hadn't gutted them."

"I didn't gut them," Hogarth said. "I thought those radios were good."

"Like hell. And cell phones? You took all the guts out of them."

"No, honest I didn't," Hogarth begged. "But I did know they were empty, you're right there. But I was desperate. I needed the money."

"Now you'll have a few other problems," the big guy said, "because you can't be bringing any more of your shit my way. You go find somebody else to pawn it off on." He turned to look at Nelson. "Are you serious about the three hundred?"

Nelson pulled a wad out and handed it to him. "Thanks for the info."

"Is that kid Hogarth took to the bus station dead?"

"We hope not," Nelson said. "We're trying to keep him alive at this point. But we think the kid saw his fellow mates kill a guy. He's trying to stay alive and to stay ahead of them.

I don't know if this weasel was part of it or if he was a go-between or if he's just slime and watched a guy get murdered and didn't do anything about it."

"Honestly, that's very much this slime's kind of work," the big man said. "But more than that, he's an opportunist. He's got his video running all the time, hoping to catch someone doing something that this slimeball can use against them. If he watched anybody kill somebody, he wouldn't help the dead guy because Hogarth here is too busy making his films. But he sure as hell would be blackmailing the living ones caught in the act. So I'd suggest you give him a good squeeze and find out who the hell he's getting money from these days. He sure as shit won't be getting any more from me," he snapped. He turned to look at Hogarth. "Remember that. No more crossing my door."

CHAPTER 11

"WHERE IS HE?" she asked Taylor.

Taylor's phone buzzed just then. He glanced down and smiled. "He's run our sneaky dude to ground. We have instructions to get the cops, the detectives in particular, and bring them to this address."

"He's really caught Hogarth?" Elizabeth asked in excitement. "That's fantastic."

"Maybe, maybe not," he said. "He needs backup." He glanced around the area. "But he also needs the cops."

"We'll call the cops," she said, "and we'll get to the address on our own."

He laughed. "A little bloodthirsty, aren't you?"

"No," she said. "A little anxious, a little worried, a little in need of some closure. He took off so fast. It was hard to know if we should have followed him or not."

"I had no intention of following him," Taylor said. "I was on babysitting duty."

It took her a moment for that to sink in. She turned and gasped. "You stayed behind to look after me?"

"Of course," he said. "That's also why Nelson didn't want you here. Our skills and abilities would be split. One would go after the killers—or the bad guys, as you would put it—and the other would stay behind and look after you."

Inside she felt a chill. "I could go back to the hotel," she said. "You don't have to watch me all the time."

"There is no way to know if this guy had a partner, if he was a decoy, or if King or Chelsea is around," Taylor reminded her. "We don't do things lightly. It's always for your safety that we would keep an eye on you. We won't chase down somebody and leave you unprotected, so that, when we come back, we must find out where you are too."

"That's hardly fair though," she said. "What if Nelson's in trouble?"

"Life isn't fair," he said in a rough voice. "You need to deal with it because your presence here has affected things. At the moment Nelson followed this guy back to his apartment. I don't know if he'll have a talk with him or if he'll lose him." Just then his phone buzzed again. "Okay, they're talking. But he still wants to hand Hogarth over to the cops." Taylor dialed one of the cops he had a number for while she watched. He relayed the message given him and the address. He finished the call and looked at her. "Are you ready to go?"

She nodded. The last thing she'd wanted was to hold back the investigation into her brother's disappearance. Of all the things that she needed, she needed answers. And yet, Taylor was right. Being here, she was cramping their style, splitting their energy. Four days with two guys focused and on target was better than four days when it was only one guy, and the other was the forced to babysit.

She'd known that but hadn't let herself think it through.

Ashamed of her own inability to see how she'd affected the investigation, she said, "I'm sorry."

Taylor looked at her with surprise and shrugged. "We're dealing with it. It is what it is."

"That sounds very sad too," she muttered.

He led the way, using the GPS on his phone to find Nelson. She wondered if this was just another goose chase.

Feeling eyes all around her, particularly after Taylor's jab about King, she stayed close to him as they walked. This was just another sign of how she had impacted the investigation. She hadn't added any value yet. Except maybe that King was more amiable to help out the guys because she'd been here. But that had also caused its own set of problems.

Despondent over her actions, she stayed silent as they moved up the sidewalk. People automatically stepped out of the way, out of Taylor's path. Like Nelson, he had that ability to create space all around him. Or maybe it was fear. Maybe people just saw him coming and moved aside to get away from him. She wasn't scared of either of them, but they had that presence. She wondered if she projected the same thing when she was in the field.

Did she give off that same power, exude that same authority when she was in her own element? She hoped so. These men were also at home on the streets. This was their world. Somehow they were like chameleons and seemed to adapt to their surroundings. Whereas she was a fish out of water here.

She had been way too friendly with King, but she hadn't seen that as an issue. Not until now. Even when they had Chelsea on the floor, Elizabeth hadn't realized just how much her own friendliness had been inappropriate. It was who she was though, and it was so damn hard to be anything other than that. Whereas these men seemed to manage to be what they needed to be in every scenario. She admired it; she envied it, and, at the same time, she wondered if they were ever confused about who they were.

It had to be difficult. Did they ever turn off completely?

She wanted to ask but knew it wasn't the time.

Finally they turned a corner and headed into what appeared to be a door next to a bar. As he opened the door, they found stairs going straight up to lodgings above. "I'm not sure anybody should be living above a bar," she muttered.

"People all over the world do," Taylor said lightly. "Particularly people who work at the bars."

She had to acknowledge that was convenient.

As they went up, a woman came down. She gave Taylor a saucy eye and shook her boobs at him. Taylor didn't even notice. Elizabeth just hurried up behind him. They climbed up to the second floor and stopped at the first door. He rapped lightly, then rapped again.

Nelson called out, "Come in."

Taylor pushed open the door and stepped in to find the weasel-looking dude tied to a chair and Nelson. Taylor rubbed his hands together. "Now this is exactly what I like to see," he said.

"Hey, you should be helping me," Hogarth said. "The guy broke into my apartment and tied me up."

Hogarth looked almost pitiful, but Elizabeth was relieved to see he didn't bear any signs of a beating. She wouldn't blame Nelson, but, so far, it appeared nobody's temper had been piqued. And not only that, potentially nobody needed a beating in order to talk.

She glanced around the small room and realized what kind of a lifestyle this guy had. There was bar food on the floor, boxes of leftover pizza on the couch, papers all over the place, dirty napkins, dirty towels. She wanted to sit down, but no place seemed clean.

Nelson motioned to the kitchen table. "Your best bet is

probably one of those chairs."

She nodded mutely, pulled out a chair and gingerly sat down.

The guy looked at her and smirked. "Hey, what's your price by the hour?"

She didn't get a chance to answer before Nelson hit him across the cheek.

Hogarth glared at him, but he shut his mouth.

Taylor asked Nelson, "What did you learn?"

"We had another visitor," Nelson said. He told them the little bit he'd learned from the pawnbroker and how that man had suggested Hogarth would more likely be into blackmail.

"You mean, you didn't help the poor victim?" she cried out. "What's wrong with people?"

Hogarth turned his glare on her. "They'd probably throw me in jail for a crime I didn't commit," he said. "Why the hell would I call the cops for anything? Even if I was dying, I wouldn't call them."

Nelson just nodded absentmindedly.

She wondered if that was his attitude too. "Well, the cops are coming regardless," she snapped. "You'll get yours for being such a lowlife."

He made a face at her and called out, "Sticks and stones …"

She crossed her arms over her chest and glared back at him. When he finally averted his eyes, she glanced around at the other two men. Nelson stood guard over the lowlife, and Taylor was on Hogarth's laptop, searching through emails. "Looks like we're talking blackmail," Taylor said.

"That's what the big guy said."

"The big guy's name is Sweets," Hogarth muttered.

"You might as well call him by his name."

"It looks like Sweets had the right of it," Taylor said. "We've got a couple emails back and forth. One of the guys is laughing, telling Hogarth to try to catch them. Another one said he'd just come pay Hogarth a visit when he came back next time, and Hogarth would get what was coming to him." Taylor looked at him over the laptop. "Not your usual expected response, I presume?"

Hogarth shook his head glumly. "Makes you wonder if they haven't done it before. But they had no intention of paying for nothing."

"Did you get a hold all five?"

"Four," Hogarth said. "I only saw four there. The fifth man was the victim."

Elizabeth hopped up, pulled out the picture of her brother and said, "Was he there?"

Hogarth looked at the picture and laughed. "Hell yes. He was standing off in the shadows, watching. If you got a problem with me not helping the victim, you should be talking to him."

"Did he try to help? To stop them?" she said a little desperately, hoping her brother had tried to do the right thing, but knowing given the circumstances, it would have been almost impossible.

"Well, he tried at first, but they beat him up and just laughed at him. Told him what would happen if he said anything. But when they were done, one of the men turned to look for him. He was still there, hiding in the shadows," Hogarth said. "That guy turned to him and said, *You're next.* I could see him in the shadows, and he kind of just melted away after that. He obviously believed him."

"We need names, and we need faces."

372

"I ain't got nothing to give you," Hogarth said.

"We don't need anything from him," Taylor said. "I'm taking photos of the emails and forwarding them to my email as well. I need about ten minutes to get this done." He worked as fast as he could with Nelson standing guard. "The cops should be here soon. How much time, do you think?"

"When you want them, they never come," Nelson said. "But when you don't want them, chances are they'll get here way too damn fast." Just then sounds of footsteps were heard out in the hall. He groaned. "Taylor, you're running out of time."

A knock came at the door. Nelson went to answer it and let in the two cops who had spoken to them down on the dock. When they came in and saw Hogarth tied up, they frowned and turned to Nelson.

He held out his hands. "This is the guy blackmailing the men who saw the murder of Peter. Don't look at me."

"Did you tie him up?"

"I very nicely stopped him from beating the crap out of me," Nelson said. "I'm much bigger and much stronger, and I didn't want him to hurt himself."

His tone was so solicitous Elizabeth almost laughed, but she managed to keep her voice and face calm and bland.

The cop looked at her. "Were you here for all of this?"

She shook her head. "We just arrived. This lowlife walked past the restaurant we were in. I pointed him out walking down the street. Nelson went after him then and caught him before we joined him."

The officers nodded. They walked over to Hogarth. "Did you see the murder?"

Hogarth stared at them without saying anything.

Nelson pulled out his cell phone and hit a button. A

video he had taken without Hogarth's knowing started to play. Hogarth's voice filled the room.

The cops nodded in satisfaction. "That's very nice. That's what we need, fine upstanding citizens like Hogarth."

"At least that proves I didn't kill him," Hogarth protested. "You got nothing on me. You can't lay no criminal charges on me for not being a great public citizen."

"That's very true," Taylor said. "But you were blackmailing the men in question."

"You knew the men who killed Mr. Patnik?" The taller cop zeroed in on the most important point.

Hogarth shrunk. "I knew a couple of them."

Taylor held up the laptop. "We've got three names here. We got a Kurt Jones, a Barry Mulgrew, and it looks like this is a Warren … I think that's Mckinley." He handed over the laptop with the emails open so they could see.

The first cop read it and whistled. "Oh, we can use this. Attempted blackmail is definitely a criminal offense."

"Big deal," Hogarth said. "So what? You throw me in jail. It's overcrowded. I act as good as gold, and I'm out on the streets in a few months."

He didn't appear to be too bothered by it. "I guess that way you get three decent meals and a bed every night too, huh?" Elizabeth asked, motioning to the place around her. "Might be healthier than this garbage."

"Hey, I didn't invite you into my place," he snapped. "Highbrow bitches like you don't know what the real world is all about."

"You're right," she admitted. "But I am learning. And I'm still trying to find information on my brother. So tell the policemen what you said about my brother being in the shadows."

Hogarth related what he had heard when the guys were threatening Chris to be their next victim.

The two cops looked at each other, then at her. "So it looks like your brother may not have had anything to do with the murder of his friend."

"He *never* had anything to do with that," she snapped. "I told you that."

"We still track down every lead."

"And when is it you start doing that?" She got up and paced the small room. "You were ready to throw my brother away for life for a crime he didn't commit. It took *us* finding this guy to get the truth."

"We still don't have all the truth though," the taller cop said. "We have to find these men and speak with them and confirm what we know."

"I've got photos," Hogarth said. "But that's only if all charges are dropped on my side."

There was instant silence in the room.

"What kind of photos?" Taylor's voice was hard. "And where the hell would you get photos?"

"It's what I do. I like to watch people. I like to keep mementos of people's actions," he said with a sneer. "Nobody ever thinks anybody's out there. But somebody's always watching. There's always somebody to catch what you're doing. Particularly if it's illegal."

"So do you have photos of the men in question with the victim?"

"Yes. He was unconscious when they carried him down to the dock," he said. "I figured he was already dead." He shot a look over at Elizabeth. "I did."

She studied him for a moment and realized what Peter's body would look like if it were being packed by several men.

She nodded. "He was probably unconscious, but, until an autopsy is done, we won't know if he was breathing the water in when they held him under, or if he was already dead."

"Where are those photos?" the tall cop asked.

"What do I get for it?" Hogarth asked in a crafty voice.

She hated the negotiations over something that could clear her brother. "For God's sake, just tell them where the pictures are."

"Hell no," Hogarth snapped. "I'm not going to jail—especially here—when I have the proof you need to clear your precious brother."

"So what do you want for proof?" she asked the two policemen.

"I already told you," Hogarth yelled. "They know how this works. I'm small fry for them. They just want the information so they can close their cases. That's all they give a shit about."

"Maybe," she said, "but what I care about is finding my brother."

Just then Taylor's voice broke through the conversations. "Doesn't matter," he said. "I just found one of them."

He held up the laptop, and, sure enough, she saw a picture. Though it was dark, it was under the streetlight of the pier as a group of men carried a body between them toward the water. There was even a date stamp on the bottom. She gave a happy sigh. "That's the proof you need to clear my brother."

The cops looked at it and whistled. "Wow, they must really hate you around here, Hogarth. The faces are barely visible but enough to see her brother wasn't part of the group. That's the photo you used to blackmail the killers with?"

"I just started with emails, hoping they wouldn't force me to go a little deeper. I would try the photos next. That would have been a harder punch for them. But I also didn't want to piss them off to the extent they'd come back looking for me," he admitted. "If I saw something, that's a different story than having proof of something."

"I don't think they would have cared one way or the other," Nelson said. "Next time they came to port, they would have looked you up."

"See? So this is a good thing. You'll pick up these guys, and I won't have to worry about them," Hogarth said cheerfully.

"Look at this one." Taylor held up the laptop, and there was Skunk standing in the shadows, just his profile and a little bit of light shining on his face as he looked at the pier with terror and confusion on his face.

"So they knew he was there. But he couldn't stop them."

"I wonder if he even tried to call the cops," one of the policemen asked. "It would have gone a long way to help stop them."

"No, it wouldn't have," Nelson said. "If they had any inkling he'd called the cops, you know he'd be dead by now."

"We would have gotten there to stop it," the cop said.

"No, you wouldn't have," Hogarth said. "You wouldn't have been there anywhere near in time. It was a done deal within minutes. I don't even know that they knew the guy was there to begin with, as I was just minding my own business. I think he followed them. And, by the time he saw what they were doing, it was already too late. He did try to stop them but…"

"I hope so," Elizabeth said. "I love my brother. And I know it's hard to do the right thing all the time, but I really hope he was in a position where he couldn't do anything but take off."

"The question we want to know is, where is he now?" asked the first cop.

"Why?" she challenged the cop. "What do you want to do with him now?"

"First off, we need to know that he's alive and well," the cop said in exasperation. "And, second, it'd be nice to confirm what Hogarth is saying."

"You mean the pictures aren't proof enough?" she asked in astonishment. "How much more proof do you need?"

"It doesn't really matter. Your brother's a missing person. We need to track him down so we can close the case."

"I have no idea where he is though," she said.

"Hogarth said he took him to the bus depot too." Nelson added. "Now whether I believe him or not, that's a different story. And, of course, his freedom from here on in will hinge on him telling the truth."

Hogarth glared at them; then finally his face fell. "Okay, so I don't know where he went. I drove him out to the edge of town, and that was it."

"What do you mean, that was it?" Elizabeth cried out. "There's no *it* in that. You could have dumped him on the side of the road because he was already dead."

"He got out of my vehicle and walked away. That's all he did."

"You must have seen which way he went then," the cop said.

Hogarth shrugged. "Not really. But he was heading toward the bus depot. So, although I didn't drop him there,

I'm pretty sure that's where he went."

Nelson pulled out his phone and called somebody. When answered, he said, "Mason, did you ever check the bus routes out of here? We have a suspicion somebody dropped Chris close enough that he could have walked to the bus stop, then moved out."

The voice on the other end spoke.

"Right, not under his real name." Nelson turned toward Elizabeth. "Any idea what other name he would have traveled under?"

She chuckled. "Did he try Skunk?"

"He would need some ID, I presume?"

Silence.

They turned to look at Hogarth, but he stared up at the ceiling, then over at the far wall. "Hogarth, did you give him a false ID?"

He glared at Nelson. "Okay, so I might have had a driver's license hanging around from some other poor guy. I just gave it to him and said he might try that. Nobody would ask for more information than that."

"And what was the name on the ID?" the tall cop asked.

"Do I have to do everything?" Hogarth cried out. "You're the cops. You do some investigating. You don't have to nail my ass to the wall for it."

"I don't give a shit," the cop said. "You can do six months and have all those pretty boys raking over your ass. If you don't want to talk, then don't talk."

Hogarth glared at them. Finally he gave in. "David Lowe. And I think there was an *E* on the end of the *Low*."

"And you just happened to find the ID?"

"I did. Some dude lost his wallet or had it lifted. When I found it, the driver's license was still in it, tucked into one of those little secret pocket flaps in the back. I just took the driver's license and kept it. You never know when you'll need an ID like that."

"So I presume this David and Chris were similar enough in looks that Chris could use it?"

"I think he was like five feet, eleven inches, blond hair, no glasses. He was pretty nondescript in the photo, and your brother's pretty nondescript in real life. Didn't take much for him to get away with using that ID."

"And he had cash," Elizabeth said. "So he didn't need to use a credit card."

The cops nodded.

She watched as Nelson relayed that message to Mason.

When he hung up the phone, he said, "Mason will get back to us in a few minutes."

The cops looked at him. "You have somebody who can check the stations?"

"Sure," he said with a smile. "So do you."

"Sure," the cop said, "but that's not really high on our priority list."

"But it is high on ours," Nelson said. "We're down here to find her brother. Obviously we wanted to know what happened to Peter, and we are well on our way to getting that done as well. Mason now has the names of the three men Hogarth tried to blackmail. We'll find from that two other men were linked to those three that led to Peter's murder."

"I said it was only four. The fifth guy was Peter himself."

"Sounds like there were seven men involved," the cop said. "Your brother, the four men who killed him, and the victim, and Hogarth."

"True enough," Nelson said smoothly. "But, having

three names, we'll find the fourth without too much trouble. And NCIS will pick them up and question them."

"So we need copies of all the photos and the statements you get from this guy," Taylor added.

"NCIS will get a copy," the cop said in a dry tone. "We don't have to give you anything."

Elizabeth could see the frustration on Nelson's face and realized how much they'd already done for the investigation. She smiled at the officers. "That's true. You don't have to, but, in the spirit of working together, it would be very nice if we could cooperate. At this point, a lot of information is flowing, and both of us have bosses who need to have case files and evidence properly logged in and tagged. You know what it's like when shit goes missing."

Both men nodded. "We'll take it under consideration," the second cop said in a noncommittal voice.

She didn't know if that was a yes or no, but she figured a little sweetness would go a longer way than some of the frustration and rage flying around the room.

A few minutes later, the cops freed Hogarth, and, with one escorting him, they led him out of his room and down the stairs.

He stopped in the hallway, protesting that the men were forcing him along. "Make sure you lock my door. I'll be back, and I'll be pissed if all my shit's gone."

Elizabeth stood, glanced around the room and said, "Wouldn't it be a hardship if all this was gone?"

Taylor chuckled. He led the way to the door. "I wish we could have kept the laptop. But the cops would take it right from the get-go, so I got what I could."

"I think you got an awful lot off of there," Elizabeth said with a smile. "We're so much closer now. All we need to figure out is where my brother got a ticket to." As they walked down the stairs, she said, "It's already lunchtime."

With an exclamation, Nelson turned to look at his watch. "I can't believe how much time has passed already. You're right. It's eleven-thirty, heading into twelve."

"So back to the hotel, or do you guys need more food?" she asked.

The two men looked at each other and shrugged.

"I suggest we pick up a couple sandwiches and go back to the room. We might even go home today," Nelson said.

"Exactly," Taylor said. "Depending on where Skunk purchased a ticket to, somebody else might pick him up stateside for us."

There was a sandwich shop on the way back. They ducked inside, picked out sandwiches they would all enjoy, had them made fresh, and, with the bags in their hands, they walked toward the hotel.

Back in their room again, sitting down at the small table, Elizabeth realized just how much she would miss the camaraderie of having these men around her. She smiled at them. "So do I get to take you guys out for a meal as a thank-you when we're back home again?"

BOTH TAYLOR AND Nelson looked at her. Nelson nodded. "I think that's a great idea."

Taylor said, "That's not fair. I'll feel like a third wheel."

Elizabeth looked at him in astonishment. "Why can't I take you out for lunch and have him along too?"

He shrugged. "I guess I can deal with it. It might be fun to see if you guys survive this or not."

She rolled her eyes at him, picked up her sandwich half

and took a big bite.

"Or I could cook for you, and we can ditch this guy," Nelson said, pointing at Taylor, laughing. Nelson was about to take a bite, but his phone buzzed. He checked the incoming text to see it was Mason. He read it and said, "Ticket was purchased to San Diego. A second ticket was purchased heading south."

"So a diversionary tactic?" Taylor asked.

"It would make sense if he did, and San Diego won't take him very far. But it will get him back to Coronado, and that's base." Nelson glanced over at her. "Which way do you think he'd go?"

"If he's running, deep into Mexico. If he's not running, then home," she said calmly. "He no longer has a place of his own, but I've told him that he can come stay with me."

"And where do you live?" Taylor asked curiously.

She beamed a bright smile at him. "I bought a house last year in San Diego. It's got lots of bedrooms, so I figured my brother could stay there if he was at home."

"Do you meet for lunches when he's in town?"

"Usually he's too busy," she said. "But you can bet after this, I'll be making a point of it."

Nelson nodded. "Nothing like trouble to bring a family home again."

Just then his phone rang. "Hey, Mason, what's up?" After a moment, he questioned, "He didn't arrive?" As he listened to Mason, explaining that they were getting the camera feeds from the bus station, it looked like her brother hadn't made it to either destination. "Shit," he said as he hung up the phone. "It'll be a while before they can track down the feeds from the Mexican side, if they can ever get it. But it doesn't look like Chris went to San Diego."

"That's where I was really hoping he'd go," she said slowly. "What if he bought *two* diversionary tickets?"

"You tell me," Nelson said. "He's your brother. What would he do?"

"I have no clue." She stared down at the sandwich as if it had suddenly gone bad.

Nelson picked his up and ate. He knew how important it was to have energy for whatever was coming. And, at this point, he had no clue what was coming. "Have you tried to call him again?"

Elizabeth picked up her phone and dialed his number. She laid the phone on the table, and they could all hear it ring and ring. Finally she stopped it and took another bite of her sandwich. "We had a summer cabin," she said. "Dad sold it a long time ago. As I understand it, nobody's living in it."

The two men stared at her. "How far away?"

"About a two-hour drive from home," she said, "so I don't really know that he would do that. But, if you think about it, he has money to get a rental car, and he could just drive home."

"It's a long drive, and he'd need ID for a rental. Even two thousand dollars wouldn't go very far."

She nodded. "Maybe a bus partway?"

"So, if he got off on a stop before San Diego somewhere, would that help him get to the cabin?"

Her jaw dropped, and she gave an enthusiastic nod. "Actually, it is south of San Diego. And, like I said, it's about two hours away. I don't know all the stops on the road from Ensenada, but he could have bought a ticket for San Diego and then got off early."

"That's what I was wondering," Nelson said. "Any way to contact somebody at the cabin?"

She frowned. "I don't think so. But there is a general store. It's possible, if he's hiding, he stopped in there to get food. He'd probably think he was safe."

"I wouldn't think so," Taylor said. "But, until we know these men have been picked up, he won't be safe."

"Maybe he isn't safe," she said. "Maybe he is in extreme danger. When they said, he'd be next, maybe they meant it. Maybe he took off right then, and they're still hunting him down."

"It's possible, but again we have to wait for further information."

A text came through just then on Taylor's phone. He checked it and said, "NCIS will be here within an hour. They want to talk to Hogarth and get the evidence themselves. They have the names of the three men, are picking them up now. The fourth man, however, is missing."

"So that's the guy who could potentially be tracking my brother."

"We don't know that anybody is tracking Skunk," Nelson said. "Keep that in mind too."

However, it wasn't long before the names came through the pipeline. They'd already finished eating and were sitting with take-out coffees, surfing on the internet as they tried to figure out a plan of what to do next. Three of the killers had been picked up, but Matt Blanc was on the loose. The three others had confessed to their part in it, but Matt Blanc, they said, was the ringleader. And he was the dangerous one. Apparently the navy had been looking into catching Matt Blanc in the act for a long time, gathering an ugly record on him as to accusations. Even NCIS was more than a little anxious to put their hands on Blanc, considered armed and dangerous, with special weapons training. In other words, he would be a hard case and even harder to take down.

"Do we believe that?" Taylor asked. "It sounds to me like they'd say anything to save their sorry asses."

Nelson had to agree. "But I think this might be somebody we need to be wary of. I wouldn't want to be your brother if this guy is on his trail. He's got a lot of special training. We need to find him, and we need to stop him now."

"And how do we do that?" she asked.

He gave her a hard look and said, "It sounds like we're heading to your cabin."

CHAPTER 12

THEY WERE PACKED up, ready to leave, when a knock came at the door.

Nelson went to the door and opened it. One of King's henchmen stood there with a worried look on his face.

Nelson crossed his arms over his chest and asked, "What's the matter?"

"I think you guys need to talk to King."

"Why?" Elizabeth asked, coming up behind Nelson.

"Why?" Taylor asked, joining them. "And why are you telling us?"

"Because I'm working for my lady," he said in a low voice. "And that doesn't always jive with King's orders."

Elizabeth understood exactly what he meant. "What's the problem?"

He glanced down the hallway. "I got to leave." And he booked it.

Taylor gave chase. Nelson closed the door and looked at Elizabeth. And she realized this was once again one of those times when, because she was here, they had to split up their team. "Go, go, go. I'll stay inside with the door locked." Nelson hesitated, but she wouldn't let him. "Go. This might be connected to Chris. We'll only have one chance to solve this."

He nodded and took off.

She closed the door behind him and clicked the lock button. She sighed. "What the hell could possibly happen now?" she muttered. She walked over to her bag, which she had on the bed closest to the connecting door, and finished her packing.

An arm wrapped around her neck and squeezed tight. Panicked she kicked out and scratched, but she couldn't breathe, and her vision narrowed to a tiny tunnel, and finally she fell to the side, almost plopping uncontrollably downward.

She was quickly picked up and tossed over somebody's shoulder. She gasped for breath, but it was as if she was paralyzed. The air was going into her lungs but not easily. She was dimly aware of being taken down one of the staircases and out in the back alley. She had no way to signal either Nelson or Taylor, no way she could call for help. Although it was still roughly daylight, it was that half-light predusk time. And, with the clouds overhead, there was very little light at all.

As he ran with her on his shoulder, she bounced with every step. It gave her a hell of a headache, but she couldn't do anything. Her arms were dangling past his butt, but she couldn't even grab his belt to shift her position. She managed a light groan, not that that would do anything.

She didn't know how long he could run like this. It seemed like forever. Her ribs were killing her from the bouncing up and down.

Finally he stepped inside another building, into the complete darkness of hell to her. She was just getting some feeling back in her arms when he stepped through a series of rooms and down a long hallway. She tried to shift, and he reached up and smacked her hard on her backside. It wasn't just a glancing blow, and she cried out with the pain and shock.

He said, "Don't move."

The message was clear. If she didn't want more of that, then she'd behave herself. The trouble was, she didn't even know what behaving herself meant here. Finally he stepped into a small room, literally flipped her over his head and dumped her on the floor where she fell and cracked her head hard. She cried out again, shuddering in pain. Then he stepped out of the way and closed the door.

She lay here, grateful to be alone. Tears welled up as she reoriented herself from the stunning pain still searing through the back of her skull. She could only hope no permanent damage had been done. The pain was crippling.

Finally she rolled over bit by bit. Her eyes opened to search her surroundings. She was in a small room, maybe a storeroom. The floor was concrete; the walls were maybe drywall or, maybe concrete too. She couldn't tell. But her heart froze when she saw the scratches on the walls.

She took several deep breaths to stem the shock rippling even now through her body. Had it been a setup from the beginning? She had to think so. And she had sent Nelson after Taylor. What were the chances they had both been taken too? Although she hoped not. Surely they were too smart for that. She was the idiot.

She'd locked one door, but she hadn't checked the other one. She didn't remember when it had last been unlocked either. But somehow the assholes had pulled a fast one on her, and there it was. She'd been taken, and now she didn't know what the hell to do. There was no sign of her brother here with her, so she could either be happy about that or worried he was hiding out in the cabin, with the other bad guy after him. It was like they had two bad guys in this scenario.

And, with that, she frowned, thinking about Chelsea's earlier comments. Had she orchestrated this on her own? Or was the henchman really one of King's men who had been used as a diversion to get Nelson and Taylor away from Elizabeth? She figured that had to be it.

"God damn it," she whispered.

Her head was still booming. But she didn't dare not take a moment to check out her surroundings, to see if she could get out. Had her kidnapper locked the door? She hadn't heard a *click*.

She gathered her energy and stood. The room swam around her. Using the wall for support, she made her way to the door. The knob turned under her fingers. She pulled it open a crack to find a bigger room. Moving slowly, keeping an eye out for anyone else, she checked for another door, and sure enough one was just to the left of her. She closed the one behind her and sidled up to the next. She listened with her ear pressed against the wood to hear if anybody was on the other side. But all she heard was silence. She crept around the door, opened it and peered out. Again it wasn't locked, just a big long hallway in front of her. Frowning, she slipped into the hall. She could hear footsteps coming toward her, so she opened the closest door and stepped inside, closing it behind her. She waited for somebody to walk past her down the hallway. Instead, she heard a scratchy voice behind her.

"Elizabeth, is that you?"

She turned, stared in shock. Her brother lay on the floor, his hands and legs both tied. She raced to his side and dropped to the floor beside him. "Oh, my God! Chris, are you okay?"

He gave her a wan smile. "I've been better. And, as much as I'm happy to see you, I'm really not happy to see you."

She understood because she felt the same way. She reached out and gently stroked the hair off his forehead.

"You want to see if you can get my hands untied?" he said, his voice raspy. "They hurt like hell."

She glanced at the ropes. They were tied so tight that the ropes were bloodstained at his wrists. Using her teeth and fingers, she pulled the knots loose to the point the ropes gave way.

He cried out but kept the sound low. He took several deep breaths, then rubbed his hands. When he could, he reached out and gave her a hug. "Thanks so much, sis. But, Jesus, I wish you weren't here."

"I wish I wasn't either," she said shakily, hugging him back. "But when you disappeared, all hell broke loose."

He groaned. "Help me with my feet, will you? It feels like my body's got no blood circulation left."

It took the two of them to get his feet untied. Then she helped him stand. He walked around, hobbling at first, and, as the blood started to move, his movements smoothed out. He could walk better and better.

Finally he gave her a fat grin. "Okay, now we're in a better position."

She smiled up at him. "Are we though? I was kidnapped from my hotel room when the two men I was with were used as a diversion, so I'd be alone. And it's my fault because I sent the one who stayed behind to watch over me out after the other one as backup. I was all about how I could handle myself," she said bitterly. "And look at me."

"I think you've done damn well," he said. "You got out of wherever you were and found me and helped me get out. So you've just doubled our chances of success."

She thought about that and perked up. "I have, haven't I?" She snickered. "The best part is, I found you. And that is the whole reason I came down here."

He walked toward the door. "Are you ready?"

"Maybe," she said. "Let me bring you up to speed." She quickly, as much as she could, told him about what had happened, what they'd found, and about King.

He just stared at her. "What?"

She nodded.

"Jesus, you know how to get into trouble."

She shot him a look. "Hey, I *was* staying out of trouble."

"I don't think you succeeded," he said.

With an ear to the door, he turned the handle and pulled it open. Motioning to her, the two crept out into the hall.

"I haven't seen any windows down here," she said, "so we must be belowground."

He nodded. "We are, but now we must find a way out of here."

There were two more doors to check. With a word of warning to her, he carefully opened the first door, finding yet another empty room. This floor appeared completely unused—except for holding prisoners.

With another shrug, he closed it again and said, "The last door's our only other option."

Her stomach heaved. "There's got to be stairs behind that door, and at the top of those stairs will be a shit ton of ugly men."

"I hear you." He opened the other door, and, sure

enough, there were stairs.

They quietly crept up the stairs, getting to the first landing, up to the second landing. There was another door at the top. And she knew that was when the trouble would begin. She grabbed his arm. "Do we have a plan?"

He shot her a grim look. "Hell no, do you?"

"No." And that was a shitty situation.

When Chris reached for the door, she caught her breath, and he slowly pulled it open.

NELSON RACED AFTER Taylor, but, when he hit the alleyway, he found Taylor standing there, turning around in a circle, glaring. "No sign of him?"

"No," he said. "None." Taylor glanced at Nelson. It clicked just then. "What the hell are you doing here?"

The two men moved back into the hotel, racing through the front lobby to see if the man had disappeared that way.

"I have no idea where he went," Nelson said. "But I want to get back to Elizabeth."

"You shouldn't have left her," Taylor said. "You know what this place is like."

Nelson shot him a hard look. "Believe it or not she's the one who chased me out here after you. She wanted to make sure you were safe."

Taylor chuckled. "I don't know about that. She's all about you. I've told you that before."

"Maybe. I think at this point, she's just all about her brother."

"And we can't blame her for that," Taylor said.

They took the stairs two at a time back up to the room. Nelson opened the door and stepped in. "Hey, Elizabeth?"

No answer. He shot Taylor a horrified look and ran through the adjoining room and then back out again. "She's gone," he said in a hard voice.

Taylor stopped and pointed. Her hair scrunchie, which she had put on that morning, had dropped to the floor. He reached down and picked it up. "She put this on this morning."

"That's not proof something's happened to her though."

"No, but she shouldn't have left without telling us."

"She wouldn't have," Nelson said with certainty in his heart. "Something's happened to her."

They both bolted from the room yet again and down the stairs. One going to the front, one going to the back, both racing out into the streets.

Nelson ran down the alleyway, but he knew in his heart of hearts he was too late. The kidnappers had had just that much of a window, and they knew this place like the back of their hands. He worried it was King. And, if that was the case, what the hell had been going on this morning with King? Or was that what the henchman's warning had been about? To get the hell out of here because they were in danger?

Maybe not that they were in danger but that *Elizabeth* was in danger. Nelson knew Chelsea didn't want anything to do with King getting Elizabeth. But would King really kidnap Elizabeth, knowing Nelson and Taylor were here and would come after King and Elizabeth for different reasons?

He pulled out his phone and gave Mason an update. "We're looking," he said, his voice hard, cold. "We just don't have any answers yet."

"Keep looking," Mason said. "I'll alert local law enforcement."

"Yeah, we're heading toward King's right now," Nelson said.

He met up with Taylor at the front, and the two ran down the street. As they got to the corner where King's place was, his henchman at the front door looked at Nelson and grinned. Nelson didn't say a word; he just walked right up, swung a hard roundhouse to the guy's jaw, and the henchman dropped to the steps.

He slammed both doors open and walked in. King raised his head and looked at him. Instead of the nice affable man, there was a snake with a look in his eyes that told Nelson how King was ready to eat him. "What the hell do you want?"

"I want Elizabeth," Nelson snapped. "Do you have her?"

King's face changed. "No, I don't." He stood slowly. "Why would you even think I have her?"

"A couple things," Nelson said. "One, because of your paramour, and, two, because of the guy who came and warned us a short time ago. And the fact that Elizabeth's now missing."

King's face went from perplexed to a hard angry red. "The streets have been warned they can't touch her," he said. "That is not acceptable."

"Why? Because you wanted her for yourself?"

King shot him a look. "You going to let me have her?"

"Over my dead body," Nelson said.

"Exactly," he said. "I could take you out, and I could keep her. But I also know I'd be bringing down a ton of heat. If she didn't come willingly, she's not one of the women you get to keep." He turned to look around, and there was Chelsea. He motioned her forward. "Did you have anything to do with this?"

She looked at him. "Of course not. I don't know any-thing about it."

He studied her for a long moment, then turned to Nelson and said, "What do you think?"

"I think she's lying," Nelson said. "She loves you." Nelson's tone softened, even though he didn't it want to. "And she's jealous as hell."

King looked from her to him and then back again. "What are you talking about?"

Nelson explained and then added, "You know Chelsea is afraid you'll replace her with Elizabeth. Chelsea knows how badly you want Elizabeth. And Chelsea seems to think she's on her way out of your favor."

"And like I said, Elizabeth's not the kind of woman you just keep," he said. "The reason I like her, the reason I want her, as you put it, is because of her softness, because of her innocence, because of her joy in life. I haven't laughed or enjoyed an hour as much as I had in the two visits I spent with her. But that's not something you get to keep forever. Like a butterfly, you can't put it in glass and expect it to thrive. The reason Elizabeth is the way she is, is because of the freedom she's been given, because of the ability to thrive in her surroundings. And her heart's already taken," he said with a snort. "Not that I really give a shit about her heart because I can't have it as it's already taken."

"You're right about her freedom and her joy," Nelson said gently. "And I'm glad you understand keeping her as a prisoner would break her spirit."

"She wouldn't give in easily to everything I would want. I'd have to take it, and that's fine in the short-term," he said, "but look at my life. I could take anything I wanted to. To have something like that *offered* to me instead, well, that's the

NELSON

gift. And it's not my gift." He shot Nelson a hard look.
"Whether you know it or not, it's your gift. And, for that, I'd
shoot you cheerfully, but I think she'd blame me regardless."

The blows were instant and hard as the truth hit Nelson.
And he realized the truth of King's words. Taylor had tried
to warn Nelson. But what he hadn't seen was how much he
wanted her himself. He ran his fingers through his hair. "The
bottom line right now is, she's gone. She's missing. And I
highly suspect you and your men are responsible."

"Not me," King said. "Although that doesn't mean one
of my men might not have. I'd have his head on a chopping
block if he didn't have a damn good reason though."

King looked around, his snake eyes once again assessing
the men in the room. Taylor did too. In the back, hiding in
the corner, was the man who had come to their hotel room
door. Nelson pointed him out. "He's the one who came to
warn us."

King turned on him. The guy shot Nelson a hard, hateful look. "Sure, I gave you a warning, and look what you do.
You throw me under the bus," he said in disgust.

"Yeah, but it wasn't a warning, was it? It was a decoy.
Because I suspect you and Chelsea had Elizabeth kidnapped.
But it would have taken at least one more man." He turned
to look around and found the other man standing in the
other corner. He pointed him out. "Chelsea's other henchman." He glanced at King to see his face had turned ugly.

He motioned the men to come forward. Neither one
moved. At that King's face turned a mottled red. He turned
to his other men, as if assessing how deep the war would be.
The other men were looking from one to the other in
confusion.

A shot rang out.

King gasped and collapsed into the chair behind him. Two more shots rang out. The two men who stood protectively beside King dropped to the floor.

Chelsea stepped forward, holding the handgun. She leveled it at two more of King's men. "You are either on my side, or you're on his. I don't give a shit which, but I won't have you stabbing me in the back after this."

The two men stared at her; one man curled his lip. But he didn't get a chance to utter a word. A bullet hole appeared in the front of his forehead, and he collapsed to the floor.

The other man held up his hands. "Hey, Chelsea, you know me."

"I know you," she said bitterly. "You're as much a part of his nightmare as anybody."

"Only because we're all in the same situation," he protested, an angry note in his voice. "You know we're all prisoners here. None of us get to have a life of our own. It's either be his man or be dead."

"Well, now it's be on my side or be dead," she said bitterly.

"*You're* the one who kidnapped Elizabeth," Nelson said.

"Yeah, I did," she said. "But what you don't know is that King has her brother."

Nelson's gut stilled as his mind spun to make sense of this nightmare. He could feel Taylor tense behind him. They both had weapons. Neither had been searched when they came in. But that didn't mean they could get to them before bullets hit them. "Why does he have her brother?"

"He took him as leverage because he really did want Elizabeth. Do you think I went to all that effort because he was just looking *at* her? No. I heard him making plans to kidnap her."

Nelson turned a hard gaze to King, who was gasping in pain. He'd been gut shot, but he was still conscious and bitter from the looks of it. He went to open a drawer in his desk but a bullet rang out, hitting him in the hand. He cried out.

"I gave you everything," she snapped, strolling slowly toward him. "And what did you give me? Nothing. More kicks, more blows, that's it. I loved you," she cried out with so much pain in her voice it almost made Nelson wince.

King stared up at her. "You don't understand how perfect she is."

"And did you hear yourself earlier? How you capture a butterfly and expect it to keep its sweetness and brightness?"

"I would have given her all the freedom she wanted," he whispered. "She wouldn't have been a prisoner."

"It's the only way you could have kept her," Chelsea wailed. "Can't you see that?"

Nelson wondered. Because, of course, that was the only way it would go. So why go to the trouble—unless it was to keep the butterfly for as long as he could. "Why did you kidnap her brother?"

King raised his gaze. "I would do a trade. Elizabeth for her brother. Elizabeth would have taken the trade easily. My men would have caught her. They were to take her downstairs until I could talk to her. I'd explain the situation. It was up to her to be willingly at my side, happy to be at my side, and I'd let her brother live. But, if she fought me, then she and her brother would die too."

Nelson shook his head. "And, of course, then that same bright joy you had found in her that matched that missing piece in your own heart would have died. You know that, and yet, you were still willing to take the chance."

"Of course I was," King said. "I can have everything, but I can't have the one willing woman I really want. But I thought I could try. I thought, if I could get her to stay with me long enough, I could get her to want to be with me. That she could fall in love with me, and we could have something together."

Nelson was shocked to think of somebody in King's situation softening to the extent he could fall in love. And yet, King shouldn't be in love with Elizabeth because Nelson himself was in love with Elizabeth. "And me?"

"You would have taken a bullet in the back of the head somewhere and dropped in the water along with your partner," King said with a casual tone. "Hell, Chelsea is still likely to do that."

"And the reason you didn't do that right away is because you didn't want to bring down more of us," Taylor said in a lazy voice from behind Nelson. "Because you know we're only two, but, when we go down, a never-ending supply of well-trained military men come and take care of business on our behalf."

King glared at him. "Do you think I'm scared of you?"

"No," Nelson said. "But I do think you were fucking broken by a woman. Not just the one who has your heart in her hands and doesn't even know it but the one whose heart you hold in your hands, and you didn't even know it."

Another shot came and slammed into King.

Nelson turned to face Chelsea. "Is that really what you want to do? Slowly tear him apart, one bullet at a time?" He could see her anger waning. But not enough. "You can still save him, you know?"

"No," she whispered. "You don't understand. There's no saving King. No matter what I do now, I'm a dead woman."

She gave a bit of a laugh. "Even among my men, there'll always be a fight to take King's place. One of these guys will try it." She raised her gun and shot the man who she'd spoken to earlier.

Nelson's breath caught in the back of his throat. He didn't think things could go any further sideways, but right now she was knocking them all off, like bowling pins in an alleyway. And he knew Taylor was just as aware of the problem. From his count, there were four men left, outside of him and Taylor. Only two of King's men stood beside Nelson and Taylor, both looking stunned at this turn of events, and there were still Chelsea's two men. King was almost gone, but it looked like Chelsea was ready to take him down completely.

Nelson said, "Is that what love is? Just anger and betrayal?"

She gave him a look that he could barely read, but he could see the pain. He could see the loss and the grief. He realized she really did care, but she also knew she was headed down a one-way street.

Behind her a door opened. It was so soft, so subtle a movement he wasn't even sure he'd seen it. It opened just a hair.

Chelsea kept talking. "You know I can't trust any of the men in this room."

Her two henchmen straightened, and one cried out, "Hey, that's not fair. We've been with you the whole time."

She gave him a half smile. "Yeah, because I made it easier on you with King. But, with him gone, what's to stop you two roosters from thinking you can take over?" She gave a broken cry. "This has been my life as long as I can remember. Nothing but discarded garbage. And I'm so fucking done with that."

And, without warning, she turned and shot twice more. The two men beside Nelson and Taylor dropped. Her two henchmen stared at her in shock. She just gave them smiles.

"Now it's just the three of us. We don't have to worry about them coming after us."

They took deep breaths, but their gazes never left her.

Nelson wondered if the group of them—her two henchmen and Taylor and him—could have jumped her. She might have shot one or two of them, but she couldn't have killed them all.

She was taking them out with so little regard for life that he knew it didn't matter what he said; it wouldn't be enough. He looked at her. "Did you hurt her?"

"Ask them. They're the ones who kidnapped her."

He shot a hard gaze at the man who had been the decoy, then turned to look at the Chelsea's second man. The other one shook his head. "I just dumped her downstairs."

"And where's her brother?"

"He's downstairs too," the henchman said. "But he's getting to be a pain in the ass to look after."

"Why is that?"

"Because every eight hours we gave him a bathroom break and water. Other than that, he gets to stay in that lovely room."

"I don't understand why King grabbed him at the beginning. And *where* did he grab him?"

"He grabbed him at the bus depot, heading back to the US, not sure what for, but figured he could use him somehow. Before he figured it out, you came to town with Elizabeth."

"Her brother was planning to go to ground and to hide

until things improved for him," Chelsea said, her voice broken, haunted. "But you arrived, and so did she. Once King saw, ... then met, her, that was it. It was 100 percent down the road for all of us."

Chelsea started to cry. She walked over to King, who was bleeding but still staring up at her, hate in his eyes. She reached out and smacked him hard across the face. "Why couldn't you have been happy with what you had? Why couldn't you have been happy with me? Why couldn't I have been enough?"

King closed his eyes.

Nelson could see he was close to death.

"You don't understand," King gasped. "When you see something like sunlight, and you reach out and touch it, and you get touched back, it's ... redeeming." He smiled a smile of sweetness and sunshine. "I may not have held on to her, and maybe nobody should, but I did get to touch her. I did get to feel what it was like, to walk in the sunshine for a moment. And, for that, I'm damn grateful." And he closed his eyes.

Chelsea cried out, "No, no, no, no. Please no."

"He could still live," Nelson said, "if we got him some help."

Chelsea reached down to touch his neck and shook her head. "No," she said, "we can't." She started to cry in earnest, as she paced, first one way; and then she got angry as she paced the other way; and then she got worried, as she sorted out what her options were.

Nelson watched as all those emotions tore across her face. "Were all the men in this room?" Nelson asked, helping her come to the right decision. "Are there others outside who will stab you in the back?"

She stopped and looked at him, and there came that weaselly assessing look. She looked around the room, counted the heads of the dead men in here, and then said, "You're right. It's just the two of you"—she pointed to her two henchmen with her gun—"with me."

"And we can take over," one of her henchmen said gently. "It's not too late for that. Nobody knows. You can take King's place. We have all the contacts. You know we've already supported you every step of the way. Instead of King, it'll be the Queen as our leader."

She looked up and smiled. "You know what? I can almost get behind that."

"The difference will be that, instead of taking orders," Nelson said, "you'd be giving them. Instead of getting beaten, you could order the beatings."

"Of course you want to be a little judicious in your orders, unless you want to end up like King," Taylor said, once again his lazy voice rolling through the room.

Nelson had always appreciated how he was in control all the time. How he seemed so calm and collected. He was always analyzing everything they'd seen to the bottom line, everywhere.

She paced back and forth and finally stopped again. She turned and looked at them with a calculating look in her eye. "The thing is, there are witnesses."

Nelson's heart froze. He had to be able to react quickly to whatever happened next.

Then behind Chelsea the door opened, and a stranger stepped out.

Taylor was talking again, but Nelson heard none of it. *Maybe not a stranger.* Nelson looked at the shape of his face, and his heart beat again. Then he saw Elizabeth step out too.

And he knew things were about to head south in a big way. If there was one thing that would set Chelsea off, it would be the sight of Elizabeth. Chelsea had tried to kill her once before, without success. But, with Elizabeth right here, right now …

Nelson stepped forward. "You know what we want. We'll take our people and leave. "If you want to live here and be the Queen of all you survey, that's up to you."

She gave a hard laugh. "Like I believe you. You don't really think I'll listen to your gibberish. You're just anxious to save your own life."

She raised her weapon, lined it up to his heart. "Two witnesses is two witnesses too many."

"And what about your henchmen?"

"They're witnesses too," she snared. "But, like they said, they've been with me the whole time."

He knew he shouldn't do it, but it was hard not to, and he needed her to believe all things were possible. Not everything would work in her favor. "Maybe," he said. "But what happens down the road when they hold that over you?"

She just glared at him, and he knew she already had thought of that. Both men would die too today. Whether they deserved it or not wasn't Nelson's job to decide. He could see that both henchmen hadn't said a word about the people behind her. They wanted her taken down as much as anybody. Nelson took half a step forward.

She held the gun back up and said, "Watch it."

He nodded. "I don't have any intention of touching you. I want your agreement that I can take my three people away, take them a long way away from you. You never have to see Elizabeth again."

Chelsea curled her lip. "She ruined my life. And I'll see

her again." Her voice was hard; she was almost gleeful, as if looking forward to it. "And I'll put a bullet right between her eyes."

And into the silence afterward came a very soft gasp.

Nelson clenched his muscles as Chelsea spun and saw Elizabeth and took a shot.

Nelson jumped Chelsea from the back as Skunk jumped her from the front. Elizabeth hit the floor, and the shots went wild, but Chelsea's hand kept clenching the trigger, as if spasmodically hitting the bane of her existence, that need to do something to take out the person she hated so much. With Chelsea finally pinned to the floor, the gun kicked out of her hand, she lay here sobbing. But her cries were half in anger and half in fury that she couldn't accomplish exactly what she wanted.

Elizabeth picked up the gun and held it out to Taylor.

He put it into his waistband out of the way. He looked over at Chelsea's two henchmen and said, "If you ever wanted a chance to restart your life, this is a really good time to get on a bus and disappear. Because we won't give you a second chance. Just being associated with what went down, you know you'll do life. I've got no bones with what you want to do after this. But you know where my vote is."

The men took one look at each other and disappeared out the front door at a hard run.

"Can you really let them go like that?" Elizabeth asked.

"Not our problem," Nelson said. "The local PD can grab them. And probably will too. Whether it's at the local bus stop or from another henchmen hideaway in town. But, with King dead, and Chelsea having taken out almost his entire conclave, the cops may not worry about these lower-level guys. And often the cops will overlook what the underlings did in order to get the bigger ones. However, the top guy, the King, is dead and Chelsea's standing in that top position and murdered a half dozen men herself and that's just now."

"I see that." She stood over Chelsea, who even now showed signs of madness. Elizabeth caught her hand in hers and said, "Calm down. It's over."

Chelsea looked up at her and spat.

Elizabeth stepped out of the line of fire. "I'm sorry for you," she said. "You didn't have a chance right from childhood. And you won't like jail much either."

Nelson pulled Chelsea to her feet, and she stood here, shaking, shivering in the aftermath. She looked at Taylor and said, "Shoot me. Please shoot me."

He shook his head. "Hell no. I don't kill indiscriminately."

"It won't be," she said, her tone dead. "I've killed a lot. I don't deserve to live. So much cleaner if you just take me out."

He shook his head. "No, you can pay the price for what you've done. Everybody here may have gotten off easy, but that was your doing. You had your chance to kill yourself, but you were all about trying to kill Elizabeth instead."

Chelsea's legs were shaky. "At least let me sit beside King so I can hold his hand and say my goodbyes."

The two men looked at each other. Elizabeth shrugged. "I can see she might need to do that."

With the men standing over her, she crouched at King's side. They could see her tears falling.

Nelson stepped off to the side and picked up his phone to call Mason. "It's over. Skunk is here." He looked to see Skunk staring out the window. "We still don't have the full story yet, but King had him kidnapped a few days ago. I guess they saw him, figured out that maybe he had some use only to find out later that Elizabeth was looking for him too. King wanted to trade Chris for Elizabeth." Mason's expletive on the other end made Nelson smile. "Yeah, I know, it's totally messed up. But we need law enforcement here, and we need several ambulances. Chelsea shot a lot of men. There won't be a whole lot to prosecute after this, just her."

Nelson heard Chelsea cry out. He turned in time to see her snatch the letter opener from on top of the desk where King had sat and plunge it into her throat hard enough that it stuck out the back of her neck. Staring at him, her eyes wide with the pain and the triumph, her features twisted as she collapsed on top of the man she'd loved and had hated enough to kill.

"Scratch that last point," Nelson said to Mason. "She won't be prosecuted either."

CHAPTER 13

E LIZABETH AND THE others, both dead and alive, had been stuck in the building until the cops and the ambulances arrived, and then the witnesses all tried to give statements. Some of it was garbled; some of it was clear, but it was obvious her brother was traumatized. Hell, so was she. The cops said they would go after the two henchmen who'd taken the opportunity to run, but they didn't appear to be too enthusiastic about it.

One of the medical technicians walked up to Nelson and Elizabeth and asked if he could check their vital signs. Nelson immediately declined and demanded that Elizabeth be looked over. She was too weak to argue. The technician measured her body temp, blood pressure, pulse rate and respiratory rate. Then he saw the blood on the back of her head and flashed a light in her eyes and had her gaze follow his finger. He carefully cleaned her wound and said she needed no stitches, but she already had one hell of a goose egg back there, which was a good sign but would be very painful for about a week. He asked her for her name and what year it was.

She laughed, then winced.

"That's a good sign," he said, "the laugh, not the wince, but I still need to hear your answers." Once confirmed, he nodded his head. "I would prefer for you to spend one night in our hospital for observation"—he raised both his hands to stop both of them from arguing—"but I understand your desire to just get away from all this."

"Thank you, sir," Nelson said.

Elizabeth nodded, winced again, and her hand immediately went to her head.

"Yes, you may travel home tomorrow. I understand you'll be riding back with Nelson to the States. Take breaks as needed, but otherwise you'll hurt for several days regardless. So take it easy, okay? And here are some pain meds to get you through tonight and tomorrow until you can see your American doctor." With a smile he was gone.

This time Elizabeth just raised her hand in thanks as the technician moved on to help the next person.

Despite being stuck here so long, they were reassured to hear King and Queen were dead. Elizabeth knew more assholes would step up and take their places. Asshole positions never stayed empty. They always filled quickly.

Her brother talked with Taylor on the other side of the room; afterward Chris contacted his commander and NCIS. It was just a huge waiting game to sort out his future, but she had hopes everyone would understand his actions. She certainly did.

Hours later, exhausted, Elizabeth collapsed on her bed in her hotel room and stared up at the ceiling. Nelson lay beside her, wrapped her up in his arms and just held her. She loved that about him; he always seemed to know what she needed. And, for the moment, it was just to be held, to know she was safe, that he was safe, that Taylor was safe, and— thank heavens—that her brother was safe too. "I can't believe it's over," she whispered.

Nelson dropped a kiss on her temple, holding her tight.

"We did it."

She smiled and kissed his cheek. "Tomorrow is four days, isn't it? We're supposed to go home in the morning."

"We'll make it," he said. "I'll drive carefully, missing all the potholes so you aren't jarred. There'll be some stuff to sort out later. And a lot of that can be done at home. NCIS and the local law enforcement here have our contact information and know we leave tomorrow. They'll call us if they need to, so it doesn't matter where we are. More important, your brother needs to go to the hospital and get checked over."

His phone beeped just then. He read the text and smiled. "NCIS just found Matt. Now it truly is over." In a louder voice he told the others.

"Yes," Chris said in a loud voice. "Damn, I'm glad to hear that."

"And on that note:"

Taylor called out, "Nelson. I'm taking Chris to the hospital. He's already torn some of his stitches on the cuts on his ankles and his wrists. Plus, I think he's got a busted rib or two. Wouldn't hurt to get an X-ray on that."

"The technician did a good job to stop the bleeding, but we should have taken him to the hospital earlier," Nelson said. He hopped off the bed and assessed Skunk. "Man, you look like shit."

"I feel it." Skunk gave him a crooked smile. "And thanks. You look damn beautiful. I'm so grateful for the rescue."

"Go with Taylor. He'll get you looked after and delivered back here again," Nelson said. "No way I'm leaving your sister alone."

"Sounds like you'll be part of the family now, huh?"

Skunk flashed him a big grin. "Told you a long time ago she was worth it."

"A long time ago I wasn't looking," Nelson said.

"You weren't looking now either," Taylor said, his smirk a mile wide.

"No," Nelson said with a big grin. "But somehow she sneaked in anyway."

"That's the way it works," Taylor said. "We'll be back in a couple hours."

"Bring food," Elizabeth called out from the other bedroom as she joined them in this room. "And bring lots of it." She gave her brother a gentle hug. "Hurry back so we can get some sleep and then go home tomorrow."

He reached down and gave her a kiss on the cheek. "Will do. That's one order I'm happy to take from you."

She smiled mistily and watched as the two left. She turned to Nelson and threw her arms around him. "Oh, my God! I still can't believe it's over."

"I know," he said. "It's hard to comprehend. Things got a little crazy there at the end."

They lay down on his bed, and she said, "I just want to sleep."

"Go ahead and sleep. Nothing's stopping you."

"Yeah, there is," she said. "You."

"I'm not stopping you," he said. "Just close your eyes."

She leaned up and kissed him hard. "You see? We now have an opportunity and plenty of time."

His eyebrows shot up toward his hairline.

She chuckled. "Are you telling me that you didn't think about it?"

"I've thought about nothing else," he confessed. "But we're on a job. Now you're injured."

"No, we *were* on a job, and I *was* injured," she said, nuzzling his cheek and chin. "But we're not now."

"Are those drugs doing the job?" he asked with a smirk. "Not sure I should take advantage like that."

Elizabeth smirked right back at him. "Chris and Taylor will be gone for *at least* two hours."

Nelson thought about it, swung off the bed, picked her up gently in his arms, padded into the other room, closed the connecting door and said, "Lock it."

She laughed. With one arm around his neck and the other arm free, she locked the connecting door. Effortlessly he lay down with her still in his arms. She chuckled and rolled to the side and tucked up close.

"Now maybe we can have some privacy too."

"Yeah? And what are your plans if we do?" she whispered teasingly.

"First, I should punish you for not staying safe inside." He shifted to the side so he could place kisses on her cheekbones and forehead. "Do you have any idea how terrified I was when I came back and found your room empty?"

Her arms snaked up around his neck. "I'm so sorry. I knew you would be terrified, but the guy did something so weird to me. It's like I was paralyzed afterward for a few minutes. He was running down the alleyway, and I was flopping like a fish, conscious but completely unable to move. It was horrifying. Then he dumped me in a room and shut the door. But he never locked any of the doors."

"I'm sorry you had to go through any of that. As for the unlocked doors, I don't think they ever needed guards, just the fear of King," he said, "because, if you think about it, King was always upstairs. Nobody would ever go past him."

"But you see how betrayal always happens from within?" she said sadly. "I felt so sorry for Chelsea."

"Don't," he said. "She might have had a rough child-hood, but she didn't have to end it all that way. Neither did she have to try to kill you."

"I think, in her heart of hearts, it's the only way she thought she could survive this. Or maybe it was her elaborate murder-suicide mission that got way out of hand. I don't know."

"I vote we don't talk about her anymore," Nelson said. "I vote we don't talk about any of this anymore." And he dropped a kiss on her lips, then on her nose, then on her chin. "I vote we talk about us."

"What? A man who *wants* to have a heart-to-heart con-versation?" she asked with a mocking laugh.

He rose up over her and came down, his lips kissing the breath out of her.

When he raised his head again, she said, "Okay. Now that sounds like my kind of heart-to-heart talk."

A chuckle slid out as he kissed her gently over and over again. Her warm breath mingling with his, stroking the fires they'd both kept banked deep inside. His fingers slid over her T-shirt to cup her breasts, his lips moving up her throat, her chin, across her cheek and down to her collarbone. He nipped her once, twice, tickled her, made her laugh and wiggle as her hands reached up into his hair, pulling him closer so she could get more of those incredible kisses. He gave her one and then another and then he was gone again.

She protested, craving his hot passionate mouth. "Maybe I want more kisses."

"And you can have more," he muttered, but his atten-tion was on her T-shirt that he'd pulled up over her chest, and the front clasp of her bra was suddenly dispensed with.

She groaned as his mouth came down over her nipple, and he suckled it deep into his mouth. "Oh, my God," she said, arching into his mouth. "That feels so good."

His hand stroked up her back, down her ribs, around her belly to cup and hold her breast. He laved first one nipple and then the other.

She twisted in his arms, so damn grateful to be alive, and even more grateful to be holding him like this. She whispered, "Did you ever think ..."

He shook his head. "No," he said, his voice thick. "But I had hoped." He drew his lips down, kissing her ribs, each one along the way. When he got to her belly button, he kissed and licked it. She chuckled and squirmed on the bed, but he slipped two hands inside her jeans waistband, popped the button and separated the zipper. He sat up, pulled her jeans off very slowly, his eyes watching as every inch became visible.

She lay here on the bed feeling beautiful as he watched her. "You're really good at this."

He looked up at her with surprise in his eyes. "I don't know why I would be because this feels like it's new, feels like it's something I've never really experienced before. It's so damn different with you." He reached up and stroked her from her nipples to her hips. She sat up with a chuckle and threw her T-shirt and bra off and lay back down. She motioned at him. "I think you should stand up and match me for clothing."

"Absolutely." He stepped off the bed and stripped down to his boxers.

She gasped, rose to her knees in front of him, her hands reaching for him as he stood proud in front of her, his erection poking out the top of his underwear. She slid his underwear down to free him, her hands gently cupping his testicles, then sliding up the long shaft.

He made a strangled sound. "None of that," he said. "Not this time."

She chuckled. "I hear you. I don't want to wait either."

With his boxers off, she lay back down again and opened her arms. He reached down, gently pulled off the tiny piece of lace that was her panties, then stopped and stared. In a fervent whisper he murmured, "Wow, you're so stunningly beautiful."

She raised a knee almost shyly.

He shook his head. "None of that." He reached down, stroked her legs, the legs that never seemed to quit, up to her hips and tiny waist before gently stroking through the reddish blond curls at the heart of her. He groaned, leaned over and kissed her navel, and then right in the nest of curls.

She gasped, grabbed his hair and pulled him toward her mouth. Her kiss was frantic. She kissed him again and again and again.

Finally he caught her face in his hands and kissed her deeply—their mouths and tongues warring, enjoying, coaxing, searing each other's passions to a higher and higher point. She tried to explore him, but he held her hands up above her head.

"I'm not kidding. Not this time." He reached down, took her nipple in his mouth deeply.

She groaned, spread her legs underneath him, wrapped them around his hips and said, "Me either. Now. Come to me now."

He took one look at her, raised himself up on one elbow, fitted himself to the right place, and holding her hips, he plunged deep.

She gasped, arched beneath him and cried out.

He gave her a moment to adjust to having him inside, and then, with his hands on her hips, he started to move slowly, then faster and faster and faster.

She twisted underneath him, urging him on, her legs wrapped around him as she rose to meet every thrust.

He caught her nape in his hands, tilted her head up and kissed her neck, down to her collarbone, as he moved faster and faster. And then he took her lips in a searing kiss as his body shuddered and shook as he tried to hold back. But just a touch of his tongue into her mouth, matching the plunge of his body, the total possession, the complete ownership— more than that, the complete surrender—was when she willingly gave herself to him and received in return all she'd ever wanted.

Her climax ripped through her, sending her over the edge. In the background she dimly heard his groan as his body throbbed and pulsed both atop and in her.

Finally he rolled onto the side, gathered her into his arms and tucked her up close.

She said on a half-groan, half-whisper, "You know what? I almost thought I would be killed earlier tonight. Then I just thought that now too."

He gave a half bark of a laugh and said, "As long as I'm killing you with joy, that's all that matters."

"Definitely," she whispered. "I so want to go home."

"Is your brother moving in with you, do you think?"

"I don't know," she said with a happy sigh. "I don't mind either way. He has to face his own bosses and get his life sorted out first. I guess the better question is, are you moving in with me?"

He reared up and looked down at her.

She smiled. "Unless you think this is a one-off."

"It's hardly a one-off," he said, kissing her gently. "But we could take things slow."

"Like we did just now?" she asked archly.

He chuckled. "Good point. We still have an hour before they get back."

"In that case," she said, wrapping her arms around him. "Let's not waste it."

He lowered his head. "Maybe that's all you want me for."

"I don't ask every man I take to bed to move in with me," she whispered against his lips. "Only the man I love."

He stared at her.

She smiled again. "I know it's early. It doesn't change how I feel though."

"I hope not," he said, "because, when I listened to King speaking about you, I could hear the exact same sentiment in my own heart." He whispered, "I love you too. I don't know how it happened, and I don't know when, and I would never have believed it could have been so fast."

She placed a finger against his lips. "No more questions, no more doubts. Let's just take it one day at a time and see where this goes."

"I can get behind that." He kissed her with passion.

She smiled, wrapped her arms around him and held him close. They'd have time to talk later. They'd have time to work out everything later. But right now, this was just for them. This was just for the two of them to enjoy. All the rest would happen in its own good time. Like any good relationship, it would only get better with time.

USA *TODAY* BESTSELLING AUTHOR

Dale Mayer

SEALS OF
HONOR
Taylor

BOOK-22

PROLOGUE

T AYLOR ROBINSON WALKED into his small apartment on base, dropped his bag on the floor, flipped on his stereo, strode to his couch and threw himself down, full length, and collapsed. He groaned, speaking out loud to the empty space, "Thank God for my own space."

A voice called from the hallway, "Did you mean to leave your door open?"

His neighbor poked her head in. Frizzy red hair from her shoulders to the top of her crown and a bright flashing grin. *Midge.* Taylor hopped up and walked over, rolling his shoulders and his neck. "It's so good to be home."

"You do travel a lot," she said with a smile. She was in her office wear, heading out to work.

He glanced at his watch. "Are you on night shift?"

She shook her head. "Nah, just got called back for an emergency. I hadn't even made it home yet, and now I'm ordered back." She wrinkled up her face. "And you know how we all love that."

"As in *not*," he said with a laugh. "I'm back from a crazy-ass trip, and I'm glad to be home."

"Rough?"

He smiled. He couldn't help it. She was more of a pixie type but always had a bright smile. He didn't know if she was sweet on him or if she just had that kind of personality, but he never would be mean to her because she was so friendly. "It was rough," he said. "No clue why but there's something about coming home with two people who just hooked up and are crazy in love with each other." He shook his head. "Not what I expected, though I should have."

She laughed. "Hey, you often have women over, so, if it's jealousy, just find another one."

"I'm not *that* bad," he protested. "I haven't had a relationship in months."

She gave him a mock look of shock. "Wow," she said with a chuckle. With a finger wave she headed down the hallway.

He stepped out and watched her stride away. She was short, maybe five feet, and always had a smile for him. He looked the other way, down the hall and across at her apartment, realizing her door was open a hair too. He would have called out to her and said something about it, but she'd already disappeared down the stairs.

With a groan, he stepped down the hall and across to her apartment and went to close the door when he caught the smell. He frowned. His heart raced. He still had his weapon. He pulled it out and nudged the door open. With the gun up and ready, he checked around the corner. The place had been destroyed, but that still didn't explain the smell. He kept going through the rooms until he got to the bedroom. And there, lying on top of the bedding, was a nude male. One Taylor recognized.

The guy worked in the supply offices. Taylor had seen him several times ... but not like this. Taylor raced back out to the hallway and down the stairs, moving as fast as he could to catch Midge. He didn't know what the hell had gone on, but no way was she walking away from a dead guy in her apartment.

She had just opened her car door when she saw him. She stopped, turned, looked up at him and smiled. "What's the matter? You missed me already?"

Her manner was so nonchalant and casual, he was flummoxed. He pulled to a stop in front of her. Her brain registered the gun in his hand, and her hands shot up.

"What the hell?" he asked. "Did you just leave your apartment?"

She shook her head. "No. I was coming home and got the call at the top of the stairs. I had to turn around and come back in again. I never made it to my apartment. So I was turning around when I saw your apartment door was open."

"Did you go into your apartment?"

She frowned at him. "I just told you that I didn't."

He took a deep breath. "Did you touch the doorknob?"

She stopped, looked at him and shook her head. "No, I didn't even make it to my apartment. Remember? I was pissed. I didn't want to head back out again."

"Well, you can't go to work. Call your boss back, and tell him that you can't make it."

"Why?" she asked. "I'll just get in deeper shit for that."

"Because you left your door to your apartment open. I went to go shut it for you."

She looked up at him. "I didn't get to my apartment. Didn't you *hear* me?"

"Your apartment door was open," he enunciated clearly. "Did you *hear me*?"

He watched her comprehension finally *click*. She swallowed hard. "Was I broken into?"

He reached out, touching her shoulder. "Are you in a

relationship with Gary?"

She stared at him. "I don't have a boyfriend. Gary who?"

"Gary Sims. He works in supply."

She shook her head. "Maybe he does, but I don't really know the man. I've likely seen him around, as we both work on base, but I don't *know* him. Not really. I work in staff records. That's not even close to his department."

"I get that," he said. "Do you know him?"

Frustrated and angry now, she stomped her foot. "I answered that already. What's this about?"

He reached out again and grabbed her hand. "He's dead in your bed—and the only thing he's wearing are three bullet holes, one in his forehead."

CHAPTER 1

M IDGE HOLLOWAY WOULDN'T believe Taylor until she saw it for herself. They now stood in the hallway, outside Midge's apartment. She stared at Taylor. Then her head started to shake, sending red curls everywhere. Her body followed. She wrapped her arms tight around her chest, but it was hard to hold back her shudders as shock set in. "I barely even knew the man," she whispered. "What's he doing in my apartment?"

"I don't know," Taylor said grimly. "But we have a very limited window to find out."

She stared at him, her fuzzy mind confused as she struggled to understand what Taylor was talking about. She glanced up and down the hallway. "This is so wrong. I'll be in so much fucking trouble."

"That you are," he said. "So, somehow, we have to clear you of this." He stopped talking and looked at her intently. "Presuming you're innocent."

Her eyes widened, and she stared at him for a moment before her temper spiked. "I had absolutely nothing to do with any of this. How could you even think I would do something like that?"

"Hey, I hated to ask, but I needed a clear answer," Taylor said, running a hand through his hair. "I'm short on sleep. It's been a rough couple of days. Look. In the last eight years that I've been in the navy, I've seen way too much shit. Not just on a personal level but globally. No, the scene in your apartment is not a new coup taking over a small country and leaving behind only bloodshed, bones and broken dreams. But, on a small scale, it's really the same damn thing. You've got somebody who wanted something, and they're using people as a way to get it. So you need to tell me how well you knew Gary."

Just then a door slammed down the hallway, and a guy turned to the stairway without even looking at them. They could hear his footsteps as he went downstairs. She looked at Taylor and whispered, "Did you recognize him?"

He shrugged. "No. I can't say that I did. You?"

She frowned. "I don't know," she said. "I feel like I'm looking at everybody suspiciously. For that matter"—she turned to look at him—"how do I know you didn't kill him? Maybe when your door was open, you had just raced away from my place."

He gave a bark of laughter. "If only I had the energy for all that. You can call Nelson and find out that I just got home like an hour ago."

"How long do you think the guy has been dead?"

He watched her with respect. "Oh, good question. Because if he's only been dead forty-five minutes, I could have killed him, but what would be my reason for letting you know a dead guy is in your room?"

She frowned, not sure exactly what his reasoning would be. "Maybe you're not a nice guy, but you're not quite the asshole who would want me to come home in the dark and see that either."

He pursed his lips with a smirk and said, "Good theory but it's a no on all counts."

She raised both hands in frustration. "Fine. So what now?"

"We call in the police," he said quietly. "And you don't touch anything."

"I'm not touching nothing," she snapped. "Except my cell phone. I have to go to work. You know that, right?"

He shook his head. "Tell them an emergency came up."

"Are you kidding? That's why I got called in to begin with. Somebody else had an emergency."

"Let me call the cops first. I'll see if you can head off to work, but I've got a pretty good idea what the answer will be."

She groaned and paced while he made the call. She heard broken bits of the conversation, but the gist was clear. She'd better stay here, or her ass was on the line.

It made sense, considering it was her apartment and all, but, at the same time, she didn't want to get into more trouble at work either. Reluctant, but resigned, she picked up her phone and called her boss.

His voice ripped through the air. "Why aren't you back here yet? I told you that we needed you."

"I'm sorry, sir," she said. "But something major is going on in my apartment building."

"Unless you're dead, dying or almost there," he snapped, "you better get your ass over here or don't bother coming tomorrow."

She gasped in outrage, but Taylor snapped her phone from her hand.

"CONSIDERING THE POLICE are standing at her apartment door and won't let her inside or let her leave, you'd be well advised to change your attitude," Taylor snapped. "I'd like your name and your rank so I can report you."

Silence followed on the other end of the phone. "Who the hell is this?"

"It doesn't matter who the hell this is," Taylor said, refusing to give an inch. "You are not allowed to speak to an employee like that, plus, she not only has a viable excuse but couldn't leave if she wanted to."

"Is she under arrest?" her boss asked suspiciously.

"No, but maybe we should be looking at you, considering the way you apparently treat her."

Again came more silence, and her boss backtracked. "Look. I've had things blow up here too."

"She works in staff records," Taylor shouted. "What could possibly blow up?"

"We've had a breach," he said. "Our computer systems have been hacked."

Silence. "Oh, very interesting," Taylor said. "Well, you'll hear about her emergency soon enough," he said. "Do you know Gary Sims?"

"From the supply department?" her boss asked, sounding curious. "Kinda but not really. No more than anybody else on base who only deals with him once or twice a year."

"He's been murdered," Taylor said.

"What? And Midge is involved? That doesn't sound like her. I didn't think she had a boyfriend," the boss said, clearly trying to make sense of the news.

"Exactly. But he's been murdered in her apartment, so you can see the problem now, right?"

"But she was at work all day. She only left the office about an hour ago."

"That will definitely help keep her ass out of jail. But, at

TAYLOR

the moment, her ass is still swinging in the air, so she needs to be here until the cops tell her that she can leave."

Midge's boss gave a heavy sigh. "What a messed-up day."

"As soon as I get it cleared here, I'll bring her to you. And then we'll see what we can figure out down there."

"What have you got to do with any of this?"

"Maybe nothing, depends if I'm assigned to this detail," Taylor said. "But chances are you won't find access to too many guys like me," he said. "I'm Taylor, Taylor Robinson. From Mason's team."

"I'll call Mason then to confirm. After all, not sure anybody on base doesn't know who he is and could drop his name easily enough." And her boss hung up.

Immediately Taylor grabbed his own phone and dialed Mason himself. As soon as he answered at the other end, Taylor said, "You'll get a call from someone in staff records. I've got Midge here. She lives across the hallway from me. We've only gotten home about an hour ago, each of us separately," he clarified. "Her door was open, and, when I went to shut it, I caught a smell that I definitely recognized."

"Hey, Taylor. How are you? Nice to know you made it back home, safe and sound," Mason said, his tone amused. "Can you do anything but get yourself into trouble?"

"Back to the problem," Taylor snapped. "The dead guy's in her bed. She's been at work all day but came home and was just coming up to her apartment, then got the call to return to work. So right now we're waiting on the military police to come and sort this out."

"And that's got what to do with me? Other than being interesting, of course. The last thing we need is yet another murderer on base."

429

"Because her boss will call you any second. I reamed him out because he reamed her out while she stood here in shock. No way in hell the cops will let her leave. You know that."

"And you threw me under the bus, why?" Then he laughed. "Whatever," Mason said. "It doesn't matter. I'll talk to him."

"Yeah, he thinks I'm a crackpot. But get this. The reason she had been called back to work was because they had a breach at the records office. Apparently their computer system was hacked. He's the head of staff records."

"What?" Mason said. "Now that is a whole different story."

"Not only a different story," Taylor said, "but I think you better let Tesla know. Because, if the staff records section has been hacked, you know somebody has gotten through one part of the navy's online defense system. So chances are, the hacker was looking for a lot more than staff records."

"We're on it," Mason said. "It's also hardly coincidental that you found a dead body in the apartment of somebody who works at the department just hacked."

"No coincidences in life, right?"

"Exactly." And Mason was gone.

Taylor turned to see her staring at him. He took his phone off Speaker and said, "I felt it would be better if you heard that. It's best if we have no secrets at the moment. It'll be tough enough coming up."

She nodded slowly. "This is big, isn't it?"

He gently brushed back the ringlet from her forehead. "It doesn't get any bigger," he said quietly. Just then the police came up the stairs. She gave Taylor a brave smile. "Are you ready for this?"

He shrugged and gave her a bright grin. "Always."

CHAPTER 2

NO WAY ANYBODY could ever be ready for this. She watched in amazement as Taylor became more formal but answered every question with the same calm serenity she wished she could have mustered but had no way to even begin to produce. She was still dealing with the shock of everything that had happened so far, and the questions just sent her into an increasingly downward spiral. She had slipped to monosyllabic answers for every question they asked. She knew they were trying to get more out of her, but she didn't know what she was supposed to tell them.

Soon it all ran together and became one long and somewhat repetitive narrative. *No, she had no idea how this guy got into her apartment. No, she had no idea why he was here. No, she had no idea who killed him. No, she lived alone. She'd been at work all day and hadn't even made it to her apartment. The first she even knew there was a problem was from Taylor. She'd been called back in to work because of a problem in her department. They must contact her boss because she wasn't cleared to tell anybody anything about her work.*

And so it continued. Finally she sagged against the wall and slowly slid down until she sat on the hallway floor. She knew it was dirty; it was probably filthy and full of all kinds of things she didn't want to think about, but her legs had turned to rubber, and she could no longer stand.

Taylor crouched beside her. "Are you okay?"

She stared up at him wanly. "No. I haven't a clue what I'm supposed to do now."

When the two cops crouched in front of her, she realized just how pathetic she looked.

"Do you need to be checked over?"

She stared at them in confusion.

"Medically," one guy said. "Are you hurt?"

She shook her head. "No. I'm not hurt, except for my heart. How am I supposed to go back in my apartment when a dead guy's in my bed? A dead guy I don't know—may have seen on base—but I don't *know* know him, but whose blood covers my bedroom."

The cop continued to write notes.

"What are you writing?" she cried out. "I have nothing to offer on this."

"You're offering lots," the one said with a smile. "Just keep talking."

She groaned and slammed her head against the wall, only to cry out and to hold her head because it hurt. Dammit. "How long until I can go back in?"

"I thought you didn't want to go back in?"

"I need clothes," she said. "I have to go to work tomorrow. So I need a suitcase and a few things out of there. Then I can leave and go sleep somewhere else."

"Where exactly would you be going?"

She opened her eyes and stared at them, her mind refusing to function. Finally she shrugged and said, "I haven't a clue."

"Well, your apartment is off-limits," the cops said.

"My clothes?"

"We'll get somebody to go in with you after forensics has

been through the place. But you can't have anything right now."

She groaned and sagged farther in on herself. She wrapped her arms around her knees and rocked back and forth.

"She's had enough," Taylor said, his tone authoritative and firm. "If you need more questions answered, I'll bring her to you at the station."

"There will be more questions," one of the cops said. He stood and handed Taylor a card. "My name is Butler. If you think of anything else, let me know."

"Video," she said. "This building has cameras, doesn't it? Security cameras?"

"It should have," the cop said. "We'll get ahold of the feed."

She nodded eagerly. "That should tell you then that I haven't been home all day."

"If you work with a bunch of people, surely they can vouch for that too?"

"Oh, right," she said. "I do. I can't even think straight anymore."

Just then she felt her body being lifted vertically. She stared up at Taylor as he helped support her upright. "That's not a good idea," she said. "I'll collapse again."

"Not a problem," he said, wrapping his arm under hers and around her ribs. "I'm taking you to my place."

Too exhausted and worn out to object, she let him lead her into his place. He walked her to a couch, where she willfully sagged onto the cushion and curled up in the corner. "What a day," she said, as she closed her eyes and sank into the cushions.

Taylor disappeared for a moment, then came back and

gently wrapped a blanket around her.

She looked up at him and smiled. "Thank you. I didn't realize I was even cold."

"Your face is sheer white," he said. "I wouldn't be at all surprised if shock hasn't taken over to the point that you're heading into hypothermia."

She stared at him but could barely comprehend his words. When he took off her shoes, she realized her feet were stone-cold. So were her hands.

He tucked the blanket firmly around her and said, "I'll put on the teakettle and get you a hot drink."

She listened with half a mind as he puttered in the kitchen. But the other half was willing to blank out so this could all go away. Closing her eyes, she called out, "Do you mind if I just nap for a bit?"

"Go ahead. Best thing for you."

But she didn't hear his words. As soon as she gave herself permission to close her eyes, she could feel that willing darkness—the space where she could forget everything that had just gone on—reaching for her. And she fell into its waiting embrace.

PEEKING AROUND THE corner, Taylor confirmed her breathing was steady. He unplugged the teakettle and poured himself a shot of whiskey instead, then went back and sat down beside her. He got his laptop and sent Mason a message. Then he contacted Nelson and brought him up to speed. Nelson's response was almost immediate.

Jesus, how long have you been home, an hour and a half?

Nah, I got in about four hours ago now. We've al-

ready been interviewed, or at least spoken to the police, but she's crashing hard. I brought her here, and she's sound asleep on my couch. The coroner is dealing with her apartment.

Does she live alone?

Rather than trying to answer everything on his laptop, Taylor pulled out his phone and gave his buddy a call. "Yes, she lives alone," he said in a low voice. "And doesn't have a boyfriend. She barely knows the victim and hasn't seen him in months."

"So she's been targeted for some reason, and it must be connected to the hack job down at the staff records office."

"But why would anybody care about getting into the staff records data anyway?" Taylor asked quietly. He moved the laptop onto the coffee table, got up and paced the living room with his phone. When he realized he was in danger of waking her up, he opened the double doors leading to his small balcony and stepped outside. "It makes no sense."

"As we currently know it, yes," Nelson said. "It may never make sense to us, but it always makes sense to the perpetrator."

"I know," Taylor said moodily. "God, all I wanted was to come home and get some sleep for a night or two. Actually get some rest."

Nelson chuckled. "Hey, as you know, it rarely works out that way."

"It'd be nice for once," he said. "As it is, she's a mess."

"To be expected," Nelson said compassionately. "Can you imagine if you'd come home to find a dead woman in your bed?"

"No, I can't," Taylor said, thinking about it. "Considering the shock, she's actually handling it very well."

"Just give her the support you can, then see if you can find somebody else to take over and get to bed."

"That's not happening. They're working on the body right now. I wish I was in there, listening to everything. You should have seen the guy though. Jesus, he's naked right on top of her bed. I don't even remember if he was tied down or not. But he took several bullets."

"So, rage or staged?" Nelson asked.

"Interesting question," Taylor replied as he leaned on the railing and stared out at the city, quieting down around him. "You know what? I'll say, *staged.*"

"That would go along with everything else we know," Nelson said.

"The bottom line is, Midge needs me for now, and probably overnight," Taylor said. "And, of course, I want to get to the bottom of this because it's right here on my own doorstep, if nothing else. What if it had been my place?"

"Yeah, didn't I just say that?" Nelson said. "Well, if it's a hacking job, it could very well be that Tesla is already working on it."

"I mentioned it to Mason, but she's probably not likely. You know the navy has a whole IT department. By the time they get into the records database, you can bet some of the tracks will have already be covered."

"I doubt it, not completely," Nelson said. "But you also know that Mason will talk to Tesla about this regardless. So he should be getting the brass and the right people on it."

"And the dead guy and the hack job are connected. I sure would like to know why she was targeted though. Jesus, she's just a young girl all alone, you know?"

"Are you feeling protective by any chance?"

"Of course I am," Taylor replied.

"Watch yourself," Nelson said, a lazy tone entering his voice. "Slippery slope there."

"Hey, it's not the same thing at all as what's happening to you."

"I hope for your sake it is," Nelson said warmly. "Think about it. Wouldn't it be great if both of us had a partner?"

"I won't say no if it happens, but she's hardly what I was expecting."

At that, Nelson laughed. "Of course not. But, if you think about it, fate has a lot more to do with that than anything. We don't always get to make these decisions, apparently. I don't think I've seen her around much," Nelson continued. "I can't remember the last time I had any reason to go to staff records either."

"If you ever have," Taylor said, "she's pretty unforgettable though. Stands about five foot with a shock of red hair. Ringlets that go everywhere."

"That sounds like fun," Nelson said with a chuckle. "She also sounds like a cutie."

"She is," Taylor said, "but I've never dated her."

"Why is that?"

He shrugged. "I don't know. It just seems too close to home."

"Interesting comment," he said.

"Whatever," Taylor said. "Anyway, I'll get going. Neither of us has eaten, and she's still asleep. I've had a whiskey, but I'll need food in my stomach before I have another one."

"Take care of her then. If you can get any more out of the forensic team, that would be good. Otherwise, we'll just have to wait and see who we can squeeze for details."

"I'm more concerned about getting details as to why she might have been targeted. What's the chance this was all some random coincidence?"

"None." And Nelson was gone.

Taylor put his phone on the coffee table and closed the glass doors again. As he walked quietly through the living room, a soft voice mumbled from beside him.

"Did you say something about food?"

He stepped around the coffee table and sat down on the edge of the couch, pulling the blanket back a little bit so he could see her face. "Are you hungry?"

She opened her eyes and smiled up at him. Then yawned. "I am. I can't quite sleep. It's like I'm in a half dozing state, out for a bit, then awake, then down again," she said. "I don't want to be a weepy female, but I can't help thinking about the poor man and what he was doing in my bed. Like, what was he expecting?"

Taylor winced. "Considering he was nude, it's quite possible he was expecting something risqué." He straightened up as a thought hit him. "Hey, do you use any of the dating sites, like Tinder?"

She shook her head. "No, I tried it once or twice, but it really wasn't for me."

"You have an account though?"

"Yeah, sure." She frowned. "But then I also have Facebook, Instagram, and all the other much more popular program apps too."

"I suppose it's possible," Taylor said, thinking hard, "that somebody used your account to set up a meet."

Her gaze widened, and he found himself staring into the most interesting golden-flecked eyes he'd ever seen. The fact that they almost matched her hair was bizarre. They were reddish-brown, too, but had little highlights in them.

She sat up slowly and said, "If I could find my phone,

maybe that would tell us."

He looked around and said, "You had it outside in the hallway, didn't you?"

She shuffled, checked her pockets and then said, "Here it is." She pulled it out, unlocked the screen and searched through her programs. "Here's one of them," she said, as she flicked it up to see her profile and held it out for him. "This is one of the ones I was trying out."

He frowned. "It's certainly a very popular one."

She nodded. "But I haven't been on that in months."

He held out his hand. "Do you mind if I take a look?"

She hesitated; it was a personal question, after all.

Whoever she had set herself up as would say a lot about who she was on the inside, plus it would also give a history of her meetings or at least the conversations between her and her matches. As he flipped through them, he said, "How long since you've been on here?"

She shrugged. Then yawned. When she could finally speak again, she said, "Months." She snuggled back into the blankets and said, "Although this is a fascinating avenue to follow, you did say something about food."

He looked at her. "It says here that you were on the site a few days ago."

Slowly she sat back up and stared at him. Reaching for the phone, she looked at the match that someone acting as her had agreed to. "Oh, my God," she cried out. "It's him, isn't it? It's Gary Sims!"

"Yeah," he said. "And, according to this, you also gave him your address and set up a meeting for today."

She raised her horrified gaze to Taylor's and shook her head. "But I didn't do it. Honest, I didn't. I don't even use this anymore! Oh, God, now they're gonna—"

He grabbed her hands and said, "Calm down, *shh*. Calm down, and we'll get to the bottom of this." But she started shaking again. Then again, if somebody had hacked into his personal life and had used it to set up a meet to murder a man, he might be in a mess himself.

He took the phone from her hand and said, "Look. I might be able to track this down, but somebody has logged into your account, so they either knew your login or had a way to find it. Where do you keep your phone?"

She just stared at him. "With me all the time. Where do you keep yours?"

"A good point," he said with a nod. "Mine's usually in my pocket. When I'm working out, it's in my locker. When I'm on a job, it's usually with me. When I'm at home, it's either in my pocket or on the coffee table." He pointed to it.

She looked to the table, then at her phone and said, "At work, it's usually in my pocket because I leave my purse in a file drawer unattended. When I'm at home, it's the same as you. It's either in my pocket or I just leave it on the counter. Or," she said, "it's on my charger."

"And where's your charger?"

"Beside my bed," she said. "That's where everybody keeps them, isn't it?"

He pointed to the kitchen counter. "I charge mine here."

She frowned. "But then, when you get a call in the middle of the night, you have to come all the way out here to answer it."

"Exactly. The only calls I get in the middle of the night are ones I need to be awake for. By the time I'm here, I'm wide awake and raring to go."

She winced. "Right. You're one of those action heroes, aren't you?"

"Hardly," he said. "But my world is definitely full of missions. In your case, if it was on the charger by your bed, the only time it's not with you," he said, "would be when you are at home." He thought about her apartment across the hallway and asked, "As you look at my apartment and think of yours, are they mirror images?"

She nodded.

"I wasn't looking to check that when I was in there, but it just occurred to me."

"What difference does that make?"

"Well, it means that you would know if anybody got in your apartment, while you were sitting on the couch, watching TV," he said, "and they couldn't have slipped into your phone while it was on the charger, unless you were asleep."

"Okay, that's just creepy. Why would you even say something like that?"

"Because it needs to be said," he replied. "Somewhere, somehow, somebody got ahold of your phone and used your Tinder account."

"But they could have done it from the computer," she reminded him.

He nodded. "What are the chances that you use the same password for your dating sites as you do for other sites?" As redness rolled up her cheeks, he nodded. "So, all the hacker had to do was find out one of your passwords for one of the sites, and they could get into all kinds of sites, correct? Do you have a laptop?"

She shook her head. "No. I'm on the computer all day at work, so I didn't want one at home."

"Okay, most people have a laptop."

She shrugged. "I have a tablet." And then she froze. "I

had a tablet," she said softly.

He leaned forward. "*Had?* What does that mean?"

"I haven't found it yet. I just thought it was somewhere in my apartment but—"

"And that's the tablet you've been signing in to all the same accounts with, correct?"

She nodded. "But they still wouldn't have known what my password was," she said.

"No," he said, "but they wouldn't need to if you use the auto login feature. Which you do, right?"

She closed her eyes and sagged into the couch. "Yes," she said, her voice barely more than a whisper.

"I want to ream you out for that," he said, "but unfortunately, you're not alone, and many people do just like you did. And, in our world of passwords, they try to minimize the problem by using the same password for many different sites."

"And then he presumably got the one he needed or logged right in because it was set to auto login and sent the message from there."

"It also means they knew who you were and probably where you worked and when. But it's interesting timing that this murder happened during the day when you were at work."

"Not really," she said, staring at him with wide eyes. "I wasn't supposed to work today."

CHAPTER 3

M IDGE GOT UP suddenly, as if demons were after her, and honestly, they probably were. She paced around the room. "I got called in," she said. "Today's Monday, but I normally work Tuesday through Saturday. The only reason I work Saturday on base is because we have so much paperwork, and they needed somebody to help get caught up, so I volunteered," she said. "I know it's unorthodox, but it's been working for us. But today the regular girl didn't show. So my boss called me in to take over her shift. Which means, I only got yesterday off, and I wasn't very happy about it."

"So, whoever set you up expected you to be home. Which also means they were expecting you to be there to open the door when your date arrived," he said.

He studied her for a long moment, and she stared back in confusion. "Well, that makes no sense. I wouldn't have let him in. I mean, I might have known him to recognize him but not enough for a Tinder hookup. Especially one I didn't even know about."

"A lot of people never know who they hook up with," he said with a dismissive wave of his hand. "The thing is, I'm just wondering if you were the target or if it was Gary. Or the both of you."

As she slowly understood, the color left her face once again, and she sank onto the couch. "Meaning, the killer would have shown up before Gary, or soon afterward, and was maybe hoping to take us both out?"

"We're making a lot of assumptions here," Taylor said with a nod. "But it does play."

"No," she said. "It doesn't play at all. None of that makes any sense. Nobody hates me enough to want to set me up with a fake date, then kill my date and kill me."

"*Somebody* hated you enough to set you up with a fake date and to kill him in your bed."

When Taylor put it that way, it was a little hard to argue. She lay back against the couch and closed her eyes, trying to let all this roll around in her head. "How did he get in?" she asked, suddenly sitting up straight again.

"Good question," Taylor said. "How *did* he get into your apartment?"

She checked the messages from the Tinder app. "The fake me didn't give any instructions on how to get in," she said. "So he was obviously expecting me to open the door." She glanced at Taylor. "What if the person who did this is a woman?"

His eyes lit with interest. "I like that," he said. "Somebody jealous of you? Or hates you? Somebody whose boyfriend preferred you over her? Or some guy who thought you were interested in Gary and wanted it to be him instead? I don't know. All kinds of angles here."

"That still doesn't explain how she got into my apartment though," Midge snapped.

"Well, there are ways to break into any place," he said. "But do you have any girlfriends who might have stayed over? Any parties where the girlfriends crashed here? Anytime you've gone away and left a key with a neighbor?"

She shook her head, then froze. "Yes," she said. "Mama

Parkins. You know? On the first floor. Her husband is the super."

Taylor nodded. "Yes, I've met him, but I don't know that I've ever met her."

Midge started to breathe faster. "What are the chances she's not okay?" she asked. "I can't imagine she would just hand over my key."

"Unless they had a damn good excuse," Taylor said. "Unfortunately, I've heard people say they were a missing lover or planning a surprise party, all kinds of excuses to get into somebody's apartment."

"Mama Parkins isn't like that," she said. "You'd know that if you'd ever met her. She's old-school. Very much a by-the-rules person."

"In other words, you don't think she would voluntarily have handed over your key?"

"No."

"Okay, let's go back over a few of the other ideas first then. Just clarify for me again, please. Has any girlfriend slept over recently?"

She shook her head.

"Has *anybody* slept over recently?"

Knowing what he meant, she shook her head.

"In the last two months?"

She flushed but stared at him bravely. "No."

He just raised an eyebrow and looked at her.

She glared. "Dating has been a little slim recently, okay?"

"Any reason why?" he asked, his gaze narrowing.

"I'm picky," she said with a shrug.

He chuckled. "Good," he said. "I am too."

She wasn't sure what to make of that.

"What about maintenance? Have you had anyone

around to do maintenance in your apartment?"

"No, I would have just called the super if I had a problem," she said, frowning. "Wouldn't you?"

"Not likely," he said cheerfully. "I would have fixed it myself."

She shot him a look. "Well, I don't have any tools and hardly would know how to begin anyway. Besides, that doesn't mean anybody else would have come into my apartment without my permission."

"In the best-case scenario, that would be true," he said. "However, say an apartment above or below was dealing with some major flooding. The repairman could have gone in there without your permission."

She thought about that, and it made a lot of sense. "Then we have to talk to the super. So that means Mama Parkins again."

"Well, that's easy," he said. "I'll make some food, and then I'll walk down and knock on the door and see if we can get any answers."

"What do you have in mind for food?" she asked, straightening again. "We can order in."

"We could," he said, "but I just came in from a few days down in Baja, and I'm tired of restaurant meals."

"I prefer home cooking anyway," she said, looking at the front door. "I had food in my fridge, but we're not allowed in there."

"I have food," he said, then walked into the kitchen ahead of her. She opened the fridge and crowed in delight. "Hey, you've got lots of good veggies here, so we can do a nice big salad, if nothing else."

"I've also got burgers here," he said, "and buns."

"Okay," she said. "I can fry them."

He hesitated and looked at the barbecue on the balcony and asked, "Do you know how to barbecue?"

She nodded enthusiastically. "Sure, if you have one." He walked out onto the small balcony, lit the barbecue and said, "While this warms up, I'll race downstairs and talk to the super real quick."

"Okay, I'll chop up the vegetables," she replied, and he disappeared.

She turned to the preparations and busied herself with the makings of a salad. While not an expert cook, eating was one thing she loved to do. And it would certainly help take her mind off this nightmare.

TAYLOR WENT DOWN the hallway to the stairs and headed for the apartment of the super. He knocked on the door, but there was no answer. He frowned and knocked again. Again, nothing. He hated to, but needing to know the answer, he grabbed the knob and turned it, but it was locked.

"Shit," he muttered, but then again they had a life too. Maybe they'd gone out for dinner. He headed back toward the stairs but caught the elevator instead because it opened right beside him. He returned to his apartment to find Midge putting the burgers on the barbecue outside. She was half done with the salad making, so he took over her spot, and she found him prepping the salad.

"Did you talk to them?" she asked.

He shook his head. "No, there's no answer. I figured they went out for dinner."

She frowned. "They don't go out much, not with Mama Parkins."

"Well, I guess I've never met her, so what's the deal? She

doesn't like to go out?"

"She's in a wheelchair and usually has an oxygen tank close by."

His dicing slowed as his thoughts ran to the most negative scenario possible, until he pulled back those thoughts and said, "Okay, I'll try again after we eat." While she took over finishing the salad, he cleaned off the table, so there was a place to sit for two, then got out the buns and burger fixings. With the salad on the table, they worked together, companionably slicing tomatoes and onions for the burgers.

"Any chance you have pickles?"

"Spicy or dill?"

"Both if you have them."

With a grin, he pulled both jars from the fridge and said, "Sounds like you like your burgers like I like my burgers. With everything."

"I like everything but heavy horseradish," she said with a chuckle. "A little bit is fine. But, other than that, no."

Before long, he pulled the burgers off the barbecue, then placed them on the buns. When they sat down for a meal together, she looked at him and smiled. "This is a rare treat. I don't have a grill, so I've missed out on the special flavor that comes with having barbecued burgers and steaks."

"We can do it again if you want," he offered. "It's much nicer to have a meal for two than just one anyway."

"It is, indeed," she said with a smile. "Sadly, a pack of steaks is in my fridge."

"Well, on the off chance that we get in there anytime soon," he said, "I suggest we have those for dinner tomorrow night."

He picked up his burger and took a big bite. Hoping she didn't notice, his mind was worrying away on the super downstairs. Taylor thought about calling somebody else but didn't want to set off alarms if it wasn't necessary. She appeared to be enjoying her burger and salad. The fatigue was still visible on her face, but at least some of her color had returned. "You're looking better," he said suddenly.

"I'm feeling better too," she said. "Food is definitely a help."

By the time they finished, another ten minutes had passed.

"Go," she urged.

He looked up at her in surprise.

"Do you think I didn't notice that you keep checking your watch? Is it the super you're worried about? In that case, you better go."

He hesitated, then nodded. "I'll help you clean up here, and then I'll walk down."

"I can clean up," she said firmly. "It's the least I can do. You go check on them. Mama Parkins is an interesting character, but I surely wouldn't want anything bad to happen to them, and you've got me concerned. So go check on them, please."

"Okay," he said with a smile. "I hope I don't need to tell you—and I forgot to last time—but please don't let anybody in."

"I won't," she said. As he walked to the front door, she said, "Hurry back."

"Will do." Stopping, he asked, "What's your phone number?" As she shared her digits, he pulled out his phone and entered her cell info into his phone. Then he sent her a text. "I've just sent you a blank text, so I'm in yours as well."

As he walked out, he stopped in the hallway and took a look at her apartment. The door was closed, and no crime scene tape was on the outside, which was typical along the base. Ignoring that, he walked to the stairs and went down slowly. His mind churned as he thought about his options if the super and his wife didn't answer again. He walked up to the door at the end of the hallway and knocked. Again, there was no answer.

He walked out the back exit and around to the window. One window was on the wall where the kitchen was. He peered through but couldn't see anything. He carried on around to the back, where they had a little patio area set up. He could see the ramp from the kitchen out onto the patio, but nobody was out there. He stepped onto the cement blocks and walked up to the glass doors. He knocked on them and again didn't see any movement. He pulled on the glass doors, and they opened.

Instantly, he could smell what he didn't want to smell. He poked his head inside and couldn't see anything. He took a few cautious steps in to check the living room, but nobody was there. He went into the bedroom and found both people were still in bed. And probably had been since early this morning. He retraced his steps and closed the patio door. Then he called Detective Butler, to whom he had spoken to earlier. When the detective answered the phone, he said, "This is Taylor. I called you earlier about a dead man in the apartment across from me."

"Right, Taylor. What can I do for you?"

"You need to come back here," he said. "I called on the superintendent and his wife. They are both dead in their bed."

CHAPTER 4

W HEN THE DOOR opened behind her, she turned, startled. But it was Taylor. She smiled brightly and said, "I took the liberty of putting on a pot of coffee."

He stared at her with a blank expression, and she raced toward him. "What happened?"

But the door stayed open, and Detective Butler stepped inside and closed it behind him. Taylor caught her up and tucked her into his arms.

She went eagerly, knowing he was distressed over something. She looked up at him. "What happened?" she repeated and turned to look at the detective. "Did something else happen? Or do you have more questions?"

"Something else happened," the detective said.

She frowned at him and then gasped. "Not Mama Parkins?"

The detective nodded. "You're the one who suggested Taylor go downstairs?"

She struggled to get her mind wrapped around what had just happened. "We were figuring out how somebody could have gotten into my apartment when I was at work. Taylor asked if anyone had a key, and I mentioned Mama Parkins. They have the super's keys, of course, but this was different. A long time ago I gave her a duplicate key when I expected someone. But she wouldn't give that key out without my knowledge. Not for any reason. She is very strict about that."

"Too strict apparently," Taylor said. "You need to brace yourself. They both have been murdered."

She stepped out of his arms, both hands going to her mouth as she stared at him in shock. Tears pooled at the corner of her eyes as she thought of the two older people who lived on the main floor in the corner. "That's not fair. They never hurt anybody. Poor Mama Parkins could barely even move." She turned to the detective. "Are we sure they were murdered? They didn't just die in their sleep?"

His face was grim. "No, there's no doubt."

Reaching a hand to her temple, she walked into the living room and sagged once again in the corner of the couch. "What is going on? That's three people in this building."

"That we know about," Taylor said. "Definitely something rotten is going on here."

"Can you give us any idea why somebody might have killed that couple?" the detective asked her.

"Only for the same reason Taylor went down to talk to them. To see if anybody had access to my apartment. If anybody had asked to get in or had wanted the keys."

"Taylor told me about your phone and the messages supposedly sent without your knowledge."

"No *supposedly* about it," she said firmly. "I did not set that up."

The detective nodded but held out his hand. She pulled out her phone, then swiped it so the password was open and handed it to him with the messages still open. He looked at it and said, "I need access to your account."

"No problem," she muttered. "I'd just give you the phone, but I need it."

"I'm taking it anyway," he said. "We'll try to get it back

to you tomorrow morning."

"Great," she said. "What else can go wrong?"

"If you need to make a call, you can use mine," Taylor said.

"What if other people need to call me?" she asked. "You know how people are if they can't get ahold of you. Just like you couldn't get ahold of the super, so you went back down again. People will be calling to get ahold of me."

"What people?" Detective Butler intervened.

"My mother and my sister," she said. "When it rings, you'll see. But please don't tell them any of this. They would book flights from Maine and be here tomorrow morning to try to get me to move back."

"You don't want to move home?" he asked.

"I came all this way to get some distance," she said with half a smile. "I don't really want to head back anytime soon."

"Any reasons we should know about?" the detective asked. "Because your place wasn't chosen at random. It appears you were targeted, and the people who got in their way were taken out."

"Is Mama Parkins even connected to Gary?" she corrected. "Isn't it too early to tell that?"

"Yes," he said, "that is true. But generally, if you get three murders in the same building at the same time, they're connected."

"*At the same time?*" She looked over at Taylor. "You said they died in bed. Wasn't that this morning then?"

"Maybe, we have to sort out time of death," the detective said. "But even within the same twelve-hour period is way too close. That's one hell of a coincidence."

"I know. I know," she said. "And that never happens here." She groaned. "I just can't believe this is happening.

They were a really nice couple. They so didn't deserve this."

"But Gary did?" asked the detective with interest in his voice.

She glared at him. "I don't know. I didn't know the man. I don't know where he lives and only know he worked at the base. I didn't even know he worked at the supply office until Taylor told me. Other than that, I couldn't tell you one thing about him."

The detective nodded. "We obviously have a lot to sort out here. At the moment, the coroner has been notified, and I've called in a team. I'm sure we'll have more questions for you." He turned and walked to the front door. "The next time you want to check on somebody in this place," he said, looking at Taylor, "maybe you shouldn't." And he closed the door behind him.

Midge looked at Taylor and asked, "What did he mean by that?"

"Well, being the person who discovered three bodies all in the same day, I'm pretty sure they think I'm either bad luck or that I'm involved." He sagged on the couch. "Like he said early on, it's been a hell of a day." Then he remembered and lifted his nose. "You said there was coffee."

She waved her hand at the kitchen. "Yeah, I made coffee, but I don't know if I can even drink any right now."

"I could use a cup," he said. "I'd like a couple shots of whiskey, but the night is young. And I highly doubt it's over, at least for me. And I don't want to smell like booze in case anything else happens."

She looked at him. "What else could possibly happen?"

He shot her a hard look as he poured himself a cup of coffee. "Just don't ask," he said. "Don't ask."

★

CUP IN HAND, Taylor sat down and put his feet up on the coffee table. He'd taken the center of the couch, with her curled up beside him. The somber mood in the room was fully justified. He knew it would be a while before he'd forget about the couple down in their bed a floor below. He laid his hand gently on her knee. Almost instantly, she covered his hand with hers. "Do you think they suffered?"

He shook his head. He had no clue, but no way would he let her think they had. "Let's hope they were sound asleep," he said. "It didn't look like they had defensive wounds or had even moved."

"I guess I should be thankful for that," she said quietly. "But this world sucks if people are taking out disabled women and their old husbands."

"Hey, it sucks for the young man across the hall too," Taylor said. "Evil appears to have no rules or regulations when it comes to victims."

"Right, and apparently I was supposed to be one of their targets too. That's what I can't stop thinking about. There was no reason for them to use my place or to include me in their plans."

"Because you survived, we can't be sure you were supposed to be part of it," he said, "but, considering it was your apartment, we have to assume some connection is there. And I, for one, am very grateful you did survive. The fact that you were called in to work is huge."

"Right," she said. "I'm sure my boss is pretty pissed off right now."

"He'll get over it," Taylor said with a half smile. "Bosses are like that." He picked up his coffee and took a sip. Like her, his mind toiled with all the bits and pieces he knew, trying to find an answer. The trouble was, they didn't have enough information yet. "So we know how they got into your place, roughly. We know how the meet was set up and that obviously Gary was happy to come see you."

"Yeah," she said, "I don't even want to think about that aspect of it."

"Then don't," he said, "but here's the real question. What did they hope to achieve?"

"By the way, were any shots fired into Gary's privates?" she asked, shifting her position so she could look down the couch and see Taylor better.

He looked at her. "You mean, in the groin?"

She nodded. "Yeah. Was a shot fired into his groin?"

"Definitely. Blood was in that area. Why?"

"Because, in a way, that would imply a woman."

"Or," Taylor said, "a male lover."

"But, if he has a male lover, why would he be coming to have a hookup with me?"

"Because lots of people go both ways," Taylor said.

"You know what? I'm not sure I'd have been happy if I'd hooked up with a guy who had just come from a male lover."

"Are you thinking of the whole AIDS thing?"

She nodded. "Yes, but not just that. What about monogamy? What about long-term relationships? A woman wants to think she is special. I would presume a man does too."

"Well, you don't do hookups," he said. "So what's odd to other people might not be so odd to you, and what's odd to you may not be to others."

She shook her head. "Doesn't matter either way, I guess. I don't know what Gary's sexuality was because I didn't know him." She brooded on the idea while Taylor studied her features.

"That's really the bottom line though, finding out who was unhappy enough to not just kill him but to fill him with bullets. Three shots."

"And you weren't home, right?" Midge asked, her brow furrowed.

He shrugged. "Until we get a time of death, I can't confirm that. But, if you're asking me if I heard the shots, the answer is no."

"When you came home, did you pass anybody as you came into the apartment building or on the stairs?"

"No, it was empty," he said, "but I was also tired and just returning from a trip. I might have passed a couple people downstairs, but I don't remember seeing anybody up here. And what I also didn't notice was your door being open."

"So, if we take that to mean it *wasn't* open at that time, since I suspect you would have noticed, then what are the chances the killer was inside my apartment when you got home?"

"Unfortunately, it's quite possible he was still there. Or she," he corrected. "And again, we have to wait for the coroner to establish time of death."

"We might have to wait for some of the facts, but the others are getting laid out pretty decently, when you think about what we've already figured out," she said.

"What we haven't figured out though," Taylor said, "is who or why."

"And both are equally important in this case." She closed her eyes and relaxed into the couch.

He studied the flush of pink on her cheeks. "Are you feeling okay?"

She nodded without opening her eyes. "Just feeling all

the shock of the day."

"Ditto," he said. "How do we find out the rest? I won't feel safe leaving you alone until we catch this guy."

"Oh, no you don't," she said, shaking her head. "You're not responsible for me."

"Maybe not," he said, raising his eyebrows, surprised by her response. "And I don't necessarily feel responsible for you, but, all the same, I don't want to see you hurt. I would hardly be an honorable man if I sat here and allowed you to go off alone and have this guy target you a second time."

She stared at him, then jutted her jaw out. "I have friends I can stay with." She threw the blanket back that she had been tucked into. "Speaking of which, I should probably go now." She reached for her cell phone, frowning when she remembered she didn't have it. Looking at his phone, she wrinkled her nose. "How did it get to be ten o'clock?" she asked as she walked to the door and grabbed her purse. "Look. Thanks for everything tonight. I'll stay with a girlfriend. Or maybe grab a hotel." She walked the last few steps quickly, as if racing away. When she reached for the doorknob, she couldn't get her hand on it because he stood in front of it.

"Stop," he ordered. "I have a spare room you can use tonight."

But she was already shaking her head. "No, no, no," she said.

"Why not?" he asked, crossing his arms over his chest.

"You've done enough," she said. "I'll be fine."

"Really?" And he stared her down. He didn't know why she was running away, and he really wanted to understand but was afraid he wouldn't like the answer. But she kept shaking her head and moving her purse nervously from one hand to the next. "Do you really think that guy doesn't know who your girlfriends are?"

She stared up at him, her jaw dropping. "Do you really think he's tracked down my friends? Do you think he'll hurt them?" She grabbed his phone off the table, so nervous, trying to dial, but she didn't know the numbers of her friends. They were icons on her phone, not memorized in her head.

He plucked the phone from her hand and said, "Stop."

But he'd done it because she obviously couldn't stop. She started beating on him. "Get away from the door," she ordered. "I have to go check my friends."

"No," he said, "you don't. Because if he hasn't found them, and if he's watching your movements, he'll find them as soon as you lead him to them."

And once again she froze.

He could see the tears and the shock welling up inside her. He pulled her in close. "Look. I'm not trying to scare you. I'm not trying to shock you. But we have to be reasonable here. Somebody died already. Three somebodies. So this lunatic could get at you. Do you think this guy will be happy with what he's done so far?"

She went stiff as a board.

He didn't know if she was afraid of him or if it was just the craziness that her life had fallen into. "I won't hurt you," he said, "and you'll be fine overnight in my spare bedroom."

She kept shaking her head. "What are the chances that he hasn't already figured out where I am? Which means, you're in danger too." She stared up at him, her bottom lip trembling. "How can I repay your kindness by getting you killed?"

He stared at her in disbelief. "I'm not some tiny female

for him to target," he roared. "I think you just insulted me."

She glared at him.

He loved how quickly she went from tears to temper. Maybe it was the red hair. Deciding to prick it further, he flicked her hair and asked, "So where's that famous redhead temper?"

"Keep pushing me," she growled. "You might just see it."

He gave her a lazy grin and said, "Promise?" He could see the red wash up her face, and she actually stomped her foot in front of him. He chuckled. "Getting there?"

"You're getting there too," she snapped. "Why would you even want to set me off in a temper?"

"Because then you stop being a scared victim," he said. "And you need to keep your head about you. You're in danger, and you need help. So get off your high horse and accept it."

She gasped at his tone and his mannerisms, and he could see the flame of red rising higher and higher. He didn't know why he was pushing it, but, since he could see she was just a hair's breath away from smacking him, he decided he might as well get smacked for doing something rather than nothing. So he caught her face with his hands, putting their lips together, and kissed her soundly. Then he stepped back and waited for the blow. But instead, she stared up at him, her eyes huge and her mouth open. He stared down at her and said, "If you don't close that mouth this second, I'm coming back for a second kiss. Don't think I haven't warned you."

She narrowed her gaze at and said, "Well."

He chuckled. "That's all you've got to say?"

"I have a lot more to say," she snapped. "But I'm still trying to figure out why the hell you kissed me in the first place."

He stared at her in astonishment. "Because you're adorable," he said. And then he watched the shock of his words hit her. He studied her for a long moment. "So did your last boyfriend and you break up in an ugly way?"

She crossed her arms as if trying to hide from him. "Why would you think that?" she snapped.

"Because now you've gone all defensive, which just underlines my question. But, if he didn't tell you how absolutely cute and adorable you are, you're better off without him. And, yes, I realize some women would be really pissed to be told that, I know," he added. "But you are stunning. For him not to have made you feel beautiful every single day is a huge shame."

At that, she started to giggle. Then she laughed. "Oh, my God," she said. "I'm not sure I've ever met anybody who could take me from the absolute edge of my temper and then throw me into a complete fit of righteous giggles."

"And why are you laughing?"

She waved a hand at him and back away, putting her purse on the counter. "Are you kidding? Nobody's ever said anything like that to me. I mean, I'm a redhead. Remember?"

"So what?" he asked. "Gingers are cute. And you are way more than cute. You're beautiful. How could you possibly not know that? Surely you've had more than the one boyfriend, right?"

She shrugged. "Yeah, I have. But that doesn't mean they were any better."

He frowned. "Meaning, they were still young and immature?"

She giggled. "You know when you have an ugly breakup,

and they say unkind things? Almost always they insult you. And that sends you looking back at the history of all those 'flattering comments,' and it makes you doubt those." She flung herself back onto the couch and glared at him. "And don't tell me that you haven't done the same thing."

"I haven't," he said, his tone curt. "There's no point in demoralizing somebody just because you want to break up with them."

"Oh, I agree," she said. "But I don't think everybody else does."

"I'm not everybody else," he said. He sat down beside her. "So, you'll stay for the night?"

"Yes, please," she said, the fatigue evident in her voice now. "I appear to be going from one end of the extreme to the other. I'm sorry for my behavior."

Such a formal note was in her tone, as if she was really serious, that he just shook his head. "Don't apologize. We're all off-center right now. And we should be. Three people died today. We should not make light of it or ignore it. Those people had family and friends who cared about them. I don't want that minimized."

"Neither do I," she said with a simple nod. "And thanks for the reminder. Because you're right. I didn't know Gary, but now I'm sorry about that. Because he deserves to be honored at his funeral. He deserved to have been liked in life. He deserved to have had lovers and friends and pets who all cared for him. Plus, parents who adored him and siblings who laughed and cried with him. It isn't fair that his life was taken away so young. I shouldn't be so worried about my own future that I forget the real problem here, which is the fact that he lost his."

"You do need to be concerned about your future," Taylor said. "We can't make light of this. And now that we know, we've got to take action and ensure you have the future you deserve. We've got to do whatever it takes to make sure you don't end up just like him."

"Somebody went to an awful lot of trouble to either implicate me in Gary's murder or was planning on taking me out at the same time," she said. "You're right about that. I just have no clue who."

"So it seems. Now, since you'll just lie in bed and worry about it …" he said and walked over to a sideboard that held paper and his laptop. He passed a notepad toward her and tossed her a pen. "Write down a list of your friends or other contacts, and let's figure out who could possibly be behind this. Think about the girlfriends you love, friends you hate, and think about the ex-girlfriends. The same with men. Think about the ones you love, the ones you hate and the ones who are now exes. Did anyone have an ax to grind? Anybody carrying a torch for you who you offended? Think about your job. Were you promoted over someone? Did you make a pass at somebody else's husband or do anything that could be misconstrued? Something that would set someone off?"

"I don't think so, not intentionally," she said. "That's not who I am."

"That doesn't matter in the least," he responded gently. "Remember? We're not talking about who you really are. We're talking about how somebody else perceives you to be. Somebody who might be a little unhinged."

CHAPTER 5

"I UNDERSTAND THE difference," Midge said, "but that'll be a hard one to crack."

"Consider any nutcases you know. And I don't mean that literally, although in a way I do. But think about anybody who's odd. Is there anybody who's too emphatic, too religious or too much of a zealot in any way?"

Midge slowly picked up the pad of paper. "This feels very wrong. Analyzing my friends in this way. Because I like them. They like me. We get along well."

"So, start with the ex-friends," he said, "friends you had a falling-out with. Can you do that?"

She slowly wrote down Diane's name. "We had a falling out a year ago," she said.

"Good. Write that down. We can get any contact numbers from your phone. Hopefully you'll get it back tomorrow, like the detective said. You know the cops will want this list tomorrow anyway, so now you'll have a jump on it."

"Good Lord," she said faintly. "The last thing I want to do is go over this list with them."

"If we do the list now," he said, "we can just give it to them, and they can take it from there."

She nodded and kept writing. "It wasn't a bad falling out, but she thought I was being too friendly with her boyfriend." She frowned, remembering the dancing and the drinking. "She was really drunk that night. She played out an ugly scene. She apologized the next day, but I didn't feel comfortable after she had completely dumped about how she really felt about me while she was drunk. It seemed to me that, if she felt that way when she was drunk, she was probably just holding those emotions back when she wasn't, and the alcohol had given her the freedom to speak her mind. I never hung out with her again after that."

"Good," he said encouragingly. "Keep going."

She wrote down another name. "Jenny was somebody I worked with," she said, then thought about it for a moment. "About six months ago she got fired, and she blamed me for it."

His eyebrows went up. "Why?"

"Because we had a lot of files that had been shifted and moved. It was her job to put them all back properly, but instead they were a mess. Totally misfiled. She'd just been through a breakup with her boyfriend, and, at the time, I wondered if she hadn't cared and had jammed the files back any old way or had been so upset that she couldn't concentrate properly and legitimately misfiled everything."

"And why would she blame you for losing her job?"

"Because she originally said she hadn't done it, and I said I saw her with the files in the filing room, putting them away. Of course everything is digital now. You have to go into the back to get older files. And they're still there, some of them anyway. We're in the process of scanning everything in, but, when someone wants information from years ago, if it's one of the files that isn't digitized, then you have to go into the back room."

"So, because you saw she had been in there, you could

give proof positive that she'd been the one who had last been touching them."

"I could confirm she had them in her hand at one time on that day. But I really don't know what she did with them after that. She might have put them down on a table, and somebody else grabbed them. I don't know. I did tell my supervisor that. She got fired anyway. Maybe because she lied."

"Okay, so that's a good reason for wanting revenge."

Midge stared at him. "So you kill three people because you screwed up at a job and got yourself fired?"

"People who do stuff like this never own their choices or actions," he said. "They are always focused on who did this to them. They're not big on taking responsibility for themselves."

She slowly nodded. "I can see that, I guess," she said. "Jenny was like that. It didn't matter what was wrong. She hadn't done it. Somebody else was always to blame. Which is stupid, since everybody makes mistakes."

"Good," he said. "Put a star beside her name and keep going."

It was painful work as she dredged through the parts of her life she didn't want to look at again. She had good reasons why she wasn't friends with these people anymore. By the time she was done, she had added three more names to the list. She handed it to him and said, "For the moment, that's all I can think of."

"Good," he said, "and, with that out of your brain, hopefully you might sleep."

"Actually I was wondering if I could impose just a bit."

"Anything," he said. "Name it."

"That whiskey you mentioned earlier. Any chance I

could have a shot?" she asked hopefully. "I don't usually, but I think it would help me sleep tonight."

Taylor was already up off the couch and headed for the whiskey decanter and two glasses. "I'm so glad you asked," he said, "because I've been dying for some myself. I wasn't going to but ..."

She chuckled. "You could have had one without me, you know."

"What I should have done was offer you one," he said with a grin. "Then we could have both enjoyed it." He returned with two beautiful cut-crystal glasses and handed one to her.

She smiled and accepted it, then took a sip of the whiskey and let the aroma float through her nostrils and through her mouth at the same time. Sitting back, she said, "This is very nice."

"It is, isn't it? A friend of mine sent it from Scotland."

"Nice to have friends in high places," she said with a smile.

"Actually he's in the industry," Taylor said with a smirk. "Not so much in high places, but well-placed friends come in handy at times."

"The best kind." She tilted her glass and clanged it gently against his. "Thank you for helping me today."

"You're welcome," he said. "Now what we both need is a good night's sleep."

She nodded and smiled, then took the whiskey and drank half of it in one go. She could feel the burn down her throat all the way to her stomach. She smiled. "I don't usually like to shoot them like that, but, man, that was irresistible."

"I'm impressed," he said. "Most people I know can't do

that."

"It's a guy thing," she said. "And very few women drink spirits neat."

"Are you going to do that with the rest of it?"

She shook her head and asked, "Do you mind if I take this while I get ready for bed?"

"Not at all. Come on," he said, then led the way to a spare bedroom barely bigger than a closet. "It's really small. I'm sorry."

"Don't be," she said. "My place is exactly the same on the other side. Remember?"

"Right," he said. "I'd forgotten that."

She walked in and turned to face him.

"So it's a good thing," he said. "You know where everything is. I don't have clothes or anything in there, but you should be warm enough. And I can give you a couple towels if you want to shower."

"A shower would be helpful," she said, and then she stopped and shook her head. "No, I think I'll have one in the morning. I don't want to interrupt the flow of sleep, and I am very tired now. Good night, Taylor." Stepping into the guest room, she closed the door.

She placed her whiskey on the night table and pulled back the covers on the single bed. She still wore her work clothes. Which, in her case today, were slacks and a dressier shirt over a T-shirt. But she would need her slacks and shirt for work again, at least for part of tomorrow, until she could get back inside her apartment, so she took them off to keep them as unwrinkled as possible. Realizing she'd never get any sleep with her bra on, she took that off too, leaving her T-shirt and panties on. She curled up under the covers, then reached over and tossed back the rest of the whiskey, replacing the now-empty glass on the night table.

She closed her eyes, hopeful the whiskey would stop any violent nightmares, but she also knew it would be hard to sleep regardless. Three people had died, and she might be a target. But she could do little about it tonight, so she tucked the covers firmly under her chin, closed her eyes and went to sleep.

MIDGE WAS RIGHT; Taylor hadn't seen very many women shoot whiskey neat before. He sat in the living room after she had turned out her light and sipped the rest of his whiskey. He stared down at the list of names she'd given him. First and last names and, in some cases, phone numbers. He brought up his laptop and searched the names. He found the first three fairly easily. One of the three had married since the time she had been friends with Midge. And another of the three had moved east about six months ago. He made notes on the list. Happily married women were rarely serial killers. The third name he couldn't find any information on. Another he found didn't appear to have made any positive changes in her world. He put an asterisk by that one. And the person who had blamed Midge for getting fired was still around. He put an asterisk there too.

His phone rang. He checked the Caller ID and saw it was Nelson.

"Hey, you holding up okay?" Nelson asked.

"Yeah," Taylor said, keeping his voice low. "She's asleep in my spare room."

"Good. I heard something on the news about the super and his wife."

"Yeah, both of them shot. Looks like first thing this

morning, while they were still in bed. They didn't look like they even struggled," Taylor said.

"Probably hard of hearing. He must have crept into the bedroom while they were sound asleep, popped the first one and then the second right away. Whichever one was the worst off would have been the second."

"Well, the woman was on oxygen."

"Jesus. That's so sad. They should have been allowed to live out the last of their days in peace," Nelson said.

"I know. And the only thing I can think of is that the murderer then gained access to Midge's apartment through them."

"Christ, learn to pick a lock," Nelson said in disgust. "They didn't have to shoot those people."

"Considering three bullets were in Gary Sims," Taylor said, "what are the chances that killing the old couple was the warm-up? Maybe the killer needed that to do the rest."

"In which case we need to stop them before they get to liking it."

"May be too late," Taylor said succinctly. "Before she went to bed, Midge gave me a list of five names. I'm working my way down the list. But I can't find anything on this one. His name is Joseph Barnes."

"What's the connection?" Nelson asked.

"She dated him briefly. He wanted more, but she didn't, and they had an ugly breakup."

"Yeah, isn't that lovely? So we have an ugly breakup, and I murder some guy in your bed so you get to suffer for it for the rest of your life?" Nelson's tone was disgusted. "It's a sick world we live in."

"I think it's also connected to that much bigger and related issue, but I haven't heard anything from anybody on the hacking of the staff records department."

"We're not likely to either. You know that, right?" Nelson asked.

"I know, but it would be nice to know what the hell was hacked and why anybody would want to get in there. Speaking of which, one of the women Midge was on the outs with, I don't see her on Facebook and find no mention of another job or anything suggesting she's still in town. And another woman got fired and blamed Midge for it."

"What? Explain that."

Taylor went through the quick synopsis of what Midge had said about her and some of the others on the list.

"Interesting," said Nelson. "That's definitely the kind of person we're looking for. But I don't know why she would have chosen Gary."

"That's a very good question," Taylor said, sitting back. "I've been focusing on Midge, but maybe we should be focusing on Gary's life. Who hated him enough to kill him?"

"Oh, I think I would have done the same as you. I would have tried to figure out who hated her enough to kill him in her bed. But you're right. We have another victim here, and he was chosen for a reason."

"Detective Butler has her cell phone, unfortunately. I wish I had it, though I'd hate to hack into it without asking her," Taylor said.

"True, but you did show Midge the app and stuff earlier, right?"

"Yeah, and I might know her password too. Stand by a second. I'm gonna grab my laptop." In no time he had her account brought up online. "Yeah, I've got it here, and I'm looking at Gary's profile. *Loves outdoor fun and games.*"

"I'll never put that down on a dating site," Nelson said,

"because gunfire and bloodshed aren't my idea of fun and games."

Taylor chuckled. "Lucky for you, Elizabeth isn't likely to ever leave you and for sure will never let you put your profile up on one of these dating sites."

"Nope," Nelson said in a smug tone. "She won't."

Taylor continued to read Gary's profile. "It doesn't say anything more than what you'd expect. Says he's thirty-four and single, looking for a serious relationship. It does, however, give his general residential area, which is also on base."

"And you know, Taylor, maybe the killer is a woman and was using the hookup app to search for anybody eligible on base."

"Yeah, Midge brought up the female killer angle too. But think about it," Taylor said. "How many guys are on Tinder here at the base?"

"Do a search," Nelson urged. "Type in Coronado and see how many pop up."

"Four hundred and sixty-two male profiles listed," Taylor announced a moment later. "*Hmm*, I thought it would be more than that. Then again, the base isn't a separate directory."

Nelson continued, "If our theoretical female killer can't single out men on the base from the Tinder search functions alone, she would have to go through all the names."

"Actually, if it was Jenny, that former coworker of Midge's," Taylor mused, "she was working in staff records, so her search would be that much easier."

"True enough," Nelson said. "I'm liking Jenny better and better for this."

"The problem with that thinking is that Midge fits better and better too, since she still works in staff records. You know the detective will zero in on that."

"So get more intel that leads to Jenny."

"She'd still need access to a weapon and that cold-blooded killer mentality to take out three people just because she hated Midge," Taylor replied.

"But that rage can grow on a person. We see it where, on the outside, they appear totally normal, but, on the inside, they're just empty."

"I know," Taylor said, remembering a few cases where he'd stared into a killer's eyes, usually in a war-torn country, and saw either a pure hatred of his enemy or the emptiness of somebody who had suffered and done so much wrong that they couldn't function normally anymore. "Jenny certainly would have had the access."

"Except her access would have been revoked the minute she was fired," Nelson said.

"Unless she's the one who hacked into the database. Just because we're assuming she wasn't into IT doesn't mean she wasn't a hacker. Or that she doesn't have a hacker for a partner. What if *that* was the reason for going into the databases to check out these local guys on Tinder?"

"That's some pretty major hacking for a revenge that she waited six months for. I don't know that it washes, buddy."

"I don't know either," Taylor said. "It probably doesn't." He leaned back and rubbed his forehead. "My head's going around in circles over this."

"Means downtime for you too," Nelson ordered. "You don't know what else will happen tonight. Three bodies so far."

"Not only that," Taylor said, "I'm pretty sure the killer was in Midge's apartment when I was here because, when I came home, her door wasn't open. Only after she stopped in to tell me that mine was open did I notice hers was too."

"Yeah, that's a little odd, isn't it? And you never heard anything? No shooting or anybody leaving?"

"Nothing. I came home, turned on the stereo and collapsed on the couch. You know what it's like when you come back from a mission. Even though home is not much, it's still home, and all you want to do is chill."

"Not to mention you weren't expecting anything unusual," Nelson said. "In a way that's even worse because you get up, thinking all is well, and then find out something major happened and how you didn't hear it. At least if you'd heard it, you would have had something to say about it. But to know you were home and somebody was over there, well that just sucks."

"Yeah, thanks for that reminder," Taylor said in a grouchy voice. "Like I needed more guilt."

"Not guilt," Nelson said. "Never that. But just the awareness that things happen behind closed doors which we aren't aware of. And that's sad. Just think about the old couple downstairs. How long before anybody would have knocked on the door if you hadn't gone after them?"

"For all I know, several people did knock on the door today. The cops said they would check the video on the building, but I suspect they'll find the video system was down or that the person is completely disguised so they're unrecognizable."

"They wouldn't have gotten away with three murders so far if they weren't at least that good," Nelson said. "Listen. Call it a night. Morning will be here fast enough."

"Thanks, man. You too," Taylor said, and he hung up. He'd heard worse advice. He headed to bed. What he needed was sleep, and he knew it. And maybe, if he was lucky, his brain, which was wired to sort out puzzles, would wake up with some decent answers come morning.

CHAPTER 6

MIDGE WOKE EARLY in the morning, feeling groggy, her mind slow to respond to the morning stimulus. When she reached for her phone, she remembered she didn't have it. She sat up to look out the window to see if she could get an idea of the time. The light was barely breaking on the horizon, so she thought it wasn't quite five in the morning yet. She collapsed back on the bed, wishing she was still asleep. She wasn't sure what had woken her up. Taylor was in a corner apartment, and hers was on the opposite side of the building.

Something had woken her. She got up, partially dressed, then slipped out of the room and walked down to the bathroom. When she walked back out, she stopped in the small apartment and cocked her head, trying to figure out what she still heard. It was coming from the hallway. Frowning, she walked over to the door and peered through the keyhole. She could only see directly in front of her. But, as she angled her view, she saw somebody close to her apartment. She froze, desperate to open up the door but knew Taylor would have a raging fit if she did that. Suddenly she wasn't alone.

He put a hand on her shoulder and whispered, "What's the matter?"

After her initial start, she pointed at the keyhole, and he

DALE MAYER

leaned down to take a closer look. Dressed only in pajama pants, he opened the door and stepped out into the hallway. Instantly footsteps ran away. Taylor went after the guy as she waited, wondering what she should do. Her door didn't seem to be open, but it looked like her intruder had left something in the doorknob, trying to open it up. There was little she could do at the moment.

But she grabbed his phone and stepped out into the hallway and took pictures of whatever it was in her door. He had gotten her apartment door open. But it was barely ajar, which explained why she hadn't noticed that from Taylor's doorway. She didn't know why anybody would want to return to the crime scene, but she stepped back, waiting and hoping Taylor managed to catch him. And, if not him, then at least the cameras caught his face, and maybe she could identify whoever it was who had just raced through the hallway. She leaned against Taylor's doorjamb, her arms crossed over her chest, waiting for Taylor to come back.

"What are you doing out here?" Taylor whispered as he came through the door to the stairs.

He was alone and wore a pissed look on his face. She turned and walked back inside his apartment. She checked the time on his phone and saw it was five-thirty. She couldn't go back to sleep now for sure and walked over to the coffeemaker and prepared to put on a pot.

He came in behind her and slammed the door, leaning against it, his eyes closed.

"I'm sorry," she said as she filled the carafe with water.

"It's not your fault," he said. "It was mine. He had a vehicle waiting. I wasn't expecting that."

"With somebody else driving?"

He nodded slowly. "Whatever the hell is going on here

478

involves more than one person."

"Oh, well, that changes things," she said. She turned to finish the coffee and pressed the button on the machine. "Do you need a shower, or do you need to at least treat your feet?"

He looked down at his bare feet in disgust. "I'll call the detective as soon as I get a shower. That's all the babying these feet will get."

"You could let somebody look after you for a change."

"When I calm down, maybe," he said. "Right now, I want to wring someone's neck. And I wish it was your intruder." He disappeared into the bathroom.

A few moments later she heard the shower going and smiled. Seeing how someone handled themselves in a conflict or a crisis was a really good way to find out what their true character was like. He had no intention of letting her bear the brunt of his temper, and she appreciated that. He was a good man. The fact that he had done as much as he had to look after her already was amazing.

She couldn't believe the speed and the power she witnessed when he'd gone after that guy, but, with a head start and a vehicle ready—she stopped and walked over to the notepad and wrote down "Vehicle?"

She'd never been that interested in knowing about vehicles. She just wanted to get in, start the engine and have it work. Other than that she didn't care.

When the coffee was done dripping, she poured herself a cup, walked over to the small balcony and stepped outside. The cool morning air brushed along her hair and her bare legs. She realized she hadn't even gotten fully dressed. She was missing her pants and Oxford shirt, but she really didn't want to get dressed again for work so soon. But the T-shirt she wore covered her butt. Probably. Matter of fact, maybe it didn't. She stepped back inside.

Taylor wouldn't be done for at least another ten minutes. She just needed a few minutes of peace and would have liked to stay outside longer, but she got some fresh air to start her day. Yet she was modest and had considered other people could see her outside on the balcony. She took several deep breaths as she returned to the kitchen, put her coffee cup on the kitchen table and did several stretches. That accomplished, she picked up her cup and headed to her bedroom, where she finished dressing. When she came back out, Taylor was stepping from his bedroom as well.

He glanced at her, noting she was fully dressed and said, "I couldn't believe it when I saw you standing there just in a T-shirt. What if that guy had come back?"

She shot him a look. "I trusted you wouldn't let him get anywhere near me," she said calmly.

He let out his breath with a hard sigh. Then he gave a clipped nod. "Good," he said, "but don't ever take a chance like that again, please. As much as I may enjoy seeing those legs peeking out from under that T-shirt, I really don't think you should be flaunting that sexuality."

"It wasn't even five-fifteen in the morning," she said. "I highly doubt anybody was out and around."

"Just that one guy to kill us," he said drily.

"I took a photo of my door with your phone," she said. "He left something in the doorknob, and the door itself is actually open."

"You should have told me that earlier. He could have come back and gotten rid of the evidence." Taylor opened the door and stepped out, with her trailing right behind him with her mug.

"Sorry."

He waved away her apology and stepped in front of her apartment door and studied it. Then he pulled out his phone and called Detective Butler, putting the phone on Speaker so she could hear as well. When a sleepy voice answered, Taylor said, "Hey, you had an intruder at Midge's apartment. He jammed the lock getting in, and the door is ajar. What I don't know is if he was leaving or if he was arriving."

"He was arriving," Midge said. "Something woke me, like banging noises. I wasn't sure what. I thought I heard something else soon afterward. And that's when I saw him there through the peephole. Well, I'd assumed he'd just arrived but ..."

He nodded at her.

The detective said, "Don't touch anything. I won't be there for at least an hour, but I'll send somebody to stand guard."

"Good enough. I'll stay here until the guard arrives," Taylor said, ending the call, as he motioned for her to step back into his place. Taylor stood with one foot in his apartment and the other in the hallway. "Can you tell me exactly what you heard?"

She shrugged. "Just what I said. Something woke me—banging noises, I think. Then I thought I heard more noises, some scratching or scraping. I don't know really, just sounds of somebody doing something. Living on base, we all respect everyone else's downtime and how we have shifts of people who work around-the-clock. Nobody should be making too much noise."

Taylor frowned, concentrating. "And, if he was trying to get in, there shouldn't have been any sounds besides whatever tool he was using to break the lock."

"But, if he had a key," she said, "why would he need to break it off in the lock?"

"I don't know, and I'm not sure if he left behind a key or if it's something else he made."

"This is so confusing," she said.

"It could also be a different person from our murderer of yesterday," Taylor suggested.

"No! There can't be two people after me."

"It must be at least two, to count the guy breaking in this morning and his driver. Could be three different people if the murderer is not this guy or his driver. But why would they be after you?" he asked with interest in his voice.

"No reason that I can figure out." She carefully put her cup on the coffee table and curled up in the corner of the couch, pulling her feet up close to her bum and hugging her knees. "None of this makes any sense."

"Maybe it does once we know more," he said. "Let the cops come. I didn't pull that out of the doorknob in case he left behind any fingerprints to be found."

She pointed to his phone and reminded him of the photos she took. He nodded and, looking at them, said, "It's possible it's a key broken off in the lock. It's possible they made a copy and left the other key downstairs with the super, thinking the cops wouldn't know why the couple was killed."

"I never even thought about that," she said. "It's a pretty funny-looking key though."

"Funny-looking keys are all over the place. Particularly if they're making the keys themselves or if they have lock-picking equipment."

She nodded. "Whatever. That's all for the cops to sort out. Do you think they'll go inside and figure out what they might have been after?"

"They will eventually," he said, "but it certainly won't be at the moment. They'll send somebody to keep watch and after that there'll be nothing for a while."

"You woke up the detective, didn't you?"

He nodded.

"He also could have been working late on the case, so we shouldn't judge."

He chuckled. "Hell, no need to judge. It's not even six yet."

She sighed and said, "It feels like I've been awake for hours."

Just when he reached for his cup of coffee, his phone rang, and he said, "It's Mason."

She listened to the conversation, at least Taylor's side, since he didn't put it on Speaker. She thought that was odd at first, but Mason was probably Taylor's boss, so why would he let her hear their conversation? She had heard tales about Mason, but she had figured they were all tall tales. Having learned more about Taylor, she wondered about that now.

As the conversation evolved, she realized they were talking about the breach at her office. She leaned forward, trying to listen. Taylor held up a hand, telling her just to wait.

When he finally hung up, he said, "It looks like the hacker went for access to the digital staff records. They didn't seem to be all that good at it in the sense that their trail was easily followed. Yet maybe that's what they intended. It looks like they opened over fifty files, and we don't know which of those were important. A forensics team is working through the files to see if anything in there might connect us to the murders."

She nodded. "And, by opening fifty, if they only wanted

one, that muddies the water nicely."

"Exactly. It doesn't look like they altered anything necessarily, but they were all saved with changes."

"What that means is, they had to have altered something," she said.

"Yeah, or they added a space or a single character, only to confuse the issue."

"I could see it if they wanted to add something or to take away something from a specific file," she said. "But this is still a bizarre way to do it. Our records are supposed to be up to date, but honestly I can tell you that they're not."

"OF COURSE I don't want to hear that," Taylor said with a laugh, smiling down at her. "Who would?"

She shrugged. "We do our best, but nothing gets done 100 percent in any one day at work. You know that."

"And then, of course, that brings us back to Jenny," he said, thinking about the murders. "She would have had access when she was still working there. She could have made all kinds of changes if she had wanted to alter the files."

Midge nodded. "She could have, yes. It's not like any time we make a change to a file that an alert goes out. Yet making changes is what we're doing. We are changing and updating files. I just finished working on several deceased members. Moving them from active to our deceased folder," she said. "So it's not as if Jenny editing a file would bring up any alert. We all have so much work to do, and we're always several days behind."

"So, say Jenny had made changes in the past, but now that she's fired, and something has gone down, she wanted to go in and undo those changes. Could she?"

"If she still worked there, she certainly could," Midge said slowly. "And I can't understand under what circumstance that would make any sense. At least not any legal circumstances."

"But three murders already is a hell of a long way from being legal," he said, "so obviously something is going on. I just wish I could figure out what."

"But she no longer has access."

"Unless she hacked in."

"Strange," Midge said. "I don't even know how hard it would be to hack in."

"Unfortunately it can happen," Taylor said. "Mason's wife, Tesla, does IT work for the government. Mostly on defense contracts, but she certainly understands hackers."

"But she's probably not part of this investigation, right?"

"Not likely. She's considered too valuable to waste her time on something like a mere hack into staff records," he said in a dry tone.

She smiled and nodded. "So you do have friends in high places. Or well-placed, was it?"

"Yeah, that was it." He chuckled, oddly happy she had remembered. "But I also work with Mason. We're both in the same unit."

"Oh." She frowned, her mind sorting through the names. "That makes you—you're a SEAL, aren't you?"

He raised an eyebrow and stared at her. *How did she know?* He was sure he hadn't told her.

She shrugged. "Remember? I deal with files all day long."

"My name just came up?"

"No," she said. "Not yours. Mason's. But I can't remember what it was all about."

He frowned, wondering why she'd need to go into Mason's file.

"Ah, I know what it was," she said with a smile.

"What?" he asked curiously.

She shook her head. "I can't tell you. Or at least not a whole lot of it. His clearance was upgraded. So his file was essentially put away, so other people can't see parts of it."

He chuckled. "Good for him. Mason's a good guy. Hell, we all are. A lot of us bust our asses every day of the year to keep America safe. Yet it always seems that a lot of the damage from sabotage and terrorism comes from our home soil. Go figure."

"You're not supposed to work on home soil, are you?"

"Not necessarily," he said. "Generally we deal with international strife and conflict. But that doesn't mean, if somebody brings the fight to me, that I won't fight back," he said.

She nodded. "That sounds like you."

"That sounds like all of us, including and especially Mason. He's even up for promotion," he said.

"I know. That's partly why I was changing the files," she said with a smirk.

He grinned at her, and then his smile widened as he realized what she was saying. "Perfect," he said. "I don't know anybody who deserves it more."

"But that doesn't help us with our current problem," she said.

"Nope, it doesn't. Are you going into work today?"

Her face fell. "What I'd like is to get back into my apartment so I can at least get some clothing."

"We can arrange that whenever Butler arrives. Because you'll probably have to go over there and see if anything else was damaged."

"I wasn't allowed in the first time," she said.

"No, that's not true," he said. "You were allowed in for a quick look, but you couldn't sort through anything because it was an active crime scene. Now that it's been dealt with and hopefully forensics is done—"

"Or they're on their way back," she added, "and then they'll keep me out of my own place for yet another day."

"You need clothes," he said. "We'll arrange to get some of your things."

"Good. And hopefully my phone too. I'm really missing my phone. I don't know how many times I've reached for it." She smiled. "Oh, and, to answer your question about work, I guess I should go in."

"It would be helpful if you did," he said thoughtfully. "And, while you're at it, think about the people who work there and about those who worked there in the past. And the fact that somebody accessed fifty files."

She nodded slowly. "Now you're asking me to spy on my coworkers?"

"Well, if a disgruntled past employee didn't have anything to do with this," he said, "what do you think about a disgruntled current employee having something to do with it?"

She looked at him for a moment, then groaned. "Oh, fine. I'll go spy on my coworkers."

He laughed. "Good girl."

CHAPTER 7

W HEN MIDGE WALKED into work well over an hour late—after stopping at the police station at Detective Butler's request and being asked another zillion questions— she felt like her insides were ragged. Although she wanted to unravel, something inside her locked it all down and tried to ignore the fact her life was falling to pieces.

At least Taylor had managed to get her phone back. Now she felt a little less like she was missing a part of herself.

When she stepped inside the office, she found complete chaos—file folders stacked on the four desks, the phones ringing incessantly, nobody here but her it seemed. She stood inside the door, bathed in an "I don't want to be here" feeling.

"There you are," her boss, Mr. Shorts, said, looking a little relieved. "We really need you now."

She walked toward him, certainly not running, but she didn't dawdle either. "What's the problem?" she asked.

"Everything," he snapped. "Two other people didn't show up for work today."

Her eyebrows shot up. "Why not?"

"I have no idea," he roared. "How am I supposed to keep this department running if all the staff is out?"

"If people get sick, they get sick," she said in exasperation. "Not a lot they can do about it."

"Then why didn't they call me and explain at least?" he shouted. He stopped, running his hands through his hair, leaving it sticking straight up, and seemed to pull himself back into control. "Look. I'm sorry. It's been pretty hellish. I really got raked over the coals this morning for the breach as it is."

"If it's an IT breach, it's hardly your fault," she said.

"They're not sure it was. Apparently the door was unlocked yesterday morning."

"That's not possible," she said, turning to look. "These are locked doors."

"And, therefore, they're also unlocked doors," he said. "It's not like we're keeping any top state secrets here. We don't have five-star security. Sure, we have security, but nobody really expects anybody to come into the filing room," he said with a disparaging tone.

He'd referred to the department like that a few times before. And she understood in a way because he'd tried to be promoted up and out but had never made it. Now he knew he was stuck here for life, and it was definitely not what he wanted. She walked over to her desk, dropped her purse into a file cabinet and hung her jacket on the back of her chair. "So, do we still have somebody answering the phones?"

He gave her a hard glare. "Yeah. Me."

She stared at the phone console and could see all the flashing lights, which was what had prompted the question in the first place. "Can I presume all those are people on hold?"

He nodded and said with a wicked smile, "But you're here now, thank God. I'll put on a fresh pot of coffee."

She wanted coffee herself, so she would hardly argue with him. She went through the phone calls and took messages, telling people she'd get back to them as soon as she could. Then she phoned both Bart and Terri to see if they were coming in. Neither answered their phones.

Not liking that one bit, she sent a text to Taylor, letting him know two more people in the department hadn't shown up, including their names and phone numbers. She was sure it was probably a breach of confidentiality, but, considering everything else going on, she didn't know where to draw that line just now. Then she logged on to her computer and changed her password.

With that done, she moved on to her emails and groaned to see so many messages had piled up. Part of her job in staff records involved responding to credit checks for anybody attempting to get credit cards, car loans, mortgages, etc. Confirmation of employment, pay scale, etc. And then personnel called or emailed about their plans and benefits, and the list went on.

And that was just people inquiring. A massive amount of updating was always needed to the files as well. It would be a very busy day. When her boss came back out again, he carried two coffee cups. He placed one on her desk and said, "I know I didn't say anything earlier, but thank you very much for coming in today."

She nodded and didn't answer him.

"Did you go to the police?"

"Talked to them yesterday, last night and again this morning," she said shortly.

When he hesitated, she looked up and said, "You really don't want to know."

He struggled, trying to figure out if he did or not, and finally he nodded and said, "You're right. I probably don't. I'll be in my office, if anybody needs me."

Then he walked down the hall. When she heard his office door go *click*, she sat back and sighed. He meant well, and he probably did have a lot of stuff to do in his office, but he rarely came out and helped them when they needed it. They were always expected to do their job regardless. But now it was down to just her, and that meant it would be a shitty day.

When she looked up again, she saw the main entrance door opening yet again. She frowned at the large man shutting the door, his back to her. And then he turned, and she saw his profile. "Good morning, Taylor," she said. "What are you doing here?"

"Well, the better question is, what are you doing, considering it's already afternoon, and you appear to still be caught up in your morning."

"As you can see, I'm the only one here," she said. "The work is backed up for days, and, with nobody to help, we'll be backed up even more."

"I passed on your message," he said, and she nodded, glancing around to see if her boss was around. So far she had seen no further sign of him.

"Good," she said. "I'm nearly ready to kill the both of them myself."

He nodded grimly. "Just change the wording on that a bit, will you?"

She winced. "Yeah, sorry."

He glanced around. "Will you take time for lunch?" It was on the tip of her tongue to refuse, when he held up a hand and said, "Don't say no. I get you're so far behind that you won't get it cleared up even this week if nobody else shows up. And I get that you've had a crazy morning, but you won't be effective this afternoon if you don't take a break to catch your breath and to get some food."

Just then her boss came storming down the hallway. "She's not allowed to leave for lunch," he said stiffly.

Taylor widened his stance and crossed his arms over his chest. "And why is that?"

"She was late coming in this morning," he said. "Her lunchtime will be her chance to work through and make up some time."

She didn't like the sound of that. Nor his bossy attitude. Sure he was her boss, but she also had rights. She'd never been much of a union person. She'd always worked through lunch when needed, but he'd gone too far.

"Considering that I was late because I had to go to the police to answer more questions *and* considering I only came in to help out," she said, "and that I should be enjoying my days off, I will take some break time, which I am duly allowed. And I will get some food, then come back and keep working. You could have hired a temp or brought in somebody to help." She shook her head and pointed at the phone lines, always lit up to max. "Or you could at least be helping with the calls."

He lifted his head and glared at her.

She nodded. "Of course not. It's not your job, is it? I'll be back in an hour," she snapped, grabbing her jacket and her purse. Then, as she walked out the door, she added, "Unless I choose to quit."

She disappeared, but not before she saw the panic cross her boss's face. She stood outside for a moment, chuckling. "That was mean," she said with a giggle. "I shouldn't have given him that impression."

"The hell you shouldn't," Taylor muttered. "You don't need to put up with that crap."

"Well, if I don't want to be out of a job, then I do need to put up with that crap," she said in a neutral tone. "And, until I find another job, I really can't afford to lose this one."

He nodded and kept quiet, which was a really good idea on his part. Because, if anybody would lash out right now at her boss, it would be him. As they drove away, she sighed into the seat and asked, "Any updates?"

"Nothing. Any idea what happened to your coworkers?"

"No," she said. "I was hoping you might know."

"I would suggest we drive past their places," he said, "but considering that you're on a short lunch break, we probably don't have time."

"Which is all crap in the first place," she said, "since I was called in yesterday as it was."

"Was that because the same two people were missing?"

She shook her head. "No, because Debbie was out sick."

"And she's still sick?"

"Apparently," she said. "Or they all got together and decided they were done working for him."

"Is he always like that?"

"He's extra-bad today," she said, trying to be fair. "But then there is just me in the office, and I walked out for an hour."

"Well, worst case, he can put a message on the phones and lock the door."

"He probably will," she said. "Or he would if he knew how, I mean."

"And I presume he doesn't?"

"He rarely handles the phones," she said. "Definitely not his thing. He panics, which is probably why he's so grumpy."

They walked into a restaurant before she even realized they were in a sandwich shop. She looked up and smiled. "I haven't been here in a long time."

"It's fresh and good," he said. He motioned to a table. "Go sit there by the window."

"What if you don't know what I want?"

"You're so tired you won't even care what I order," he said with a laugh.

She grinned and nodded. "Isn't that the truth?" Dropping into the chair at the table he'd pointed out, she put her purse and jacket in the chair beside her and propped her chin on the palms of her hands. She was tired. Sleep had been difficult last night, tossing and turning with thoughts of the three people who had died. All with a connection to her. That she was central to this, she understood, she just didn't know why. Very quickly she was joined by Taylor, as he sat down in the chair across from her.

"So what did you order me?" she asked.

"A clubhouse," he said.

Her eyebrows shot up. "That's one of my favorites, but I rarely eat them because of the extra bread."

He shot her a look and growled in a dark voice, "Don't ever let me hear you talk about dieting."

She shook her head. "No, I've been blessed to not have to diet. But a lot of bread is in a club."

"Carbs are good for you," he said in response.

She shrugged and settled back. "I won't argue the point with you today. Like you said, I'm too damn tired."

He nodded in satisfaction. "That's what I figured."

Just then the waitress arrived with two cups of coffee. Midge pulled one toward her, grabbed the cream and poured in a liberal amount.

"You think that will keep you awake?"

"No, I'm just hoping it'll wash down the nasty taste of

the coffee my boss made this morning." Laughing, she continued, "Because that's another thing he doesn't do well."

"Not a lot of bosses do," he said, "because, so often, the secretaries do it for them."

"That's definitely the case here." As she relaxed a bit, she could feel her energy drifting down her toes. "Lord, I wish I didn't have to go back this afternoon," she said. "I could go home and go to sleep." Instantly she froze and then groaned. "But then again, look what I'd be facing." She raised stricken eyes to him. "Do you think they've released my apartment yet?"

He leaned across and grabbed her hand, pulling it away from the coffee cup as he said, "I don't know if they have or not. I can ask, but you also have to come to terms with the fact that your bed is ruined, as is your bedding, and your place needs to be thoroughly cleaned, as in professionally."

"Oh, God," she whispered. "I didn't even consider that. But he was shot in my bed, and all that blood would have soaked through, wouldn't it?"

Taylor nodded. "And it probably got into the carpet too. We also don't know if anything else might have been taken, since we never did get a chance to look that closely."

She reached up to rub her temple. "It wasn't even a very old bed," she muttered.

"I highly suggest you get yourself a new one regardless," he said. "Even if it's secondhand, I doubt somebody would have been murdered in it."

She gave a shudder. "No way," she said. "Even if it has to be a super cheap one, I'm getting a new one."

"Good. You probably just need the mattress and box spring. We can probably use the frame and headboard. But honestly, I don't know what the blood splatter will look like on the headboard and on the night tables."

She swallowed hard, images flashing into her mind. "I don't even want to think about it."

"To get back into your apartment," he said, "not only do you have to think about it, you have to deal with it."

She stared at him. When a cough sounded beside them, she looked up to see the waitress, holding two plates. Taylor let go of her hand, and the waitress set down the plates. "Thank you."

After the waitress left, he glanced at Midge and said, "When you're done with work today, I suggest I pick you up, and we'll go bed shopping."

She gave a broken laugh. "First, let's find out if I can get into the apartment. Because otherwise I can't arrange anything."

"As soon as we can get in," he said, "I have a couple guys I'm pretty sure will help haul out the bed and whatever else isn't salvageable, if you'll trust us on that." He looked at her with a piercing stare.

She nodded. "Please, if you can get that out of there before I have to see it again, I would really appreciate it."

He nodded and said, "I don't know about the floor though."

"I don't suppose blood comes out, does it?"

"It comes out but not very well, and it will soak through the carpet and the padding to the floor underneath."

She didn't know what to think of that. The apartment wasn't hers after all; she rented it. "I guess we have to talk to the landlord. Though, since it's base housing, maybe they will take care of it."

"That's another phone call I can make. But I will have to tell them that I live there with you. Otherwise they won't talk to me."

"True," she said. "That might cause undue complications, considering the circumstances. Just check it out and, if they insist on me calling them, I'll make the call from work this afternoon."

He nodded. "Tuck into that," he said, motioning to her sandwich. "I want at least two-thirds of that gone before we take you back to work."

She stared down at the monster sandwich and said, "If I leave anything, I'm taking it with me." And, true to her word, she did take the last quarter of it back. It was just too much for her to handle. But she knew she could be hungry again by midafternoon. She walked back into the office, and Taylor left her with a promise to make a bunch of phone calls and to get back to her.

As she tried to open the door, she found it was locked and laughed. Of course her boss had done exactly what Taylor had suggested. She unlocked it and stepped into the room. It was odd to have the place so empty like this. She really wished the other two employees, Bart and Terri, had called in, or had at least answered her voicemail message so she understood what was going on. They were both normally very reliable, so she didn't get this issue at all.

She sat down at her desk, her box with her leftover sandwich sitting off on the side with her purse, as she ran through the phone calls ringing through. With that done, she put the phone on Silent, so she could ignore them for a bit. This was not the time for her to get lost in one million phone calls. Or messages. She'd deal with those later, after she'd gotten some of the highest priority backlog issues resolved. Bringing up her email, she got back to work. About an hour later she stood and walked around, stretching out her arms and her neck.

She hadn't seen her boss since she returned and figured he was probably either napping in his office or he'd left as well. In a way that would make the most sense. When the chips were down, he was definitely the kind to take a hike. And maybe that was a good thing because not everybody did well under stress.

She walked to his office and tapped on the door. There was no answer. She tried the knob, and it was unlocked, so she pushed it open and froze in her tracks. He sat there like always, and, at first, she didn't understand. He looked the same as he always did, but like he was sleeping. The only thing different was the hole in the center of his forehead.

TAYLOR ANSWERED THE phone, still sitting in the parking lot outside the gym. He had stopped in to talk to Mason, and they'd had a couple minutes of conversation. Then Taylor had made a few phone calls and was just making another one when his phone rang. Thinking it was somebody responding to one of his questions, he answered it.

"Get back here. Please," Midge said, her voice terse and on the verge of panic. "He's dead."

Taylor froze and then asked, "Who's dead?"

"My boss. He's dead. Somebody shot him in the forehead."

"Have you called the police?" She took several deep and shaky breaths, and he could hear the panic she was desperately trying to hold back. But he was already driving in her direction. "Where are you right now?"

She gave a strangled laugh. "I'm hiding. In the supply room."

"Are you in danger? Is someone else there?"

"I don't know," she said. "Please get here fast." And, with that, she hung up.

Swearing softly, he flipped through his contacts and dialed Detective Butler's number.

"Now what do you want?" the detective asked in exasperation. "And, if this call is about yet another dead body, I don't want it."

"Neither do I," Taylor said in a harsh voice. "But apparently Midge just found her boss in his office. Dead."

The detective's voice turned businesslike. "Where?"

He gave him the address and said, "She's hiding in the supply room."

"Is somebody in there with her?"

"I don't know," Taylor said. "I'm about seven minutes away. I think she's scared that whoever did this to him might still be there."

"I'm on my way," the detective said.

Taylor snorted and said, "Doesn't matter. I'll be there way ahead of you." His next call was to Mason, and he brought him up to date. "I don't know what Colton's doing," Taylor said, "but we might need to pull him in to give me a hand on this."

"Not a problem," Mason said in a calm voice. "He's here with me and heading to your place right now."

"Send him to Midge's office. That's where we're going. And, if we can get there before the cops do," he said, "we'll have a chance to case the joint first."

"Done," Mason said. "Obviously this is getting worse, not better. I don't want Midge returning to that office again."

"Hell, neither do I," Taylor snapped. "The whole office

needs to be shut down. Two other people didn't show up for work today either."

"Names?"

Taylor gave him the names. "And the only reason she worked yesterday was because somebody else had called in sick. As far as the department goes, she's the only one active right now."

"If she's the only one, then she shouldn't be anywhere near that place."

"Give me two minutes," Taylor said, "and she won't be."

Hanging up the call, he pulled into the same parking spot where he'd dropped her off earlier, then dashed out of the Jeep and ran to the glass doors. Pulling open the door, he stepped inside. He didn't have a weapon, but he stopped for a second to listen. There was nothing. Not even sounds of her. He walked down the hallway and saw the open door and inside was the boss, just as she described. A beautifully centered hole right in the middle of his forehead. He still couldn't hear anything. "Midge?" he called out. "I'm here."

He opened the next door, and it was the bathroom. He stepped into another room and saw it was the lunchroom. At the end of the lunchroom was a small door. He opened it. As he did so, he heard a half shriek. He looked down to see Midge curled up at the far end of the shelves. When she saw it was him, she scrambled to her feet and hurled herself toward him. He braced himself for the impact, but she was so small and so light, he hardly felt it. He wrapped her up in his arms.

Picking her up, he carried her back out to her desk, walking past the boss's office quickly so she didn't get a second look. But he needn't have worried since her face was buried against his neck. At her desk, he sat her down and tried to get her to release her hold on him and said, "The police are on the way. I need to know from you exactly what happened."

She shook her head and refused to let go of his neck or to lift her face from his chest.

He didn't blame her one bit; she'd been through a lot. He sat down and pulled her into his lap again and just held her. If this was the only thing he could do for her right now, this was what he would do. Her boss was dead, and Taylor highly doubted anybody else remained in the office. Only one person mattered to him right now—her. After a few moments, he rubbed her back and asked, "Can you tell me what happened now?"

She pulled back and stared at him with haunted eyes. "When I returned from lunch, I sat down and started working on the most critical backlogged email requests. Before I knew it, about an hour had gone by, and I was getting stiff and tense, and even my jaw was clenching. I put the phones on Silent, so I could get some things done rather than just add to the list, but I could still see the flashing lights as calls rang through, trying to get ahold of us. It felt so weird to be alone in the office, and it just hit me how alone I was. I stood and stretched and walked to my boss's office. I figured maybe he was sleeping. I knocked lightly, then turned the handle and pushed the door open, while in the back of my mind wondering if the sneaky little bugger had gone home and had left me holding the bag."

Taylor nodded in understanding. From what he'd seen of her boss, that sounded very likely.

"Of course the front office door was locked when I came back," she said, frowning. "Which now makes no sense. And there he was. At first I thought he was asleep. I didn't understand what I was seeing, and then I couldn't look away. I dialed you immediately, and then, I don't know, some sound or something weird scared me." She was shaking, her voice breaking as she tried to tell him exactly what happened.

"And I just thought about where I could hide, so I ran to the supply room and curled up in the corner. I called you again because you didn't answer the first time," she said and then gave him an accusatory stare, as if he was supposed to be off the phone, waiting for her call at all times.

Ironic, since he'd been making calls on her behalf. But he didn't say anything, he just massaged her shoulders gently and asked, "Did you hear anything else?"

She shook her head. "No. No, I didn't. By then I was so panicked it seemed like every sound was amplified to the point where I was afraid somebody was coming in the door. I couldn't tell if I was hearing people upstairs or if someone was right outside. She shuddered and asked, "Why is this happening? What is going on?"

A voice from the doorway behind her said, "That's what we want to know." Detective Butler walked toward her. He raised his eyebrows at Taylor, who motioned down the hallway.

When they came back, Butler's face was grim. "You want to start from the beginning?" he asked. "We need to hear it again. And likely again after that."

She lifted her face and stared up at Taylor, and her expression broke his heart. "He's dead," she said blankly, the shock very obviously setting in. "They're all dead."

"All of them?" the detective asked. "Who is *all of them*?"

She stared at him, bewildered for a long moment, and then said, "I don't know." She motioned toward the entire office. "Where are they all? What's happened to everybody?"

"That's exactly what we need you to tell us," the detective said.

Hopefully sooner than later, Taylor thought. Yet she wasn't in any state to do it right now. Taylor wrapped her up in his arms and tucked her tight against his chest. He looked over at the detective and asked, "May I take her home?"

The detective hesitated, then nodded. "Might as well. We'll come by in a little while. See if you can get her lucid again."

Taylor gave a small snort. "Four bodies in less than twenty-four hours? With another two or three employees unaccounted for? It might take longer than *a little while,* Detective."

Butler had the good graces to look ashamed. "I get it," he said. "Go ahead and take her home. We have a lot to deal with here." And then he stopped and said, "Wait. What did you touch when you came in?"

Taylor pointed to the entrance door and then said, "The supply room door. Other than that, it would have been anything I touched right here. Oh, and I was here earlier, before lunch, when I picked her up but didn't go past the front desk there."

The detective nodded. "Okay, thanks. Take her to your place, and we'll be in touch."

CHAPTER 8

M IDGE HEARD THE detective's words in the back of her mind, and she understood Taylor was lifting her up and carrying her outside. When the fresh air hit her, she lifted her head and said, "I'll be fine."

He gave her a snort. "It'll be a while before you're fine, sweetie."

She struggled to get out of his arms, trying to stand, but he refused to let her. "My car is here," she said. "I want to drive it home."

Another voice from behind her said, "You're not driving anywhere, miss."

Taylor turned and said, "Midge, meet Colton. Colton, meet Midge." And yet another man pulled up behind him. "And this is Troy. He's another one of our guys."

Troy nodded with the gentlest of smiles she'd ever seen. "Good afternoon, ma'am."

She loved him immediately. With a sigh, she said, "Nothing is good about it, as much as I wish there was." She looked over at Taylor. "Do you think they would drive my vehicle home for me?"

"Good idea. Don't worry. You can trust them with it." Fumbling in her purse, he found the keys he'd scooped up when he'd grabbed her things and handed them to Colton. "Meet you guys back at my place."

Both men nodded.

Taylor opened the door to his Jeep and helped her into the front seat, then closed the door and walked around to the driver's side. She sat there, numb, and hadn't even thought to buckle up. But he did. Reaching over her, he grabbed the seat belt and pulled it around to click in tight. Then he started the engine and drove carefully back to his place. His mind reeled with questions, but it wasn't the time, and it wasn't the place. Besides, there didn't appear to be any answers right now. Back at his place, he parked and walked around to her side. Once he unbuckled her seat belt, it was like she woke up from a nap.

She looked up at him and smiled. "I really will be okay, you know?"

"I know you will," he said gently. "But how long it will take is the real question."

She hopped out on her own and reached for his hand before he led her inside to the elevator and up to his apartment. She was relieved to see his place was completely normal. The last thing she wanted was to see any ruckus here, as she already felt like she wasn't safe anywhere. If his place remained untouched, then at least she could think of it as a safe haven.

She walked over to the couch, where the blanket was folded in the same corner she had grown accustomed to. Wrapping the blanket around her and putting a pillow under her head, she curled up and closed her eyes.

TAYLOR HOPED SHE would sleep. Knowing the guys were on their way, he put on a pot of coffee and tossed some beers into the fridge. Then he walked toward the small deck and opened the glass doors wide. He stepped outside and took several deep breaths of fresh air. Something rotten was happening on base. And he didn't have a clue why or what. Hearing knocks at the door, he walked over and opened it. "Since when do you guys knock?" he joked. "Normally you barge right in."

"Yeah," Troy said with a grin. "But we didn't want to scare her."

"I appreciate that," Taylor said, with a nod toward the couch. "I'm hoping she'll nod off, if she hasn't already."

As they studied her, she murmured something and snuggled deeper into the couch.

"She's had a shit day, hasn't she?"

"Yeah, the past twenty-four hours have been one nightmare after another. So, the beer isn't quite cold yet, but the coffee is hot. Which do you want?"

They both asked for hot coffee, with Troy adding, "That'll give the beer time to cool."

Taylor took them out on the small balcony. They stood there out of Midge's earshot, so she could sleep, and quietly went over the details. At least the few details he had.

"Seriously? That's four dead people in less than twenty-four hours," Troy said, his voice hard and angry. "What the hell is going on?"

"We don't know," Taylor said, fatigue in his voice. "Tesla has been on it too. Because something in the staff records data was hacked. Certain files were accessed, and all we have to go on is a theory involving Jenny, a disgruntled employee, who blamed Midge when she got fired."

"Do you think Jenny's the one involved?"

"We don't have anything that proves it either way. It would be nice if we could get a definite lock on one suspect and their motive though."

"Of course Jenny makes a decent suspect because she had access and could have done all kinds of things to the files. It's possible and, even likely, that she still has computer access, plus a key to the records department, even though her credentials should have been canceled."

"Midge suggested Jenny might have taken somebody else's access codes. Which means Jenny could have never really lost access at all. She could have been getting together whatever information she wanted this whole time."

"But it's not as if the staff records contain any top secret files," Troy said, trying to get up to speed.

"No, they don't," Taylor said. "And the department is constantly updating the files. Midge is always providing employment information for banks and finance companies for mortgages and things like that. When new information comes through, they update the files. Sounds like the records are mostly all electronic now, except for a relatively small batch of paper files still waiting to be scanned."

"Sounds boring."

"It is, though she seems happy enough. I'm not sure she wants something more challenging right now, although it seems like maybe the challenge is in managing the volume of work, rather than the work itself. Plus, her boss seemed like a dick."

"Right. Besides, somebody has to do the job. Otherwise you and I could get stuck with it," Colton said, laughing at his own joke.

Troy rolled his eyes at that. "They'll be sorry if they ever put me into a job like that. It's amazing how much paper I can drip coffee all over, and that's without even trying," he said with a cheeky grin.

"There has to be a reason why someone would even think access to the staff records data would be helpful."

"The only thing I can think of," Troy said, "is if getting access to staff records somehow gives them a back door into something else that's more valuable."

"That was the premise I think Tesla is looking into. But you realize a whole IT department is supposed to be working on this breach. I don't know this for sure, but I rather imagine she would have gotten frustrated at the slow results. I haven't heard anything from them either."

"You let Mason know about this from the get-go, so I'm sure he's discussed it with Tesla and the brass to see what the hell's going on. This isn't a small case now."

"I don't know if the base is on full lockdown," Taylor said, shaking his head. "It should be, but you and I both know information flows slowly sometimes. As do decisions."

"Well, a lover's tiff is one thing, but killing an old couple to get a key to Midge's apartment shows a decided lack of handy skills, like lock-picking," Troy said. "So I'm thinking it won't be anybody with any military training."

"Not to mention the fact the first-known victim's groin was shot up," Colton said, "so I'm leaning toward a female."

"And a disgruntled female employee would also go back to make sure she shot her boss for good measure," Taylor said. "Although I only spoke to him twice, I wanted to punch him out myself. I'm sure he had plenty of enemies."

"Yeah, especially whoever sentenced him to a job like that," Colton quipped. They all had a good chuckle, a welcome release of tension.

"So, I'm really liking the idea of Jenny as a suspect. But, for all this conjecture, we need something that'll prove her involvement," Taylor said, leaning on the railing and taking a deep breath.

"That'll be the hard part," Colton added, "because, if she's had access all this time and is any good with computers at all, then maybe she's already closed off any trail showing she was there."

"But we know," Taylor said, "that, no matter how good they are, they always leave something behind."

"True enough," Colton said with a nod.

"However, we still have the guy trying to break into her apartment this morning. And his driver. So it's not just Jenny. She has help."

Just then they heard a sound. Taylor turned to see Midge sitting up.

CHAPTER 9

"**Y**OU KNOW I can hear you guys just fine, right?" she announced. "And, although I had my eyes closed and was resting, I wasn't asleep." The men just looked at her without saying a word. "It's not as if you were discussing classified secrets or anything. And you made a summary that makes sense. But I don't know that Jenny has the balls to do all this."

"How about her anger?" Troy asked, walking in to sit down on the couch beside her. "Is she angry enough, mean enough or revengeful enough for something like this?"

"The problem is, I don't know her that well," Midge said, looking first at his coffee and then back over at the pot. "She did have a mean streak, I guess. But it was just little stuff. You know? Office stuff, … like Jenny would take the last cup from the pot of coffee and not put another pot on. Leaving me with a full set of busy phone lines when Jenny went off for lunch, instead of taking five minutes to help. Saying she'd done a bunch of work, and then you'd discover she hadn't done any of it. She was definitely not *coworker of the year* material," Midge said with a tired smile. "Not by any means."

"Did anybody ever stop by at work to see her?" Taylor asked. "Like a boyfriend, family members coming to take her out for lunch—anything like that?"

"Or did you ever see her anywhere else but work?" Colton added.

"Did she get picked up by anybody?" Troy asked.

"Easy, guys, one question at a time." She sighed and cast her mind back. "I'm not sure that I did see anybody else actually wanting to see Jenny. Again she's not somebody I particularly liked, so I did my best to ignore her."

"And you still have no idea why the other two people didn't show up for work?" Taylor asked.

"Nope," she said, "and actually it's three people. I don't normally work on Monday, so I usually would have been at home when that guy was killed in my apartment. But Debbie, the person who was supposed to work on Monday, didn't show up, so I got called in. And two others, Bart and Terri, didn't show up today. I was hoping the cops would check it out by going by their places. At least we'd know they were like seriously hungover or something, and that's why they didn't show up or answer their phones."

"Did they call in sick?"

"No, they didn't, and that's why my boss was so upset. I heard Debbie called in sick yesterday."

"Do you know if anything else was bothering your boss?"

"This morning, it could have been anything. Taylor saw him, and he wasn't very friendly, although that wasn't so uncommon for him. But he was very agitated today. I wondered if he figured he was doomed to be in staff records for the rest of his career because of the security breach."

"That would do it," Colton quipped.

They turned to look at Taylor, and he nodded. "Can't say he was terribly friendly. He was adamant Midge shouldn't be allowed to leave for lunch."

Both men drew their eyebrows together.

Taylor added, "They were getting so far behind, her boss wanted her to work straight through."

"Which I have done many times," Midge said, "and I would have this time too, but I needed food."

"And I had ridden over to take her out for lunch," Taylor said. "We weren't even gone the full hour. I took her back because she felt guilty about the work."

"The problem with that workload," she said, "is that there's supposed to be at least four of us. No way I can get caught up if it's just me."

"Interesting. Could you have gotten fired over this?" Colton asked. "Not that I can see why you would, but, if somebody was fired and blamed you, maybe they're doing their best to return the favor and get you fired."

She chuckled. "You know something? If they did fire me right now, it would be a blessing. Because something is rotten in that department, and I don't have a clue what it is."

"You won't be going back until it's cleared up," Taylor said. "So it doesn't matter how far behind they are because it's about to get worse."

Midge groaned and said, "It'll take weeks to get caught up if I'm not there daily, at least trying to keep up."

"It'll take weeks anyway," Troy reminded her gently. "Remember that."

She nodded, then got up and walked into the kitchen, where she poured herself a cup of coffee. It was the last cup. After the others waved off her suggestion of making more, she shut off the pot and came back and sat down again. "The thing is, none of this pertains to the poor man who died in my bed yesterday. And, other than a theory about getting a key to my apartment, how could any of this—the dead guy in my apartment and my office being hacked—possibly involve that sweet couple from downstairs?"

"Well," Colton said, "we don't know how or why yet, but there will be an explanation. We just have to get to the bottom of it."

"And fast," she said in a sharp tone. "This guy's leaving a mess of bodies in his wake, and, well, I really don't want to be the next one."

JUST THE THOUGHT of her being the next victim turned Taylor's blood to ice. He walked over and sat down beside her. Patting her hand and linking their fingers, he said, "I told you that isn't happening."

She raised her eyes to his and said, "I know. But I didn't expect my boss to get shot while I was at lunch either."

"As much as it's hard to think along those lines, we do have to consider the fact your boss could have been an entirely different issue."

Troy and Colton shared a nod.

She stared at him and then shook her head. "No way. Not when we have three other bodies and a hacker involved."

"I know it doesn't look that way, but you know we have to look at every angle. And that also means we have to sit back and let the police do their work."

She glared at him. "Did you walk through that place? With all the paper files collecting everywhere, how would the cops find anything?"

"They'll fingerprint anything suspicious or anything commonly touched, like the front entrance doorknob and the like," Troy said.

"It's a public office," she said tiredly. "You saw that front counter, right? Hundreds of people come in that office. If they fingerprint that front counter, it will just bog down their investigation."

"What about the boss's door?"

"Well, mine will be there for sure," she said, "because I thought maybe he was sleeping, so I opened the door to check. It was strange, like, all of a sudden, the place felt empty. I hadn't noticed up until then because I'd been so buried in work. Well, I did put the ringing phones on Silent. And then it just seemed to take a little bit of time for that sense of unease to trickle through my brain. Apparently I'm really slow these days." At that point, she yawned and sank back against the couch.

"You're exhausted," Taylor said, studying her face with worry. "And you should be on medical leave as it is. Finding one body is enough. But finding out you were set up, somebody was killed in your bed, friends of yours in the building are missing, and then your boss is murdered—probably while we were out for lunch—is reason enough for a mental breakdown. And we don't want to go there."

"I'm not the kind to have a breakdown," she said, jutting out her jaw firmly. "And don't even make me sound like some weak-willed woman who needs to see a shrink."

He snorted. "Weak you are not," he said, going for a smile. "No way I'd make that mistake."

Just then was a knock on the door.

She groaned and said, "What is this? Grand Central Station?"

He patted her knee as he stood and walked to the front door. Sure enough, it was the detective, just as he expected. Letting him in, he directed him to the living room. As the man walked through, Taylor caught the dismay on her face before she quickly managed to school the look. He understood how she felt, but the sooner they knew everything there was to know, the faster the investigators could get on with it. Taylor introduced Butler to Colton and Troy.

The detective was gentle with her, asking as many questions as he had in their last interview. By the time he was done, Taylor could see her energy was gone as well. He let the detective out, realizing it had only been a forty-five minute visit this time. Taylor turned to find her curled up in the corner of the couch, her head on the pillow and the blanket wrapped around her again. He went to the fridge and pulled out three beers this time. As he carried them into the living room, he could hear her deep and rhythmic breathing, and he realized she had fallen deeply asleep. The men stood and walked onto the balcony, and this time he closed the door, so she wouldn't hear their conversation. Popping the tops off the beers, the three men sat in silence.

Finally Troy said, "This is the damnedest thing."

"Isn't it though?" Taylor replied. "I've never seen anything like it."

Colton looked up from his phone. "The base has been placed on full lockdown, by the way. They have no suspects at this time, according to all the newscasts."

"I forgot to ask the detective if they checked the video feed from the records building. There should be images on both ends." He sent the detective a text. The answer came back almost immediately. *"Feeds were damaged in both,"* he read aloud. *"No information to be had."*

Street cams? Taylor texted back.

We're on it, the detective sent back. **It'll take time.**

But Taylor was chomping at the bit. "Does anybody else

around here have access to cameras? Somebody who could see who might have left my apartment building in that first hour when I got home? Or who had been at the records office when she was gone that one hour for lunch?"

"The street cams should definitely show us something," Colton said as he pulled out his phone and began to make a call. Soon it was evident that the call was to Mason.

Taylor brightened at that, saying, "If Mason could get us access, that would be great."

Troy said, "The police detectives are completely overwhelmed and probably don't have the manpower they need for a deal like this. But you know it'll take an official assignment in order to get all that, and you're not allowed because you're too close to the scene. For all we know, you're on the suspect list."

"I already thought of that," Taylor said humorously. "But the last thing I'd ever do is shoot some guy in a woman's bed."

"Right?" Troy said. "Ridiculous."

Taylor thought about it long and hard and said, "The question is, why would someone shoot the boss?"

"Because either he was in on this from the beginning and wanted out," Troy said, "or he was in their way."

"Or," Taylor added, "somebody hated his guts and wanted revenge."

Troy inclined his head. "Or that," he said. "Some real shit is going down on this base lately. And I don't like this trend. It used to be that we saw the bad guys overseas. Now it seems like we're finding them everywhere we turn."

"I know," Taylor said. "The thing is, this time we're not even on a mission. I just got back from Baja with Nelson, what was it, yesterday? And now look at me."

"We're supposed to be going out next week," Troy said. "Elizabeth is apparently getting a chance to do her thing in the delivery system for the new warheads."

"So what are we doing with them?" Taylor asked with interest. "Although I think we're about due for more diving practice. That would be very nice. I'd like to get back to something that's halfway normal."

"Nothing's normal about this," Colton said. "Mason says the IT group is looking not only at the hack job, but they're also looking at the cameras. And they were deliberately sabotaged."

Taylor shrugged. "But we already knew that. What we really need is to follow the traffic cams further out, those not disabled, to see who came and went from both places during those hours."

"Mason said the military police are on that."

Taylor glared at him. "I hate having my hands tied like this. Too much bureaucracy is involved here."

"There's always bureaucracy," Troy said mildly. "We do what we can do within the law. And, when we can't, sometimes we just have to go our own way."

Taylor wasn't sure if a suggestion was in there or not, but he was interested in anything Troy had to say that would get them through this. "If anybody has any idea how to proceed, I'm all ears," he said. "Because, right now, I can't see anything except the reality that Midge is the first one on the detective's list of suspects. And the next one on the murderer's hit list."

"If that was the case," Troy said, "the shooter would have waited for her at the office."

Taylor nodded. "I thought of that too, and I'm not sure why she wasn't taken out. Unless they still need her for something."

"But what?" Colton asked. "She has no higher security clearance than anybody else and no better access than the others."

"Say they need her to be the fall guy," Taylor said slowly. "They need somebody to be guilty. So it looks like it was her boyfriend in her apartment. Then she went into work and shot her boss. What do you want to bet her own personnel file was altered to show confrontations, a bad attitude and threatening behavior at work? Showing a history of suspensions and anything else somebody can plant to make it look like she was predisposed to do this?"

Silence.

Then Colton finally spoke. "Well, that would be really shitty if that's the case. Because then somebody is deliberately laying breadcrumbs pointing at her, setting her up. And you're right. If she's alive, she makes the perfect patsy for this. But who hates her so damn much they would kill all the others to make her look guilty?"

"I don't think they killed the others to make her look guilty," Troy said. "I agree this has a very personal touch to it. But I think all those other people had to have played a part in this too. What we really need—and could work on ourselves—is the connection between all four of these dead people."

"All four?" Taylor said, rolling the idea around in his head. But then he nodded. "You're right. We assumed killing the old couple was to get the key to Midge's apartment, but we don't know that for sure. For all we know, a much bigger connection is here." He grinned and said, "Did you guys bring your laptops?"

Troy held up his phone. "I don't need any more than

this."

Colton said, "I've got mine."

Taylor tiptoed back into the living room and checked on Midge. She still slept soundly, so he took his laptop and brought Colton's outside too. "Are you guys okay to work out here?" he asked and left the question open.

Both men nodded. "Particularly if you've got more beer," Troy said conversationally. "I can guarantee I'll stay until it's gone."

Colton chuckled. "Don't listen to him. He says the weirdest shit, but really he's all heart."

"I know what he is," Taylor said. "He's a big old teddy bear."

Troy glared at him. "Don't pull that shit on me," he said. "I'm as big and as tough as the rest of you." Settling into his chair, he hooked his feet up on the end of the railing and started working on his phone. Taylor chuckled as he opened up his search menus and typed in names. "So we've got one elderly couple, one young man, and another man at least a decade older. What's the chance they're all related?"

It didn't take Taylor long to start making bridges between them, and he whistled. "So the guy in her bed is connected to her boss? Uncle and nephew."

"No shit?" Colton said, raising his gaze to look at Taylor. "That's a connection the cops need to know about."

Taylor answered, lifting his gaze to stare ahead of him. "The boss was really ugly today. Like really mean. If he was like that all the time, I can't imagine she'd have stayed."

"If he just found out his nephew was murdered, that would make anybody pretty ugly," Troy added.

"And," Taylor continued, "if you were in a plot involved with your nephew, and suddenly he's been murdered, you might start wondering about yourself. If the plan from the beginning was to blame Midge, then you'll be very angry when your own nephew is the one who's been murdered. It would also explain why Shorts didn't want Midge to leave at lunchtime. Maybe the killer was supposed to take care of her, and, when he found out she wasn't there anymore, took care of the boss instead."

CHAPTER 10

WAKING UP SLOWLY, Midge felt the aches in her body from her strange position. She was still curled in a tight ball on Taylor's couch and, with that, came the flood of memories of everything that had happened. She closed her eyes again, letting the images wash over her. So many people had been murdered and without any plausible reason or explanation. That just blew her away. Since her boss had been killed, Midge worried she had been the intended victim, and, when they couldn't find her, they had killed him instead. Unless the killer was just so angry that he was ready to take out anybody in his path as an outlet.

What if she hadn't gone out for lunch? Would her boss still be alive? Or would she be dead too? She had no decent answers. The never-ending circle of questions was overwhelming.

"Hey," Taylor said quietly. "How are you feeling?"

"Like I've been bludgeoned, not my boss," she said sadly, noting Colton and Troy were gone now. "I'll admit. I didn't like the man. But I never would have wished this on him."

"I'm sorry," he said, "and I'm doubly sorry you had to be the one who found him. It's one thing to know somebody who was murdered, but it's another thing when it's you who comes across the body."

She nodded slowly. "At least I didn't have to see Mr. and Mrs. Parkins. There was just something almost artificial about seeing my boss like that. It was surreal, like I couldn't understand what I was seeing. I guess it was shock and disbelief that it could be the truth."

"I think that's a normal reaction," he said. "I didn't want you to sleep too long. Hopefully you can go to bed and get some real sleep tonight."

She gave a broken laugh. "It's not even close to bedtime, is it?"

He shook his head. "Actually, it's not. But I was hoping we could get some food into you."

She stared at him, and then a stupid thought hit her. "I didn't bring the leftover sandwich home."

"That's okay," Taylor said with a half smile. "It certainly lends credence to your tale about having gone out for lunch with me."

She stared at him blankly for a moment. "I guess they'll probably even question that, won't they?"

"The cops have to," he said, his tone almost apologetic. "They can't leave anything unturned."

She straightened and winced at her sore muscles. "Man was not intended to sleep like a pretzel."

"Nor as a tiny ball," he said with a chuckle.

She took several steps around the coffee table and headed for the bathroom. There she stared at her tear-streaked face and the shock still present in her eyes. The disbelief at how completely sideways everything had flipped. She washed her face and, using the hand towel, patted it dry. When she stepped out, Taylor was in the kitchen. Her stomach rumbled as she sniffed.

"That's a good sign," he said. "At least in my world, if

you've got an appetite, it means you're dealing with things."

"I guess if you're really in shock, you're not even interested, are you?"

He shook his head. "Not usually. I don't have a ton here, and I don't think it's wise to go out shopping with you, much less leave you behind all alone, but, if you're up for a simple meal like chicken Caesar salads, I think I can make this stretch."

"If you can make a chicken Caesar salad," she said, "you're way the hell ahead of me. And I happen to love that, by the way."

"Good," he said. "I've got two chicken breasts, but one is on the small side."

"Perfect," she said in a dry tone. "I'm on the small side myself." Then she stopped. "You'd eat both of them usually, wouldn't you?"

He flashed her a wicked grin. "I'm not on the small side, so the answer there is definitely a yes. However, I'm more than willing to share."

But she worried. "What if you're still hungry?"

"Don't you worry about me," he said. "If so, I've got other food."

She looked at the chicken breasts and saw the small one was about half the size. She nodded. "Okay, let's do that. May I help?"

He nodded and took several items out of the fridge. One of them was a big head of romaine which he put in the sink. "If you want to wash that, then we'll be good to go. I'll light the barbecue, and we'll toss on the chicken."

Watching him work in the kitchen was a wonder. Perhaps partly because she had never developed much of a rhythm in the kitchen herself. Not that she wasn't willing to try, she just hadn't bothered so far. As she ripped up the lettuce, Taylor pulled together a dressing in his blender. She smiled as he held out a taste on a spoon. "That is delicious," she said in amazement. And she looked at it and frowned. "So you don't even buy a bottle of dressing?"

"No point in buying a bottle when you can make twice as much for half the price, and it's way better," he said.

She snorted. "You maybe, but not me. I probably would have forgotten to put the lid on that sucker and had dressing all over the kitchen."

"That's how I learned to put the lid on," he said with a chuckle. "That's exactly what happened to me."

The chicken breasts took longer to cook than she expected, but, by the time he brought them in from the barbecue pit, complete with beautiful grill marks, the aroma had her appetite working overtime. "I can't believe how hungry I am," she said. "Smelling that chicken brought it on."

"That's a good sign," he said with a smile. He served up two large bowls of salad, already tossed with his homemade dressing, sprinkled them both with parmesan and then spread the chicken, now diced, over the top. Then he handed her a fork and carried the large bowls to the table. She sat down and tasted it, then moaned in delight. "Oh, my God," she said and then didn't talk much as she was too busy eating. Before she knew it, she stared at her empty bowl in amazement. Looking at him, she saw him frowning, first studying his bowl and then hers. "I'm sorry," she said. "You're not getting enough to eat, are you?"

"I was just thinking the same thing about you," he said. "You inhaled that."

She nodded and laughed. "I did. It was fantastic. Thank

you."

"Do you need some of mine?" he asked, nudging his bowl closer.

"I definitely appreciate the gesture," she said with a teasing smile, "but I'm fine. It's all yours."

"Hey, I offered," he said. As if giving her another chance, he nudged it a little closer. "Going once. Going twice."

She pushed the bowl back toward him firmly. "It's all yours. Now eat it," she said in a firm voice.

He shrugged and proceeded to finish it while she sat back and watched him.

"It's really a joy to see somebody eat well," she said.

Surprisingly, he agreed. "I hate taking somebody out for a meal at a restaurant only to have her pick at her food. Too much fat, too many carbs, but the worst is when she leaves three-quarters on the plate and says, 'I'm dieting.'"

Midge laughed out loud at that. "Not me. I'm always hungry," she admitted. "I don't eat a whole lot because of my size, but it seems like I go through it fairly quickly."

"Also due to your size," he said. "You obviously have a very high metabolism to stay so slim if you aren't doing anything to work on it."

"Maybe if I was getting proper meals all the time," she said, "I wouldn't be quite so slim."

"We'll have to see what we can do about that," he said with a teasing tone.

"You'd hate it if I was chubby," she said.

"Ha," he said. "I think you'd look adorable with a little extra weight on you."

"What? So I'm not adorable now?" she challenged in a mocking tone. But he knew she was teasing. Once he was done, she got up, grabbed his bowl and hers and started to wash the dishes.

"Hey, you're my guest," he said. "You don't have to clean up."

"You cooked," she said, "so I can certainly clean up. And it was an excellent meal, so thank you for preparing it."

With the dishes done, he led her to the small balcony, where he sat her down and said, "I hate to offer you more coffee," he said, "because you've already had a fair bit."

"I know," she said, "but I would like something warm. I'd have said something cold, but every time I think about what's going on, I get chilled."

"I'll put on the teakettle," he said, "though I'm not sure what I have for tea."

"I'm sure we can find something," she said, "even if it's just hot lemon."

He disappeared and then came back a little later.

"So," she said, "did you and your buddies come up with any answers while I was sleeping?"

"Several theories but, without evidence, we can't really go in one direction or the other."

"I keep thinking, if I hadn't gone out for lunch, maybe my boss would still be alive."

"And I keep thanking God that I took you out for lunch because chances are you'd be dead if I hadn't."

"I know," she said, "that was my second thought."

"One of our thoughts was that, considering how your boss didn't want you to leave for lunch, maybe it was his job to keep you there."

"You mean, to be killed?" she asked, horror threading through her voice. "Why would he do that?"

"First, we don't know that he did," Taylor said. "And,

second, if you were to be killed, it doesn't make sense that it would have been there. Personally, I think they were looking at you to carry the blame for whatever the hell was going on."

"Well, they already tried that," she said, "and it didn't work."

"Of course not," he said. "So why is it that they're not trying again? Well, they probably did, because, if they were after you, maybe they were trying to force you to do something for them. And, if that wasn't the answer, maybe they were hoping, by killing your boss, you would be in hot water again."

She shuddered. "That's not just a lot of hate," she said, "that's a completely sadistic attitude."

"It is, indeed," he said, "and definitely not one we want to consider, but we have to."

"Is there anything we can do though?"

"We spent some time trying to map the relationships between all the victims."

She studied him carefully, the question evident in her face. "Relationships?"

He nodded. "We set aside our assumptions and started from scratch and discovered, for example, that your boss and Gary were actually uncle and nephew."

Her jaw slowly dropped. "Really?"

He nodded. "Really."

She shook her head. "I had no idea."

"I know," he said, "and we don't know who else, if anyone, might have known each other or been related to each other. But, if your boss was acting ugly, it might well have been because he had just found out his nephew was dead."

She gasped and said, "Yes, he was so upset, and we

didn't really understand why."

"Exactly."

"We're still looking for a relationship between Gary and your boss to the old couple downstairs."

She shook her head. "I thought they were killed to get keys to my place?"

"That was our first thought," he said, "but that doesn't mean it's necessarily right or that it's the whole answer. It's possible it has nothing to do with any of it, and something else altogether is involved."

She sighed. "I can't imagine Mr. and Mrs. Parkins were involved in anything mean or ugly. They are way too nice. Or were, I guess."

"Maybe so, but that doesn't mean they aren't somehow connected, like, what if they refused to do something and that got them killed?"

She couldn't believe there would be a connection at all. After a few moments of silence, Midge spoke again, her voice much softer. "That's a little too much of a coincidence, isn't it?" she asked slowly. "Two people, blood relatives. One killed in my apartment, and one killed at my place of work? And on a day that no one else happened to be there."

In a very gentle voice, he said, "Now you can understand why the cops are interested in you, right?"

"Are they on their way here again?" she asked, a perfect segue.

He winced. "Yeah, they are."

She nodded dully and stared out across the balcony. "Well, I guess it's a good thing we ate a light meal," she said. "I'll be wanting to throw up when the questioning starts."

"I told them that you weren't doing that well, and they needed to keep their questions short."

She waved a hand. "We have to do whatever we can," she said. "Four people are never coming back and have no chance to do anything. The sooner the cops figure out it wasn't me, the sooner they can move on. I also need to know what I'm supposed to do about my job."

"I would presume you are to wait for permission to return to work. I can confirm that for you," Taylor said, texting Mason. "Somebody will track that information down and let me know."

"Did they ever find out what happened to my coworkers?"

"Not that I've heard," he said. "We'll ask the detective when he gets here."

She nodded, and Taylor stood as the teakettle whistled. "What can I get you?"

"I don't even know if I want anything anymore," she said, depressed. "Anything that goes into my stomach now will just want to come back up when they start in on me."

"Hey now, you didn't do anything wrong," he said firmly. "Remember that, and don't let them treat you as if you're a suspect."

"I *am* a suspect," she cried out, jumping to her feet. "Two men—one in my bed, one in my office. Not to mention the couple downstairs. That all means I'm involved and a suspect. I just don't know how or why."

Taylor grabbed her by the shoulders, then gave her a very gentle shake. "I get that. And honestly, the cops probably do too. Sure, they're looking for a connection, but what they're really looking for is what you know—even if you don't know that you know it."

She stared up at him and blinked.

"Did you get that?" he asked.

531

"Yeah," she said, "surprisingly, I did. That actually makes sense." He walked into the kitchen, and she followed him. "So, did you figure out if you have any tea?"

He opened a drawer and said, "A collection of stuff is in here. If you find anything you like, help yourself."

She sorted through the drawer and mulled over her options, eventually choosing an Earl Grey because she had seen some milk in his fridge. She made herself a cup, and, when it was ready, she took it out to the balcony and sat down again. Then hopped to her feet, walked back over and grabbed her phone. "I wonder how we can find out what other relatives either of them had."

"Why?"

"Well, somebody hated them enough to kill them," she said. "I get that maybe they hated me more and wanted to set me up for this. But the thing is, I can't imagine someone killed these two men in cold blood just to make a point."

"People have done that many times over," he said calmly as he stood at her side.

"I know that," she said, "but I want there to be another reason. I don't want to spend the rest of my life looking at every stranger, wondering if he'll shoot me to prove a point."

Just then came a knock on the door. She froze and then sagged in place. "It's the cops, isn't it?"

"Good, if it is," he said forcefully. "The sooner they get here, the sooner they can leave." Turning, he headed back into the apartment.

She put down her phone and sat quietly, waiting.

TAYLOR OPENED THE door and smiled at the detective and another officer. "She's not been awake very long, but we did get a bite to eat. She's sitting on the balcony, having a cup of tea."

The two men nodded, and he led them to the small balcony for yet another set of questions. There wasn't a lot of room, so he deliberately sat down beside her as the two men stood. He watched as they assessed the color in her face, as if wondering if she would cry or explode at them.

"I told her that you were coming," he said. "So, let's get some of these questions answered, so you can move on to the next task."

"We don't have too many more, so it won't take long." Butler turned to Midge. "We've confirmed you had lunch with Taylor at the restaurant. And that he dropped you off at the door of your office. The video cameras and security systems for the front entrance were disabled, so we don't have any clear view of when you arrived. But Taylor says he watched you walk in the door."

"There should be a security code tracking system," she said. "I had to use my key to get in because the office door was locked."

The two cops straightened. "It was locked? Because the back door wasn't."

Midge nodded. "Yes. I unlocked it, wondering if my boss had gone out for lunch himself or had just locked the door so he didn't have to deal with anyone who came in. However, I didn't check the back door. I just sat down and got to work. The phone lines were buzzing like crazy. I answered a few to clear them. Then I put the system on Silent, so I couldn't hear it. It's been an absolute nuthouse there, and, in an office of five, it was only me. I started in on the emails and some of the work, trying to prioritize the most critical. Then it seemed to me that everything went really quiet. Like, all of a sudden, I realized something wasn't quite right. It wasn't right that I hadn't seen or heard from my boss in all the time I'd been back. Nobody had come in or left. I got up and went back to his office. I knocked, and, when there was no answer, I tried the door and pushed it open. That's when I saw him."

"Exactly what did you see?"

"He was sitting in his chair, like always, leaned back a little. First, I thought he was asleep. It was surreal as I noted a bullet hole in his forehead." She exhaled, as if trying to stay calm. "I'm pretty sure it's exactly the same as what you saw."

"Did you happen to check if anybody was in the place? Either when you first arrived or at this point?"

She gave him a shocked stare. "The only thing I was looking to do was staying safe."

"And yet, you didn't run back outside."

Midge frowned. "No, I didn't. And I don't know why. Instead, I ran into the storage room and hid and called Taylor."

"So, from that position, you don't know if anybody left the office, do you?"

She shook her head. "No. I don't. I guess I should have run out to the front and stopped anybody from coming in." She held out her hands, palms up. "I really have no idea why I did what I did," she said, "but that's what happened."

"Taylor, can you confirm the position of her boss when you saw him?"

Taylor nodded. "Yes. It was just as she said. I didn't see anybody when I arrived, not more than ten minutes after her call, I think."

"Ten minutes can be a long time," the officer said.

"That's true," Taylor said. "Do you have any reason to

believe somebody else was in there?"

"While I was there?" she cried out. "Is that possible?"

"We don't know," he said. "We're just trying to see if there was time for somebody else to have arrived. The body was just as you described it when we got there. So, maybe there was someone, and maybe there wasn't."

"Or are you thinking somebody hid in the room, and, with her coming in, they couldn't leave?"

The detective shot him a look, and Taylor knew they were wondering that very thing.

"But, if the security cameras were down, you have no way to know if anybody was there or not. Correct?"

"Correct. Though a woman did see a man fleeing the building about ten minutes before you called us."

"Meaning, he would have been somewhere in that office the whole time I was there," Midge asked, "and then heard me go past the office and hide in the storage room? And then he ran out?"

"It's possible," the detective said.

She shuddered. "Jesus! Why the hell didn't I just leave? I could have called you from outside," she cried out, looking at Taylor. "What's wrong with me?"

"Look. In retrospect, you shouldn't have been in that office in the first place," he said, "not with everything that's been going on."

"And yet, you wanted me to spy on everyone there?" she said, half humorously.

"Only to find out that nobody was there," he said, "so that didn't work out so well, did it?"

She looked at the two cops. "Did you track down my missing coworkers?"

"That's still in progress," the detective said, "and I haven't heard an update."

"Do you know about Gary Sims and my boss being related?" she asked, almost throwing it out as a challenge. To see whether Taylor and his buddies had done as good of a job as the cops, or if the cops had already found that out.

The detective looked up at her and said, "Really?"

She glanced over at Taylor.

"Apparently," he said. "We ferreted that information out about an hour or so ago. Looks like they were uncle and nephew."

"Do you know anything about the relationship?"

"No," Taylor said.

"No," Midge confirmed.

Taylor continued, "We didn't know anything about it at all until we started searching, looking for any connections between the four victims."

The detective pursed his lips, then nodded. "Good angle," he said. "On the surface they all look like they have nothing to do with each other. But evidently they do. Did you find any connection with the other two?"

"No, not yet anyway," Taylor said. "But it seems to me there has to be something more involved for all four of them to be killed like that."

"And yet, we were under the assumption maybe it was to get access to her apartment."

"That made sense to me at first too," Midge said. "But, the more I thought about it, killing is an extreme answer if you're just looking for a key. Maybe they couldn't have broken into my apartment, but they sure as heck could have just crept inside the manager's apartment and grabbed the keys and left. They didn't have to walk up to the bed and shoot them." She blew out a breath. "Do you have anything new about any of this to add?" she asked. "Have you found anything out?"

Both cops shook their heads.

She groaned. "I just want this over with."

"Well, in that case, I highly suggest you stay in one place. Because it seems like, wherever you go, people get killed," the detective said, his voice hard. "And please don't leave town."

Midge stiffened and glared at him. "Do you really think I killed those four people?"

"I don't know what to think yet," he said. "What I can say is that I have no reason to take you off the suspect list. And that's just as important as trying to put you on it. You have no good alibi for when this guy was supposedly killed in your apartment and how you didn't know anything about it. Yet you were home and seen by Taylor here right around the time he was killed."

"No," she cried out. "I told you that I was *coming* home, and then I got called back into work because of all these hacking problems and a sick employee. I'm not supposed to do overtime, and I was already not supposed to be working that day."

"Yes, but according to the clock, you left work at your normal time, or a little bit early. Actually ten minutes early, which would have put you back at your apartment. So, what if you came home, shot him and then left? Then you realized maybe you'd left the door open, or maybe you needed an alibi, so you stopped here at Taylor's to tell him his door was open. That gave you an alibi for just getting home, and then you turned around and walked back out again. We didn't get a chance to talk to your boss about you being called back into work, so we only have your word for that."

Taylor watched as she started to shake, looking shocked. He grabbed her hand and asked, "Where's your phone?"

She looked at him, not comprehending.

He spotted the phone on her lap, then snatched it up and said, "Unlock it."

She quickly did as he asked, then handed it back to him.

"So did Shorts call you or text?"

"He called me," she said in a daze.

Taylor looked through her recent calls. "What is the office number there?"

She shook her head. "I can't even think. I'm sorry."

He looked it up on the website and said, "Well, no incoming calls from the office to you show up on your phone, at least not the published number."

She stared at him confusion. "What? Are you serious?"

He nodded.

"So, he used his own phone to call me? I don't understand that."

"It doesn't matter right now," Taylor said. "What I need to do is find the call."

She went through her calls and pointed out the one. "This one. See?" She passed it back to him. "And look. It came in just as I was coming into the apartment."

"What did you do from the time you left work to the time you got home? That's a five-minute drive at the very most," the detective said.

She twisted around to look at him. "I went to the bank. My face should be on the security video there. I went in and took out some cash."

"Why didn't you use an ATM machine?"

"Too many people are robbed at those or have their card number stolen by some illegal reader attached to the machine. I don't like using those machines," she said. "Most of the time I just get extra cash back when I buy something. Most of the stores let you do that. This time I stopped by the bank and took the money out." She shrugged. "I've certainly done it many times before."

"So then you came home?"

She nodded. "Then I came home."

"If you took cash out, will it still be in your wallet?"

She frowned and said, "Yes, I would imagine so. Any reason why it wouldn't be?"

In a voice very patient and slow, as if speaking to somebody who might be a little slow herself, he said, "And how much money did you take out?"

"I took out two hundred dollars."

"So, if we open your wallet, will we find that money there, proving you did go to the bank and take that money out?"

Taylor winced as she understood what the detective was saying.

She glanced at him. "Well, I could go get my purse and check for you, but then you would probably accuse me of putting money in there right this moment to confirm my story." Turning to Taylor, she asked, "Would you mind getting my purse for me?"

Silently he got up and walked into the kitchen. He understood why the cops were doing what they were doing, but it was hard to watch. He picked up her purse from where it was, still sitting on the kitchen counter, then brought it out and handed it to her. She rifled inside and pulled out her wallet. She opened the wallet, and, with the cops there looking on, she made an exaggerated movement and pulled out two hundred dollars. Ten crisp twenty-dollar bills. She laid them out for the cops to see.

They nodded, acknowledging the point.

She put the money back into her wallet and looked for the receipt, then pulled it out. She handed it over to them. "I always get a receipt when I go to the bank."

The cops smiled. "Good," they said. "This has a time and date stamp on it."

They took a picture of it and returned it to her. She put it back into her wallet. Taylor could see she was calming slightly now that they believed her.

"So, you came up the stairs and down the hallway, and when did you get the phone call?"

"Somewhere around the top of the stairs," she said, "and I was talking to my boss, and he said he had a really big mess and needed me to turn around and come back."

"And that's when you saw Taylor?"

She nodded. "Yes. His door was open. I hadn't even made it to my place, which, as you know, is still down this hallway a little bit farther. So I just called through Taylor's open door and told Taylor his door was open and asked if he wanted me to close it. That's when he came out and talked to me."

Taylor confirmed exactly what she said. "After we talked, then she turned away to leave. I was out in the hallway, still standing there, staring after her," he said. "Admittedly I was tired, having just come back from a mission, so I was a little groggy. But that's when I recognized that her door was open."

Although the cops were probably relieved, they were also frustrated. Because, if she was in the clear, they had no idea who shot Gary Sims.

"Therefore," Midge said, her voice hard, "I didn't have

enough time to leave work, come home, shoot Gary Sims *and* go to the bank. Or go to the bank, come home, shoot Sims and then leave. And, with Taylor's door open, no way he wouldn't have heard."

"True enough," Taylor said. "I think I must have just missed whoever was in your apartment."

"And we don't have an ID," she said, "on the guy who tried to break into my apartment later, right?"

"Nope. And the security system is busted, so no way to track that down."

"And yet," she said, "traffic cameras are all around the base. So there must be a way to track them."

"We're on it," the detective replied.

"How *on it* can you be?" she cried out in frustration. "It can't take this long. The same vehicle had to have been at my place and at my work."

"But it wasn't," the officer said, using a sharper tone. "We've already searched. Now we're tracking different vehicles, hoping we'll come up with a pair working together."

Midge sat back, fell silent and stared out at the view beyond the railing.

But Taylor didn't think she saw any of it because it looked as if she had just checked out of the conversation. Standing up, Taylor said, "Gentlemen, if you don't have any other questions ..."

"No, we have a bunch of leads to keep working on," the detective said. "Now that we've confirmed she couldn't have been home, that backs her off the top of the suspect list."

Taylor knew that was how they would look at this until the real murderer was caught. "I'm glad you got that," he said. "We'll keep looking into relationships to see if we can find anything else."

"Please share the information," the cop said. "I get that she's pretty traumatized by this whole thing. But the only way it'll ever be over is if we can catch the guy who did this."

Taylor led them back out to the hallway, then closed the door and locked it behind them. As he stepped back onto the balcony, she hadn't moved. She still stared at the view. Only now there was a mulish jut to her chin.

"What are you thinking?" he asked, sitting down beside her and reaching for her hand. He was doing a lot of that lately. Locking his fingers with hers, he marveled at how tiny she was.

"I'm thinking they don't give a damn about finding the guy who actually did this. I look like a good suspect, so they're focused on me."

"That is quite possible," he said, "but can you really blame them?"

"Yes, I can," she snapped. "They could have been tracking down all kinds of stuff all day long and yesterday. Instead, all they could see was me."

"Don't forget it's hard in cases like this," he said. "If the street cams *and* the security cameras are down, there isn't any way for them to know who was here. They have to wait on forensics, and that'll take time."

And, just like that, she sagged in place and waved a hand. "Ignore me," she said. "Apparently I'm incredibly unstable at the moment. I don't mean to be a bitch, but I feel like they came here ready to accuse me, and, if I hadn't gone to the bank and gotten that receipt as proof, they would still be looking at me instead of for the real killer."

"It's possible," he said. "But that doesn't mean it's the only reason." He looked around and said, "How about we go for a walk? You could use some exercise and a chance to slow down that mind of yours so you'll sleep tonight."

She shrugged. "Sure. Why not? It's not as if I have anything else to do."

Not exactly the response he had hoped for, but he'd take it. They got their shoes back on, and, as they stepped out in the hallway, she looked toward her door and frowned. "Dammit! I should have asked him if I could go in and get some clothes," she fumed.

"We can text him," he said, then led the way to the stairs, and, within minutes, they stood outside in the fresh air.

She looked at him and smiled. "I want to go down to the beach."

He nodded, texting and walking as they moved toward the walkway. With the text sent, he pocketed his phone and reached for her hand. Together they strolled in the evening air.

"How is it that everything can look so normal?" she asked softly. "And yet, you know something so incredibly ugly is going on. And that even now I could be watched."

"That would imply you were a target. Seems like they've had ample opportunity to take you out, and they've chosen not to."

"That is just as confusing," she said. "I don't understand any of it."

"I'm just grateful they haven't," he said, squeezing her fingers.

She smiled and looked up at him. "Would you have even noticed me if all this hadn't happened?"

His eyebrows shot up. "I noticed you a long time ago," he said.

"And yet, you never asked me out?"

"You never gave me any indication you were open to being asked out," he said drily.

She laughed. "Good point. I haven't been into dating lately. Life hasn't been too much fun."

"I get that," he said. "And I've been really busy too. I've been on steady missions back to back, plus, I had training. Although there's lots of leisure time, sometimes I just want to come home and collapse."

"No dating for you?"

"A little tired of the dating scene," he said, his tone short. And then he laughed. "A lot tired of it actually. All I wanted was a relationship that would last more than a few nights or a few weeks. But it seems like I no sooner got started, when something blew it up, or I found out I couldn't really tolerate the person I'm with and backed out myself."

"Dating's not much fun. Especially in today's age, when a date seems to be all about the photo for social media, and everybody's on these bloody dating apps." She stopped and looked up at him. "I showed the cops the app, didn't I?"

He nodded. "You did. They're following that lead too."

They walked a little farther, and then she asked, "Any chance my boss was on there?"

"If he was single, I wouldn't be surprised," Taylor said. "But I really can't see that the old couple would have been."

She chuckled. "No. I think they were very happy just to be together."

Sharing a sense of the sadness, he squeezed her fingers gently and said, "At least they went together."

She nodded. "Yes. At least they went together." As they walked along in comfortable silence, they saw nobody else. "Did you—well—did you ever think maybe we're being followed?"

"I've considered it," he said cheerfully. "We'll deal with it if it happens."

"Where do you get that confidence from?" she asked. "It seems like just so much could go wrong, and yet you are always in control, as if, whatever it is, you'll just handle it."

"My confidence comes from my work," he said succinctly. "Nothing quite like being dumped in the middle of a war-torn country where you're on a mission to track down some bomb-maker or terrorist leader. You don't know what's coming at you, so you end up learning to deal with whatever it is. That attitude has held me in good stead, no matter where I was."

"Got it," she said. "Well, I haven't had a lot of experience with that, working in staff records and all."

"Are you kidding? Your job seems more exciting than mine this week."

At that, she laughed. Then she apologized but started laughing again. "It seems so wrong to be laughing, but, God, it feels good."

"We're human, and, as such, we have to do whatever we can just to cope sometimes. If that means laughing in order to ease the pressure so we don't blow our stack, then that's what we do."

"You're a nice man," she said, squeezing his fingers.

"I don't think any guy likes to be called a *nice* man," he said boldly. "Hot? Yes. Sexy? Absolutely. Dangerous? Always. Bad boy? Yes, ma'am. But *nice*? Not so much, you know?"

And that started her howling with laughter again.

He grinned, loving to see it. This was exactly what she needed. A chance for a release, a chance to let go. A chance to just relax.

She started giggling. "*Nice* isn't such a bad word," she said. "It's not like I said you are a good man or dependable, or—you know—the kind you take home to meet your parents."

"I'll have you know I am all those things, but somehow they don't seem like compliments when they come from you."

Midge stopped walking and turned to look up at him. "That's too bad," she said in a soft voice. "Because I meant them exactly that way. You are a great person. And I really want to thank you for looking after me. I don't know what I would have done without you." In a surprise move, she reached out to kiss him on the cheek, but, at the last moment, he turned, catching her lips with his and gave her a proper kiss.

CHAPTER 11

T HE KISS REACHED inside and shook her to her soul. She didn't want to let him go. Something about those warm lips coaxing a response from hers had her wrapping her arms around his neck and holding him tight. She hadn't expected this to happen, but, of course, she should have. She had been watching him for some time. When she had seen his door open just the other day, although it was the neighborly thing to do, she had to admit to wondering if he was home and if it would be a chance to see him again.

She had met him in passing several times, but that had been it. His looks had always attracted her, but she and Taylor hadn't really had a chance to connect before, beyond smiles in the hallway, but this was different. His arms came around her back, and he hugged her tight. And she let him. God, she couldn't get enough of him. As if everything that had been going so wrong in her life had suddenly reasserted itself to being right. Nothing felt as good or as correct in this moment as being in his arms and kissing him as she was.

When he finally pulled back, she laid her head against his chest and said simply, "Wow."

She could hear the rumble under her ear as his laughter rolled up his chest and out through his mouth. She looked up at him and grinned. "Honestly, I didn't expect that to happen. At least, not like that."

"Well, you should have," he said comfortably, showing no signs of letting her go. He held her gently in his arms, and, of course, she nestled herself right up against him.

"Something is so very solid and dependable about you."

"Ouch. Here you go with more insults," he murmured.

"You could say a lot of other things too, you know?"

She chuckled. "I could," she said. "But it might go to your head then. I like you the way you are."

At her words, he opened his eyes wider and said, "Of course. I live to serve."

She snorted. "Maybe because you're in the navy and maybe because that's what you do. Particularly being one of those big badass SEALs."

"Many of us are, here on base."

"Sure," she said. "Also newspapers of all kinds are online as well. I keep up with everything that's going on around here."

"Yeah?" he said, looking skeptical.

"Of course I do also work at staff records, so I may have looked you up."

He stopped and stared.

She shrugged. "Hey, you are interesting."

"Just what is in my file?"

"Nothing much," she said. "Like a very detailed résumé."

"Okay, well, that's a little unnerving. Have you ever checked out your file?" he asked.

She shook her head. "God, no. That would be the most boring thing ever. Nothing interesting is there. At least not until recently."

"But, if somebody wanted to, they could go online, get into your file and fix it so something unpleasant was in it, correct?"

She gave him a hard frown. "But why would they?"

"Consider the current circumstances," he said, "and maybe you should rethink that question."

"*Mmm*," she said. She gently stroked his shoulders and down his arm. "I think I've had enough of that thought for today."

"I don't blame you," he said, his tone serious but light too. "Are you ready to go home?"

"Maybe," she said, "but maybe not. It's nice out here on the beach."

"It is getting later."

"I know," she said, "but, when I go back, I have to face the reality of seeing my door again. And knowing all that awaits me."

He squeezed her fingers and nudged her back the way they'd come. They strolled slowly along, listening to the waves crash on the beach. "I don't come down here enough," she said. "I go to work and come home, and it seems like I do nothing else."

"I think everyone gets into a rut," he said. "We get into a routine, and it's hard to break it sometimes."

"I need to," she said, "because apparently life is shorter than we imagine it, and the last thing I want to do is end up dead without ever having really lived."

There wasn't a lot he could say to that. But she clearly meant what she said. Being out here in the not-quite moonlight was like they were on a date, trying to forget about all the nastiness the last two days had exposed her to. It was really nice.

"I needed this, Taylor. Thank you. I didn't know it, but you did, and, for that, I thank you."

He chuckled. "You're more than welcome. I figured we needed to get out and shake away some of this for a while."

"Too bad we have to go back," she said with a sigh.

"It won't be that bad," he said.

She shrugged and let him lead her toward the apartment. As they walked back inside, she looked up at the stairs and the elevator and said, "I guess there isn't any elevator camera, is there?"

"I would imagine the cops checked," he said.

"I wonder," she replied, "and it's not that I want to mock the police. But I think they're a little on the busy side. They've got three separate crime scenes, and three separate murders of four people. It would be easy to miss a detail like that."

He pulled out his phone and sent a text. "Now they won't," he said with a smile. "Do you want to take the elevator?"

She shook her head, "No thanks. Stairs for me." They headed up, with her a step ahead of him. She didn't know if he was still keeping an eye on her or if he was watching the way she walked. She wanted to think it was the latter, but she wasn't that much of a fool.

At the top of the stairs, he opened the double doors and took a look down the hallway. She realized he was still protecting her, which was almost a letdown, since she'd been thinking he might be actually watching her as she walked. He motioned for her to go into the hallway. Together they walked to his place, and she deliberately avoided looking farther down toward her door. He unlocked the door, and the two of them went inside. She yawned as she crossed to the living room, where she sat down on the couch. Then she yawned again.

"Looks like it's about bedtime for you," he said.

She nodded. "I know." She looked at him and whispered, "I don't suppose you have an extra toothbrush and toothpaste I can borrow, do you?"

"Oh, crap, we should have gone and gotten you a few things that you need."

She shrugged. "That's what I was planning to do with the two hundred bucks today. I didn't want to tell the cops this, since it's none of their business, but I put myself on a cash budget, so I could figure out how much I'm spending. There was a line at the ATM, so I went into the bank. But, when the cops were asking me all those questions, my brain completely froze, and I felt nothing but panic."

"They would have understood if you'd explained it."

"Maybe they would have," she said, as yet another yawn escaped. She struggled to her feet using the couch, then used the wall to hang on to, as she made her way to the small spare bedroom. "Man, I didn't think I would make it this far."

"Hang on. I've got a spare toothbrush in here somewhere. He pulled it out and then handed her the package. She unwrapped it and walked into the bathroom, where she washed her face, brushed her teeth and used the facilities. Then, when she stepped out, she said, "I'm too tired for a shower now."

"You'd feel better though," he said.

She leaned against the doorjamb, pondering her options. "If I'd done it before we went for a walk, my hair would even be dry."

"Well, it would be mostly dry," he said with a smile. "You do look really tired though."

She nodded. "I think it'll have to be in the morning."

She slowly made her way to the bedroom. As she sat down on the bed, she realized she hadn't even shut the door. He stepped up behind her and asked, "Do you need any help? You're worrying me."

She gave him a wan smile. "All of a sudden it's just too much again. It feels like I've done nothing but sleep all day, but here I am, right back to being exhausted again."

"That's a combination of the stress, shock and depression over what's happened," he reassured her gently. He pulled the blankets back on her bed and said, "I feel like I should tuck you into bed. You're like a little child who's so lost right now." If there was anything to motivate her to move, it would be that. The last thing she wanted was for him to see her as a child. She straightened up, attempting a bright smile. "I'm fine. You can go."

He walked back toward the doorway, still frowning at her. She shooed him away and said, "Don't worry about it. Once I get some rest, I'll be fine."

She took off her shoes and socks, while he waited, watching. As soon as he stepped around the corner, she shucked off her clothes. She slipped under the covers and pulled the pillow toward her. She had to admit to being way more tired than she had expected. It didn't make any sense. She briefly wondered if he'd put something in her tea. But it tasted just like tea, and she'd been the one to make it. Maybe it was the walk in the fresh air—or even the kiss.

She didn't know, but something had suddenly sapped her strength. She closed her eyes and started to nod off. She heard him talking to someone, either on the phone or at the door. She didn't want to hear any more; she just wanted it all to go away. But then she heard him say something about her staying another night, so she listened more carefully.

"She's staying until this is buttoned up," he continued. "No way she can be alone right now."

She frowned at that. It bothered her to think she was so needy and in such difficulty that she had to be looked after. She was normally very independent, and to be in this position was unusual. Anything unusual, new or different was uncomfortable. Still, there wasn't a whole lot she could do. She punched the pillow and rolled over, but now her mind wouldn't stop.

It made her even more upset to realize he might view her as needy. Finally she sat up and made a strangled sound of frustration. He was there at the doorway in an instant. He frowned at her, and she frowned right back at him. "I don't need looking after, you know?"

His eyebrows shot up toward his hairline. "What brought that on?"

She shrugged and waved her hand. "Whatever phone conversation you just had."

Understanding lit his gaze. "Ah, so you figure, because I was talking to somebody about you staying here, that means I think you're helpless, and I have to look after you."

"Yes," she said defiantly. "That's exactly what I think."

"So, let's say that's true," he said. "What difference does it make? What possible difference does it make if I do think you should be looked after right now? You know the work I do. You know the man I am. I will hardly send you out into the cold to a girlfriend's apartment, only to have the both of you end up dead by morning."

"There you go again," she said. "I could stay other plac- es. If I'm not welcome here, I don't have to stay."

"Of course you don't have to stay, but you are welcome here," he clarified. "And you're not my prisoner." He walked in and sat down on the bed. "Where's all this coming from?"

"I don't know," she cried out in frustration. "I was almost asleep, and then I heard you talking, and it just made me angry."

He reached out, pulled her into his arms and held her. "Look. You've been through something terrible, and it's not over yet. You need someone to help you, to give you some care and to help keep you safe. I'm right here, and I want to do it. It's not a chore, and I'm not feeling used or abused. I'm happy. Now, would you please just get some sleep?"

"No," she said. "I can't. You woke me up."

"Nothing could have woken you up if you were out," he said. "Chances are, you just hadn't quite made it to sleep yet, and then your brain wouldn't stop again. Now you're worrying about everything."

"Of course I'm worrying," she said. "Just think about how much has gone wrong."

"Yes," he whispered. "But it's not wrong right now." He wrapped his arms a little tighter around her until she was curled up against his chest.

"I could probably go to sleep like this," she said, humor in her voice. "But that's hardly fair to you."

"Well, you would fall asleep," he said, "and I could put you back in your bed, like a child."

She snorted at that. "I'm hardly a child," she said as his hand slid to her hip and slowly stroked her waist and up to her ribs.

"Definitely more than a child," he said. "You're all woman."

Hearing the thickening of his voice, she smiled and squeezed him gently. She knew it was taking a risk. A big risk actually. Because she didn't do relationships on the cuff like this. And having known him for a couple days at this level was not the same as actually going out and dating. But it hadn't been the first time she'd made a decision to go to bed early with somebody. Though rarely on a first date. Back in her younger years, she had been a little wilder and had enjoyed the party scene now and then.

But she'd always found it to be an effective way to find somebody. For those moments when you were lonely and cold, it was great. But she wanted to wake up to this guy in the morning and not feel that same emptiness she had always felt before when she'd done the same thing. Regretfully she started to pull back.

He hesitated for a moment, and then he let her.

She looked up at him and smiled. "I'd still rather you respected me in the morning."

"What the hell does that mean?" he asked, frowning.

She shrugged. "I've found, anytime I go to bed with somebody without really being in a relationship, it doesn't work out. It's great in the moment, but it's not for the long-term."

"And you're not into 'in the moment' kind of relationships?" he asked, his head tilted to the side as he studied her in the half light.

She shook her head, her curls flying riotously around her head. "No," she said. "I haven't been for a long time. I guess, if I'm looking for anything, it would be a relationship. The kind of relationship where somebody would be there long-term."

"And do I not look like long-term material?"

Since honest curiosity was in his voice, she wasn't sure how to answer him but wanted to be honest in return. "I don't know," she said as she looked up at him. "You should probably leave."

"And why the change just now?" he asked, not under-standing.

"Because what I want is what I shouldn't have."

"And what do you want?"

This time she gave him a hard glance. "Don't be ob-tuse."

He gently stroked his finger down her cheek. "It's not that I'm averse to it ..." he whispered.

"Oh, no. Don't you dare say 'but,'" she said, "because that means you're not interested. I've heard it all."

He gave up on his strangled explanation, then swept her into his arms, grabbed her hair gently and tugged her head back.

When he lowered his mouth this time, she could feel the passion from deep inside.

She murmured something, uncontrollably wrapping her arms around his neck and kissing him back with all the ferocious passion she'd been withholding. She was drowning in heat, raging fires and relentless hormones. It seemed wrong in so many ways because of all the senseless death around her. But, at the same time, it was a celebration of life. A celebration of something special they had discovered. A precious spark she wanted desperately to protect and to foster into something more.

When she found herself flat on her back, the sheet no longer up to her chest, and hot skin was against hot skin, she realized he had swiftly moved them past several stages all at once, and she hadn't even noticed. When she finally tore her mouth free, gasping for air, she stared up at him in the darkness. Her eyes were wide, and his were gleaming.

"You are deadly," she whispered. But she was drowning

every word with kisses on his face, her hands stroking through his hair and kneading the muscles at the back of his neck, as she reached up and closed his mouth with hers. He swept his hands down her body, pulling the sheet completely away from between them.

And, when she lay back down again, it was to have him come down on top of her. Her hands toured his back, finding he no longer had pants on either. Or boxers. She moaned, her legs spreading and wrapping around his hips, stroking against the hard ridge between them. She couldn't get enough, and she couldn't stop writhing against him. Her need drove her so hard.

"Easy, sweetie. Take it easy."

She shook her head. "I can't," she said. "I can't."

He eased off to the side, lying beside her, his fingers gentle as they tried to soothe her instead of increasing the passion. She shuddered with every stroke, every touch. He slid his hand across her breasts, cupping them and feeling the weight. Reaching over, he gently latched his mouth on top. When he suckled, she cried out, her back arching against him.

He slid a hand down, stroking it gently under the elastic band of her underwear. She moaned. When he stroked his fingers over the soft cotton right at the V of her legs, her hips thrust up hard against him. He gently rubbed back and forth, the material causing a fiction all its own, and she couldn't handle it.

All of a sudden her body exploded as an orgasm ripped through her. She lay shuddering and gasping, her body still rolling with pleasure as he disposed of the scrap of material, then fully stroked her plump lips, smoothing the moisture up and over the tiny nub. She jerked and moaned as her body surged once more against his fingers.

He shuddered and whispered, "You are dynamite."

She shook her head.

"Yes, you are," he said. "Liquid fire." He suckled her breasts, first one, then the other, his fingers stroking up her ribs in a slow caress, his tongue stroking across each bone, finding the ridge and the valley between.

When he hit her navel, he stopped and kissed all around it. But she was already shuddering and shaking in his arms. When he hit the soft curls at the V of her legs, she cried out, her hands clutching his hair. Desperately wanting what he was offering, yet knowing it would send her cascading again, but this time she wanted him with her. When he finally touched her with his tongue, she exploded once more.

She cried out, "Please," and this time he latched on and suckled her hard. And once again she exploded, quivering on the bed, desperate to have him inside her. She whispered, "Please, come to me."

And he was there, easing himself into her as if afraid her swollen tissues wouldn't accept him. But instead, she was so eager, so wanting that joining with him. And her body, already so hot, exhausted, but ready for him, made that journey inside easier than both of them had expected. Finally he was seated at the core of her. He leaned over and kissed her, their lips and tongues dueling gently in the night.

When he started to move, she thought she had died and gone to heaven yet again. She couldn't believe how much this man stirred her senses and stoked the fire within. She moaned gently as he moved inside her, picking up the same tempo and surging up against him. Once again she could feel that same passion, that same ocean rising within. Only she knew the joy that was coming, and she drove toward it, letting him take the lead, until once again she was cascading over the cliff.

Only this time, in the recesses of her mind, she heard him cry out as he journeyed over the cliff as well. To find his own climax. When he collapsed beside her, she couldn't stop trembling. With an oath, he pulled her tight against him.

"Are you cold?"

She shook her head but could barely speak. He pulled the covers up over both of them and just held her tight.

"I'm fine," she whispered.

"You don't seem fine."

"It was just so good," she whispered.

"Good," he said, pure satisfaction in his voice as he kissed her gently. "Now, will you please go to sleep?"

She gave a tiny chuckle and closed her eyes. Her body replete, she curled into his body, and finally she slept.

SO, THAT'S WHAT it was like to be immersed in liquid fire, Taylor thought as he lay here, his heart still slamming against his chest, even long moments later after she'd fallen asleep. He'd never seen anybody so responsive, open and honest with her passion as Midge. Unbelievable. He cuddled her gently, her body now completely relaxed and wrapped around him. She was tiny, like a china doll. But apparently every inch of her was full of nerve, and she was like nothing he'd ever seen before. It had been the most incredible lovemaking he had ever participated in, and he wanted to do it all over again.

Even though his body was tired, humming and throbbing, his mind was unable to leave his thoughts alone. But she was so exhausted herself that she was already out cold.

And he knew she needed that first and foremost.

He should have been honest earlier. He had noticed her many times. Yet it always seemed like the wrong timing. He was either leaving for a mission or knew he was heading out soon. He knew lots of guys who took the opportunity to go out and have one-night stands, just picking up somebody at a bar, but that wasn't what Taylor wanted. Like her, he wanted an actual relationship, and it never seemed to happen because he always kept putting it off, thinking the timing would be better *later*. But there was really never any better timing.

But tonight she had taken it into her own hands, by asking if he'd noticed her, and he was damn happy she had. She was special. What was going on in her life was such a nightmare. She was tiny and defenseless against any assault, lacking any training or martial arts skills. She would be an easy mark.

Just then she murmured restlessly in her sleep.

He kissed her gently and whispered, "Sleep. You're safe. Just sleep."

She relaxed, draped against him again. He smiled at the knowledge her body knew him. Her subconscious knew him. There might be resistance in that temper of hers, which he happened to really like. But, so far, she had been dealing with some of the worst scenarios possible. It was his job now to help her get through this so they could find whoever it was going after everybody in her circle.

Taylor wondered for a long moment if they had taken the wrong tack. Maybe she just happened to have shitty timing. Maybe it was all an accident or a crazy coincidence. He knew many people didn't believe in those, and he wasn't sure he did either. But he was happy to look at any and all options if it meant keeping her away from a killer. He shifted in the bed, and, hearing her murmur of protest, he smiled, and his body relaxed.

If he could grab a little sleep himself, it would help. He doubted she would sleep through the night without waking up. If he had his choice, he'd love to go at it again whenever she woke up. He wanted to feel that same response. He didn't think anybody had ever been quite so honest with him. Anybody who was not worrying about how he would see her or how he would feel about her emotions. It was such a unique experience that he couldn't wait to delve back into that fire again.

He closed his eyes, letting his body drift deeper and deeper into the darkness. Only as he started to go under did he hear her murmur something.

"Chances, chances."

He frowned, thinking about that, but she was obviously asleep. He peered at her and gently nudged her to see if she was awake, but obviously she was out.

She murmured again. "Chances."

"What the devil?" he said, and it stopped, but he took her words with him as he nodded off to sleep.

When he woke up several hours later, it was the first thing on his mind. As he rolled over, he found her beside him, her eyes wide open. He smiled down at her gently, and, as she reached up to kiss him, he met her halfway. She snuggled into his arms and yawned. "Can you sleep some more?" he asked.

"I've woken up several times," she said. "Each time I managed to go back to sleep, but I'm not sure I could this time. I think I'm slept out."

"Good," he said. "Now maybe you can tell me what the

hell *chances* means to you?"

She twisted in his arms and said, "What?"

"As you were nodding off to sleep last night," he said, "you kept saying, 'chances.' It seemed important."

She lay here, frowning, as if figuring out what he was talking about. Then she shrugged. "I'm not sure."

"You said it several times though." He hated to be so insistent, but often the subconscious brought up the answers they needed. The conscious mind had a habit of burying everything, so it didn't have to deal with issues.

"Do you know anything about *chances*?" he asked. "It would be a good name for a casino."

"Oh," she said, gasping. She sat up and stared at him. "It was a *chances* lottery."

"What are you talking about?"

"We had an office pool. Started several months ago when the lottery had grown to a really big payout," she said, frowning down at him. "And we were buying lottery tickets. Chances tickets. But not for every lottery drawing. Only for the great big ones."

"And?"

She shrugged. "I don't know. We all put money into a pool. There was some drama about bringing other people into it. Apparently somebody wanted to bring in a family member or something, but, since it was an office pool, and they didn't work in our office, how could they?"

Midge made it sound like a reasonable workplace exercise, but Taylor had an inkling of what could be going on here. "Did everybody in the office put in for it?"

"I think so," she said, "it was pretty expensive too. We had to buy so many tickets for so many draws or something. I don't know for sure. I think it was fifty dollars every time, and I put in, just like everybody else."

"Any chance one of those tickets won?"

She frowned. "I doubt it," she said. "I never heard from anybody about it."

"That doesn't mean one of the tickets didn't win though," he said.

"I guess," she replied. "I don't even know where the tickets are."

"Who arranged it?" Taylor asked.

Her mouth opened as if to answer, and then she snapped it shut and just stared up at him mutely.

"Your boss did, didn't he?"

CHAPTER 12

"Yes, HE DID." Midge nodded. "It might have been his son or his nephew that he wanted brought in on the deal too."

"Is there any chance Shorts would have done it without you guys knowing about it?"

"I don't know," she whispered. "We all just paid the money. If he added another person to the pot on the sly, he might have done it without us knowing, although we voted against it."

"But that's not very effective if nobody is checking up on what he did. I presume he bought the lottery tickets too?"

She nodded.

"I also need to know when this was," he said.

"I guess we started it months ago. But the latest big lottery event was last week," she said. "Actually, I think the draw was this weekend."

He slowly sat up and said, "I think we need to check that out."

She scoffed at the notion. "It's almost impossible to win a lottery drawing. I would hardly think that's the problem."

"But what if you won? And what if Shorts knew all of you had shares in it? What if he didn't want to spread the shares around?"

"What's that got to do with his nephew dying in my bed

though?"

"If you went to jail and had no clue about the ticket, you wouldn't come back at Shorts or his nephew Sims, would you?"

"Probably not. I wasn't exactly sure when the drawing even was, and I never saw a ticket."

"So, as far as he's concerned, you gave him fifty dollars, and, if he returned your fifty and said he never bought any tickets, just for the sake of argument here, and, if you wind up going to jail, you'll never think anything about it. Will you? Meanwhile, he has a winning lottery ticket that he pockets, and it could be worth a lot of money."

"But what about his nephew? What about Mr. and Mrs. Parkins?"

"I don't know how the Parkinses fit in, but I think Shorts cut Sims into your office lottery," he said.

"Maybe so. But what about the other coworkers?" she asked. "This doesn't make any sense. And how does it have anything to do with Jenny?"

"When did you first start buying these tickets as a group?"

She stared at him, and then a flush rose up her cheeks.

"It was while Jenny was still employed there, wasn't it?"

Midge nodded slowly. "That was part of the stink because she didn't want to go in on the tickets."

"So what if she didn't and what if you guys won?"

"She'd be the only one who didn't get a share," she said softly. "And that would just add to her hate. But she's not going to kill off everybody else," Midge said, "because that would just leave me with an even bigger share of the pot."

"Unless she can get her hands on the winning ticket and makes sure you don't."

"It all seems very convoluted."

"Money always does that," he said with a smile. "People will do anything sometimes in order to get what they want. In this case she lost her job, and, for all you know, she could have had a relationship with somebody, and that broke up too."

"She was in a relationship," Midge said, frowning. "With one of her coworkers."

"One of the ones who didn't show up for work?"

She nodded. "Yes."

"So we definitely have to track him down. He might be helping her."

"That's a horrible thought."

"Just think about it. For every person in that lottery pot who doesn't show up to get their share of the earnings, then the pot gets bigger and bigger for the others."

"But I'm still here."

"But you don't really know anything about it, do you? You don't know who has the tickets. You don't know when the drawing was. You don't know if you won or not."

"No," she said, "I don't." And she stared at him nonplussed. "I guess I'm too naive. I assumed that, if we won, somebody would tell us. Or at least tell me. I still think you're grabbing at straws." She swung her legs over the side of the bed and stared down at him. "Damn, I can't believe I'm even saying this because I really want to crawl back into bed with you, but I need a shower."

He lay here on his back and tucked his hands up underneath his head. "I don't have a problem if you take a shower," he said with a bright grin. "I may have a problem though if you decide you want to shower alone."

She gasped in delight. "Beat you there," she said, giggling, and took off for the bathroom.

When she finally emerged from the bathroom, she was exhausted again. But in a good way. Her body hummed, and, although she was tired, a certain energizing feeling remained inside. She looked down at her dirty clothes she was forced to wear again today. "I should have asked to put on laundry last night."

"Butler didn't respond to my text earlier on this. Let's call the detective right away," Taylor said. "Surely we can go in and get you some fresh clothes."

She looked up at him hopefully. He walked around in his boxers, cell phone in his hand, as he talked to Detective Butler. She went into the kitchen and put on coffee, amazed at how different the world looked after a night with him. Just knowing and having that hope in their relationship had given her a whole new perspective on life. Yesterday she'd been depressed and so worried. And right now it was as if she'd been given a new lease on life, and she didn't want to do anything that would cost her that new beginning. It was way too precious.

With the coffee dripping, she turned to the fridge to see if she could find anything for breakfast. They really needed to go grocery shopping. She'd moved in on him, eating up his food, and had yet to offer to help. Hell, she wasn't even any good at cooking.

But she could fry a couple eggs. She brought out eggs and some ham, then found some buns, so maybe she could make breakfast sandwiches. Moving carefully in the kitchen because she wasn't used to this, she put the buns on to toast and fried up the ham and then cracked in the eggs. By the time he joined her in the kitchen, she was almost done.

He stared in wonder. "I thought you couldn't cook?"

"I can fry an egg," she said, "and that's about the extent of it."

"This looks marvelous," he said, motioning at the pan full of eggs.

"I'm making sandwiches," she said, and he watched as she stacked up the ham and then the eggs on the buns and then covered them with the tops. She handed him a plate with two breakfast sandwiches and got one for herself and sat down at the table. "What did the detective say?"

"Yes, you can go in. You're only allowed to take a couple changes of clothes though."

"That's fine," she said. "I was hoping to not even have to go into the bedroom. But I'll have to. There's no way out of it."

"And," he said, "he wants to hear more about the chances thing."

She froze in the act of taking a bite and set the bun back down on the plate. "Damn. I wish you hadn't told him about that."

"Midge, we have to. We don't know if all this came about for a different reason, but maybe somebody found the ticket and realized it could be worth a fortune. Or whether it was all because somebody had already cashed in the ticket. Or whether they didn't even buy the ticket to begin with. Murders have been committed over much less. And right now we have an awful lot of murders going on."

She picked up her egg sandwich and took a bite, her thoughts in a muddle. She hadn't even given those stupid chances lottery tickets a thought. They had been doing a lottery pool for just the few big lottery contests over several months now. She hadn't even heard the others joking about it. And why was that? The other workers were often talking about stuff like that.

But she'd been so overworked and overwhelmed, and the place had been sliding under the onslaught of work without even half the staff they needed. It had become a very grim place to work lately. Not exactly what she wanted on a long-term basis. Now she had no clue what would happen to the records division. Eventually she finished her sandwich and sat back with a happy sigh. "Happy body, happy tummy. And with the coffee, ... perfect."

Taylor chuckled. "I liked the order you put that in."

"It was a great night," she said, "and the shower scene definitely topped it off." She'd picked up her coffee and took a sip, watching as he plowed his way through his two sandwiches. "Should I have made you more?" she asked.

He shook his head. "No, this will be just fine."

"So, what are we supposed to do from here then? We can go grab some of my clothes, which I'm grateful for, so I can finally get changed. But then what?"

"We'll go to the office to see if we can find any information on the tickets."

"What about the cops? Don't they want to know?"

"Yeah, we're to contact Detective Butler if we find anything."

She sighed. "Well, I guess that's better than having to go to the station or trying to meet them at the office. But the minute I walk back into that office, you know the place will just overwhelm me with the sheer volume of outstanding work."

"But you're not going there to work," he said. "We're going there to see if we can find out anything."

"They should check Shorts's home as well," she said. "For all I know, he kept the tickets at home."

"We'll go find out." After a second cup of coffee, he held out his hand and said, "Come on. Let's go get you some clothes."

They made their way across the hall to her apartment, and he pushed open the door. The smell was dark and musty. She wrinkled her nose. He nodded and said, "Come on. Let's get some things out of your dresser."

She walked into the bedroom, her eyes studiously avoiding the bed. She focused on the dresser, then quickly walked over to the closet and brought out one of her beach bags. Moving back to the dresser, she got out underwear and bras, then several changes of clothing. Back at the closet, she found a pair of sneakers and a pair of sandals. As a last thought, she grabbed a sweater. She moved quickly back out to the living room, where Taylor stood in the doorway, waiting for her.

He held up a tablet. "Is this the one you're missing?"

She laughed. "Yes, it is. Good, then no one stole my phone or my tablet."

"Exactly. I'll leave it here though in case the police want to check it out."

"Fine." She sighed. "I almost managed to get out of there without even looking."

"Good," he said. "You did really well."

As she stepped out of the bedroom, he closed the door behind her. She looked around at the rest of her apartment and said, "I don't even know what to do now."

"That's all right," he said. "We'll figure it out. Let's take your things back to my place, so you can change. Then we'll head to your office and see what comes next."

TAYLOR KNEW WHAT he wanted to come next, but this nightmare had to stop before he gave more time and energy to his personal pursuits. It also wasn't fair to make a serious move on her when her whole world was in chaos. He needed to just be here for her for the time being.

Strange how things worked out. He thought again about all the times he'd noticed her before but always in passing and with really crappy timing. And now, the more he was with her, the more he liked her. Hell, it had gone way past that point.

Timing was everything though, as he well knew. So much craziness was in her life right now that it made no sense. First though, he needed to get her bag back to his place, where she'd stay until this was over, then head to her office.

He closed and locked her apartment door firmly behind her, then let her into his apartment again. After dumping the bag on the floor by her bed, she turned and wrinkled her nose. "We have to go, don't we?"

Understanding filled him. He walked closer and tugged her into his arms. "Yes," he whispered against her head. "We do. But it doesn't have to take long. Go ahead and get changed if you want to, and let's get this over with."

She stepped back, looked up at him and smiled gently. "You're a good man."

He narrowed his gaze at her.

She chuckled. "It was a compliment, not an insult."

"Are you sure?" he asked suspiciously, though he let her see the twinkle in his eye.

"It's a good thing," she said with a laugh. "Trust me."

"It sounds boring as well."

"Well, girls go for the bad boys, but, when they grow up,

they realize *nice* is the way to go."

He hadn't heard that and wasn't sure she was right, but, if she was happy, then, hell, who was he to argue? He reached out a hand. "Now come on. No more procrastinating. Let's go."

She shot him a look of mock outrage as she brushed past him. "How did you know that's what I was doing?"

CHAPTER 13

PULLING UP TO the parking lot at the office felt strange. Off somehow. Detective Butler stood there, waiting for them. Midge glanced at Taylor. He shrugged. "Standard procedure. You can't be allowed to go in there and take something that might prove to be vital evidence."

"*Vital evidence*," she answered slowly. "I never would have dreamed anything in my office was even important and certainly not vital."

"It's important in that it's one step of a long series of paperwork. Unfortunately it's a thorn in the side of nearly everyone, but it's also necessary when we need to keep track of people and events in our life and our employment."

She nodded. "I get that." She unbuckled her seat belt, opened the door, then hopped out and slammed the door, maybe a little too hard. At Taylor's sharp look, she shrugged. "Can't say I'm terribly thrilled at being back here."

"Did you consider the ramifications of that long-term?"

She ignored him. Because honestly, she didn't want to consider the ramifications long-term. If she had to come back here on a regular basis, it would be beyond hard. It felt strange to her even now. She'd have kept working long enough to sort out her future, but it would have been as short term as she could make it.

She also couldn't quite understand why nobody seemed

to be alarmed about the other employees still missing. So she had to assume the employees had been found or at least the cops had communicated with some of them. Detective Butler, his face trained on hers, asked, "How are you doing?"

"As well as can be expected," she said, trying to keep her voice firm and clear. But despite her efforts, it got husky at the end. The last thing she wanted to do was break into tears right now. She stopped and said, "Did you finally get ahold of anybody else who works here?"

He shook his head. "They're still working on it."

"But somebody has gone to their homes, right?" she asked, her voice sounding sharp, even to her own ears. "Please, let's not find out three more employees from around here are dead too that we don't even know about yet."

Butler's gaze narrowed, but he didn't seem too perturbed at her words.

Taylor reached out and gently stroked her shoulder. "Take it easy," he said. "I highly doubt that has happened."

"But we have no way to know, do we? Four people dead that we know of, and, when you get to that number, what difference does three more make? Particularly if we're talking about a multimillion-dollar lottery ticket."

The detective looked at her and said, "You didn't mention that earlier."

"I didn't think of it earlier," she said and stared at him steadily. "You know what? You could probably ask another couple dozen questions that would spark up other information I've completely forgotten about or thought wasn't important. I don't even know the details of the whole lottery-ticket drama."

"Interesting," he said as he motioned toward the office door. "Shall we?"

With him as an escort, they walked in, and she stopped for a moment, sniffing the air experimentally. It wasn't that it smelled any better, but it didn't have that same smell, that metallic-and-something-else smell that she found hard to describe. She walked to her desk, then sat down and pulled open her drawers.

"Do you have the ticket? Or is it tickets?" Butler asked.

"It's tickets. We put in for a pot and bought a bunch of them," she said. "I never saw the tickets, outside of my boss holding up a few. I just wondered if I had a notation here that I'd bought them and when." She pulled out several other drawers and eventually found her small black notebook. She popped it open on the desk and flipped through several pages. "Here it is. I bought the last of them on June fourteen," she said. "See? Here's the note. *'Pd. $50 to Shorts for chances lottery.'*"

She heard both men sucking in their breath. She looked up at them. "Clearly that means something to both of you? What's going on?"

"For a seventy-five-million-dollar lottery drawing this past weekend," the detective said succinctly, looking at his own notepad. "That's worth killing over."

She stared at him, her jaw open, eyebrows raised. "That is a lot of money."

He nodded. "Do you know where the winning ticket is?"

She frowned. "I never saw a ticket. I gave the money to my boss. We all did, as far as I know. He went out and bought several tickets for the group, I assume."

"You didn't ask for a photocopy of them or anything?"

She frowned, concentrating. "I think he was supposed to email it or something." She brought up her emails and sorted to show only those from her boss. "Give me a minute. I have literally hundreds of emails from him."

"Did you search further for mention of lottery tickets?"

She did a couple more searches and then laughed. "He wrote down *Retirement Plan* on the subject line."

She opened the email and, sure enough, found a receipt and a copy of the tickets. She sent it to the printer, and, when she could hear the machine moving behind her, she walked back there to find both men crowding around the printer. Pulling the sheet of paper out, both men got excited at having an angle to work.

"Well, it looks like it could be a motive after all," Taylor said.

"We don't even know if it's a winning ticket," she said. "It could be a partial winning ticket. There were a lot of smaller prize payouts too."

The detective took the ticket and headed off to one side of the room, where he made some phone calls. Taylor looked at her and asked, "You want to print off another set of those? I can help track these down."

She walked back to her desk and sent another copy to the printer. He stayed where he was, waiting for it to come out. Then he took a photo of it and sent it to Mason. "We should get answers on this one pretty soon."

"But what if we don't find the ticket?" she asked.

Taylor pointed at the photocopy and said, "Surely nobody's stupid enough to cash in the big lottery ticket, as long as you have a copy of this, and you're alive and well."

She froze when he pointed out that harsh reality. "Let's find out if any of these are really a winner and how much the payout is first," she said. "I just don't see that it's worth killing for. There were five of us, for Christ's sake, so it would still be an incredible amount of money for each one."

"Fifteen million each," he said, "versus seventy-five million alone."

"What the hell would anybody do with seventy-five million?" she cried out, raising her hands in frustration. "That's a stupid amount, excessive, and nobody needs that much."

"Half would go to taxes right off the bat."

She stopped. "Really?"

He laughed and nodded. "Really. And then you have decisions to make with the rest of what you won."

"So out of fifteen, that's still almost eight million," she said. "So that means all of us could retire."

"Maybe that's what happened to all your coworkers," he said. "Maybe they retired rich."

"But could they have gotten the ticket and claim the prize money without me?" she asked. The thought not only hurt her feelings, but it pissed her off. That was a hell of a lot of money. How could anybody be so greedy to cut her out of it?

"We'll find out soon what the winning numbers were, either from Mason or the Butler," he said. "But let's see if we can find the original ticket."

"If my boss had just turned it in," she said, "then there won't be a real ticket. Or my missing coworkers turned it in?" she asked, thinking about them. "If they had the ticket, and they turned it in without me, or him, I can see that making him pretty angry too."

"I hadn't considered that," Taylor said approvingly. "That's a hell of a reason for murder."

"But I would still be entitled to my portion, right? And it's still in my email inbox."

"Did everybody get a copy of that email?"

She brought up the email again and shook her head. "No, he just sent it to me. Of course, that doesn't mean he didn't also send one to everybody else individually—or sent blind copies—but I did ask him for a copy at the time."

"And he sent it to you, so I'm presuming he had honest intent on his part at the time, but, what happened after that, we don't know," Taylor said. "Because, if that money is still out there, ready to be claimed, the five of you are now four of you."

She swallowed hard. "That's an ugly way to look at it."

"Maybe," he said, "but that's the truth."

The detective stepped over. "The prize money has not been claimed, though they got a phone call about it."

"What does that mean?" she asked.

"It means somebody called to say they have the ticket and asked about the procedure for claiming the money."

"Of course they didn't get the name of who was claiming it, did they?" Taylor asked.

Butler shook his head. "No, although they would have to provide the ticket and identification if they tried to get the prize money. So far, they haven't."

"When was the phone call?" Taylor asked.

"Two days ago," he said. "Potentially that phone call made it real to the point they decided to kill everyone."

"It still doesn't explain why the old couple was taken out."

"Not yet, it doesn't," Taylor said quietly. 'Unfortunately, when it comes to big money, it doesn't take that much motivation to take someone out."

"It's even more important now that we find those coworkers," the detective said. "We are searching for them but no luck yet. Meanwhile, let's search for the original lottery tickets."

"Want my help?" Taylor asked.

Midge jumped to her feet. "Me too?"

"You can help," the detective said cautiously. "But you can't touch anything."

Taylor just stared at him.

Butler raised his hands, palms up. "Okay, okay. You know what I mean. When you find something, you call me."

With that, Taylor and the detective started to search the first desk in the employees' area. Rather than get caught up in the nightmare of evidence and tampering with it, Midge just stood back and watched. They went through Bart's desk first. After finding nothing, they went through Terri's desk, which revealed nothing.

"Can you log into their profiles?" the detective asked Midge.

She nodded. "Yes, we use a system in the event of computer glitches where we use each other's logins to get in to complete the files." She sat down, brought up the computer and signed on, using Terri's login.

"Go to the email and check for that same retirement planning subject line," Butler said.

"Nope, it's not here," she said, checking emails from her boss. "And again, I have hundreds of emails to sort through."

"Search for *lottery tickets.*"

"Holiday fun?"

After she had tried all their suggestions and still hadn't gotten anywhere, the detective nodded and said, "Okay, we'll get forensics to go through and give it a closer look."

Taylor turned to Midge and asked, "What are the chances they think you don't know anything about it? Or that they don't think you were part of it?"

"We joked about it being all five of us. That we'd have to find ways to split the money nicely and take care of all the legalities. And that we couldn't all quit our jobs at the same time," she said, "because the department would be completely empty. Bart used to joke, saying he dreamed about *calling in rich.*"

"Instead of *calling in sick*, is that it?" Taylor asked. "What do you want to bet he's sick trying to figure out how he can get ahold of the money?"

"Well, now there's only four of you," the detective said. "But we have to find out if anybody else was involved."

"Well, let's go check the boss's computer then," she said.

"Can you log in?"

She stopped in the hallway, then frowned. "I'm not sure." As she went around to the computer, she froze, seeing the bloodstains on the office chair.

"Take it easy," Taylor said, then turned to look at the detective. "I presume forensics has been all through the place?"

He nodded. "Absolutely. But let's move the chair out of the way."

They removed the big office chair from her sight and gave her a different chair to sit in. Perched awkwardly on the edge, she brought up his computer and tried several different times to log in. Shaking her head, she said, "Nothing's letting me in."

"Good," the detective said. "You shouldn't have access to everybody's computers, for crying out loud."

"We should also have a computer system that doesn't freeze up when two of us are working on the same database," she snapped back. "We have deadlines and people yelling at us because we haven't gotten back to them. Plus, with a dozen phone calls waiting, we're on the go all the time. We do what we have to do to keep functioning."

The detective opened the drawers beside her. "Did Shorts ever keep his desk locked?"

"No clue," she said. "I can't say that any of us got along all that well, especially with him. So, when our day was done, the last thing we wanted to do was check to see if he had locked his drawers."

"A lot of times," the detective said, "people do exactly that. They want to snoop into other people's things to see if they can use something. Like something they can write them up for or otherwise get them in trouble with."

"Wow. Well, I choose the 'live within your own space and ignore what others are doing' motto," she said sarcastically. "Plenty is going on in my life. I don't need to be snooping into his."

She caught Taylor's odd look and realized that, to him, her world was very plain and basic. She showed up at work, did her job and left, and she didn't have a ton of extra things going on. And he was right to a certain extent, but that didn't mean she wanted to insert herself into other people's business.

"Hey, I prefer not to pry," she said to change the view he may have had. "I didn't mean that my world is so crazy that there's no space for curiosity. But I also don't believe in crossing boundaries."

"And checking your boss's office is doing that?" the detective asked, writing down notes.

"Of course it is," she said. She had no clue what he could possibly be writing, but it was always unnerving to have somebody in authority write notes, as if about you. While she sat here, studying the detective, Taylor checked the rest of the drawers.

"I'm not seeing any tickets," he said as he lifted the last of the files and froze. "Well, would you look at that."

Underneath was a clear plastic file folder, and it was flipped upside down. It had stuck to the bottom of the last manila file folder, and, as Taylor had lifted the file folder, it had dropped back off. Lifting it up, he held it for the detective to see. "I say we now have ourselves a megasize motive."

The detective's face lit up when he saw it.

Midge said, "I want a receipt for that."

The detective looked at her and frowned, earning a glare from Midge. "Oh, no. That ticket doesn't just disappear now."

"It's going into evidence," he said.

"That's nice," she snapped. "I just want it to be noted that it's mine."

"Oh, it's noted already," his voice went soft. "And that people have died for it already."

"So say you," she said. "What I know is, I have a dead boss and somebody who tried to frame me for murder. That's pretty personal. And, if that ticket is the reason my life has been turned upside down, it's not leaving my sight until I know what the hell is going on."

"Or until you get to cash it in. Is that the idea?" the detective asked, his own tone hard. "Maybe all your protests of innocence were just a ruse until you could get your hands on this."

She snorted. "Not likely. I do have a copy in my email, which I hadn't even thought of until you brought it up. What I have now is a detective I don't know from Adam trying to take possession of a ticket that is potentially worth a lot of money."

Just then Taylor's phone rang. He refused to move between the two of them, the ticket still in his hand.

"MASON, DID YOU hear?" Taylor stared at the ticket in disbelief. He'd never known anyone who'd won a decent-size lottery prize. This one was unbelievable. "It's a seventy-five-million-dollar lottery."

"Bingo," Mason said. "That's a hell of a lot of motive."

Taylor looked at the detective, with Mason still on the phone. "So, this ticket in my hand could be the sole winning ticket for the whole seventy-five-million-dollar payout."

Butler got a call too, flipped through his notepad and wrote something down. Hanging up, he read off the winning numbers, while Midge compared that to the email copy of the lottery tickets now in her hands, so Taylor could check the original tickets in his hands.

Midge gasped in shock to find a match.

Taylor looked at her and smiled. "Right. Okay, Mason, we have possession of the original winning ticket now, and I'm taking a picture of it," he said and sent it to Mason. Then he said, "Midge has asked for a receipt from the detective as well."

"Smart of her," Mason said. "That's the only proof she'll have that he actually picked it up from her custody."

Taylor thought about it and nodded. "The request sounded odd, given the circumstances." His gaze was on Midge. She just glared at him. "Do you think she's involved?" Mason asked.

"No. I think she's upset enough about all the other inexplicable things going on here that she didn't want to have the ticket disappear too."

"I like her all the more," Mason said. "She needs to stand up for herself. If that ticket goes missing, all kinds of hell breaks loose."

"Right. Well, now you know," Taylor said. "And I'm wondering what the legal aspect is as to whether or not it even needs to go into police evidence."

"I don't know," Mason said. "Let me talk to Alex." And he hung up.

As he put his phone away, Taylor said to Butler and to Midge, "Mason will check with a friend of ours as to the legal aspects surrounding this ticket."

"I obviously must take it into evidence," the detective said. "I acknowledge Midge has a partial right to it. Other than that, it's not an easy case."

She looked at the detective. "That's quite true. But I would be much happier to bring it down to the station myself."

He hesitated.

"Why are you hesitating?" she asked, her tone sharp. "Unless you have something to do with this?"

"I don't like what you're suggesting," the detective said.

"And I don't like what you're suggesting." She stood up and snatched the original tickets from Taylor's hand and said, "I will take it down."

"You're not taking it from this office," the detective said.

Taylor placed a hand on her shoulder and held up a hand in front of the detective. "Hey, hang on here a minute. Midge has a claim to it. We know that. What we must do is find all the other people who also have claims to it."

"And," Midge snapped, "we have to make sure this detective is in no way connected or has the opportunity to cash this in."

"Now that we have photocopies of your claim," Taylor said, "and you'll surrender this for a proper receipt, he can't cash it in."

"Good," she said. "And where the hell are the rest of the people involved in this?"

"Maybe you should tell us," the detective said, his voice ugly. "I don't like what you're implying at all."

"I don't like what you've been implying all along either," she snapped, "so don't get all hissy with me. You were just accusing me, so maybe now I'm accusing you. How do you like it?"

Taylor chuckled. "I don't know where you got your backbone all of a sudden," he said, "and you're sure not too particular about picking your battles, but this one apparently matters."

"A lot of people are dead," she said quietly. "And that means we have to be even more vigilant."

Just then several people entered the main office. "Taylor, you in here?"

Midge watched the detective's face. He stiffened, and his gaze went to the ticket in her hand. She narrowed her eyes and shook her head. "You don't get to touch this ticket. Do you understand me?"

Colton barged in, along with several other men who stood at all the exits. "So it's true? A winning lottery ticket is at the bottom of this thing?"

"A partial winning lottery ticket apparently," Midge said tiredly. "It was an office pool. According to Taylor, the payout is seventy-five million. There were five of us, as long as somebody didn't sell off more shares."

"Oh, now that's an interesting thought too," Colton

said. "What if somebody sold more to someone outside the office group? Or someone got angry that they wanted in and couldn't be?"

"All those scenarios and more are what I'm wondering about," Midge said, "but unfortunately the detective here hasn't tracked down any of my three missing coworkers. Since my boss and his nephew are both dead, I'm wondering if Gary was allowed to buy into the pool, only to be killed by a person who thought they should have gotten more. Then they killed my boss as well. And, of course, with less survivors, the odds just look that much better."

"But they'll look even better still," Colton said, "if there are less than four."

She nodded. "That's exactly my problem. As long as this ticket is an issue," she said, "so is my life. And I don't want that hanging over my head."

Colton turned to the detective. "Have you gotten anywhere tracking down her coworkers?"

The detective just glared at him. "This is an official investigation. I get that somehow she seems to have turned this into some circus, and you're all playing along, but that's not how it works. I want you all to come down to the station. Especially her, and I want that damn ticket."

"You can want all you like," Midge said. "The fact that you refuse to give me a receipt means you're not getting it."

Colton stiffened beside her. "Of course the station will give you a receipt for that ticket. And they will be responsible for the seventy-five million, should they lose it."

She snorted. "All he wants to do is give me a bullet," she explained.

At that, the detective just stared at her. "You can't possibly think I'll try to kill you?"

"I don't know what the hell's going on," she snapped. "But right now, I find it very hard to trust you."

She stood, with Taylor and Colton at her side, and said, "Let's head to the station, shall we? I'm sure your supervisor won't have any problem giving me a receipt for this ticket."

Taylor had to admire her gumption. While Colton disbursed the others with him to return to base, Taylor led her out to the vehicle and said, "You hold that ticket close."

"I've got it," she said, fatigue evident in her voice. "I just can't believe this is all over money."

With his voice low, Taylor said, "It's one of the biggest reasons people hurt each other. In this case it's a lot of money, but I've seen terrible crimes committed for far less."

"But there were five of us," she said. "That's fifteen million each. And I get that we lose half to taxes and all, but still, seven and a half million? That's far more money than I've ever even imagined having."

"Would you have been happy with that?"

She laughed. "Absolutely. I'd have counted my blessings and tried to figure out an alternate plan for the rest of my life. That is plenty for someone to change their whole life with."

"How does it make you feel to realize that now only four people split the prize?"

"Well, don't ask me to do the math," she said. "So it's not enough to go buy anything in the world, thank God. It's not enough to do anything but enjoy my life. If I handle it wisely and invest it properly, I can enjoy a long and happy life without having to stress over making ends meet," she said. "Beyond that, I certainly don't want anybody else killed to increase the pot. I'm happy enough to have my portion and don't need or want anybody else's."

"The question is," Colton said, "do the others feel the same way? Or have they already set plans in motion to make sure the pot keeps growing?"

"What happens in a case like that?" Midge wondered out loud. "Do the remaining winners still get the rest of the lottery winnings? And the person who was doing all the killing? Does he still get his portion?"

Taylor shook his head. "Once he goes to jail, I think he forfeits his winnings."

"I don't know," she said, "and that's really not a court case I want to go to. We bought these tickets to dream about a chance for a brighter future. The last thing I want is to have no future at all."

Down at the station, she handed over the original ticket and received a receipt. As soon as the officers there understood what was going on, the ticket was placed in the safe.

Then Taylor turned to her and asked, "Now what?"

"I want to track down my coworkers," she said in a low whisper.

Colton, standing beside her, nodded. "That should have been done from the beginning."

"According to the detective, they've been trying."

Colton's lip curled, and she shrugged. "I have no clue. But I suggest we make inquiries ourselves."

They stepped out of the station, and Taylor looked at Colton. "Two vehicles?"

Colton nodded. "Yeah, I think, in this case, it's probably best. Troy has gone to Terri's house to take a look. If anything looks off, he'll call. I'll follow you at a distance."

Taylor studied his face for a long moment. "You know something I don't know?"

"My instincts are screaming at me."

Taylor snorted. "Mine too. But we're getting there," he said, "and pretty quickly, I'll bet."

Colton nodded. "Yeah. Crunch time. Keep an eye out."

Taylor nudged Midge out of the station and back to his vehicle. When they hopped in, he asked, "Do you know where any of your coworkers live?"

"No, but I'm sure your buddies do," she said. "Let's just drive. I have a terrible feeling about all this."

Taylor chuckled. Just then the phone rang. It was Troy.

"Nothing at Terri's place. We're heading to Lockview Street. That's apparently where Bart lives."

"We'll meet you there," Taylor said. As he drove, weaving his way through the traffic, he watched Colton pull in a few vehicles behind him. Just far enough back to not be obvious and close enough to keep an eye on them.

"What do you think will happen to my job?"

"The staff records department can't be shut down for long," he said. "I'm sure right now the brass is trying to determine the best way forward. Your department might get absorbed by another with management in place, but they will still need staff to handle it."

"In theory, four of us still work there with the boss. Just nobody is showing up, and now we can't," she said.

He glanced at her, hearing her depressed tone. "Stay positive now," he said. "Colton was serious when he said this is likely to be crunch time."

"What does that mean?"

"It means we'll likely get to the bottom of all this today."

She brightened. "Do you think so?"

"Now that we know what the motive is, yes."

They pulled up in front of a series of condos and hopped out. "I wonder why he doesn't live on base?" Midge asked.

"A lot of people don't like living on base. Also, a lot of government housing is off-base, and that's another option. But this appears to be private property." They walked up to the front door and contacted the super. No answer there. They pushed Bart's buzzer and waited for him to answer. Nothing. As they stood here, somebody came out of the building. Taylor held the door open for them, and Midge said, "Thank you," then ducked inside, letting the others in behind her.

"That's the problem with this kind of security," Colton complained. "It's way too easy for someone to get into these places."

"But it wasn't that easy," she said. "We still had to wait for somebody to come out."

Bart lived on the third floor. By the time they stepped out of the elevator and walked to his door, they still had no answers from anybody else as to what was going on. Midge knocked on the door and waited for someone to answer, but there was nothing. She glanced up at the men and frowned. Then she knocked harder. Still no answer.

Taylor and Colton exchanged hard looks. Colton stepped forward and in front of her. Taylor brushed her back ever-so-slightly, and then suddenly the door popped open.

"Did he leave it unlocked?" she asked.

"No," Taylor whispered, and, with a nod toward Colton, he opened it.

With Taylor keeping Midge in the hallway, Colton stepped inside and called out, "Hello? Anyone at home?" He did a quick trip through, while they waited. When he came back, he shook his head and said, "Nobody home."

Taylor could feel the fear and panic drain away from her.

"Oh, thank God," she said. "I was petrified you would

say he was in there, dead."

Locking the door, they retraced their steps to the car. "So that's two of three, still missing," Taylor said. "Another lives about five minutes from here in a rented townhouse."

"That's Debbie, right?" Midge said.

"Yes."

They drove there, and, following the instructions to the right number, they knocked on the front door. Again there was no answer. This time Midge stepped back and looked at Taylor with an eyebrow up. He just shrugged, and Colton moved to the door.

"So, he does that better than you or what?"

Colton chuckled. "Hell no, he's as good as I am."

"Actually, he needs to practice," Taylor said, chuckling. "So we're just helping out."

And the door opened. Colton stepped inside and called out, "Hello? Anybody home? Hello?" Once more, he walked through the bottom floor as the others waited. He came back through, shrugged and pointed to the upstairs. Taking the stairs two at a time, he came back down almost as fast.

She expected him to step outside, saying it was all clear, but he didn't.

Instead, he looked at Taylor. "Call in a team. Looks like she's dead."

CHAPTER 14

"SERIOUSLY?" MIDGE CRIED out. "That can't be true. I had to go into work because she was sick," she said, turning to Taylor. "Why did somebody not do a welfare check?"

"We'll have to check with the cops for that," Taylor said. He held up his hand as Detective Butler answered the phone, his voice a little stiff from the confrontation earlier.

"We've been checking on the other coworkers," Taylor said. "You guys do your job really good. We're over at Debbie's place right now. She's dead," he said, "so you need to bring a team in now."

The detective made a strangled exclamation and said, "I'll be there in ten."

As Taylor terminated the call, Midge looked at him and said, "He can't be here in ten. It took us twenty."

"It's just a phrase," he said soothingly. He pointed to the big swing set. "You might as well sit down. We're not going anywhere soon."

She raised her hands in frustration. "I thought you said Troy was coming too?" she said, looking over at Colton.

He nodded. "He's meeting us here. He already checked out Terri's place."

"Alone?" she asked, her voice turning to a squeak. "That doesn't sound very smart."

DALE MAYER

"He's a big guy, and he's well-trained," Colton said. "Besides, you're the one in danger. So we needed to have an extra man with you."

"I still don't get it," she said. "That's another one down." Her mind went to the lottery ticket, and she winced. "So now only three of us are alive to claim the ticket. And, no, I'm not trying to divvy up the lottery pot in my head. But I'm worried because of Bart and Terri."

"Exactly," Taylor said, and just then his phone rang. It was Troy.

"I've just run around the building. No sign of them. You've got Colton there. I'm doing another pass around the neighborhood. See if I find anything."

She listened to the conversation and understood Troy would meet them here. She looked at Taylor and said, "So, two are still missing."

"Correct. Let me ask you something. Are those two in a relationship?"

She stared at him blankly. "I don't think so, but I have no way of knowing for sure."

"Do you think either of them have any relationship with Jenny, the disgruntled ex-employee?"

"I thought you guys had given up on her with the new lottery-ticket theory," she asked suspiciously. "Or do you just treat everybody like they're suspects?"

"To a certain extent, we treat everybody as if they're suspects," Taylor said. "Unfortunately, when it comes to cases like this, they often are."

"As far as I know, there are no relationships, but again I don't have any way to confirm or deny it."

He nodded. They sat here in silence, waiting for the cops to arrive. Midge groaned when Troy pulled up first. "Do the cops ever do anything in a timely manner?"

"They're doing the best they can," Taylor said. "They have a lot of red tape, and Butler has to get a team together. Just because he could get here faster doesn't mean the coroner and the forensic team can."

"Does the forensic team come from the military or do they bring in outside people?"

"I imagine they start with their own team. But, if it gets to be too big or too much, they'll go outside for help."

"Well, this makes five murders now," Midge said, watching the cops arrive. "If they haven't solved it in the first twenty-four hours, it seems like they need to get some help in."

"Thanks for the advice," the detective said, his voice hard. "If I could be sure you weren't contributing to the body count, I would feel better."

"I have witnesses here," she said, "I didn't even go in the house."

"Who went in and found her?"

Taylor said, "Colton did."

The detective and Colton exchanged hard looks. "Where is she?"

"Top right bedroom," he said. "Looks like a bullet in the head."

"Which would follow the same pattern we've already seen," Taylor said. "We checked Bart's place, but no one was there. And Troy went over to Terri's place. Nobody was home there either."

"Which brought up the question that they are potentially missing together," Taylor said smoothly. "You did say that a male contacted the lottery corporation about the winning ticket, right?"

The detective nodded. "And that could be your missing Bart."

"It could be." Just then Taylor's phone rang. He put it on Speaker.

"We found Terri's vehicle," Mason said. "It's in a parking lot in an alleyway behind a store."

"That's a good start," Taylor said in relief. "Maybe from there we can find her."

"Don't need to," Mason said. "We found her. With a bullet in the forehead."

Midge stared at Taylor. "The next time you have bad-news phone calls like that," she said faintly, "don't bother putting them on Speaker on my account. I'd just like this whole nightmare to go away. Terri didn't do anything to anybody. There was no reason for her to be killed."

"She either knew too much," Taylor said, "or she was involved, and they decided to cut the numbers down even more."

"So what about Bart?"

"No sign of him yet, but we're still looking. But, the longer this goes on without him showing up, the more suspicion gets thrown on him," Butler said.

The others all nodded.

"So now you're wondering if he's in this alone," Midge said to Taylor.

"He might be," Taylor said. "But he could also have a girlfriend. Do you know anything about that?"

"He hasn't had one that I've known about for a long time," she said. "He went out with Jenny a while ago, but I don't know how serious it was. They were quite friendly though."

"So did Jenny and Terri have anything to do with each

other?" Colton asked.

"I don't know," Midge said.

Taylor added, "But we need to find out. And fast."

"You mean, before somebody comes after me?" asked Midge.

"The fact is, you are one of the only remaining members of that entire office," the detective said coolly. "With your name and proof of that, you get a portion or all of the ticket."

She shook her head. "I didn't have anything to do with that damn ticket."

"Well, it sounds like the rest of the office did, and at least some of them knew it was a winner. Now they are slowly taking out everybody else in the group."

"No," she said. "What about Gary?"

"We don't know his connection yet," Taylor said. "It's quite possible your boss cut him in for a piece of the pie."

"If that would piss off anybody, it would have been Bart," Midge said. "He's got a hell of a temper. But none of that has anything to do with the fact that Gary Sims was killed in my bed. There's no logical reason for that."

"Except you were supposed to be home that day," Taylor reminded her. "And I can see that they might have tried to make it look like a love affair gone wrong. They'd kill you, and then make it look like you'd killed him. Like a murder-suicide or something."

She stared at him. "And that just might have worked, if I'd been there."

"Oh, yeah," he said. "Nobody would have even known you'd had a part in the ticket at all." Taylor turned to the detective. "I presume you have an all-points bulletin out on Bart?"

"We do now," he said. "But that still doesn't explain the old couple."

"Actually, it does," Troy replied. "They were Gary Sims's aunt and uncle. Not a relationship that's well-known as he was adopted. They are his birth mother's family and were close."

"So Mr. Shorts cut them in for tickets too?" Midge asked. "This was an office pot. What was he doing bringing everybody else into play?"

"We don't know if he *did* cut them in. It's possible he told them about the win though, and that might have messed up someone else's plans," Colton said mildly. "Maybe Shorts really wanted to help out the old couple."

"Or," Taylor said, "Shorts never got the fifty bucks from the Parkinses and had no intention of cutting them into the tickets."

Midge rubbed her forehead. "They were old already. In ill health. It's not fair that somebody cut them down like that. They deserved to enjoy their last few years on earth."

"Agreed," Taylor said, and all the men nodded in agreement. "But, when it comes to money, nobody plays by the rules."

"I can't believe Bart would be like that," Midge said. "I mean, I know he had a temper and all but ..."

"What is he like?" Taylor asked.

"One hundred percent into everything," she said with a laugh. "If we were making a change in the office, he wanted to change everything. If the boss wanted to change out desks, the next thing he knew, they'd changed out the carpets, chairs, computers and everything else. The whole place got revamped. That was Bart pushing it. Very passionate, very dedicated."

"Did he like his job?"

"I don't think any of us liked our jobs," she said. "Not exactly the kind of job to like, you know? But he was good at it. He'd show up and do his job, and he'd leave. He was always joking, laughing, and he was a dreamer. And he dreamed big. He wanted to sail around the world. He wanted to have a sailboat and just take off. He already had a name for it too. *Baldie*. After a dog he loved and lost." She shrugged and laughed. "We used to tease him about it all the time."

"You didn't care about the tickets?" Butler asked Midge.

"They did an office pool. I put in for it and forgot about it. It never even occurred to me until it came up yesterday or whenever that was."

"And that's when you remembered about the ticket?"

"Yes, when Taylor was asking details about the lottery we'd played. But you already know all that."

"Okay, so an awful lot of people are involved," Taylor said. "But really, the bottom line is, we need to find Bart, and I'm not ruling out this Jenny person who was fired."

"Tell me again about her," the detective said.

"Jenny used to work with us at the records department, and she was definitely a little off. She didn't do a good job and was always on the edge of trouble. She ended up getting fired over six months ago and blamed me. She was quite friendly with everyone else though, particularly Bart."

"Was she now?" the detective asked. "In that case, let's pick her up as well."

He walked a few steps away, and Midge wondered how much police work was actually just making phone calls. Because he didn't seem to do a lot except be on the other end of a phone. It was frustrating for her to be sitting here on the sidelines, expecting something to happen, but, so far, it had just been boring stuff. Except they kept tripping over dead bodies.

She said, "I'll walk the sidewalk here a little bit. I need to shake some of this off. It's pretty damn depressing." Taylor frowned at her, but she ran lightly down the few steps onto the sidewalk and then just paced back and forth as she tried to wear down some of that pent-up anguish inside. More cops arrived just then with a team. And while she was happy to see them, it was also difficult to be engulfed in the system once again. Questions were being answered, she was being brushed aside, only to be poked and brought forward again. Finally, she asked, "Are you guys done?"

"No," Detective Butler said. "We might need to do some of it in the morning."

She sat down on the bottom step, waiting for the chaos to end. When this was over, she wanted nothing to do with the police for at least another thirty years. As she sat here, she looked up and down the street and then saw a car like Debbie's was down there. She hopped up and studied it, thinking maybe it was her coworker's car.

Taylor came up to her and asked, "What are you doing?"

"I think that is Debbie's car," she said. "But maybe not."

He looked at it and then called the detective over. They checked the ownership. Taylor shook his head. "No, it's not."

"Of course not. That would be too easy." Midge shrugged. "It's Bart car that we need to find."

Just then came a shout from the house. Midge watched as Taylor walked back up to talk with Colton at the doorway. She leaned against the car, waiting for them to be done. A couple men walked by and then a woman. Everybody was curious about what was going on in the house.

When somebody clasped something over her mouth and grabbed her from behind, she tried to fight and kick but couldn't shake them off. *Chloroform.* Made her weak and go quiet. She was tossed into the back of a car. She couldn't move. She couldn't even speak. The vehicle drove away slowly, but the hand over her mouth didn't ease up, and she succumbed to the drugs.

"Okay, I'll head back in and see if I can find out more," Colton said.

Taylor ran down to the bottom of the steps and turned toward where he'd just left Midge. But there was no sign of her. He looked around, seeing a bunch of people standing there, and he asked, "Did you see that short redhead standing here somewhere?"

They looked at each other and back at the car, and one said, "I think so."

Another said, "I think she was right there, leaning against the car."

He looked at the car and then swore. It wasn't the same car anymore. At least the one in front wasn't. The car that looked like Debbie's was still here, but now a truck was parked in front of it. He called out to the crowd, asking for whoever owned it. One of the guys walked over and said, "Yeah, it's mine. Why? What's the matter?"

"Did you see the car that was here before you pulled in?"

"It was pulling away, so I was just happy to get a spot."

"Did you see a redhead?"

He frowned and said, "Yeah, I think somebody helped her get into the back of the car. But I don't know for sure. I was too busy trying to get into the parking spot. With all this shit going on, no way I can even get into my own place."

"Don't suppose you caught sight of the license plate, did you?"

The guy shook his head.

Taylor ran to Colton and the detective to explain what the problem was.

Colton said, "I took some pictures of the parked vehicles on this street. Let me see if I've got the license plate." He brought up the photos on his phone, and there was a corner of the license plate. "Okay, we've got the make and model and we've got one letter on the end."

"Well, that will help some," the detective said, "but not a lot."

Taylor wanted to follow the kidnappers, but how was he supposed to know where they had gone? "What do you think he'll do? Go back to Bart's place? Or go to Jenny's?"

Colton asked, "You're still stuck on Jenny being involved?"

"Until I have a reason to believe otherwise, yeah," Taylor said. "I can't get it out of my mind. Particularly since a winning lottery ticket is involved, and Jenny knows the woman she hates is getting seventy-five million dollars. In that case, Jenny's hate is growing."

Colton said, "Come on. Let's go." With the two of them in separate vehicles, Taylor headed first to Bart's place, where he did a quick search, then left for the only address they had for Jenny. He spoke to Colton on the phone as he drove. "Please tell me that the detective has an APB out on that vehicle."

"Well, he does, but the place is pretty overrun. I think some festival is in town. The traffic here is just brutal."

"We've got to find her," Taylor demanded. "This doesn't make any sense. Why didn't they just shoot her, like the others?"

"Whatever the reasoning," Colton said, "we can be grateful. We can't walk back from a fatal bullet, but, if there's any reason they want to talk to her or something, then we have some time to set up a rescue."

"Says you," Taylor replied with a snort. "We haven't had any luck getting ahead of this. Everything we do is just playing catch-up."

"This is our time to catch up. We've got a lot of people looking. Mason's got half a dozen men out searching for that vehicle, and Butler issued the APB. Somebody will see it somewhere."

"But will it be before they drop her dead body somewhere?" Taylor asked bitterly.

"She really got to you, didn't she?"

"Yeah, she did," he said. "And that's got nothing to do with it. The fact of the matter is, I'd feel shitty if it was anybody. But it's her, and she's been targeted right from the beginning. I told her that I'd keep her safe, and instead I lost track of her. How the hell did they manage to sneak in and steal her away?"

"It was likely very easy," Colton said. "Once all the on-lookers gathered, it would have been just a quick jump and grab. She's small enough that they could have picked her up, put chloroform over her face or injected her with a needle. She would have gone down in a heartbeat and would have been theirs from that moment on." Colton paused and added, "I've got another call coming in. I'll call you back."

Taylor pulled over in front of Jenny's condo. It was a weird set of condos, more like townhouses from the looks of it but maybe not. He wasn't sure as he studied them and frowned. Whatever. He hopped out and walked up to the front of the building where Jenny's number was. The door was open, with workmen inside. He checked the number again and then just walked right in, and nobody even questioned him. She lived on the main floor. Well, that was easy for a change. He walked over to the number 123 and pounded on the door. When there was no answer, he knocked again and then again.

A stranger walked up and asked, "Hey, what's going on?"

"I'm looking for the person who lives here," he said. "We need to talk to her regarding an investigation. We've got a young woman who's been kidnapped, and we think Jenny has information on the woman's whereabouts. Have you seen her lately?" Taylor asked.

He shook his head. "I'm the caretaker here. No. No, I haven't. Not at all, probably for at least two days."

"Seriously?"

The guy nodded.

"I suggest you use a master key so we can make a quick wellness check."

At that, his jaw dropped open.

"Look. I've got five dead bodies. We need to know if she's alive."

That jump-started the caretaker, and he opened up the apartment. "I could get into a lot of trouble for this."

"You could," he said. "Or maybe you'll get an award for being a hero."

"I can't let you in," the caretaker said.

Taylor shrugged and said, "Go in and do a quick check. Make sure she's not in the bedroom or bathroom. And be prepared in case it's not a pleasant view."

"I served over in Iraq," he said. "I've seen plenty." His voice dwindled as he disappeared into the kitchen, the living room and then over to the bedroom. He came back and said, "She's not here."

"She's not in the bathroom?" Taylor asked.

He shook his head. "It's empty."

"Good," Taylor said, and he bolted out the front. Then he stopped, turned and said, "Do you know what kind of vehicle she drives?"

"Yeah, a Pontiac Sunfire. After losing her job several months ago, she crashed her vehicle. The insurance didn't cover much, and she ended up with an old beater. That girl has had a run of bad luck," he said. "I sure hope she can turn that around to something good now."

"She ever talk to you much?" Taylor asked. "Has she ever mentioned a girl named Midge?"

The caretaker's face lit up. "Yeah, that's the one she hated. Since she got her fired from her job and all."

"Well, Midge is the woman who's been kidnapped," Taylor said. "She's small, about five foot tall, with long red ringlets. She was taken not very long ago. But five other people in her sphere have all been murdered in the last couple days. I'm really terrified she'll end up dead too."

"I can't remember the license plate," the caretaker said. "We did have words over where she was parking a couple times. Because she isn't too particular about following rules, so I've had multiple complaints about her."

"Did they write down the license plate?"

He nodded, pulled out his phone and said, "Got another one here just the other day. Here it is." As he rattled off the series of numbers, Taylor tapped them into his phone, encouraged when it ended with the letter he expected. Heart racing, he sent a message to Mason, Colton and Troy. "Okay, that might be the one we're looking for."

"She was pretty angry at that woman," the caretaker said.

"Yeah, I hear that," Taylor said. "Let's hope she's not so angry she does something stupid."

"Did that woman really get her fired?"

Taylor looked up from his phone and shook his head. "No. Jenny did something wrong at work. That's what got her fired."

The caretaker shook his head. "Everyone likes to make up stories to minimize what they really did. If people would just be honest from the get-go, things would be easier."

"True enough. We keep hoping, but humanity is in a messed-up state these days." Taylor headed out. "Now we need to find a place where she would hang out," he said out loud to nobody in particular.

The caretaker followed him outside. "You could go to her mom's place and check there," he said.

Taylor turned to look at him and frowned. "Why her mom's place?"

"Her mom passed away, so the house is empty."

"Do you have an address?"

He gave it to him. "It's only a few minutes from here." He pointed. "Go down to the end of the block, then take a right onto High Street. Go down about five blocks and take another right, so you're just completing a square, and it's in there. Her mom passed away about five or six months ago. It's almost out of probate, and then she wants to sell the house. I think the For Sale sign is already up in the front yard."

"Got it," Taylor said. Then he opened his phone and

called Colton and brought him up to speed.

"I'll meet you there," Colton said. "Troy is coming too, and I'll tell Mason."

"Good enough," Taylor said. "Be there in five."

CHAPTER 15

MIDGE WOKE UP from whatever had happened, knowing she was in real trouble. Deep trouble. She rolled over, only to get a hard smack across the face. She cried out in pain and lay here, stunned for a long moment.

"Go ahead and try again," a familiar voice invited. "I can keep doing this all day."

"Why would you do this to me?" Midge asked, lifting a hand to hold her swelling cheek, surprised to see her hands and her feet were not bound.

"I've thought of nothing else," Jenny said. "You got me fired. Then I lost my vehicle, and I'm about to lose my apartment too. All because of you."

"I don't know what you're talking about, Jenny. I didn't get you fired."

"Yes, you did," she said. "You told them that I was hacking into the files and changing information for money, depending on who needed what. Somebody trying to get a mortgage may have needed their wages to be higher than what they actually were. No problem. I changed it. For a little extra money, I'd even arrange to call the lenders and give them proof positive these people were making what they needed. Maybe somebody else needed an extra degree in their background? No problem. I added it." She scoffed. "It was a good gig. And you're the one who screwed me out of it."

Midge lay frozen in place. "I had no idea you were doing all that," she said in bewilderment. "Why?"

"Why not? Our department is dead. Just full of dusty old files, and people they can't move anywhere else. Like you. It's not like you ever got promoted. You were completely ignored and overlooked."

"I never tried to get promoted," she said. "And I was happy there."

The other woman laughed in disbelief. "Are you kidding me? No way."

"And all of this is because you lost your cushy little job where you were cheating the system and lying for other people for a little extra money? Did they even find out about what you were doing?"

"Not from me," she said carelessly. "But when I hacked into the files, I figured I could keep working, even though I wasn't there anymore. I'd always had remote access anyway, and I knew several people's logins, so I just kept doing it. And then somebody upgraded the system, and, when I tried to get back in again, it was much harder. But I got somebody in the office to give me a hand, and, of course, at that point, he got in a bit deep too. But it would be an easy out for all of us when we realized one of the office lottery tickets was a winner."

Midge lay here, absorbing all this news. It had never occurred to her that somebody in staff records would be altering records for money. And, of course, she now knew who in the office had been helping Jenny.

"So this isn't even about you getting fired. This is about that stupid lottery ticket, isn't it?"

"Seventy-five million is hardly stupid," Jenny said cheerfully. "No way you'll be getting any of it. Sorry. Seventy-five million for two sounds a hell of a lot better than seventy-five million for three."

"You weren't even part of the office pool, were you?"

"I was," she said. "Bart got a share for me, the same as bloody Shorts there bought a share for his nephew."

"So actually seven of us won?" she asked.

"Yeah. But we decided very quickly no way it would be big enough to share. So I arranged for you and the nephew to die. You were supposed to kill him and then turn the gun on yourself. It sure wasn't hard to get into your Tinder account and set up a meet." Jenny laughed. "It was supposed to look that way anyhow. Of course, I did the killing. Something I really was looking forward to. But you weren't there. Of course you weren't there. You're never where you're supposed to be on time."

"Sorry if I messed up your plans," Midge snapped. "How was I supposed to know you had all this murderous planning going on behind my back?"

"Well, you probably couldn't know," she said cheerfully. "It's not like I give a shit anyway. This is much better. It will be much more personal, and I won't have to worry about you ever getting out of it."

"So you lured Gary to my place to make it look like a lover's dispute and to get rid of two of us?"

"It did. Well, it should have. But it didn't quite work out that way."

"And the old couple?"

"Yeah, well, you see our boss and his nephew told them all about it. How they had all these tickets, and they were going to win." She laughed. "Besides, I hated them anyway."

"What are you even talking about? They were harmless."

"No, they weren't," Jenny said. "I tried to live in that building a couple years ago. I was there for about three months and got my ass kicked out. So I was totally okay if they were gone. Besides, we couldn't keep them around, knowing they knew about the winning tickets. We couldn't allow anyone to know, or they'd tell the cops that people in the office pool were mysteriously dying. They would have just caused trouble. And come on. They were old. We should have been paid to do it really."

Midge just stared straight ahead. She couldn't even see the sick woman's face. Her mind was too overwhelmed with how carelessly Jenny was talking about taking somebody's life. "Is it so easy to kill then?"

"Gets easier every day," Jenny said. "Those two damn women from the office. Jesus. It was nice to shut them up. Of course, Bart didn't necessarily want to do those two. But I wasn't having any of that shit."

"So you had to take them out. They had done nothing to you and, like me, probably didn't even know the ticket was a winner. But you still had to take them out?"

"Debbie knew. She was bugging Bart about looking for the ticket so she could check it. She said she had a really good feeling about it. Bart and I knew at that point we would have to do something about it. The ticket had to be ours and ours alone."

"Sorry if a few people got in the way of your seventy-five million," Midge said slowly. "You could have been just as happy with a portion of it, you know?"

"Never. But I will be now. With just Bart and me."

"It's not like Bart will be happy sharing with you," Midge said with a laugh. "Why would he? You've killed off everybody. You know what? If he gets rid of you, nobody will know anything."

There was a moment of silence, and Midge didn't even see the blow coming. But it snapped against her head, sending her flying forward into the side of whatever space she was in. It was weird, like some closet. Yet big enough that she was knocked around in it, but not big enough that she could roll over and get to her feet.

"I wouldn't keep saying things like that if I were you," Jenny said.

"Or is that the way you're thinking about Bart," Midge said when she could. "After all, you did kill all those people, and he knows about it. Maybe you should get rid of him, so he can't cause you any trouble."

"He loves me, and I love him," Jenny said, her voice hard and callous. "Like you'll come between us. Do you think everybody else didn't already try?"

"I didn't even know you were having an office romance," Midge said. "I'm extremely obtuse apparently, and unaware of everything going on around me."

"Isn't that the truth." After a moment of silence, Jenny asked, "Did you really not turn me in to the boss?"

Midge shook her head. "I didn't know you were doing anything. I saw that you had the files and hadn't put them back properly, but I didn't say anything to him."

"Yeah, I was going to put them back properly, but I didn't get a chance. That's the thing. I was trying to do things covertly, since it took time, space and energy to get it all done at the right time. It was getting a little hectic there. Of course I took on more jobs than I should have. I should have kept it to no more than one a day, and sometimes it was three and four."

"How the hell did they find you?"

"Bart was doing a little bit of the same thing himself. And word soon got out that a couple people in staff records would make changes for a price."

"That is amazing," Midge said, still stunned at their audacity.

"Yeah, it was a great gig. An excellent supplemental income, hidden within a regular job. Of course I had to keep the tedious day job in order to make all the excellent extras, but that was okay. Until I got fired ..."

"Okay, so why am I here now?"

Jenny snorted. "Are you telling me that you really can't figure that out?"

"Well, your one attempt to kill me didn't work, and I presume just the three of us own shares in the seventy-five million now," she said warily.

"Right," Jenny said. "And you can bet, if I wasn't sharing with seven or five, I'm sure not sharing with you. We're just waiting for the heat to die down, so we can get the ticket, cash it in and go."

An odd sound came from behind the two of them. Then Midge heard Jenny talking with somebody else. Suddenly Midge was picked up and dragged out into the middle of what looked like a bedroom. She glanced around and asked, "Did you say you got your mother's house?"

"Yep. She passed away, and I'm the only one left. It helps to keep things in perspective. I used to have a sister, and I'd have to share this with her. But, with both of them gone, it's all mine."

Midge hated to ask, but in her heart of hearts, she had to know. "Did you kill your sister, so you didn't have to share?"

"She was almost dead anyway. She was a drug addict, killing herself slowly with every shot. The last six months she actually sped up the process. I just made sure she had some pretty ugly drugs one day. She overdosed. It was simple."

"That must have devastated your mother."

"It did, and it sped her to the end. I didn't even have to kill her. Which is good because too many deaths would get a little suspicious. She died of a heart attack and left everything to me."

Jenny's voice held such a note of satisfaction, almost a sense of things having been righted, as if Jenny had finally gotten what was coming to her.

Midge tried to shift so she could turn around and see where she was and actually see Jenny. But she got another blow across the head for her effort. She collapsed back down, gasping with tears in the corner of her eyes.

"You know what? I'm liking that whole hitting part," Jenny said. "I've got a lot of rage inside me, so I can just unleash it all on you."

Another smack came across her face and then another. Midge struggled with herself, fighting to maintain consciousness. The blows were getting harder, as if Jenny was really giving herself the freedom to let loose.

A sharp voice behind them said, "Stop, Jenny."

Through her ringing ears, she heard Bart's voice.

Jenny shrugged and laughed. "She's so freaking useless though."

"We said we weren't doing this. It leaves scars and forensic evidence."

"So, we beat the crap out of her and drop her in an alleyway Dumpster," Jenny said. "What's the big deal?"

"The cops are all over the place," Bart said. "We said we weren't going to hurt her."

"Why? Are you sweet on her?" Jenny asked, her tone

hard. "You know I won't tolerate that shit."

"No, I'm not sweet on her," Bart said in exasperation. "She's a bloody Goody Two-shoes. Who the hell wants to be around her?"

Even through her physical pain from the beating, Midge could feel that statement cut deep. Was that how the office had been? Was that what she didn't understand about everybody she worked with? How absolutely bizarre was it that all of this was going on?

Bart chuckled. "We need a better solution for killing her. And it can't happen too quickly. Remember that. There are an awful lot of deaths lately."

"So, just one more and we grab our ticket, cash it in and bug out of here," Jenny said. "It doesn't get any easier than that."

Midge vaguely wondered how they would react if they found out the ticket was in the safe at the police station. When Midge opened her eyes, she saw both people had moved into her viewing area. Jenny ran over to Bart and threw her arms around his neck and kissed him passionately. Bart didn't appear to be holding back at all. She watched in disbelief as the two of them made out right in front of her. She wanted to roll over and vomit, but she knew she'd just end up lying in it. As it was, her stomach was heaving with the heat and the pain throbbing through her head.

"Or you could just kill each other," she whispered, "and save us all the effort."

Jenny laughed. "Why the hell would I do that? Bart knows exactly who and what I am," she said. "He needs me."

"He knows you are the killer. So, with you dead, he's on easy street," Midge whispered, trying to reach to the rational part of Bart's mind.

Bart chuckled again. "Hey, the least she can do is kill you first." And then he laughed, like it was the biggest joke ever.

Jenny smacked him lightly, thinking it was hilarious too.

But Midge had to wonder. It sounded like something serious was in his voice. As if maybe that was his plan after all. She could only hope Taylor found her in time. She knew he would be after them as soon as he could. But how long would that be? They'd been here at least fifteen or twenty minutes, and she didn't know how long she'd been unconscious. She coughed, feeling the acid rising from the bile in her stomach. Her chest heaved as she struggled for air. When she finally collapsed back down again, gasping, she whispered, "May I have some water?"

Bart said, "Sure." And he disappeared.

Jenny dropped down at her side. "We'll just throw it all over you," she said.

"If that's what makes you happy."

Bart came back, and, reaching out, he grabbed Midge under the neck and sat her up. He held the glass for her as she reached up with her hands, taking it and drinking it. As soon as she was done, Bart pulled it away and laughed.

"Just in case you were getting any ideas about smashing the glass in my face," he said.

She shook her head. "The only thing I want to do is live."

"Sorry," he said regretfully. "That is the one thing I cannot do."

"You could," Midge said. "You could take care of Jenny, grab the money and run all alone, keeping the seventy-five million for yourself."

He laughed, a big belly laugh this time. "She said you

were trying to turn her against me."

"You mean, turn you against her," Midge said. "I really don't care which one of you turns against the other. It will happen eventually anyway. She's a real liability. But why the hell would you give away half of all that money?"

He stared at her now.

Midge nodded. "Think about it. I don't even want any. Go ahead and take it. Run. Cash the check, lose half of it to taxes, and the rest is yours. Free and clear." Then she dropped back down again, feeling her chest heave and her head boom.

Bart stared down at her for a long moment.

Meanwhile, Jenny got angry. "You're not listening to her, are you? I told you that's what she would try to do."

He nodded, and said, "Of course I'm not listening to her. She's a fool." He walked into the kitchen, at least Midge thought it was a kitchen.

She could hear water running, and then she heard sirens. They seemed to be getting closer. While she was wondering how to stay alive a little bit longer, Bart came into the room again. Smiling down at Midge, he grabbed Jenny's neck, and—in a movement she thought for sure no one but Taylor could do—Bart snapped Jenny's neck like a chicken. Dropping her body beside him, he said, "Good idea. See ya," and he took off.

Midge lay here in disbelief, staring at Jenny's lifeless body beside her. With Bart gone, she managed to get to her feet. She didn't have her phone, but Jenny still had hers. Midge grabbed it and phoned Taylor. "Please come," she gasped.

"We're less than a minute away," he reassured her.

"If you're looking for Bart, he's trying to find the ticket, cash it in and make a run for it."

"I think we see him up ahead. I'll be there in a minute."

She collapsed beside Jenny and just stared. Midge didn't even want to touch her, but she knew she needed to see if Jenny was dead or alive. When she pressed her fingers against Jenny's neck and couldn't find a pulse, Midge got to her feet, then slowly made her way out of the room.

At the front door, she could hear a hell of a battle outside. She stepped out on the front porch just as Taylor rammed his fist into Bart's face. Bart went down and didn't get back up. She gave out a cry and raced toward Taylor. He opened his arms, and she fell into them. He held her by the shoulders and took a good look at her face.

"Did he do that?" He looked ferocious, like he was ready to beat the shit out of Bart now, even though he still lay unconscious on the ground.

Stopping him, she said, "No, he didn't. It was Jenny."

He raised his eyebrows and looked at the house. "Then I need to meet with her."

He let her cuddle against his chest, her face so hot and puffy it was tight. She whispered, "You don't have to. Bart just snapped her neck. He wasn't going to share the ticket. He was going to keep it all for himself."

Taylor held her gently in his arms, his hands stroking up and down her back. "I'm so sorry, sweetheart. I'm so sorry they got to you before I could get here."

"It's okay," she said. "You and Colton were right. It was all coming down today. I'm not terribly impressed with the way it happened." She pushed back ever-so-slightly and said, "And my face hurts like hell."

"Was it as we suspected?"

"Partly," she said. "But Jenny had a side gig going, altering staff records for people who needed higher incomes for employment verification, like when applying for mortgage loans. Or adding extra educational credits or degrees to their background data. I'm sure what she told me was just the tip of the iceberg. Bart got wind of the money she was making, and he was doing it too.

"After she got fired, she managed to keep doing it remotely, until they changed the IT passwords, and Jenny couldn't get in anymore. She's the one who was hacking in. She was desperate to complete the work she had agreed to do, and her customers were getting angry because she wasn't doing it. Then, as soon as she managed to hack back in, she found out about the ticket because she'd been in on it too, probably because of her relationship with Bart. So, at some point, she and Bart decided those winnings were just for the two of them at the end of the day."

"And what made Bart decide to take it on alone?"

"I persuaded him that sharing with her was a really bad idea, since she did all the other killings. Plus, the taxman would take half of it already. He figured he was getting half of seventy-five if just he and Jenny shared the winnings. But, when I reminded him it would only be one-quarter after taxes, he didn't like the sound of that."

Taylor gave a rough exclamation and then folded her gently in his arms. "Back to greed on all counts."

She nodded. "Even worse, apparently Jenny killed her sister so she wouldn't have to share her future inheritance. Her mom was already sick. Then her mom, after being traumatized by the death of one of her daughters, had a heart attack and passed away pretty quickly too. Leaving the mother's house all to Jenny."

"Wow," Taylor said. "Apparently after Jenny killed

once, it just got easier."

"I think it's worse than that. She looked forward to it. She wanted to beat the crap out of me and throw me into an alley Dumpster," she said painfully. "I don't think she would have stopped hitting me. She was a real liability to him as well."

"Good thing Bart stopped her then," Taylor said. "Saved me from doing the job."

Midge reached out and stroked his face. "I wouldn't want you killing somebody for my sake."

"Don't you worry, sweetheart. If somebody were to come after you like they did and were still alive to tell about it, I'd make sure I took him out. Bart here isn't getting off lightly either. Not only did he kill Jenny but he participated in all the other murders."

"To their twisted logic, the old couple had to go. They weren't even part of the pool, but they knew my boss and his nephew were getting all that money. Since they knew, ... they had to go. Plus, Jenny already hated them. And you were right. I was supposed to die in my apartment. Jenny had it planned that Gary would be found in bed with me. They would set it up to look like I'd killed him and then killed myself, distraught over what I'd done."

"And you know what? That might have worked," Taylor said. "Except Debbie called in sick."

"The trouble is, she probably didn't call in sick," Midge said. "I think she was killed, and then Jenny called it in so nobody would come looking for her. That call is what took me to work that day, so Jenny actually foiled her own plans without realizing it."

With a big chuckle, he tucked her up close and said, "It doesn't matter anymore. It's over."

Midge snuggled in close and said, "I hope only good things come in our lives from now on."

"It's all what we make of it. So how about we only make good things happen for ourselves?"

She looked up at him, then said, "Really?"

Leaning down, he said, "I'm willing. How about you?"

She touched her lips against his and whispered, "For you, always. I haven't seen anybody more interesting in a long time."

"Well, no need to be looking now," he said, "because I'm here. And I don't share well." He gave her a grin and said, "Now let's go get that face of yours taken care of. We have things to do, and they have nothing to do with all this murder and mayhem."

"That sounds good to me," she said, and, without another look at the disaster she'd left behind, he led the way to the Jeep. From here she knew things would only get better and better. After all, they'd been through the worst now, and she looked forward to seeing what good things would come their way.

EPILOGUE

C OLTON EDGEWOOD BOARDED the military plane on the first leg of his journey overseas to the Thule Air Base in Greenland. He was okay with that, but, at the same time, he hadn't been home long enough to really get his feet under him. And, after helping Taylor these last few days, it seemed like such a rush job. Colton had really planned on staying home on base at Coronado for a week at least.

He'd served in a unique position in Afghanistan—as a liaison for one of the joint military teams, pulling together group training of "friendly" wars, all in a mission to foster peace and to further everybody's education and skills. So now he was headed to Greenland for a similar operation.

Greenland was a strategic site for the US Air Force, and he didn't expect to be there for too long and would be heading off to Africa afterward, at least as far as he understood. For now. His orders were never firm for long. He'd get one step on a journey but would never quite know where he would go from there.

Still he'd never been to Greenland and was looking forward to it. With a population of fewer than sixty thousand on the whole island, it was a unique corner of the world, where nobody actually owned their own land, instead buyers were granted the right to use it, and everybody worked together to make their society the way they wanted it. The population was mostly native people, and Colton really appreciated the different viewpoint they brought to the world.

He shifted position. He was the only one on this military flight, along with a ton of cargo. He wished he could have ridden in the cockpit, but, with room only for a pilot and a copilot, Colton definitely wasn't small enough to squeeze between them up there. The trip was long but uneventful.

Just as they prepared for a landing, he heard a large explosion on the left side of the plane. He bolted from his seat and stuck his head in the cockpit to take a look in that direction. The left engine was on fire. He swore.

The copilot glanced at him and said, "Take your seat."

He nodded but grabbed three parachutes instead, in case they had to abandon the plane. He made his way forward again to see the pilots calm and controlled but issuing instructions to the base as they approached. "I've got two parachutes here, in case you guys need them."

"Hopefully not," she said.

Katie. Katie Winslow. Somebody he'd known for a few years and had flown with a couple times and once even had shared an overnight stay. That had been a hot and heavy night; then they both showered the next morning and carried on with their individual lives. But to see her here and now just put another human face on this. He didn't recognize the pilot.

Katie looked at him again and said, "Take your seat, Colton."

At that, he nodded, grabbed his parachute and buckled it on, then took a seat. He couldn't buckle in with the chute on, but he wasn't letting go of it. At the moment, the parachute seemed more critical than the seat belt.

The plane careened to the side and slipped downward at a rate that was more than a little nauseating. He caught his breath, following the safety procedures that he knew they would go through now. He had been in similar situations before. Not exactly this but … He leaned forward to look out the cockpit window, hoping to see land in the distance. Regardless, if the pilots had put out a Mayday call, they could jump and get free and clear of the plane, if headed for a crash.

Katie joined him, holding onto a nearby strap, and said, in a curt but controlled tone, "We have to bail."

"Understood." When he rose, he immediately fell as the plane shifted again to the side. "What about the pilot?" he yelled over the loud din, scrambling to his feet once more.

"He's coming," she said, righting herself as well. She quickly grabbed her parachute, and he helped her strap it on.

The two of them made their way to the cockpit, where the pilot still tried to guide the plane. She called out to him, "George, come on. We're done."

He nodded. "I know," he said. "I just wanted to make sure we got out to the ocean, where this doesn't come down on anybody." Finally he bolted toward them and, with their help, quickly got buckled up in his parachute. He looked out and said, "It won't be that easy to get out of here. It's going to be hard to get clear of the plane."

"I know," Colton said, as he struggled against the downward angle of the plane to reach the emergency door, kicked it open and basically tossed Katie out.

The pilot raised his eyebrows and shook his head. "Damn, this is the first time for me."

He didn't get a chance to say more because Colton already had pushed him outside in the frigid air. He jumped out right behind them. All Colton could do was watch the plane dive, flames shooting out behind it, as it beelined for the deep dark ocean below.

He turned to see the two parachutes now floating above him. They'd gone from an ugly and dangerous situation to an uglier and deadlier one.

Nothing was easy about landing in the Arctic Ocean— hypothermia would set in within twenty minutes. Then it wouldn't matter who came to rescue them – it would already be too late.

This concludes Book 22 of SEALs of Honor: Taylor.

Read about Colton: SEALs of Honor, Book 23

SEALS OF HONOR: COLTON BOOK 23

His next flight becomes a fight for his life ... and the life of the two pilots.

Colton is helping out on a training session in Greenland, currently in midair. The copilot is a woman he knew intimately and had planned to reconnect with, only life never seemed to give him that window. His flight turns into a nightmare as the engine blows, and he, along with the two pilots, are forced to abandon the bird and jump into the Arctic Ocean.

Kate Winnows might not have been overjoyed to see Colton as her only passenger, but she's darn happy he's here when all hell breaks loose. She'd never forgotten him. Had hoped to reconnect but, like him, her life was busy, finding each of them all over the planet. Now she needs him to help her save her reputation, her job and possibly her life ... again. And, if she can make it happen, she wants a second chance to show him what he means to her.

Especially when they find out the crash was no accident but just the tip of the iceberg in a case involving blackmail, drugs and ... murder.

Find Book 23 here!

To find out more visit Dale Mayer's website.

https://geni.us/DMColtonUniversal

Author's Note

Thank you for reading SEALs of Honor, Books 20–22! If you enjoyed the book, please take a moment and leave a short review.

Dear reader,

I love to hear from readers, and you can contact me at my website: www.dalemayer.com or at my Facebook author page. To be informed of new releases and special offers, sign up for my newsletter or follow me on BookBub. And if you are interested in joining Dale Mayer's Reader Group, here is the Facebook sign up page.
http://geni.us/DaleMayerFBGroup

Cheers,
Dale Mayer

COMPLIMENTARY DOWNLOAD

DOWNLOAD a *__complimentary__* copy of TUESDAY'S CHILD? Just tell me where to send it!

http://dalemayer.com/starterlibrarytc/

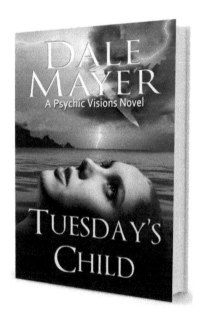

About the Author

Dale Mayer is a *USA Today* best-selling author, best known for her SEALs military romances, her Psychic Visions series, and her Lovely Lethal Garden cozy series. Her contemporary romances are raw and full of passion and emotion (Broken But ... Mending, Hathaway House series). Her thrillers will keep you guessing (Kate Morgan, By Death series), and her romantic comedies will keep you giggling (*It's a Dog's Life*, a stand-alone novella; and the Broken Protocols series, starring Charming Marvin, the cat).

Dale honors the stories that come to her—and some of them are crazy, break all the rules and cross multiple genres!

To go with her fiction, she also writes nonfiction in many different fields, with books available on résumé writing, companion gardening, and the US mortgage system. All her books are available in print and ebook format.

Connect with Dale Mayer Online

Dale's Website – www.dalemayer.com
Twitter – @DaleMayer
Facebook Page – geni.us/DaleMayerFBFanPage
Facebook Group – geni.us/DaleMayerFBGroup
BookBub – geni.us/DaleMayerBookbub
Instagram – geni.us/DaleMayerInstagram
Goodreads – geni.us/DaleMayerGoodreads
Newsletter – geni.us/DaleNews

Also by Dale Mayer

Published Adult Books:

Hathaway House

Aaron, Book 1

Brock, Book 2

Cole, Book 3

Denton, Book 4

Elliot, Book 5

Finn, Book 6

Gregory, Book 7

Heath, Book 8

Iain, Book 9

Jaden, Book 10

Keith, Book 11

Lance, Book 12

Melissa, Book 13

The K9 Files

Ethan, Book 1

Pierce, Book 2

Zane, Book 3

Blaze, Book 4

Lucas, Book 5

Parker, Book 6

Carter, Book 7

Weston, Book 8

Greyson, Book 9

Rowan, Book 10

Caleb, Book 11

Lovely Lethal Gardens

Arsenic in the Azaleas, Book 1

Bones in the Begonias, Book 2

Corpse in the Carnations, Book 3

Daggers in the Dahlias, Book 4

Evidence in the Echinacea, Book 5

Footprints in the Ferns, Book 6

Gun in the Gardenias, Book 7

Handcuffs in the Heather, Book 8

Ice Pick in the Ivy, Book 9

Jewels in the Juniper, Book 10

Killer in the Kiwis, Book 11

Lovely Lethal Gardens, Books 1–2

Lovely Lethal Gardens, Books 3–4

Lovely Lethal Gardens, Books 5–6

Psychic Vision Series

Tuesday's Child

Hide 'n Go Seek

Maddy's Floor

Garden of Sorrow

Knock Knock...

Rare Find

Eyes to the Soul

Now You See Her

Shattered

Into the Abyss

Seeds of Malice

Eye of the Falcon

Itsy-Bitsy Spider

Unmasked

Deep Beneath

From the Ashes

Stroke of Death

Ice Maiden

Psychic Visions Books 1–3

Psychic Visions Books 4–6

Psychic Visions Books 7–9

By Death Series

Touched by Death

Haunted by Death

Chilled by Death

By Death Books 1–3

Broken Protocols – Romantic Comedy Series

Cat's Meow

Cat's Pajamas

Cat's Cradle

Cat's Claus

Broken Protocols 1-4

Broken and... Mending

Skin

Scars

Scales (of Justice)

Broken but… Mending 1-3

Glory

Genesis

Tori

Celeste

Glory Trilogy

Biker Blues

Morgan: Biker Blues, Volume 1

Cash: Biker Blues, Volume 2

SEALs of Honor

Mason: SEALs of Honor, Book 1

Hawk: SEALs of Honor, Book 2

Dane: SEALs of Honor, Book 3

Swede: SEALs of Honor, Book 4

Shadow: SEALs of Honor, Book 5

Cooper: SEALs of Honor, Book 6

Markus: SEALs of Honor, Book 7

Evan: SEALs of Honor, Book 8

Mason's Wish: SEALs of Honor, Book 9

Chase: SEALs of Honor, Book 10

Brett: SEALs of Honor, Book 11

Devlin: SEALs of Honor, Book 12

Easton: SEALs of Honor, Book 13

Ryder: SEALs of Honor, Book 14

Macklin: SEALs of Honor, Book 15

Corey: SEALs of Honor, Book 16

Warrick: SEALs of Honor, Book 17

Tanner: SEALs of Honor, Book 18

Jackson: SEALs of Honor, Book 19

Kanen: SEALs of Honor, Book 20

Nelson: SEALs of Honor, Book 21

Taylor: SEALs of Honor, Book 22

Colton: SEALs of Honor, Book 23

Troy: SEALs of Honor, Book 24

Axel: SEALs of Honor, Book 25

SEALs of Honor, Books 1–3

SEALs of Honor, Books 4–6

SEALs of Honor, Books 7–10

SEALs of Honor, Books 11–13

SEALs of Honor, Books 14–16

SEALs of Honor, Books 17–19

SEALs of Honor, Books 20–22

Heroes for Hire

Levi's Legend: Heroes for Hire, Book 1

Stone's Surrender: Heroes for Hire, Book 2

Merk's Mistake: Heroes for Hire, Book 3

Rhodes's Reward: Heroes for Hire, Book 4

Flynn's Firecracker: Heroes for Hire, Book 5

Logan's Light: Heroes for Hire, Book 6

Harrison's Heart: Heroes for Hire, Book 7

SEALs of Steel

Geir: SEALs of Steel, Book 6

Jager: SEALs of Steel, Book 7

The Final Reveal: SEALs of Steel, Book 8

SEALs of Steel, Books 1–4

SEALs of Steel, Books 5–8

SEALs of Steel, Books 1–8

The Mavericks

Kerrick, Book 1

Griffin, Book 2

Jax, Book 3

Beau, Book 4

Asher, Book 5

Ryker, Book 6

Miles, Book 7

Nico, Book 8

Keane, Book 9

Lennox, Book 10

Gavin, Book 11

Shane, Book 12

Bullard's Battle Series

Ryland's Reach, Book 1

Cain's Cross, Book 2

Eton's Escape, Book 3

Garret's Gambit, Book 4

Kano's Keep, Book 5

Fallon's Flaw, Book 6

Quinn's Quest, Book 7

Bullard's Beauty, Book 8

Collections

Dare to Be You...

Dare to Love...

Dare to be Strong...

RomanceX3

Standalone Novellas

It's a Dog's Life

Riana's Revenge

Second Chances

Published Young Adult Books:

Family Blood Ties Series

Vampire in Denial

Vampire in Distress

Vampire in Design

Vampire in Deceit

Vampire in Defiance

Vampire in Conflict

Vampire in Chaos

Vampire in Crisis

Vampire in Control

Vampire in Charge

Family Blood Ties Set 1–3

Family Blood Ties Set 1–5

Family Blood Ties Set 4–6

Family Blood Ties Set 7–9

Sian's Solution, A Family Blood Ties Series Prequel
    Novelette

Design series

Dangerous Designs

Deadly Designs

Darkest Designs

Design Series Trilogy

Standalone

In Cassie's Corner

Gem Stone (a Gemma Stone Mystery)

Time Thieves

Published Non-Fiction Books:

Career Essentials

Career Essentials: The Résumé

Career Essentials: The Cover Letter

Career Essentials: The Interview

Career Essentials: 3 in 1